GUARDIAN
UNRAVELED

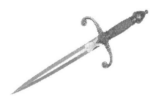

A FALLEN GUARDIAN NOVEL

GEORGIA LYN HUNTER

GENRE: PARANORMAL ROMANCE

This book is a work of fiction. Names, places, characters and incidents are either the product of the author's imagination or are used fictitiously. Any resemblance to actual people, living or dead, businesses, organizations, events or locales is entirely coincidental.

For my late parents, George and Ann
I miss you both so much,
Love you always.

***

Jen
"Thank you" is not enough for all you've done...
and do.
Love you, girl.

GLOSSARY

Absolute Laws: Forbidding the mating between mortal and immortal. If broken, the couple is executed.

Ancients: The mystical forces that watches over all realms.

Archangel: Michael-Leader of the Fallen Guardians (also referred by the Guardians as "Arc." A term coined by Týr, and used by the others)

Blood Demons: A species of demons who live on blood, but like the high of human blood. Since human souls aren't meant for them, the souls die after a few days, forcing the demoniis to seek new ones. But consuming human blood along with the soul, extend the soul's life a little longer.

Celestial Realm: Home to the divine angels.

Dark Realm: Where the species with dark souls dwell, demons, demonii, wyvern (a seven-foot tall lizard-like creature), etc. Along with other amorphous entities like Caligos and Jaedas who steal corporeal bodies—Caligos thrive on emotions, and steal human bodies. They don't eat or drink. Jaedas prefer immortal bodies to inhabit.

Demonii: Turned demons. When they first steal a human soul, they lose their dark ones.

Demons: A species of supernatural beings with dark souls who resides in the Dark Realm.

Empyreans: They were created in the image of the divine angels but enjoy a more carnal life. Two level denizens: High-level—the Lords (With vast powers)

Lower-level—the working class (limited or lesser powers)

Hedori-Lower level, but gifted with stronger powers when he was elected as a protector to the crown prince

Georgia Lyn Hunter

of Empyrea.

Fallen: Angels who fall, and give up their wings and stronger abilities when they leave the Celestial Realm.

Fallen Guardians: A formidable group of fallen immortal warriors, banished from their realm, who swore fealty to Gaia to protect humans from supernatural evil. And resides on Earth. Some of whom are referred to by their pantheon's name.

Gaia: A powerful mystical Being who watches over Earth and mankind.

Nephilim: Half angel offspring born from human females and divine angel mating.

Otiums: A species of demons, more docile in nature. Many of whom escaped the tyranny of their world to dwell on Earth. They usually live below the radar in the human world, not keen to draw attention to themselves.

Others: A collective term for other supernatural beings, e.g.: gods, faes, vampires, etc.

Pantheons: Where the gods of various religions dwells.

Psionics: The human descendants of the Watchers. (All females)

Rogues: Angels who refuse to lose their wings and stronger powers. They escape the Celestial Realm and go into hiding on Earth.

Seraphim: The highest-level angels who oversees all things.

Sins: The Seven Deadly Sins. Created by an Ancient mystical force for justice and balance of the realms.

Tartarus: Where immortals' are incarcerated.

Throne: Third level divine angels, created for war.

Urias: Spawned off Chaos, Creator of the Empyreans.

Watchers: Higher-level angels who were tasked to

watch over fledgling mankind, but fell in love with mortal women.

Whitefire: An immortal flame that can cause untold destruction. Used to destroy the wings and abilities of angels who fall.

***

Name pronunciation:
Dagan: Day-gun
Týr: Tier

Prologue

1483 BC

Days…endless days.

Gray skies. Impossible heat. Yet there was no sun.

Dust caked his eyelashes and lined his mouth. Dagan could barely see. He swallowed—or tried to, but couldn't. His throat had long since dried up, and his swollen tongue had stuck to the roof of his mouth.

Trees shimmered in the distance. Water. Shoving back hunks of grimy knotted hair covering his face, he pitched toward the oasis, craving the relief. As he neared it, the mirage flickered and vanished, revealing an unending sea of lifeless, gray, arid landscape. No water or shelter, just a few bone-dry trees and sand.

No! The denial reverberated in his head. He had no idea how long he'd been here…months, years since he started chasing the mirage. A never-ending cycle trapped in this godsforsaken place where nothing survived. Except him.

His knees gave way. He fell to the scorching sands, a husk hovering close to death, one he could never seek.

"For the lifeblood you shed, death is too easy for

you..." An emotionless whisper. *"Eternity will be your reminder bound to your need—a prison you cannot escape—a curse you'll regret when it matters the most. It will be your downfall..."*

At the familiar words, Dagan forced his eyes open. Pain tore through his eyelids, maybe his lashes were ripped out. He didn't know or care as he searched the desolate place. There was no one around.

A strident hiss pierced his ears. A violent flutter of leathery wings erupted near him. Dozens of red eyes. They swooped down in a harsh screech, viciously tearing at his belly. Unimaginable agony ricocheted through his body. He bared his teeth at the huge monstrous black birds, fists lashing out with feeble hits, his strength that of a babe. Dry lips split apart. Blood seeped.

Blinded by hunger, he grabbed one of the avians by its featherless neck and bit hard, ripping out its larynx. Blood flowed down his chin. He gagged, retching out the gore. And his parched tongue finally unglued from the roof of his mouth. Some of the blood slid down his throat. He flung the bird aside, swiping at his lips, wanting the metallic taste gone. With no water, he sighed and closed his swollen eyelids...

When he awakened again, his torn belly and dry peeling skin had healed. He had no idea how much time had passed.

The days drifted past. There was no sign of the grisly birds, and he withered away once more, back to just skin shrunken over bones as he crawled the never-ending desert, his hunger raging.

Raucous noise and furiously beating wings exploded around him, shattering the stillness.

The vampiric vultures were back...

Georgia Lyn Hunter

Chapter 1

The rhythmic thudding of hundreds of heartbeats crowded Dagan's head.

Thump, thump, thump… Hypnotic. Enticing. The draw dangerous, inevitable, if he'd let it.

It was always this way when he first appeared on patrol. Primitive urges locked down, it should be a night like thousands of others in his long life. But this one, the worst.

All Hallows Eve was a damn pain in the ass.

Hunkered on the rooftop of a warehouse in the Bowery, he coolly eyed the noisy line of humans snaking the sidewalk of Club Nocte, waiting to gain entrance.

Why would Blaéz ask him to check out this area first?

Besides the foolish mortals disguised as what they imagined went bump in the night—hell, they sure made it easy for the real scourges lurking within the depths of the decrepit backstreet to lure them in and snuff out their feeble little lives—he didn't sense any sign of supernatural disturbance.

Dagan scanned the alley again, his focus narrowing on a couple. The male dressed in a long, black cape, his arm thrown over the shoulders of a nun in a short habit, hurried the female along. Moonlight underscoring his face pale and a red mouth with pointy canines. Count Dracul. Of course.

The twosome headed deeper into the disreputable area with no idea of the dangers that prowled the night. With demoniis out in droves hunting prey, it was always a mess leading up to this night.

Despite the distance, he could clearly see and hear the wannabe vampire. The idiot pushed the nun against a wall, hands fumbling under her tunic. "Let me sink my fangs into you, pretty one…" His voice deepened, probably his idea of vamp talk. Dagan's lips twisted in cynicism.

"Yes, my dark prince." The nun laughed, arching into him, her black veil falling back and exposing her smooth, tan neck. "Bite me—make me immortal."

The man snickered, sucking on her neck instead. Lost in their world of make-believe, she had no idea of the true danger lurking nearby. How absurdly effortless it would be to walk up to her. *He* wouldn't even have to say a word, and she'd be his for the taking.

Go. It's what you want, the dark thoughts unfurled in the pits of his mind, coiling tighter around him. *Satisfy the hunger that plagues you.*

His powerful mental shields shuddered. His fangs lengthened.

No! He was a Guardian, sworn to protect these reckless humans, not kill. With shaky hands, he pulled out a half-smoked cigar from his pocket, put the thing between his lips, and struck a match on the wall. Palms

Georgia Lyn Hunter

cupped around the flame, he lit it. Inhaling deeply, he let the scented, sedative smoke saturate his lungs and cloak his thirst.

For now.

As he blew out a thin stream of smoke, the acrid sensation of insidious evil coasted over his skin. The mystical Gaian sword tattooed on his biceps stirred in warning. His gaze sharpened, rapidly sweeping past Dracul and his nun, honing in on the two figures lumbering toward them. They slowed near the recessed doorway where the couple tugged at each other's clothes.

"By Hades," the tall demonii rasped in delight. "I do enjoy this time of year more than any other. I want her."

"What the—?" The man pivoted. "Get lost, assholes!"

Guttural laughter ripped the air. "We cannot oblige. See, we want not just her but *you,* too." The shorter, heftier demonii punched the human in the face. The tall one snatched the woman around her waist and licked her face.

Dagan killed his smoke. Before her screams tore through the night, he immobilized the four with his mind. Pocketing the cigar, he flashed down, freeing the humans from his hold.

He summoned his pulsing weapon. In an eddy of gray smoke, the obsidian sword took shape, the mystical inscriptions glowing briefly as he swung the deadly blade, decapitating both demoniis in one lethal stroke. They fell to their knees, bodies disintegrating within seconds.

"Whoa!" the man gasped. "That's so cool."

Dagan pivoted. The couple gawked at him in a

drunken stupor, like he was a savior or something for rescuing their foolish asses. Grim Reaper would be more fitting.

"Leave," he snapped, letting his eyes glow.

Without a word, they stumbled off. In their inebriated state, they'd undoubtedly assume it was all part of the Halloween scene. As he dismissed his sword, an eerie, icy sensation slid over his psyche. Not demoniis…something else.

Motionless, he waited, letting the cerebral wave surround him, then a crackle, like ice shattering, fury slid over him. And he knew.

There you are, asshole…

It had been a long damn wait for the psychic killer to show up again.

Slipping through the shadows, he followed the strains of violence abrading his mind. None could hide their psychic signature from him for long, yet this mortal he'd been hunting for several months had done just that. This time, he'd get the slippery bastard.

He passed a rundown motorcycle club with flashing neon lights. The stares that came his way from the bikers hanging outside didn't bother him. His extreme six-foot-eight height, and his waist-length hair he usually wore in several warrior braids always drew notice.

Moments later, he slowed, the trail dead-ending outside a warehouse. The scent of fresh blood beckoned him like a beautiful siren and his jaw clenched. The alley remained quiet, but not for long. Two homeless humans began bickering deeper in the alley.

Before they arrived and mucked up the psychic vibration of his prey, Dagan studied the three dead

Georgia Lyn Hunter

bodies. Two were reduced to nothing but fleshy meat-sacks, bones and muscles pulverized. Blood and gore dripped out of their ears, nose, and mouth. The other had been stabbed in his side. If it were just the knifed man, Dagan would have walked. Humans killing each other were not his problem.

The pile of rags with the knife wound shuddered. A low moan left the vagrant as he stumbled to his feet and tripped over the bodies. He cursed drunkenly. "B-bastard, tryin' to take my food."

"Hold it." Dagan grabbed his arm. The ripe fumes coming off him had Dagan keeping his breathing shallow. "What happened?"

The homeless clutched his bleeding side. "He t-took my cart, stabbed me—"

"Who else was here?"

"Want my cart back. Satan. He kill 'em bodies. Three bodies. Pooffff—one gone." He swung his arms wildly, spittle flying everywhere. Dagan hastily evaded the saliva rain. "Gonna use his weapon...kill—kill!" He made stabbing motions. "Want my cart back—want my cart." He zigzagged off.

It had to be a demon. Only they were pulled back into the Dark Realm at the time of true death.

One of the dead snagged his attention, though. Frowning, Dagan lowered to his heels near the pulverized body and slipped his hand beneath the man's shirt. Sure enough, he found the telltale ridges that ran down his shoulder blades where wings should have been. A Fallen.

Shit. This killer would be dangerous to not only the human populace but the Guardians, as well. In a flash, the last moments of the man's life passed through Dagan's mind...

A surge of fear exploded as he rose into the air. He couldn't breathe. His skull compressed. Unrelenting pain spread. "Don't—don't do it..." a plea, then resonating silence... Death.

Nothing to point Dagan to what the killer looked like or who it was. However, the same bitter iciness he'd been tracking these last months prevailed in this place.

He mind-linked with Aethan, needing the Empyrean's abilities to clear out this psychic killing before the human authorities came across the bodies and led them down a path that would cause Michael to go bat-shit crazy. *Downtown. Have a mess here.*

The killer struck again? the warrior asked.

Yes. Two bodies.

On my way.

As Dagan rose to his feet, another scent teased his nose, fruity with a hint of spice...and something more. He drew it inside him, studying the new clue.

Rage, so much rage...yet, beneath it all, like a mile of grit, despair and anguish abraded him.

A familiar shift in the air and Aethan took form beside him. The cold moon highlighted the warrior's multihued blue hair he'd pulled into a ponytail and glinted off the small silver hoops in his earlobes.

Hands on his hips, Aethan surveyed the death scene, expression grim. "With this kind of power, we'll all be at risk."

Didn't he know it? With a nod, Dagan dematerialized, tracking the fading vibration.

***

Shae Ion blew away the strands of hair dipping into her eyes and stared through her viewfinder at the homeless man seated on an up-turned crate a short distance away. Several stray cats circled between his legs. The moon cast a pale light on the moment, giving the scene a raw, realness to it. Despite his poverty, the old man dropped crumbs of whatever he was eating for the strays. Her camera shutter whirred as she captured several shots for her *Nightlife* series.

As a freelance photographer, she traveled to places the world forgot existed. Besides, *National Geographic* demanded the best, and she needed her work to be gritty and beyond exceptional to get their attention. More, being self-employed gave her the time she needed to search for her mother.

She lowered her camera and rubbed her burning eyes. Six months had passed, and still nothing. Hiring a PI had been a waste of time. He'd come up with not a single lead. Now she'd been reduced to this. She only hoped Harvey came through for her.

A gut-wrenching thought knocked the breath out of her lungs. *Oh, God, please, don't let her be dead—*

Rough hands grabbed her shoulders. Her Nikon crashed to the asphalt. Her heart slamming against her ribs, she jabbed her elbow into her assailant's throat and spun around.

The guy stumbled back. His eyes glowed, streaked with red. "What's a pretty little human like you doing all by her lonesome in this place?"

"Waiting to stake your ass." She gave the demon a wide berth, the iron blade she'd concealed in the back waistband of her jeans now gripped in her hand. Oh, she knew what he was. Born with extrasensory awareness, it made her cognizant and wary of the demon-kind living in this world. Otiums, Harvey called them. They appeared human and preferred a quiet life. It was why they'd defected to Earth and away from the cruelty of their world. But then every species had assholes who terrorized the innocent.

"Wanna play, little human?" he taunted and leaped for her.

Going low, Shae struck out with her weapon, slicing him across the chest. Growling, he dove for her, knocking the blade from her hand. She countered with a flying kick. He grabbed her foot, yanking hard. Using his body as leverage, she flipped backward through the air, breaking his hold and landing on her feet.

In a move she didn't even see, his fist struck her in the solar plexus, sending her flying to the filthy ground. She lay there, unable to breathe, scalding pain scouring her body, so sure she'd fractured her ribs.

"Shae?"

At the horrified voice, she simply shook her head, eyes squeezed tight.

"Hell, I'm sorry—"

"I-I'm okay…will be…" she wheezed. Crap, even speaking hurt. Had this demon really been a malevolent one, he would have taken her blood, her soul, whatever he wanted from her by now.

"Hold still." Harvey, her best friend, laid his hand on her chest, and a slight warmth spread through her at his healing power.

When her lungs functioned again, and it didn't feel like her ribcage was being pried apart with a chest spreader, she opened her eyes and stared into a lean, handsome face. Red-tinged, caramel-hued eyes watched her anxiously.

"Thank the dark gods! I'm really sorry about that last punch, I didn't mean to hit you so hard."

She grimaced, rubbing her chest. It wasn't something she'd willingly want to experience again. "It's okay. I wanted to learn how to fight your kind, so I have to accept all the bruises that come with it. Thanks for the healing."

"No problem." His expression still edged with worry, he tunneled his fingers through his dark hair. "With the places you go, and now what you want to do, I have to be sure you're ready for anything."

She sat up and blew out a rough breath, disarraying the reddish strands of hair falling over her face. "Don't judge me because I'm a girl."

"It's not *that*. It's because you're human."

Right. Her lips twisting wryly, she took the hand he extended, and he pulled her to her feet. She picked up her camera. Darn! The casing had cracked, but at least the rest of the expensive equipment appeared intact.

"Here." Harvey handed her dagger back, then pulled on his leather jacket he'd left lying on the crates near the wall, covering his bloody shirt.

Remorse flooded her. "I didn't mean to hurt you."

"It's nothing. I'll heal."

She dropped her things into her backpack. "How did you find me?"

"Where else would you be when RockinHell is in town? *RockinHell*." He snickered at the band's name. She smacked his arm. "Don't be mean. Why don't you accept the band manager's invitation and play guitar for them?"

He snorted. "You gotta be kiddin' me. Play with *that* loser?"

"Ash's okay—"

"Forgive me if I trample all over your rose-tinted glasses. The guy's an asshole. He can't see what's right in front of him. He'd rather have a revolving door to his bed than you. Hell, if it was me, I'd tell the others to fuck off and come after you."

Grimacing, she glanced at her scraped knuckles then swiped the blood on her jeans. "It's been a long time, and I'm okay, honest. C'mon—" She hooked her backpack over one shoulder and her arm through his. "Let's forget this and go have a drink."

"S'pose it's better than stalking."

She huffed out a laugh. "You give me crap about Ash, and that's where *you* were this evening?"

Harvey was head over heels for a human girl who had no idea he existed. And he was too terrified to even approach her because of what he was.

"More like every evening. Pathetic, right?" Disgust etched his features.

Smiling, she changed the subject. "Did you manage to get me a name?"

"You sure about this?" Lines of concern creased his brow.

"Stop worrying. Let's face it, Harv, it's been six months, and I've tried everything to find her…" She inhaled a shaky breath. The seedy places she'd gone to, flirting with men, demons, and Fallen just to get a lead. "This is the only way to find my mother."

"Fine. Remember, summoning an Edge demon isn't only risky, if they like the way you look, some of them will demand a shag instead of your blood in payment."

She snorted. "All they're getting is money, never *that*. If it's my blood…" She thought about it. "It's a small price to pay."

"Okay, then." He pulled out a folded piece of paper from his jacket pocket and handed it to her. Excitement hiked, causing the heat that had recently plagued her to surge in response. She ignored the latter, staring at the name. Finally. "Thank you."

"No prob—shit," Harvey cursed, his gaze darting to

the entrance of the backstreet. "Shae, forgive me but I must leave. It won't end well for me, not with *him* here." His body shimmered.

"Harvey, wait! Who?"

"You're in no danger, just go back to the club…" His voice faded as he vanished.

What the hell had scared him off? Harvey wasn't the type to run. She stilled, prickles of awareness skating over her skin. It made her tummy dip, and not in a fearful way.

Shae pushed the paper into her jacket pocket. The sensation continued to assail her, growing sharper. Cautiously, she traversed the length of the alley then slowed. There. Deep in the shadows, a tall, dark figure slumped against the wall.

Leave—run! Her cautious side yelled. A low, tortured groan reached her, reverberating through her mind and clawing at her to help. Aw, crap!

Shae dug into her knapsack, found her blade, and slipped it into the back of her jeans. At least it wasn't demons, or worse, their turned brethren, the soul-sucking demoniis. Taking comfort in the feel of her weapon, she inched closer.

***

Dagan cut into another gloomy backstreet. *Aaand* found himself back in the alley where he'd started his patrol.

Farther up, more inebriated humans geared in their Halloween get-ups stumbled out of Club Nocte. The long line remained, partygoers braving the chill, waiting to get inside.

He scanned the place, but the vibe he'd been tracking had gone cold. He bit back a curse. Just great. Except for the demoniis he'd killed earlier, there was nothing that pricked at his senses.

He headed in the opposite direction, deeper into the alley, away from the noise, and staggered to a halt. A mouth-watering scent flooded his senses.

Blood. Fresh human blood.

The seductive aroma seeped through him, tightening his body and saturating his mind like a compulsion. His jaw clenched, his incisors throbbed.

He whipped around, scanning the alley. Pain stabbed his belly, shredding his gut. Hunger took hold. He fell against the wall, struggling against the temptation, eyes shut tight. It took every ounce of willpower he possessed to plant his booted feet on the asphalt and not go after the faint ambrosia trail.

Sometimes, he regretted killing that first damn bird which had bound him to his deadly thirst, but he understood too he couldn't have deviated from that fated path any more than he could stop breathing.

"Are you all right?" a husky voice asked.

His gaze snapped to her. She was tall for a mortal, yet the top of her head barely reached his shoulders. He could clearly make out her alabaster features in the gloomy alley, and the noticeable, bumpy Y-shaped scar running down her cheek. He didn't care how good she looked, right then, all he could think about was just how delicious she'd taste...blood infused with strawberries and spice. Decadent.

Familiar.

The predator side of him thinly leashed, he fought for control—battled not to sink his fangs into her carotid. His eyes slit in warning. "Leave!"

"Look, I'm just trying to—"

"I don't need help!" Damn do-gooder humans.

The coppery nectar tugged at his senses, tempting

him to will her closer so her rich, warm plasma could slide down his throat. And there, on her left hand, he found the source of his doom. Blood smeared her scraped knuckles.

His fangs dropped. *Shit.* He held his breath, reached into her mind, and willed her gone…but hit a wall.

What the hell? He could compel anybody.

With his control fading fast, he snarled, "Get the hell away from me if you want to keep breathing."

Stormy gray-gold eyes widened. Then she stunned all hell outta him and glared right back. "Is that supposed to frighten me? A pair of fake fangs? Shouldn't you be out there with all the other cretins scaring the innocents tonight instead of hiding in the shadows like some pleb?"

At the taunt, Dagan didn't think, he hauled her to him, raking those "fake fangs" down her neck, bruising the skin a little, a hair's breadth past her carotid.

The girl squeaked and slapped her palms on his chest. "What the hell?"

His arm banded around her waist, and he sucked on her fast-beating pulse, his saliva already healing the bruised skin. Unable to let her go just yet, he settled for running his tongue over her silky, warm flesh. She smelled of cinnamon and strawberries, a taste he'd long forgotten. A light brush of her psychic powers skipped over him.

She yanked free, surprising him with her agility, and drew back her fist. He saw the punch coming and let it, hoping it would clear the damn haze in his head. She nailed him straight in the face.

Fuuuck! Stars exploded in his skull, stunning him senseless with the power of her blow.

"Don't ever fucking touch me like that!" Her slanted

eyes glowered like a wildcat's in the dark. Shaking her fingers, she stormed off, muttering in disgust. "What the hell was I thinking trying to help that barbarian? I should have just left."

Dagan stood there, dazed, his blood strumming.

What the hell was *he* thinking? He hadn't lost control like that in millennia.

The urge to go after her, taste her skin again, and satiate his hunger rode him hard, except it would lead to her death. At the thought, something inside him bolted shut.

He rubbed a shaky hand over his throbbing jaw, his damn twitching cock betraying him, then pulled out his cigar—and cursed. He'd left her with memories of his near lapse. Dropping the smoke back into his pocket, he took off after her fast-disappearing figure.

As if sensing him, which surprised him considering he was thousands of years old and an immortal supernatural hunter, she spun around. Before she opened her mouth, he captured her furious gaze. Eyes the color of thunderclouds lit with gold specks lost their turbulence to stare blankly at him. The oddest sensation crept through him. This felt so wrong. He wanted her to remember him. Yet it didn't stop him from what he had to do. First, he grasped her hurt hand and laid his palm over her bruised knuckles, letting his restorative power heal her. Then he scrubbed the unfortunate encounter from her mind.

"Oh…" She blinked those stormy-hued eyes at him a moment later, her brow creasing in confusion. Then shaking her head, she pivoted and ambled off toward the noisy club, leaving behind her luscious scent.

Dagan watched her retreating form. And like his feet had a mind of their own, he found himself keeping to

Georgia Lyn Hunter

the shadows and following her. She thumped on the metal back door. It opened. Smiling at whoever answered, she slipped into a dimly lit corridor. With a thought, he kept it from locking and entered unnoticed.

"I'm so glad you came, Shae." A lanky blond sporting a mohawk hurried toward her and crushed her to him in a hug. "I missed you, doll."

Dagan's teeth clacked down, his eyes narrowing at the male touching her.

"I'm fine, Ash." She smiled, stepping away from the human—which probably saved his life. Yeah, rules had to be followed, and killing mortals was a big no-no.

She is not yours.

No, she wasn't. Could never be.

Reining in the possessiveness that had sprung up out of nowhere, he dematerialized from the club. He didn't mix with mortals, let alone stalk them. Undoubtedly, he was losing his mind from not feeding.

He dematerialized to the Catskills Mountains. As he reformed in the dense forest, he instantly picked up the coppery odor of a wounded animal, its lifeblood pulling at him. He followed the trail, then it all turned fuzzy. He was at the cougar's neck, incisors tearing through flesh and sinew. A red haze filled his mind as blood, warm and thick, flowed into his mouth. He ravenously gulped the liquid nourishment when a shuddering breath cut through the bloody miasma.

No! He reared back, his heart thundering against his ribs in horror as the dying animal collapsed to the ground. Fuck! He scrubbed his unshaven jaw. Normally, he didn't kill the creatures, but this scene drove him back to his blood-crazed past. Instead of the big cat, human bodies lay around him.

Numbed to his very soul, knowing what he was truly

capable off, he flashed to the rapidly flowing river nearby and dove into its icy depths. But nothing could wash away the guilt.

He was a killer. It had become his way of life, a cycle he had no way of ending.

Chapter 2

An hour before sunrise, Dagan reformed on the castle's portico on their island estate just off Manhasset Bay on Long Island Sound. Not because he would poof when caught in sunlight, but because it was time to knock off from patrolling.

He opened the giant wooden front door into the foyer. The recessed orbs highlighted the floor-to-ceiling stained-glass windows on his right. As he headed for the grand staircase, Blaéz appeared at the top, his mate tucked to his side. At her flushed face, it didn't take a genius to know where the warrior's first stop had been on his return from patrol.

Once from the Celtic pantheon and now a fellow Guardian, the warrior's precognition was unequaled. Blaéz nodded at him. It was still a shock to see those cobalt blue eyes when they were once the color of glaciers after losing his soul while imprisoned in Tartarus. But finding his mate had changed all that.

Darci smiled in greeting, her hazel eyes a startling contrast to her tan face. The rare times their paths crossed, she was friendly. Always.

He didn't get that. Echo, Aethan's mate, had avoided him like the plague when she first met him. Not this female. So he merely nodded and jogged up.

"Dag, wait," Blaéz called out.

He glanced back.

"Anything unusual occur tonight at Club Nocte?"

Dagan narrowed his eyes.

"I don't imagine I'll get a straight answer." A smirk rode Blaéz's face—one Dagan didn't care for. "But I'll hazard a guess that tonight was different. Later." The warrior strode off with his mate, his heavy boots thudding in the marble hallway like a deadly omen.

A pair of wild, gray-gold eyes set in a pale face surrounded by wavy, coppery-red hair seeped into his mind.

Damn the Celt and his annoying mind games!

That female was *not* an anomaly in his night's work.

Jaw clenched, he strode for his quarters on the third floor, in the wing opposite Aethan's.

There, in his dimly lit cavernous bedroom, Dagan shut himself away from the others—and the damn world.

Undrawn, ebony drapes revealed the bank of windows opposite and the still dark sky. The wall sconces cast an obscure light over the circular turret living room, dimly illuminating the single couch and a flat-screen TV—one he never used, which for some reason Hedori, their butler, seemed to think he needed. The gloomy, silent quarters suited his mood.

He opened the door on the far side of the fireplace and entered the darkened room. The earthy smell of wood hung heavy in the austere space as he trampled across the wood shavings and sawdust to the small

Georgia Lyn Hunter

fridge near the window. Snagging a bottle of water, he gulped down half the contents, his gaze roaming the place.

The room held nothing but a bench, a table with assorted tools, and a few blocks of wood. Several completed sculptures of varying sizes depicting animals and birds took up space on the floor. He didn't bother with shelves since they all eventually became firewood.

Gulping down the last of the water, he tossed the empty bottle into the trash bin. Despite the thick walls and the fact that he was three floors up, voices carried to him from the kitchen, along with feminine laughter.

Since their escape from Tartarus, he'd never joined the warriors at meal times. Didn't see the point when he didn't consume solids.

Restlessness crawling through him, he changed into sweats and a t-shirt and swapped his boots for sneakers. He jogged down the narrow side stairs, cut through the rec room to the terrace, and took off in a hard run across the manicured gardens, past the lake, and into the dense evergreens edging the estate—the shadowy canopy of trees taking him back to another dark time…in Tartarus. *Gray skies, sweltering heat and endless wastelands—impossible hunger shredding his belly…*

Breathing hard, Dagan shut off the dark memories, no good would come from remembering.

At the burn in his calf muscles, he slowed to a stop on the pebbled shores just off the north side of the soaring cliffs bordering the estate, and inhaled deep lungfuls of the cool, briny air. Minuscule waves fell in a gentle swish on the shore. Hedori's sleek white sailboat moored farther down, bobbed on the calm waters near the boathouse.

As the night skies gave way to splashes of orange and pinks as dawn approached, a low disembodied voice reached him. *Dagan?*

Kaerys.

His lips flattened. He swiped the sweat from his face with the back of his arm.

He'd called her several days ago, and she'd ignored him. He knew why, too. The last time he fed from her, she'd been all over him, but he'd stopped her, simply wanting to eat and get back on patrol. She'd been furious.

"You would deny me again, after all I've done—after I saved you?" she cried. "You broke our betrothal, yet I forgave you. I waited five centuries while you were imprisoned..."

Kaerys always used the guilt card. Her cold-shouldering him wasn't anything new either. Despite her being a minor goddess of chaos, vengeance would have been a more suited title. She could be callously vindictive when things didn't go her way and took delight in making him pay. Tied to her as he was by his blood need, he didn't have many choices.

He pinched the bridge of his nose and exhaled wearily.

Dagan?

Not in the mood to talk to Kaerys, he willed the gateway closed. Unfortunately, he'd have to relent soon since he needed her blood to keep his fucked-up DNA working and his power level recharged before his abilities flatlined. In his line of work, he had to be at full strength.

A sudden wave of power, though tamped down, briefly surrounded the island. The archangel had arrived.

Dagan dematerialized and took form near the imposing stone castle covered in ivy. A streak of gray rushed through the open rec room doors, only to skid to a halt on the terrace. Its fat belly dragging on the granite tiles, Echo's pet crouched, the warning to stay the hell away from him clear in those unblinking amber eyes.

What? Dagan remained where he was, two stairs down, and stared coolly at the feline with the ginger ruff. *Think I won't bite you?*

With a plaintive meow, Bob slunk sideways from him and sprinted to the other side of the terrace, disappearing into the bushes to watch Dagan from behind a potted shrub. Since scared cats weren't on his menu, Dagan jogged up the steps and into the rec room, retrieved his black cigar case from the wet bar, and made his way to the Arc's study. The French doors were flung wide, and the cool breeze, a mixture of the briny Atlantic Ocean and flowers, drenched the small room.

The leader of the Guardians wasn't at his desk but outside on the small patio, his inky hair pulled back in a haphazard half-ponytail. Michael sat on the edge of the wooden table, stroking a euphoric Bob.

He looked up, his shattered irises appearing as if prisms of light were glowing from them. "Everything okay with you?"

No, just fucked in every way. "Yeah. Fine."

The Arc's eyebrow lifted, but he didn't ask questions. After all, Michael had seen him at his worst, a monster held in the throes of bloodlust. He hadn't judged, instead found a way for Dagan to survive without killing again. So, yeah, he owed him big time.

Footsteps echoed. The others appeared moments later.

Aethan leaned against the doorjamb while Blaéz claimed one of the wrought-iron chairs. Týr, the other. Dagan didn't even glance at *him*. The enmity between them was too old, and something that could never be put to rights or healed, not with the spilled blood of innocents between them.

"Any repercussions since taking out the skin club?" Michael asked, folding his arms. And Bob let out a disgruntled meow.

Dagan recalled that particular incident from a year ago at Club Illudo—or the Sin Club as it was called. An immortal had been killing human females through autoerotic asphyxiation. Dagan had finally caught the bastard in action before Aethan turned everything to dust inside the club—demons included—with his formidable power of whitefire. The Fallen had been badly burned and close to death, and still he'd threatened Dagan with retribution. He was probably well acquainted with Purgatory by now.

"I checked it out tonight." Aethan freed his bound hair. "It's exactly as we left it, just rats and 'roaches occupying the place now. Can't believe the shit some of these immortals resort to for ultimate gratification, killing the innocent."

Dagan's stomach heaved. He's been responsible for far, far worse.

Retrieving a cigar from his black case, he lit it and inhaled deeply. Even the sedative smoke couldn't dull his remorse. He understood if he fed on a human again, he would revert back to that repugnant creature he'd once been, steeped in endless bloodlust. And, this time, he'd suffer the consequences.

Georgia Lyn Hunter

He leaned a shoulder against a wooden trellis covered with thick, creeping vine. "The psychic killer's back," he said, changing the subject. "Two more bodies tonight, the third a demon, but he'd already been pulled back to the Dark Realm when I got there. A homeless man got caught in the middle of the fracas, suffered a stab wound. Said something about Satan killing people."

"Yeah, I came across him after I got rid of the bodies—called me the devil," Aethan added with a wry smile. "Probably caught a flicker of my power."

"Nah, it's the hair." Týr smirked, reaching out to stroke an abandoned Bob. The feline rose and dove onto his lap, settling there with a happy purr.

Snorting, Aethan continued. "The vagrant was still mumbling about Satan using his weapon for revenge, then about someone stealing his worldly goods. The guy reeked like a defunct distillery. He was probably hallucinating from the blood loss. I healed him and sent him off."

Michael's brow furrowed. "So, two humans and a demon dead?"

"No." Dagan blew out a spiral of smoke. "One of the dead was a Fallen."

"That's a first. Why would the killer target Fallens now?" Blaéz asked.

Dagan shrugged. Hell, he had no idea what the fucker was up to. "There is something else…" He frowned. The girl's scent reminded him a lot of the psychic killer's, but gut instinct said no. And as much as he didn't want to talk about *her*, he had a job to do. "While tracking the killer last night, I came across a female. Human. She smelled almost identical to the one at the death site—"

"Rage?" Aethan cut in, his gunmetal grays narrowing. "Think she could be psionic?"

Dagan understood why he asked; his mate was the first of the Watcher's descendants to rise. Mortals born with vast powers from long-dead angels, something no human should ever possess.

He shook his head. "Not sure about that, though I did pick up a faint psychic impression from her."

Why else would he react the way he had?

Blaéz smirked but merely said, "I've been keeping an eye on this situation with the human authorities. They're conducting an investigation into the disappearance of those humans from earlier in the year. The female needs to be watched."

Michael slowly nodded. His brows slanted in a frown as he scratched his whiskered jaw. "If this situation grows too dangerous, it will soon bring notice to us. The Celestial Realm won't be pleased." He glanced at Dagan. "Find her and keep an eye on her."

Dagan's fingers tightened on his cigar case. Damn the Celt and his idiotic suggestions.

"Why would those snobby assholes be interested in what goes on with our lowly investigation?" Týr asked, Bob forgotten on his lap. With a rumble of displeasure, the cat hopped off and waddled indoors.

A heavy sigh barreled out of the archangel. "Because even though Zarias was the leader of the Watchers, there were some amongst his band of angels who wielded immensely dangerous powers. The M.O. of these killings bears a striking resemblance to Zarias' second in command, Laius. When the female's calm, you'll probably get a false reading. It's best to have her in a contained place to be certain."

Calm? Dagan frowned. Hell, she'd been furious

when she punched him in the face.

Psychic? A mere whisper of it.

A killer?

Hardly.

***

Shae pulled on her black boots and laced them, her gaze on the folded piece of paper on the bed. She should be excited about this, right? One step closer to finding her mother.

Except she couldn't get her mind to focus because of this sense of unsettling disquiet she felt. It had plagued her last night and the entire day while she holed up in the developing studio downtown, as if she should remember something. But the memories continued to elude her.

She rubbed her temples. Harvey had met her in the alley, and he'd put her through the wringer, testing her fighting skills. *That* she recalled. He'd given her the demon's name, but something had disturbed him, and he'd bolted out of there, saying something about being in trouble. And then she stopped at the club. So, what was she missing?

Ugh. She huffed out an annoyed breath at hitting a blank, sending the strands of hair dipping into her eyes into disarray.

Her cell rang. She grabbed it from her nightstand. Harvey. "Hey, you okay?"

"I'm good. Sorry I had to bail last night. I just wanted to avoid someone who'd kill me without a second thought if he saw me."

Her stomach dipped in anxiety. "Who—why?"

A heavy sigh coasted down the line. "Because I got in the way of his job. I had to rescue my idiotic kin, who took to joining a group of blood-demons. He was caught with them while they fed from humans. My kin hadn't done anything, but regardless, he would have died. There's no reasoning with those cold Guardian bastards."

She wiped at her damp brow with the back of her hand, her temperature rising again. "I'm happy you're safe but don't ever scare me like that again. Harvey, let me call you back. We can meet up to summon the demon, 'kay?"

"Sure, later."

Dropping her cell on the bed, she rose. The room tilted. Dammit, she sat down again. With shaky hands, she snatched the frosty, plastic bottle with the glucose solution from the bedside table, unscrewed the top, and swallowed some of the concentrated mixture. Having to deal with sudden dips in her blood sugar was bothersome as hell.

Sweat beaded on her brow, her mind buzzed, and her heart pounded too fast. She drank more of her ice-cold liquid and inhaled deeply, trying to calm down... Finally, the heat eased a little, as did the hum.

Shae collected the things she needed: cell phone, the folded paper, some cash from the bedside, along with a roll of Dextrose candies, and pushed them into her jacket pocket. Covered for her evening, she headed out, skirting the marble podium in the corridor with the priceless Ming vase, and ran down the stairs.

Uncle Lem had gone on an overnight business trip to Chicago, but he'd be home soon, and she needed to leave before he coaxed her into staying and having dinner. He was the one person she couldn't say no to. But she had a demon to summon, and it was nearly ten p.m.

In the kitchen, she grabbed a slice of toasted brown

bread with cheese and ham from the microwave. As she ate, she dumped the dishes into the dishwasher with her free hand, switched on the machine, then shoved the last bit of her sandwich into her mouth. Still chewing, she hurried into the living room, determined to be gone before Lem came back.

The study door opposite the living room opened. "Shae?"

Aw, crap. She swallowed her food, slapped on a smile, and pivoted. "Uncle Lem, you're home early."

"Yes." His sea-blue gaze twinkled. "I got in a little while ago and came straight here to pick up some papers for the office. I have a late-night conference call."

In his mid-forties, average height, with short, light brown hair and angular features, Leamas Hale was one of those men who looked good in anything he wore. But he favored suits, and it flattered his lean frame.

She'd known him since she was a little girl. He'd been her father's best friend. After her dad had died several years ago, he'd been there for both her and her mom. But just thinking of her father, and pain burrowed deeper.

"Shae?" Lem crossed to her, anxiety creasing his brow. "What is it?"

"Nothing." Before he started with the questions, she asked the one thing guaranteed to stop them. "Did you find her?"

A tinge of pity flashed in his eyes. "She doesn't want to be found, Shae. If she did, wouldn't she have contacted you?"

Despite hearing her own thoughts from Lem's lips, pain still seeped into her. To be responsible for driving her own mother away, perhaps she deserved to be abandoned and alone.

"It doesn't matter, I want her found. Then she can tell me to my face that she hates me instead of leaving you to do her dirty work—*how could she*?" she cried, unable to hide her bitterness. "*Nine* years after Dad died, *now* she—" Shae pulled in a deep breath and turned away before he could reach for her. She didn't want comfort, didn't deserve it. "I'm sorry, I shouldn't have yelled."

"It's all right." He awkwardly patted her back. "You are her child, you're distraught at her sudden departure from your life."

A child? Harsh laughter escaped her. Right. One she could no longer stand to look at. There was nothing else to be said, was there? Her mother hated her for sending her father to his death.

"Shae, your mother was quite distressed at what happened the night before she left."

"What?" She spun around to him, feeling as if an iron fist squeezed her chest. "Mom left because of the accident?" And not because her father had been mugged and killed when he stopped to buy her ice cream?

He nodded. "I didn't want to tell you, but seeing you hurting this way... That evening your laptop exploded, with glass splintering everywhere"—his gaze settled on the scar on her face—"and she hit the wall across the room, it terrified her."

"But she said...she said it wasn't my fault." A whisper of pain. "And I don't have any new abilities, except for sensing Others. It was a glitch."

"I know, child. However, before she left, that was what she told me. She couldn't get over losing your father and then that... I'm sorry." Lem's lips twisted in

Georgia Lyn Hunter

sympathy.

Swallowing hard, Shae slipped her hands into her jacket pocket, her fingers squashing the piece of paper with the demon's name. No matter. She'd find her and hear for herself. *Then* she'd close that part of her life. "I have to go. I'll see you later."

Instantly, Lem's expression morphed into a stern one. "I don't like you out on the streets alone, Shae."

He made no bones about the fact he thought her career choice *dangerous*. Well, it was—not that she'd tell him. She didn't want Lem worrying himself into an ulcer or worse, a heart attack. He was all she had left.

"I'm not working tonight, Uncle, I'm going to the club."

Nothing showed on his face, but she sensed his disapproval. Whatever his feelings were toward Ash, she was grateful he kept them to himself. She didn't have many friends. *Many*? She stifled back a harsh laugh. It was just Ash and Harvey. After her father's death, Lem had had her home-schooled, so friends weren't a priority.

Shae left and made her way to the penthouse elevator. The moment the door closed, she inhaled deeply, squeezed her eyes shut, and struggled to center herself as the cage carried her down in death-defying speed from the eightieth floor. The moment the elevator opened, a little dazed, she stumbled out, reached for a candy in her pocket, and popped the thing into her mouth.

A little steadier, she cut through the elegant foyer with its marble pillars, smiled at the older doorman, and stepped out into the busy street. Harvey wasn't on duty tonight. Who knew the part-time doorman of The Tower would become her best friend? She'd known him since she moved into the penthouse, when he'd befriended a lonely fifteen-year-old who'd just lost her father.

Her gaze swept the street, searching for a cab. At the sight of a tall, familiar, fair-haired man standing a short distance from her, she hastily hid behind a group of people also waiting for a taxi.

Aza. Her uncle's right-hand man and business partner was talking to a heavyset demon. A few of Lem's business associates were Others, but he never invited anyone home. Except Aza. A Fallen.

Sometimes, Shae wondered about her state of mind when she accepted his offer to search for her mother in exchange for a date. Sheesh, she'd been such an idiot and she realized the truth too late as the weeks passed and he didn't find anything. He just wanted her.

Sure, he was good-looking, but something about him made her uneasy. After three months and a few dates, she'd rescinded the offer and took to avoiding him. Yeah, Harvey had called her crazy for agreeing to the Fallen's deal.

A taxi glided to a halt, and she hastily climbed in before Aza saw her. Inhaling a thankful breath, she settled back in her seat and scratched her left wrist. She pushed her silver bracelets aside and frowned at the redness covering the small tattoo there—an intricate series of knots with one side open. Ugh, she hoped she wasn't getting a rash on it.

Her cell beeped with a text. She pulled it out of her jacket pocket. Ash.

You coming to the club, doll?

She bit her lip then typed back. *On my way.*

Great. See you soon.

Ashton Stiles was not only her friend but also an

amazing guitarist and the frontman for RockinHell. The demons living in this world probably got a kick out of the name. Harvey sure did.

A while later, Shae hurried down the alley toward the warehouse that had been converted to a nightclub. Stopping in front of the graffitied back entrance to Club Nocte, an unsettling awareness crawled through her, like she should recall something about this place.

Warily, she rubbed her neck and studied the alley. A shiver darted along her spine. She banged the heavy, metal door, and a tattooed bouncer opened up and waved her inside.

Avoiding the groupies hanging out in the corridor near the backstage area, she made her way into the noisy club instead, still a little uneasy. And at the sudden blast of music, she stumbled into two guys.

"Hey, beautiful." One smiled drunkenly. The other one's gaze rested on her cheek. "Dang, girl, that thing sure ruins the look."

Asshole. Instantly, her hand went up to block the scar on her face. Oh, she was aware of it, and it hurt when she smiled or when some dickhead spewed out shit like that. Uncle Lem had said she could get it fixed with a good plastic surgeon, but she'd refused—not until she found her mother. The scar her reminder of what she was responsible for.

Smoothing her long, wavy hair over her cheek, she texted Ash, *I'm at the bar, need a drink.*

And got an immediate response. *See you in a few.*

Ash's band usually played the second half of the night so he had time. Shae pushed through the throng of people, squeezed in between a heavyset man and another guy, and ordered her drink. The moment she got her vodka tonic, she gulped back some of the fiery liquor, the burn soothing her a little, and watched for Ash.

She'd met him six years ago during his short stint at University, and they'd become fast friends. For a moment, she'd thought he liked her, too. But that had just been her imagination. Considering his notoriety when it came to women, it was probably for the best. So she'd shut away those feelings and moved on. She'd dated, but her one serious relationship had ended a year ago.

Then, all the craziness started. With the constant heat swirling inside her—and her mother taking off—socializing had been the last thing on her mind…except for those few dates she'd had with Aza.

Shae took another sip of her drink. As her sight adjusted to the flashing laser light, a man half hidden in the shadows of the dimly lit seating area adjacent to her caught her attention.

So tall, with his arms folded over his chest, he surveyed the dance floor, his face barely visible. The people around him gave him a wide berth where he stood near the steel railings, probably at the perilous air he seemed to exude.

As if sensing her stare, his head turned, and he went utterly still. Goosebumps spilled across her skin. Hastily, Shae shielded behind a bulky guy and his girlfriend walking past, her heart thudding rapidly. How she knew he was looking at her, she had no idea.

Ugh, with all the madness she'd had to deal with recently, she was probably overreacting. She'd never seen him before. He had to be looking at someone behind her.

Her head buzzed. She set her glass down and rubbed her temples. Hazy images that'd haunted her sleep last night resurfaced, seeping through her mind. A blurred face…lips kissing her throat. Heat flowed through her body, desire awakening—*noooo!*

The air in the club drained. Her lungs shut down. Unable to breathe, she shoved and pushed her way through the crush of bodies, desperate to get to the entrance before she passed out.

After what seemed like forever, she stumbled into the cool night. Some distance away from the congested entrance, she slowed down and pressed her back against the grimy wall, desperately inhaling the rancid air. *Havta calm down, havta calm down…*

A scrawny cat hissed, darting past her, almost yanking her heart out of her throat. Jesus! She rubbed a hand over her face then popped a strawberry Dextrose into her mouth. She retrieved her cell from her pocket to text Ash that she was leaving, only to stop and stare at her hands. In the moonlight, her pale skin appeared chalk-white. No wonder people thought her fragile, breakable. That was their first mistake.

"Dammit, Shae, you don't go taking off like rabid dogs are after you and scaring me," Ash groused, stomping up to her, his lean face creased in worry. "It's not safe out here. Didn't you hear me yell after you? And aren't you staying for the show?"

Meeting his concerned gaze, she realized then that it wasn't Ash's fault but hers for prolonging this insanity—for meeting up whenever he called. She settled for, "I was, but Harvey wants to see me. Go back to your fans, Ash. I'm leaving."

His lips tightened briefly. He didn't like Harvey, which she didn't get. It wasn't like he knew what Harvey was or that Others inhabited this world, too. "Fine. Let me call you a cab at least—"

"Yo, Ash," one of the band members yelled. "The manager wants to speak to you."

He glanced in the direction of the club's back entrance and cursed under his breath. "Give me a minute, okay?" He hustled off.

Shae sagged against the building. God, she needed a break, a moment of peace. No buzzing heat in her mind, move past Ash and find a way to locate her mother.

It wasn't such a tall order, was it? She slid her eyes heavenward to the night sky. No answer there. Guess she was all on her own, then. Pushing away from the wall, she took a step toward the main street and froze at the tall, dark figure heading her way.

Him.

The man from the club.

Instinctively, she shrank back into the shadows. It wasn't as if he were even aware of her, just because she was of him. Her cell rang. Harvey. "Hey."

"You didn't call back?"

"I'm sorry, things got a little hectic."

"No problem. I'm guessing you're at Club Nocte. Be there in ten minutes. We can catch some of RockinHell, and then do the summoning at midnight."

Shae rubbed her shaky palm down her short skirt, her mind all over the place, too rattled to think clearly. "I want to more than anything, but it's been an exhausting day. Work and other stuff, you know"—like strange dreams of a man kissing her throat— "Tomorrow night would be better."

"Okay. But I'm working tomorrow. I get off at eleven. How about I meet you at Club Nocte around 11:30?"

"Sounds good, I'll see you then." She ended the call.

Looked up. "Dammit!" She jumped back, her heart crashing against her ribcage, her cell falling to the asphalt with a sharp clatter.

He stood right in front of her.

The urge to run grew. Instead, she scrambled after her phone. Thankfully, it had stayed together.

"A moment."

At that low, accented voice, something inside her stirred awake. Muscular, leather-clad thighs filled her view as she straightened. Even with her five-foot-eleven height, the man towered over her. Her gaze trailed up, up, up. Dressed entirely in black, he appeared as if he belonged to the night.

Dark. Mysterious. And very, very dangerous, the realization seeped into her.

Stubble darkened his jaw. Inky hair woven into several ropey braids hung past his waist. But his sculptured features appeared as if cast in bronze, his expression about as readable as the same metal. Yet a raw sensuality etched every line of his cold, handsome face. His compelling magnetism slithered around her like a net slowly reeling her closer.

However, the piercing stare of those cold, citrine eyes had her thoughts skidding back to reality. Yellow was supposed to be warm, but his were like frozen fire. *Other.*

Shae shifted back a step, her cell clutched tightly to her chest. *Leave—get-out*, the warning whopped around in her head. She'd never been one to disregard her sixth sense. Without speaking, she stepped around him but found him in her path. Crap!

Warily, she eyed him. Instinct warned her that he wouldn't leave until he had whatever he'd come for. His nose flared slightly as if breathing *her* in?

"Shae?"

He knew her name? No, no! Her heart slammed violently against her ribs, it actually hurt.

She tended to avoid Others. Uncle Lem said it was safer because most usually came with a crap-load of trouble one could not avoid. Thank God she hadn't told him about Aza.

"Who's asking?"

"We need to talk."

There was intent to compel behind those cool words. It pushed through her mental shields, urging her with gentle force to agree. Hurriedly, she tightened her mind's defenses. She had to get out of there before Ash came looking for her and got caught in the crosshairs of whatever this was.

Shae tried to cut past him again but he moved so incredibly fast, blocking her way once more. Uneasiness crept into her. Demons could do that, Harvey had shown her so she'd be aware of what she was dealing with. But this man's eyes didn't possess any tinge of red.

"I don't have time, my date will be here any second," she lied.

"We can do this here, now, or the hard way."

"Are you threatening me?" she snapped, despite fear crashing through her.

Those yellow eyes became slits of irritation, like he hadn't expected her to...what? Fight back? She had so little control of what was happening in her life, she'd be damned if she allowed a stranger to take away her choices, too. She became then aware of how quiet the alley had become—just him and her—when he suddenly grabbed her, hauling her to him.

"What the hell?" She yanked at the arm holding her

Georgia Lyn Hunter

against a wall of rigid muscle and breathed in his warm, masculine scent…sandalwood with a hint of leather and cherry tobacco. Her blood warmed, and desire stirred, unsettling her—*no*. She fought harder, shoving at his chest.

"Stop." The low, clipped order halted her struggles like nothing else did. He wasn't looking at her, but appeared to be scanning the gloomy thoroughfare. Then she felt it, an eerie slide against her skin. Her stomach churned, the urge to flee tearing at her. Danger was closing in on them.

"Let go!" she cried, hitting and clawing like some wild animal. A sharp, whizzing sound echoed. The man spun her around, slamming her against the wall, and he jolted.

Shae gasped.

His furious gaze glowered like a living flame as they pinned hers. Pain shimmered in her mind. Then everything went dark.

Chapter 3

Dagan swept the difficult female he'd willed to sleep against him and scanned the alley again. There was no one else in the area except them. But the burning sensation in his back told him differently and had him gritting his teeth in annoyance.

His wound would heal as soon as he got the bullet out. But he needed the evidence and couldn't do so now. Whoever had taken a shot at the girl had vanished. Yeah, it had been meant for her, because no one would dare shoot at him, not if they wanted to live.

Using his psychic senses, he tracked mentally…and picked up a fast-disappearing trail. He studied it, absorbing the acrid odor of sulfur and fear. Demon. Asshole probably hadn't expected *him* to show up. He was going to enjoy the scourge's death.

Dagan shifted Shae's slight weight in his arm and picked up her fallen cell phone with his free hand.

Thudding footsteps broke the quiet. "What the hell are you doing?" a male barked. "Let her go!"

He straightened, recognizing the human as the one

from last night, the one whom she'd been hugging, and cut him an impassive stare. The urge to wring the man's neck for leaving her alone with a damn sniper after her took hold. If he hadn't been hanging around this place, waiting for her, she'd be dead.

"I'm taking her with me."

"You aren't taking her anywhere!"

He didn't have time for this pesky human's interference. Dagan simply held the man's gaze and took over his mind. "Go fuck up your life like you usually would" was his preferred directive, but Gaia would kick his ass for that. *You've already seen her home. Now leave.*

The guy's belligerent expression vanishing, he ambled back to the club entrance. Women rushed him. He put his arm around a brunette's waist and they disappeared inside.

Date? Right. Dagan glanced at the female in his arms and shook his head. Pushing her cell into his back pocket, he stepped deeper into the shadows, and with the castle in mind, he dematerialized them both there.

A few minutes later, he reformed on the portico, willed the massive front door open, and entered the foyer. About to head upstairs, Dagan paused. With her conflicting psychic vibrations, he changed direction and headed down the marble-tiled corridor to the stairs that led to the basement. The floors there gave way to plain, dark tiles and an unadorned passage leading to the training arena. The once painted walls were bare, gray stones again. Hedori had probably given up on maintaining the surfaces here. At times, their powers escaped, and it did some real damage despite the arcane magic protecting the place.

With a thought, Dagan retrieved a black exercise

mat, dropped it against the wall, and laid her on it. This place was safest for now.

"If you're the one I'm searching for," he told her sleeping form, "I'm not surprised you have a hit on you." He moved a swathe of silky hair away from her face, his fingertips brushing her cheek, and frowned at the rough, uneven, Y-shaped scar there. Slightly pink, it stood out on her pale skin. Had to be recent.

Hard to imagine a person this fragile could be a ruthless killer when she appeared to have more damages to herself. But then in his long life, and with all he'd seen, nothing much surprised him anymore.

He glanced at the colorful, wavy strands he'd been caressing between his fingertips, a blend of deep reds, light browns, and hints of gold. She stirred awake. He dropped his hand.

Feline-tipped eyes the color of brewing storm clouds with specks of sunlight blinked at him. She sat up and scrambled back. That stubborn chin rose, accusation flashing in her eyes. "What the hell did you do to me?"

Sent you to sleep and dematerialized with you. No, he didn't think that would go over too well. He said instead, "You're safe."

"Safe—*safe?*" she snapped, her face a delectable shade of red. Then she glanced around the place, and her color drained. "You *kidnapped* me? Brought me here because I wouldn't *talk* to you?"

"If you want to give it a label, then sure."

She looked like she wanted to punch him again. Her soft mouth tightened. A deep inhale followed as if she were struggling for control.

No way could he leave a psionic, if she were one, on the loose. Shit would not just rain down on them but explode everywhere, and he definitely could do without that. He scanned her again and, despite her temper moments ago, he picked up nothing, just a slight hum of her psychic abilities that resonated though his psyche.

Hell, he'd rather she was psionic, then he could hand the wildcat over to Michael and be done with this deadly temptation. But he needed answers first.

"Those dead men in the alley last night. Tell me about them."

***

Shae inhaled deeply, counted to ten, and prayed a madman hadn't abducted her.

He remained hunkered down in front of her, eyes cool, his powerful forearms braced on his muscular, leather-clad thighs. Small scars marred his tanned fingers he kept loosely clasped in front of him. He wore a wide, corded leather band on one thick wrist and several narrow ones on his other. His black t-shirt stretched across his broad shoulders like a second skin, the short sleeves revealing bulging biceps. On his left one, he sported a sword-like tattoo made up of a myriad of intricate designs. It was unusual, like nothing she'd ever seen.

With those clothes and his long, ropey hair, he dressed like an extra from a movie shoot or something.

"You can't keep me here," she tried to reason with him. "You have to let me go. My uncle will be frantic and calling the cops by now."

"Not until you answer my questions. Those dead men?"

She scowled, all thoughts of being calm and rational flying out the window. He'd accosted her outside the club, kidnapped her, and now he expected her to answer his damn questions? "Just what the hell are you talking about? What dead men?"

Sure, he was infuriatingly good-looking, but then so was Ted Bundy.

At the thought of the serial killer who'd charmed and murdered several college girls, Shae sprang to her feet and bulleted for the door. He grabbed her around the waist. Crap, she'd forgotten how fast he could move.

"Lemme go!" She hit him, but he merely swept her into his arms like she was some delicate freakin' daisy and carried her back. Furious, she bit him. Hard. And hoped her teeth did some real damage to his biceps.

An annoyed grunt escaped him. "Stop that, you little hellcat."

Like a bag of unwanted grain, he dropped her on her butt, back on the mat again.

Pain jarred up her spine, and she clenched her teeth. But the three angry, red streaks scored on his powerful forearm had her blinking.

She'd done that? Shocked to her core at her dreadful behavior, Shae opened her mouth to apologize but when she met those burning yellow eyes that had taken on hints of orange, a spurt of anger cut through her guilt. "This is kidnapping. I'm gonna have your barbaric ass thrown in jail!"

"Try. When you're ready to talk, scream. Maybe I'll hear you, maybe I won't." His eyes like flint, he stalked out, shutting the door quietly behind him, only to stride back inside. He crossed to the far end of the room, grabbed all the swords from the stand there, and walked out again. Leaving behind a small fridge. Right then, she wanted to fling the appliance at his arrogant head. Except he looked like he could break her neck with just one hand.

She had to get out of here before he came back.

Jumping to her feet, she ran for the door and tried the handle, not surprised to find the barbarian had locked her inside. Her teeth ground in frustration. She glanced around the barren place. Where the heck was she?

A basement in a warehouse? Another state? This place could demand its own zip code. It was freakin' huge. But getting that knuckle-dragging brute to tell her anything…hell, it would be easier if she simply wished for wings.

The interior, though well maintained, had high rectangular windows that she had no hope of squeezing through. Recessed lights were embedded in the ceiling and rugged stone walls flowed around her. Yep, trapped.

She paced the slate-colored tiles covering the floor. Sweat beaded on her brow and neck, the heat inside her rising.

Why the hell was she feeling this way? Like a lit detonator about to go off?

With trembling fingers, she retrieved a barrette from her jacket pocket and pulled her waist-length hair into a high ponytail, trying to cool down. Shae hurried to the small fridge and found it stacked with energy drinks and water. She grabbed a bottle of water, unscrewed the top, and drank some, fighting to calm down so the dizziness wouldn't take over and make her black out.

Wouldn't that movie-reject be thrilled at how weak she was?

As she stomped back to the black mat, his question bounced around in her head. Dead men? She didn't recall any, but there'd certainly be one tonight when she got her hands on *him* and strangled him with his damn hair!

***

Dagan left the basement, frustration riding him hard. Sending a telepathic message to Michael that he had the woman, he strode into the empty kitchen. With the other warriors still out on patrol, only their females and Hedori would be around.

To be sure, he scanned and found Echo in the library with her tutor, and Blaéz's mate in her quarters. Good. Or those two would go poking their noses in his business if they knew another female was here. They wouldn't care that she could be a dangerous psi. Best the little hellcat remained in the basement. Once Michael confirmed what she was, then he would be done with this.

His thumbs hooked in his back pockets, Dagan stopped at the open French doors and stared out into the moonlit night, inhaling deep breaths of cold air. Yet nothing could wipe out the tightness in his body or the compelling scent that seemed determined to haunt him.

He rubbed his forearms where she'd scratched him. Hell, she'd bitten him, too! He checked his arm. The little hellcat's teeth had punctured his skin but hadn't drawn blood.

His pocket vibrated. Pulling out her cell, he frowned at the abridged message. Ash Stiles. This had to be the human who was with her. *I hope you're okay, doll. How about lunch? Call me.*

At the shimmer in the air, he pushed the phone back into his pocket as Michael took form, his aviator shades perched on his head.

"I have the female—" *Who made me lose control.* No need for Michael to know how he'd reacted to her or what he'd done. Or that he'd been on a short fuse ever since to go after an innocent human and break his neck. "Her name's Shae. She has the conflicting vibes of a psionic and something else I can't quite isolate. And someone took a shot at her."

"Where is she?"

"Basement."

About to enter the kitchen, Michael paused, cutting him an amused look. "Yes, it would be safer down there."

Of course, it was. The Arc didn't have to deal with the hellcat.

They both flashed to the basement. Michael put on his shades, shielding his fractured irises he never revealed to humans. Dagan willed the locks open and stepped inside. A bottle came flying at his head, drenching him before falling to the floor with a thud.

"You locked me in this damn place, you-you barbarian!"

The urge to gag her grew. His lips thinning, Dagan swiped the water off his face then followed the Arc to where she was, realizing he was no longer the focus of her ire. Her attention had shifted to Michael.

What was it about Michael that made the females go all gaga soft and shit? And not fight and scratch him? The Arc was dressed the same as he was, in leathers, but he wore one of his moth-eaten t-shirts, this one in a faded navy. Strands of hair had escaped his bunched ponytail, and a day's stubble darkened his jaw.

Suspiciously, she eyed the both of them. "Who are you people? What do you want from me?"

The Arc lowered to his haunches as if that would make him less intimidating. She scooted back, pressing defensively against the wall behind her.

"I am Michael. I'm sorry that you are being held in our training quarters. I'd like to take you to a more comfortable place to talk. Can I trust you not to…throw things?"

A faint flush tinted her skin. Was the wildcat embarrassed? Yeah, right.

She nodded. "Hello, Michael. It's good to know some of the leather posse has manners." She shot Dagan a dark look, her antagonism back in spades.

He didn't react, merely watched her. If she was psionic, then her stubborn little ass was now Michael's responsibility.

"Good. Come." In spite of Michael's relaxed expression, Dagan sensed his amusement as he walked out of the arena. She followed him like some purring, happy little kitten. Claws hidden.

Dagan followed the hellcat.

She'd tied her jacket around her waist, revealing a black sleeveless top that exposed her pale, slender arms. As they took the stairs up, his gaze lowered past her short gray skirt to her long, sexy legs. On her feet, she wore a pair of battered, lace-up, steel-toed boots. Perhaps sensing his stare, she cut him a sharp look over her shoulder. He waited for her to say something, or to kick him down the stairway with those deadly boots.

She did neither. Instead, she simply dismissed him with a toss of her head, her high ponytail flipping back and nearly whacking him in the face.

He followed her into the massive kitchen lined with oak cupboards and a gray granite counter. A center island separated the dining area.

Shae stopped abruptly when she saw Hedori. Only Dagan's quick reflexes saved him from crashing into her. He sidestepped her and crossed to the open doors, hoping the brisk air would clear his lungs of her fruity spice scent.

"That's our butler," Michael said. "Hedori, this is

Shae—?"

"Ion. Shae Ion."

Their all-around handyman, butler, and protector gave her a half bow. "I am pleased to meet you, Ms. Ion."

Her lips curved in response. "It's Shae. You have pretty eyes."

Usually quite stoic, Hedori's *pretty* eyes glowed, apparently, a goner for her. "Ah, thank you. Would you care for something to drink?"

"A soda, please."

Hedori inclined his head and went to get her more ammo to fling at his head.

Don't rush her, Michael telepathed him. *She's on edge. Give her time to relax, lower her guards. She has extremely strong shields.*

Very well.

"When you're done with your drink, we'll meet in my study," Michael told her. She didn't say anything as the Arc nodded at him and left.

Hedori handed her a glass of fizzing, orange drink and was graced with another smile. She sipped her soda, then totally ignoring him, she wandered past him, stepped outside and stared into the darkened garden where insects chirped in dissonance. "This is so lovely, tranquil…"

Her voice held yearning, and her shoulders drooped as if in dejection. Dagan wanted to go over and soothe her.

"You'll be safe here," he said instead.

Her back stiffened. She spun around, eyes spitting fire. "How am I safe when *you* abducted me, brought me here against my will—and where is *here* anyway?"

"You should be thankful I did, or you'd have had a

bullet in you."

"Oh, right. I'm supposed to believe this…this fanciful tale that someone took a shot at me when you did your mumbo-jumbo and put me to sleep?" She narrowed those feline grays at him. "Don't ever do that again! And how do you know the bullet was meant for me? With your charming personality, I'm sure there must be scores of people after you."

Just to shut her up, Dagan tore open his shirt. It was ruined anyway with the damn bullet hole. He felt a small measure of satisfaction at her wide-eyed stare…then her gaze slowly swept down his torso before gliding up again. *And* wouldn't you know it, his damn cock stirred awake, not like it ever rested when she was around.

He cut her a flat look and stalked from the kitchen, the bullet an annoying twinge between his shoulder blades. A shocked gasp left her. Good, she'd seen the bloody hole in his back.

Dagan jogged upstairs to his quarters. In his huge, gray-and-black-tiled bathroom, he willed the slug out, and it clattered to the floor. With the ruined shirt, he wiped his back free of blood, tossed it aside, and picked up the bullet.

A prickly sensation slithered through him as he studied the thing. This was no ordinary lead ammunition but a hollowed-out slug with a liquid center made to explode and immobilize the victim. Whoever was after Shae didn't want her dead, but they didn't seem to care if she was hurt.

He'd see about that. Despite her annoying the hell out of him, he refused to have her harmed while under his watch.

Snagging another t-shirt from his closet, he pulled it

Georgia Lyn Hunter

on and headed downstairs. Frowning, he glanced around the silent, deserted kitchen, then at the open French doors.

Dammit! He sprinted outside and came to a dead halt.

She crouched on the porch, stroking Bob, who lay like a furry rug on the tiled surface amongst the potted shrubs, purring and enjoying her touch. More irritation flowed that she'd scared the crap out of him.

Inside the castle, she was safe. But outside? Not so much. Shit could fly right to their doorstep. He'd learned that when demons had followed Blaéz here several months ago, leading to a deadly fight, and Blaéz almost losing his life.

The cat blinked its amber eyes, pinning him with an unwavering stare as if warning him not to interfere in his moment of bliss.

"Are you done?" he snapped.

"In a sec," she retorted, "I'm petting the cat. What's your name, my feline friend?"

"Bob."

"Hey, you speak. But you sound an awful lot like him." She stuck out a thumb behind her. "That's too bad, 'cause I like you." Another scratch under the thick orange ruff surrounding Bob's neck, then she rose to her feet and faced him. "Are you taking me back after this *talk*?"

"So whoever took a shot at you can finish the job?"

"You sure are a ray of sunshine, aren't you?"

Refusing to let her jibes prod a retort from him, which he was sure was her intent, he merely said, "You are in danger. Only a fool would disregard that. Follow me."

***

Shae glared at his retreating back, finding it hard to believe that anyone wanted her dead, but if that were true, then she'd barely escaped with her life. And he'd put himself between her and the bullet. Damn.

Exhaling roughly, she hurried after him, through the kitchen and down a long, winding corridor. Fine, she'd listen to what they had to say, and hopefully, find out what the hell was going on because this year just seemed to grow worse and worse.

Not wanting to think of that, Shae found her gaze drifting over his wide shoulders and down his tall figure. It was his swaying, ropey hair that held her attention.

How long would it be if he left it untethered? Would it caress his tight ass?

Oh, she'd love to see that. Just because he aggravated her like no one else could, didn't mean she couldn't appreciate a sexy man. Ugh, she guillotined the thought.

As if sensing where her gaze was, he cut her a narrow-eyed look over his shoulder. She gave him a disarming smile.

Nope, no reaction from those austere features—his face would probably crack if he so much as smiled anyway. He opened a door into a small study and waited for her to enter. She stopped short in the doorway of a room loaded with testosterone and gaped.

Michael was there with three other equally tall men. At her entrance, they turned. Man, these guys all had one thing in common. They were knock-you-on-your-ass gorgeous. Even her abductor fell into that category with his dark, brooding looks. Of course, being Others, they would be.

"Shae?" Michael motioned for her to enter, still

wearing his dark shades. "Please, sit." He waved a hand to a leather armchair adjacent to the stone fireplace.

Um, no way. No matter how good-looking they were, she refused to trap herself in a chair surrounded by these men.

"I'll stand, thank you." She remained near the entrance, well aware that escape was an illusion. If her abductor were able to move as fast as he did, chances were, so could these guys. And didn't that just make her want to—ugh, yeah, stay put—get this over with.

He handed something to Michael then strolled over to the open door leading out onto the terrace.

He hadn't even told her his name, the louse. And she wasn't about to ask.

"Dagan, you know," Michael informed. "That's Týr." He nodded to the stunning blond with eyes the color of melting toffee. "Aethan, with the hair. And Blaéz," he indicated the guy with the buzz cut and deep blue eyes.

Day-gun? Her gaze flickered his way, and she found him watching her, arms folded across his chest. His expression remained cool, remote, but his eyes burned with a dark heat that made her tummy dip… Maybe it was the heat of hate. She hadn't exactly been nice to him. But then *he* seriously needed an attitude adjustment.

She greeted the others with a quick hello.

The men nodded. She refocused her attention on Michael, who placed a small metal slug on the mahogany desk. Frowning, she stepped closer. About to pick it up, a callused hand grasped her arm, startling all hell out of her. "Don't touch it."

Rattled at Dagan's sudden appearance, she pulled

free and wrapped her arms around her waist. "What's going on? You snatched me from the club, then informed me that someone took a shot at me—which is highly unlikely, considering I'm nobody."

"That's not just any bullet," Michael said, picking up the cartridge. "It's one only a supernatural being would use."

"Supernatural?" she repeated.

"It wasn't accidental," Dagan said then. "It was meant for you."

Shae froze. After everything she'd been through this past year, she didn't need any more talk in riddles. "What are you saying? What's wrong with the bullet?"

"It's spelled, meant to immobilize until retrieval. It's one demons are fond of using."

At Dagan's blunt words, a sickening pit opened in her stomach. She grasped the backrest of the chair she'd declined moments ago. "Who—" She licked her dry lips, taking in the other men who hadn't said a word yet. "Who are you people?"

"We are warriors—Guardians of this world," Michael said. "We keep mortals safe from supernatural evil and have done so for the past three and a half thousand years."

"Guardians of…" she breathed, feeling as if the air had been sucked out of her lungs. Instantly, her gaze darted to Dagan. No wonder he acted like the world owed him a favor. She glanced back at Michael. "Demons?"

"Yes, though not all are evil, at least not those who now live in this realm. But demoniis—"

"I know about them," she finally admitted. "They steal human souls to revive their dying ones. My best friend is a demon, he told me. Why me?"

Georgia Lyn Hunter

"We have no idea. But we think there's something about you that caught their attention. We try to protect mortals with strong psychic abilities. And until we can determine why they want you, it will be safer for you to stay here while we handle this situation."

God, all she wanted was to find her mother. She did not need evil demons after her.

Shae rubbed a weary hand over her burning eyes, wishing this were all some bad dream. But six months was just too long to not wake up. And, yet, despite her skepticism at what Michael had revealed, somewhere deep inside her, she felt the truth of his words. "I can't just stay away, my uncle will worry."

"Call him. Make an excuse," Dagan's quiet voice cut through her cloud of fear. "Far better than making him a target, too."

Oh, Lord, if whoever wanted her dead was desperate enough, they could use Lem as bait. She refused to put the only family she had left in danger. "All right. But I have to go back, get my things and leave a note for him."

"Dagan?" Michael asked.

Those cool, yellow eyes met hers. "Let's go." He tilted his head to the terrace and stepped out.

Even though she'd rather run in the opposite direction from his arrogance and archaic ways, he was familiar, and he hadn't gotten mad at her despite her dreadful behavior earlier.

"Damn pestilence!" one of the Guardian's muttered. "They should all be eviscerated."

"Indeed," someone else added.

"Then we'll be out of a job," the blue-haired guy, Aethan, drawled.

Shae hurried past the annoyed warriors and onto the

porch. Dagan took her hand, startling her. But strangely enough, it soothed her as well. Obviously, she must have lost her mind. The man was about as calming as a washing machine, all turbulence. Open the door, and he'd probably wreak havoc.

"Wait." She hastily untied her jacket from her waist and pulled it on.

"Dag, you need company?" Aethan asked.

"Nah, he's got this one covered," the buzz cut guy drawled.

The blond, however, watched Dagan with a look Shae couldn't fathom…remorse edged with pain?

Dagan ignored them and grasped her hand again. "Address?"

She told him. The next minute, everything became a swirling sensation as the looming mansion vanished.

Ohhhh crap! Her stomach heaving, she grasped him tightly around his waist and buried her face against his chest, breathing in his unique and warm male scent.

All too soon, they took form in a backstreet near the chrome and glass building of The Tower. And she was clinging to him like a vine. Hastily, she let go, straightened her top and, evading the reeking dumpsters there, headed for the front of the building, all the while aware of his quiet, dark presence following her.

Harvey was still on duty. His warm smile slipped when he looked behind her, wariness spilling off him. She couldn't blame him. Dagan was about as friendly as a tiger with his space invaded.

"Hey, Harv," she called out. She had to find a way to get into town tomorrow evening to meet Harvey, without her shadow, because she doubted Dagan would calmly accept her summoning a broker demon.

Georgia Lyn Hunter

At the penthouse elevator, she slowed. Then, gritting her teeth in determination, she stepped into the suffocating steel space. With Dagan there, she really hoped she didn't lose her shit.

Shae squeezed her eyes shut and leaned against the wall, arms wrapped around her waist as the cage bore them up, claustrophobia making her stomach churn. She tried desperately to center herself like she usually did...

"Shae, look at me!"

The urgent voice came from a distance. Someone was shaking her. She blinked her eyes open and found Dagan in front of her. Concern flickered in his bright eyes.

Oh, no. Not again. Embarrassed warmth flooded her face. "I'm sorry, I don't like enclosed spaces."

He let her go. "So you create a windstorm to break through?"

She frowned in confusion. "What the heck are you talking about? I don't *create* anything. I just shut my eyes and pray it ends, fast. I'm grateful this is the penthouse elevator so no one sees me losing my mind."

He eyed her thoughtfully as the doors slid open. Shae hurried out of the deathtrap and made for the penthouse at the far end, then unlocked the door and entered the condo. She was halfway across the room when she realized Dagan hadn't followed.

Spinning around, she found him standing at the doorway. "Well, aren't you coming inside? Or do you need an invite like a...a vampire?" She couldn't resist the taunt, or stop her grin when his sexy mouth tightened.

"In a minute." A cold snap.

Who knew she could ruffle the feathers of this big,

bad, uptight warrior?

He cut her a cold stare before pulling out his phone. A hazy memory of lips kissing her throat stirred again. Her smile faltered. But when she found him watching her, she blinked away the images and smirked. "Okay, then. You hang out there and ghost the place, I'll go pack."

Chapter 4

Vampire? Dagan ground his teeth at the word. He wasn't one, at least not in the way books and legends depicted. He could walk in sunlight, into churches. Stakes wouldn't kill him. His life was eternal.

But he was a killer, had taken so many lives. Consumed by darkness, the madness taking over, seeking, always searching…

Bodies writhing in blood, he drank deeper and harder until every last drop was drained. And, still, the thirst gripped him…

Jolting free from those crippling memories, his emotions locked down, he made his call. He hadn't bothered about the surveillance cameras on this floor since he'd already hazed them all the moment he entered the building.

Hedori answered on the second ring. "Sire? How may I help?"

He pulled his gaze away from the empty staircase Shae had gone up. "I need the Ford here. Park behind The Tower." He reeled off the address. "And come up to the penthouse floor."

"Be there in a flash."

Dagan slipped his cell back into his pocket. Yeah, the Empyrean would be here in a flash. Literally. He, fortunately, could transport *anything* with his abilities.

Unlike Dagan. He couldn't dematerialize large, non-organic things. It was why he needed the truck to cart Shae's luggage. Besides, he liked driving, and it cleared his head, something he needed right now.

He studied the flickering mystical wards keeping him from entering the apartment. Shae, it appeared, had no idea about the protection spell. *He* could break through, painful and doable, but that would only alert whoever had put them up in the first place. Since creating wards wasn't something he did, he left it to the Empyrean who was ace in building the defense layers.

A few minutes later, the elevator opened. Hedori stepped out and strode toward him, his gaze already shifting to the doorway, clearly sensing the ward. "Shall I undo it?"

"Yes. But once we're done, put it up again."

Hedori nodded.

"One other thing, can you get me more smokes?"

"Yes, of course," he said, his focus on the doorway. As Hedori set to work using intricate hand movements and murmuring soft words he didn't catch—mostly because he wasn't interested—Dagan waited impatiently, his gaze back on the stairs Shae'd gone up. He didn't like the idea of her alone up there while he was stuck out in the corridor.

Whoever had put the wards up seemed determined to keep immortals away because only humans could cross the threshold. "How much longer?"

Hedori didn't respond. A minute passed, then several

more, before he lowered his hands. "It's done."

Dagan entered the penthouse. The place screamed opulence. He hadn't pegged the hellcat as one to like this kind of overdone abundance when she dressed in battered boots and simple clothing. But what did he know?

He jogged upstairs and followed her light, tantalizing scent down the hallway until he found her in the last bedroom, pulling out a froth of silky things from a drawer.

"The door's there for a reason."

He ignored her tart comment and strolled around the huge, lavish bedroom, stopping at the window overlooking the park. He leaned against the windowsill and watched her pack. She pulled out a...he peered at the name—Dextrose pack—from the bedside drawer and tossed them into her suitcase on the bed.

"What's that?"

"For my low blood sugar."

He frowned. He hadn't smelled any illness on her. "You're sick?"

Those stormy grays snapped back to him. A feminine eyebrow rose in a taunt. "Why? You gonna use your superpowers and cure me now?"

He merely stared at her. She rolled her eyes and dropped a pile of clothes in a case. "I'm fine."

He wasn't sure what exactly went on with that since immortals didn't get sick. "Is it a risk factor?"

A long, drawn-out sigh followed, like he'd asked her the fate of the universe. He waited.

"Depends on how you look at it. As long as I have my meals regularly and this close"—she pulled out the pack of Dextrose she'd thrown in her suitcase and waved it at him—"I'm good. So, no worries that I'll be dropping in a dead faint at your feet."

"Good to know," he drawled. "Who else lives here?"

A shrug. "Uncle Lem. He's at work, late-night conference call. Then there's the chef and maids, but they don't live here."

"Your parents?"

"My dad died several years ago." A flash of pain crossed her face and disappeared just as fast. "Mom took off earlier this year. Wanted her own life."

Bitterness laced her tone as she zipped her luggage. She shouldered her knapsack, grabbed her jacket from the bed, and headed for the door, dragging the single suitcase behind her.

He frowned, following her. "Is this all you're taking?"

"I'm leaving for a few days, not a vacation. I have everything I need until this mess is sorted out."

Guess she'd learn differently soon enough. Dagan took the bag and knapsack from her. Her mouth opened then closed. The hellcat, speechless? That was a first.

Yeah, he may be a bastard, but he did have some chivalrous qualities…when he remembered.

She put on her jacket, slid her hands into the pockets and frowned. "My cell, did you see it?"

He retrieved it from his back pocket and handed it over. "You dropped it outside the club."

"Thanks."

In the living room, she got a pen and a sheet of paper from a drawer in the small table there and jotted a note. He could easily read it despite standing a few feet away.

Uncle Lem, I'm taking off for a few days. Work. Forgot to tell you earlier.

Will call you soon.

Georgia Lyn Hunter

Shae.

Nothing to worry about there, he let it go.

She put the folded paper against the small vase on the table just as the Empyrean entered.

"Hedori?" Confusion crossed her expressive face. "I didn't know you were here, too."

"I was in town, thought I'd give you a hand with the luggage," he covered smoothly.

"Thanks, but I'm all set, just one teeny-tiny case," she said smiling.

Dagan followed her outside, and needing her distracted while Hedori put the wards back up, he said, "Here are the rules while living at the castle. You cannot just up and run back to the penthouse or anywhere you like. You cannot—"

"Whoa, hold it!" A flash of temper brightened her eyes. "Who died and made you my keeper?"

He lifted an eyebrow, didn't bother to point out that he'd just saved her ungrateful hide. But she seemed to get the message when her seductive mouth became a thin, unhappy line. He continued, "Do anything I don't approve of, I will lock you back in the basement."

Her delicate jaw tightened. "God, you're such an arrogant butthead!"

He rested a shoulder against a marble pillar, and found himself holding back a smile. "None would dare call me that to my face."

"You'd probably beat the crap out of them."

"No. I'd just kill them."

Her lips wavered, almost in a smile, then pressed back into an annoyed line. Hedori nodded from behind her. Dagan drawled, "Glad we got that cleared up. Let's go."

She wheeled around and stomped back to lock up,

but his heightened hearing caught her soft mutter. "You're a damn pain in my ass."

Naturally, his gaze slid lower to said behind. He had to stifle the urge to slide his palms over those tempting mounds. His hand tightened on her luggage instead.

Penthouse secured, she stalked past him, and as they entered the elevator, he said, "Pain in the ass or not, I'm all you have right now, little girl."

"Little girl?" The scowl returned. She stabbed a finger at the button for the ground floor. "I'm nearly twenty-five."

"So?" He leaned against the metal wall as the doors slid shut.

"So? What do you mean *so*?" Those feline-tipped eyes glowered fiercely. His entire nonchalant attitude appeared to rub her the wrong way. Something he couldn't help but savor when around her.

His gaze drifted over her striking features, spotting twin splashes of red on her cheekbones. Hell, if he was honest, her compressed lips made him want to slowly suck them back to a quivering softness. Instead, he lifted a shoulder in a careless shrug. "I call it as I see it. The scratching, the biting, need I go on?"

"God!" She spun away and glared at the receding floor numbers on the side panel, one booted foot tapping impatiently. "Can't you go any damn faster?" she growled at the elevator. The door glided open, and she stormed out.

Mission accomplished, he thought wryly, following her. At least she hadn't panicked from claustrophobia and let loose her abilities while trapped in a confined space. He frowned. Powers it appeared she had no idea she possessed. He grabbed her arm when she headed for the front of the building. "Not that way. Back entrance."

Pulling free, she marched in the opposite direction. Moments later, he stepped out into the cool alley, scanned the street, and found the double-cab, elevated truck parked a short distance from The Tower.

Dagan dropped her bag and knapsack onto the back seat. An icy sensation crawled over his skin, followed by a bile-inducing sulfuric stink. He wheeled around, pushing Shae behind him.

"Hey—" A sharp gasp followed, then she whispered, "What is that?"

Yeah, she'd sensed it, too. "Trouble."

***

Shae cautiously examined the shadowy backstreet. The dim lamp affixed to the looming building cast a small circle of light over the back entrance. The prickles on her nape grew. Familiar with this eerie sensation, she knew what it meant. Demons.

"Maybe they're the Earth ones?" God, she hoped so. This night was turning out to be the third worst of her life.

"No."

One single word, and her shaky hope crumbled. A smoky shimmer in the night air caught her attention, and a sword took form in Dagan's left hand. Strange symbols glowed briefly on the black blade. If she hadn't believed he was immortal before, she sure did now. Heck, in a dark street, none would know he palmed a deadly weapon. But his eyes, they blazed like a predator's in the night.

Two figures stepped out of the gloom, their irises sparking red. "Give us the girl," one of them lisped, stopping several feet away.

At the guttural demand, fear swamped her. Crap, she

didn't have her blade with her—wait, she had the *other* one, but she kept that in her knapsack. Then everything happened as if in fast-forward. Dagan leaped at the demons, sword swinging. He decapitated one. The head fell with a sickening thud to the asphalt and rolled toward her. Her heart in her mouth, she jumped back as the body and head shriveled and vanished.

The remaining demon's hand glowed red. "Did you think we'd come in pairs?" He flung a deadly hellfire bolt at Dagan.

"I'm surprised you can think at all." Dagan ducked the fiery red missile that blasted a dumpster to smithereens. A cacophony erupted. Several more scourges took form, swarming the backstreet like insects, grunts filling the air.

"You. Come." A demon darted for her, eyes gleaming like neon red moons.

"No, you fucking don't!" Dagan flew in front of her like a deadly force of nature, his hair flying around him like whips. He beheaded the demon with a single swipe of his blade.

"Get in the truck," he snapped, pulling her out of her frozen state. He spun back to the remaining demons fanning out.

Her breath hitching, she smacked a hand on his back. "Give me a switchblade or something. I can't stand here defenseless."

"Don't have one. Just get in the damn truck!"

Rely on someone else to keep her ass safe? Not happening. She wasn't totally helpless. Harvey had been a good teacher.

Keeping one eye on the fight, she eased backward and opened the truck door. As she reached for her knapsack, a slant of moonlight gleamed off a length of black metal lying on the floorboard. She grabbed it instead—a dagger. Thank God!

Shae wheeled around, weapon braced. Oh, shit! Her heart thundered in her ears. So many of them surrounded Dagan. He fought hard and bled from several cuts on his biceps. Damn monsters!

Furious, she darted forward.

"Shae, get the hell back," he snarled.

"No, I can help!"

A demon flashed in front of her and grabbed her upper arm, grinning like a jackass. "Got you."

Teeth gritted at the painful grip, she plunged the blade hard into his ribs. A raucous screech erupted from him, and he punched her in the face.

Her head snapped back, agony exploding in her skull. Goddamn bastard! Something inside her shifted and crashed, letting loose a storm. Heat exploded like a volcano. A red haze stealing her mind, she dove for the demon.

In the distance, a terrifying roar filled the alley, like some violent animal set free. "You dare hurt her?"

Shae barely heard any of it. Feeling as if she'd stepped away from the fight—like she was viewing a fast-moving movie clip—she watched the girl in the darkened backstreet fight. Her features too pale, her red hair streaming out like flames, she whirled and struck, her furious cry erupting in the alley like a death knell. The girl shimmered and disappeared...then reappeared behind another demon, her blade flashing before she faded again...

Shae. A familiar voice slipped into her mind, tugging at her. *Follow my voice. You have to come back—c'mon, you can do this.*

She latched on to the compelling tone and slammed

back into cognizance. And swayed. Strong arms grabbed her.

"Are you okay?"

Inhaling harsh gasps of air, she became aware of her surroundings, of how dark and silent the place was. Not even a stray cat skulked. She twisted in Dagan's arms, her gaze darting around and settling on the pile of disintegrating bodies, then lowered to the dripping, bloodied dagger she still clutched.

Oh, dear God! What had she done? Trembling like a blade of grass, she flung the weapon away. Her terrified gaze rushed to him. "I killed them—I *killed* them all."

"If you hadn't, I would have. They were scourges from Hell, death's always in the cards for them. C'mon, let's get out of here." He hurried her to the truck.

Something warm dripped down her mouth and chin. She dashed it away with a trembling hand and stared blankly at the blood coating her fingers.

When she couldn't seem to move, Dagan picked her up and put her on the seat. She bit back a whimper, her entire face aching. Hell, the scar stung viciously like glass slicing her open again.

Gingerly, she touched the bridge of her throbbing nose. "Oww."

He gently removed her hand and held his open palm an inch from her face. A glowing, blue light seeped out. She grasped his thick wrist. "What—"

"I'm healing you."

Oh, right. Warmth tingled through her skin. His eyes glowed brightly, a hint of red seeping into them. She blinked. His gaze lowered, dark lashes shielding his irises.

Georgia Lyn Hunter

Moments later, the ache in her nose and jaw receded. He pulled off his t-shirt and carefully wiped her mouth and chin. Ugh, she must have imagined the red eyes.

"Keep your head back and hold this under your nose."

Inhaling deeply, she did as he instructed. He buckled her in then smoothed a stray strand of hair away from her cheek, startling her. "It'll be okay."

He shut the door and rounded the hood to the driver's side.

How could it be *okay*? Even though Harvey had been teaching her to fight demons, she hadn't killed any, not until today. And now she'd taken out several of them. Bile rushed up her throat. She swallowed hard, unable to stop the shivers spreading through her body.

An hour later, as they headed toward Manhasset Bay, though it was close to early morning, the night seemed to grow even darker. Shae stared through the windshield, the headlights illuminating the shadowy road.

"What exactly are your abilities?" Dagan asked, pulling her out of her troubled thoughts, his gaze on the road.

"I don't know. I could always sense demons and Others, but a few months ago, something changed."

He cut her a sharp look. "Explain."

Shae lowered the shirt from her nose. "I was working on my laptop...I'm a photographic journalist. This buzzing heat started inside me and grew. Then, I don't know what happened, but the laptop exploded and the vase and wall mirror in the room shattered. The blast flung everything across the room." *My mother included.* "Soon after, I realized that when I'm scared or angry, an energy rises inside me. But never like *this.*"

He didn't say anything for a moment. She glanced at him. The light from the dashboard highlighted his stern features and bare, ripped chest. The sight distracted her. No matter how upset she felt, she was woman enough to appreciate his masculine perfection. Hell, she wanted to explore each muscle with her fingers, her—

"What about teleporting?" his voice pulled her back from dangerous thoughts.

"What?"

"Teleporting. You appear to have that ability, too. You vanished and reappeared behind the demons you eliminated."

"I don't know anything about that."

Christ. She rubbed her burning eyes, trying to wipe away images of those bloody bodies lying on the asphalt before they disappeared, not wanting to remember how easily she'd taken lives. Deep down, she understood that they would have killed her and Dagan with no remorse and she'd had no choice, but still...

Fog engulfed them as they drove along a bridge for several minutes before they hit solid ground again. Then huge, wrought-iron gates glided open, and Dagan drove through. Tall evergreens lined the road, the tops disappearing into the starless night. The truck's bright headlights were the only things breaking the thick gloom.

Moments later, they left the dense trees behind, moonlight casting a silvery glow over the rolling, landscaped gardens. Shae simply stared.

Yes, she lived in luxury, but this ivy-covered, gray stone castle with its sweeping towers, turrets, and crenelated battlement set against the backdrop of the dark sky took her breath away. Lights backlit the windows, adding to the magical aura. "This is so beautiful."

Dagan's gaze flickered briefly over the building but he remained silent as he brought the truck to a halt in front of the portico. Shae glanced at him. For some strange reason, she wanted to ease the grimness from his expression.

"You live in a fairytale, so what are you? Prince or beast?" she teased.

A nerve pulsed on his jaw. He jumped out and opened the back door, retrieving another t-shirt from a duffle bag there. He pulled it on, hiding his sexy body once more.

Shae climbed out and wiped her face again with his shirt. Hopefully, she'd gotten rid of all the blood.

"Your face is clean. You're beautiful," he said quietly, shocking her. "C'mon." He headed up the stairs and held open the enormous front door.

Shae stepped into the marbled foyer and gaped at the sweeping grand staircase. A crystal chandelier illuminated the gorgeous stained-glass windows on one side depicting angels, knights, and their women. It was as if she'd stepped into another world.

But Dagan didn't give her a chance to admire them or the lush plants and armored statues there. He ushered her down a winding corridor, and the smells of something savory drifted to her.

She stopped at the entrance to a huge kitchen with a sea of oak cupboards and gray granite tops. A small flatscreen was mounted in the corner near a window. The French doors were still open, and the familiar aromatic smell of thyme and other herbs wafted inside, adding to whatever was cooking.

A slender, attractive woman with honey-toned skin and a cap of choppily cut ebony hair leaned against the island counter talking to Hedori, a half-eaten carrot stick in her hand.

She glanced at them. Curious mismatched eyes met Shae's. Wow, but her eyes—one a fiery amber and the other cool like an ice-covered lake—held an otherworldly glow, yet she appeared human. Not that Shae had met any immortal woman. But there was something ethereal about her.

"Shae, this is Echo," Dagan introduced her. "Aethan's mate. Echo, Shae Ion."

Echo seemed startled that he'd spoken to her but she gave Shae a friendly smile. "Hiya, nice to meet you."

"Thanks." Not sure what else to say, Shae settled for the truth. "It seems I'm going to be staying here for a while. Someone took a shot at me with a spelled bullet."

Echo's face lost all color. Then, just as fast, she appeared to pull herself together. "You can't be too careful. Those things are really dangerous. You'll be safe here."

Dagan spoke to Hedori and said something about showing her to a room—probably in the basement.

"I'll do that," Echo offered.

Dagan hesitated, then nodded before cutting Shae a sharp look as if to say *behave*.

If she hadn't just been through such a harrowing experience, she might have smirked and said something to irritate him. But she recalled the care he'd taken with her afterwards, so she remained silent.

Still, she relished the way his eyes narrowed suspiciously and couldn't resist shooting him an innocent glance as she followed Echo. Oh, yes, he'd wonder what she was up to, and that made her smile.

Chapter 5

"Did you pick up any impression of who could have put up the wards?" Dagan asked Hedori the moment the door shut behind the females.

Despite Shae's mischievous look, which was probably to annoy him or maybe to cover up her shock at what she was capable of, worry took hold. This new ability of hers to teleport would be a problem if she didn't learn how to lock down her power.

"No, but I'll recognize it again, and it's definitely not demon-borne." Hedori scooped the sliced carrots into a bowl. "There's always a distinct signature to the species it comes from."

"Someone like us, then?"

A nod. "There's more." Anger seeped into the male's usually passive features. "One of the bedrooms…so much anguish and despair in there." His orange-green eyes blazed, which was rare in itself since the Empyrean was more laid back than the rest of them. "Female. And it's not the girl."

Dagan frowned. Shae had said her mother took off.

What had happened?

The door opened, and Michael strode inside, along with Blaéz and Aethan, back from patrol. Týr followed moments later and dropped onto a chair, his expression tense as if he were riding the edge. Whatever.

"Is she the killer, then?" Blaéz asked, pulling out a chair and dropping down.

Killer? Dagan hesitated. Her slaying those demons earlier with a dagger didn't mesh with the more dangerous M.O. of killing with the mind. "I don't think so. But whether she's psionic or not, I'm not sure. Echo would need to confirm that."

Aethan dragged out a chair then stopped dead. "Where's the female?"

"With your mate."

Gunmetal gray eyes sparked a dangerous white. "Dammit, Dag, you let Echo be alone with a killer—a would-be psychic killer?" he snapped.

Damn pain-in-the-ass mated males. Shae wouldn't hurt a fly. Hell, she was weighed down with guilt at ending those assholes from the Dark Realm.

"She's no killer, Aethan," Echo said, entering the kitchen. "She's terrified of what's happening to her."

"You don't know that for sure." Aethan cut her a dark look, sat down and pulled her onto his lap. "Until then, keep away from her."

Echo rolled her eyes at her mate's order as Elytani, their newest Guardian recruit who was still on probation glided in. Despite her six-foot height, with her pale hair and delicate features, Dagan wasn't convinced she could handle this life. But hell, Shae, a human, had just proven him wrong. However, unlike the other females here, Elytani appeared quieter, didn't speak much.

Darci entered the kitchen behind her. Her unusual sunflower-hued eyes swept over them and settled on Blaéz. "You wanted me?"

"Always, *a leannan*." He held out a hand. Frowning, she took it and lowered onto the seat beside him.

"Echo, will you be able to decipher what Shae is?" Michael asked. "Human with the usual abilities or…"

She shook her head and moved off Aethan's lap to the chair next to him. "Her aura's too faint for a proper reading. And she's really scared. Her laptop short-circuited several months ago…" Echo repeated what Shae had told Dagan. "I don't have to tell you how scary that is to someone who barely had any powers. When Aethan found me, even *I* wasn't prepared for all this—" She waved her hand around them. "And what followed."

Michael leaned his palms on the enormous table, his shattered blue irises sparking an eerie silver. "We have to know for sure, one way or the other, if she's responsible for those deaths in the alley before anything else happens. And if she possesses any other abilities."

"She can teleport, too," Dagan said. "Several demons confronted us on the way back. They wanted her. She took them all out in seconds, and there were easily a dozen of them. I think it's the first time the ability manifested…" Recalling her terror, his gut twisted. He couldn't protect her from what she was. She had to learn to adapt, fast.

Michael frowned. "So she can also manipulate time?"

He had no idea—hell, he'd stood there in a dazed awe, watching her. "I don't think so, but she's really fast when her ability takes over. There's more. Her apartment has the kind of protection wards only an immortal would use. No, it's not demon."

"You think it could be this kin of hers?" Blaéz asked, playing with Darci's hair.

Dagan shrugged. "Doubtful. She senses Others, and she would have said something."

"Maybe. But ask her anyway to be sure," Aethan said, sliding his hand down Echo's back as if needing the contact.

Dagan nodded and wondered if he'd ever want someone as much as these two warriors did their mates. They'd both been prepared to give up their lives for their women. Shae's face flickered in his mind. No. He'd given up wanting things he could never have long ago. His path was a dark, deadly one, and a mate was the last thing he needed.

"BTW," Týr said, tilting his chair back on two of its legs. "Been hearing whispers in the alleys about a man seeing the devil and a white light appearing and bodies disappearing. The cops are trawling the area now."

"Damn, should have wiped the drunk's memories," Aethan muttered, glancing out the open French doors. "There's still time to find him before the sun rises." He pushed to his feet.

"One last thing…" Michael straightened, his eerie blues skimming over them. "Someone needs to shadow Shae and guide her into this life and what it means if she does turn out to be psi. As it stands, chances of her going back to her old life don't look good."

Dagan slid his hands into his pants pockets. No one stirred. The mated warriors wouldn't. That only left… He met Týr's impenetrable dark gaze.

"I have to get back to the penthouse. Need to check out a few things before morning." Dagan stepped outside. Yet he didn't move. The thought of her with another ignited a raging fire within him. He rubbed his stubbled jaw. Shit.

Without turning, he said, "I found her, I'll do it."

He dematerialized to The Tower, taking form in the backstreet. Crouching on the asphalt, he studied the rugged surface where the fight had occurred earlier, allowing the vibes to slide over his psyche.

Who the hell wanted Shae?

At the prickles cascading over him, he eased into the shadows, letting them conceal him. A familiar stench drifted to him, one he'd marked for killing not twelve hours earlier.

A hefty, dark-haired demon appeared in the alley, shoulders hunched, his gaze darting around the place. Then another, taller, blond male joined him. Dagan frowned. There was something vaguely familiar about the latter.

"What the hell happened?" he snapped, grabbing the demon by the throat. "A simple job, and you fuck up again?"

"She was with one of 'em. The same one who took her last night."

"You mean—"

The demon nodded. "He killed the first two minions, and *she* killed the rest. One minute, she was cowerin' behind him, and the next, like a cyclone, she killed everyone. I sure wasn't stickin' around."

Dagan sauntered over. Both turned. The tall, thin male instantly vanished, and the stockier one's form wavered. Before he flashed, Dagan grabbed him and slammed him against the wall.

The demon wailed. "What the hell, man?"

"Talk. Why do you want the girl? And who's the

Georgia Lyn Hunter

Fallen?"

"I-I ain't speakin', asshole."

Obviously, a local demon. "We can do this the easy way, or the hard way."

"Look, man, I was just mindin' my own biz, and you come up and scare the shit outta me—"

Dagan smashed the demon's face into the wall. Bones crunched, a screech of pain echoed. "You do realize I could kill you and none would care? This is the human world. Give me a name. Lie, and I'll just take what I want from your mind. Trust me, if you want to live a normal life, then you don't want me inside your head."

He didn't have Blaéz's ability, but most of these fucks didn't know which Guardians possessed said deadly power.

"You're bluffing."

"You're right." With his mind, Dagan pinned him to the building wall. The demon's weapon hidden beneath his coat floated into the air. His eyes widened as the tip of the blade pierced his throat. "But I *can* kill you without touching you, or...I'll make you kill yourself. Either way, you'll die."

"No-no," a whimper tore free. He grabbed the hilt and tugged, trying to pull it out of his neck. "I can't tell you, he'll k-kill me."

Dagan folded his arms over his chest and stared at the scourge who'd dared to shoot at Shae. At just the thought of her getting hurt, rage tore through him. He let the dagger plunge deeper. An agonized scream ricocheted in the backstreet.

"*You* took a shot at her last night." Cold, brutally cold. "Was it on his order?"

"No. Not kill. Only wanted to retrieve her. He says

she belongs to him," the demon tripped out in a guttural moan. "He goes by Aza," he sniffed. "I think there's something going on with the Fallens."

"What?"

"I don't know. Now free me," the demon whimpered.

"Sure." Dagan let the blade slide out of the demon's neck, then whipped it around and sliced clean across, decapitating the fucker. There were no second chances with him.

***

Dagan took form on the rec room terrace. Too close to the edge, an unexplained restlessness riding him, he headed for the basement, hoping a workout would settle him.

In the training arena, Týr was going through a furious, solo workout with a broadsword.

Dagan changed into black Gi pants and retrieved a katana from the stand. It didn't matter that they never spoke, he needed a fight, and this one would be…cathartic to a degree.

He strode to the center. Týr slowed, eyes narrowing. No nod of acknowledgement. He stepped back, exchanged his broadsword for the other katana, and strolled to the middle of the mat.

Dagan lunged. Týr didn't avoid him but met him head-on, their swords clanging, the sound bouncing off the walls. Memories of another time took over...

Arid lands stretched out for miles, and impossible heat surrounded them in the Sumerian temple, now home to the Goddess of Life. Inara was barely eighteen and too young for this immense responsibility, but she was the chosen one.

The fierce sun beating down on him, Dagan swiped

Georgia Lyn Hunter

the sweat from his brow as he worked his way along the perimeter of the temple and the surrounding buildings. The lush new life that had sprung up in the temple yard didn't escape his notice. It was because of Inara. She'd touched the dead plants on her arrival, and life had flowed back to the place.

Her caress gave life.

But she was too playful, didn't want to be sequestered at so young an age—or accept her calling.

Needing to check on her, he headed back for the temple. In the foyer's cooler interior, he scanned for her. "Inara?"

"In here."

Dagan stepped into the living area. His jaw hardened at the sight of the soldier slouched on the couch sipping wine. The male jumped up, the pewter goblet flying to the floor in a dull clunk. "My pardon, sire—"

"You're released from duty. Get out."

As the soldier scuttled away, he cut his sister a narrow-eyed stare. "They are here to protect this temple and you. You are not to indulge in this frivolousness, Inara. You have your handmaidens for that."

"You're too serious, ahu." She pouted. "Brother, I will die if I don't have something else to do with my time other than focus on my duties. There's no harm, they know this."

He didn't care. Her life was far too important. His sister needed to understand this. When he got back from patrolling the borders this evening, he would sit her down and explain the danger she put herself in with her playful ways.

"We will talk tonight."

Laughing, she waved him off, her hazel eyes gleaming with mischief. "I cannot wait."

With his gift of telepathy, it was easy for him to communicate with the other protectors. Dagan headed out and mind-connected with Týr, his second-in-command and the only male he trusted to be at the temple when he wasn't around. I'm leaving to the borders.

I'll be there. *Seconds later, Týr took form on the temple portico, the sun gleaming off his light hair. He sprinted up the stairs and slowed when he saw Dagan, the twinkle in his pale brown eyes fading. "What's wrong?"*

"I had to dismiss another soldier."

Týr shook his head, grunted, "Maybe I'll just kill the next one who forgets his duty."

"Keep her safe, Týr."

"Always."

Much later, the noon sun scorching him, Dagan swiped the sweat from his brow as he patrolled the boundaries. Eyes narrowed, he perused the area again, unease riding him. "Seth, Nikkos," he called out. "Let's go to the outlying lands. Something doesn't feel right."

They flashed to the remote terrain surrounding the temple. As they reformed, a cloud of dust in the distance had him stilling. Dagan shielded his eyes with his hand as a lone rider approached on a huge destrier.

"Who the hell is that?" Seth muttered, shading his eyes, too.

Dagan's warning radar roared inside him like an alarm. "Halt," he yelled, but the rider continued in blatant disregard.

Georgia Lyn Hunter

Sword summoned, Dagan leaped into the air and straight at the rider, taking him down. Debris flew all over as their bodies landed with a hard thud on the dusty ground.

Cold, blue eyes met his. With his pale skin and shoulder-length, ebony hair pulled into a queue, he didn't belong in the desert. Dagan wasn't in the mood to interrogate, not when it came to his sister's life. He attacked. The male met him strike for strike. The male's countermoves held the precision of one well versed in war. He was powerful.

Before questions formed, the pale warrior cursed and leaped away, his gaze scanning the area in front of them. "I am Blaéz of the Celtic pantheon, assigned as protector to the Goddess of Life. We have trouble."

Dammit. *Of course! He'd been watching out for him.* Trouble? *Dagan pivoted, scanning the area. A sudden haze spilled over the place, and more figures appeared. Red eyes flashed. Dagan stumbled back.* Demons. Here?

Fiery hellbolts whizzed past them. Dagan ducked. With his mind, he seized them, flinging them high into the air. His power was such that they didn't reappear.

Blaéz flew into the horde, hacking off heads.

A hissing sound echoed in the fracas, and a bolt hit Dagan in the back. He stumbled. Fury exploding, he wheeled around and struck out with his mind, splitting the demons in two. Then it all suddenly stopped. The demons vanished, leaving only a thick, dusty haze behind.

Inara! *Dagan flashed to the temple, panting hard. At the sight of the blood and the broken bodies of the handmaidens on the floor, a tortured cry ripped from his soul. "No—Inara!"*

He raced to her room. More carnage surrounded him. Gore soaked the bed sheets dragged to the floor. Several slain soldiers lay there amidst the crumpled bodies of the handmaidens, their sightless eyes staring at nothing. It hurt to breathe. Tears glazed his eyes.

A groan pierced the pain in his mind. Dagan whirled toward the sound. A huge form pushed off the floor, climbing to his feet as if drunk.

"What the hell happened?" Týr groaned, rubbing his eyes.

Dagan dove at the warrior, slamming him into the opposite wall. "For all that is holy, Týr, tell me she is safe," he pleaded. "Tell me you kept my sister safe."

Bleary, pale brown eyes blinked and looked around. Anguish swept over his lean features, and Dagan knew. An agonized cry tore free. He swung his sword in a deadly arch and sliced the carotid of his best friend...

The tinny sound of a sword falling to the floor brought him back. Breathing hard, Dagan stumbled away, fighting to shut off the images that still haunted him to this day, eons later.

Heavens knew he'd paid the price for his crime by being imprisoned in Tartarus.

His gaze fell to the droplets of plasma spilled on the gymnasium floor. Týr stood there, blood seeping from deep gashes on his heaving chest, anguish distorting his usually perfect features. "*Bróðir,* forgive me."

The Norse's words hit him hard. They'd been best friends—brothers—once. Drawn together in the unforgiving world of their pantheons when they'd squired as young boys at the Gates of the Gods, the political powerhouse of all deities. Later, Dagan had shunned his old life to become protector to the new Goddess of Life, and Týr had, too. In all that time, he'd never spoken of his past or his kin. Dagan hadn't pried.

Swiping the sweat from his brow, he realized he not once asked Týr what had occurred all those centuries ago. He'd only understood that Týr was responsible for Inara's *death*—or so he'd thought then. And in his anguish, knowing he'd failed in keeping his dying mother's wish to protect his sister, he'd sliced the throat of his best friend, nearly killing him—which is what would have happened had they not been yanked out of the temple to the Gates of the Gods for judgment in that precise moment.

It tortured him daily, wondering what else he could have done to save his sister. Where he'd fallen short. But it was too late—too fucking late for anything. The desolation in him deepened.

"Dag—"

Shaking his head, he strode out before the pain roiling inside him erupted and he tore everything apart with his bare hands and hurt the people who mattered.

And the bastard, Týr, did.

He just couldn't forgive him.

***

An hour later, showered and changed, Dagan took the stairs up to Michael's quarters on the fourth floor, knocked, and entered.

"Dressing room," Michael called out.

The Arc's quarters had the same layout as his. He headed for the first door next to the fireplace. Michael stood in the middle of the room with closets on one side and a mirrored panel on the other. He re-hitched the towel slung low on his hips. A brow rose. "What's up?"

"I found one of the demons who attacked Shae and me—the same one who took a shot at her. Took care of him. But the Fallen he was with escaped." Dagan leaned a shoulder against the doorjamb. "It seems the Fallens are rallying together for something big. You know anything?"

Lines furrowing his brow, Michael opened his closet. His back bore two deep, lumpy, lengthwise scars where his wings should have been. "I've heard rumblings about them gathering here. I trolled through the city a few days ago, but nothing seemed amiss. At least not so far."

"You do realize they could be hiding whatever it is they're up to when you're around?"

Michael had probably been behind a lot of those Fallen losing their wings. Revenge was always in the cards when it came to them.

A nasty grin broke over Michael's face as he dropped the towel, got a pair of jeans, and dragged them over his muscled thighs. "Hmm, so their vendetta's probably with me. We shall see... Besides, I don't want to tip my hand just yet, I have bigger fuckers to reel in."

Undoubtedly more runaway angels, but Dagan didn't ask. He had a shitload to deal with right now, he couldn't worry about the other aspect of his job. Shae was who mattered, and she had no idea of the danger nipping at her heels.

He got back to the issue at hand. "This Fallen wants Shae."

"I'm not surprised. Kicked from Heaven and losing their more powerful abilities, they would look for ways to compensate—gain power again. Take Shae to Romania. It'll be safer for her there, and buy us some time."

Dagan rubbed his jaw. Hell, he wanted to leap at the

chance to go back to the place he regarded as home, but his Guardian oath stopped him. "No, with trouble stirring again, you need me here. I'll keep her safe, but it's my duty to see this to the end."

"Understood." Michael's fractured irises glowed as he pulled on a navy t-shirt. "But she's far more important. They obviously know we have her now— we'll keep an eye on the penthouse. You need to leave, trouble already heads this way. I'll remain here for the duration or as long as it takes to end this. With the kind of abilities she wields and her burgeoning powers, she's vulnerable right now."

Dagan glanced behind him through the bank of windows. Weak, early-morning light seeped into the bedroom, daybreak mere minutes away. "One more thing." He refocused on his leader. "Inara?"

When Michael freed them from Tartarus, he'd told Dagan he freed her, too. But she'd disappeared, never to be seen again.

The Arc exhaled heavily and shook his head. "Still nothing. It's been three and a half millennia. Wherever she's gone into hiding, she's secreted herself well. She *is* the Goddess of Life, Dag, she won't be found if she doesn't want to be."

He didn't care. She was his sister, and he'd failed her once. Not again. "When this is all over, and Shae's safe, I'm taking some time off. I have to find my sister, *I* need to know she's okay."

With a slight incline of his head, Michael acknowledged his wish.

Dagan headed out, only to stop on the third-floor landing. He had no idea where Echo had put the little hellcat. He scanned the castle and instantly picked up her psychic vibration, the damn thing rolling through him like an inherent caress.

Mouth tight, he pulled out his cell, recalling her number—yeah, he'd checked after the human texted—and sent her a message. *Come down to the rec room.*

He jogged down to the ground floor and headed for the rec room. It was empty, but cheering from a recorded ball game playing on the flat screen echoed in the place. The Celt was probably around somewhere.

Dagan retrieved his spare cigar case from the wet bar in the corner and removed a smoke. He threw open the French doors, stepped outside, and sat on the top step leading out to the rolling lawns as day broke. Cigar lit, he inhaled a fragrant lungful of smoke and stared into the gardens, his mind on everything that had occurred.

A soft, furry slap flicked his side as he blew out a spiral of smoke. Dagan glanced down and cocked an eyebrow at the overweight, gray feline. "You hit me with that fluff of yours again, I'm going to shave off all your hair. Understand, cat?"

Bob ignored him. With another flick of his tail as if to show Dagan who was boss, the cat stalked past him and down the few steps, tail held high. He prowled through the plants, his focus on the birds perched on a low branch.

Dagan shook his head. Cat probably had snark for breakfast with that streak of bravery.

"*Come down to the rec room.* Really? Did it occur to you that this place is massive and I could get lost—which I did until I smelled your smoke?" Her husky but frustrated voice stroked his senses, shoving all his need receptors to the forefront. He shut his eyes at the effect this human girl had on him.

Another deep inhale, then Dagan killed his half-smoked cigar, pushed it into his pocket, and rose.

Georgia Lyn Hunter

"We're leaving."

"Again?" Her brow furrowed. "Why?"

"I'll explain later, but we need to go, now."

"Where?"

"To the Guardians' other abode."

She blew out a tired breath. "Great, more migrating. I should have been a bird. Fine, let me get my stuff."

"No time. I'll have your things sent over."

Pulling on the last reserves of his psychic energy, he parted the mystical veils, and a shimmering gateway appeared. At her wide-eyed stare, he grasped her hand and stepped through the flickering portal.

Chapter 6

Shae disliked it when Dagan flashed with her, but stepping through an eerie opening splitting the air unsettled her more.

As she stumbled into sunshine, exhaling a relieved breath, the crack in the dimension closed with a soft hiss behind her. The icy chill here seeped beneath her jacket. Shae hastily let go of his hand and buttoned up her jacket.

Tall, spindly trees grew sporadically along a shallow riverbank, and the cool, earthy smell of damp soil drenched the air. Boulders covered with varying shades of lichen were clumped about. In the distance, a mountain range meandered into a forest and beyond. Heavy clouds enclosed granite peaks.

She searched the place for signs of habitation, a village, or even a hut. Nothing. "Where are we?"

"Romania."

It made sense why he'd open a portal. "So where exactly is your house—" She broke off and peered at the mountaintops as the clouds drifted apart for a second. Far, far up, there was something. Shae gaped. "Is that it?"

He grunted.

The Guardians' abode appeared like a disjointed series of blocks with towers which were stuck to the rock face of the soaring cliffs. Then the clouds merged, hiding the buildings once more.

"Whoa!" Laughter spilled free. She pivoted to him. "Are you competing with the eagles for home space?"

His mouth twitched, and her tummy tripped. She wished he'd stop doing that. She didn't want to like his smile, too, not when his handsome face was already so damn distracting.

"C'mon." He slid his hand around her waist and drew her close. Again, her body appeared to dissolve. Crap! Shae grabbed him, eyes shut tight. Moments later, they reformed on the sky-high courtyard. She bit back a moan, so darn grateful that he hadn't let her go or she would have landed face-first at his feet.

Midday sunlight spilled over the building. From a distance, the place had appeared charming with its mismatched turrets and balconies meandering along the rock face of the mountains.

Up close? The abbey-like building didn't welcome or captivate.

It loomed. Menaced. Made her want to hotfoot it out of there.

She shivered and rubbed the goosebumps flooding her arms. "This looks like an abandoned…monastery?"

"It was. After a minor tremor destroyed part of the building, we convinced the previous residents, the good monks, to take the dwelling we'd procured at that time, and we moved in here." He headed for the arched, black, wooden door.

Frowning, Shae followed him. It seemed they hadn't bothered putting things to rights after the quake either. The courtyard sported spidery cracks in the dusty granite surface that crept into the main building. She entered the cool foyer and warily eyed the spindly fissure on the worn floors. "How long have you lived here?"

A shrug rolled off those broad shoulders. "Since the fourth century.

Whoa! "And you didn't think to fix this place up in all that time?"

"Why?" He cut her a questioning look. "It's been stable enough."

Okaaay. Hopefully, the building wouldn't slide off the mountain anytime soon. "So, where's the church?"

"The worship place was on the other side of the monastery and collapsed after the tremor."

Ugh. That wasn't very reassuring. But if they still resided here, it probably—*hopefully*—was safe.

Shae slowed to a stop and simply stared. Soaring walls and a faded, patchy biblical ceiling fresco that had suffered some damage through the passage of time surrounded her. Sunlight streamed through the dome-shaped windows into an enormous split-level living room of sorts.

On a wooden coffee table lay a spilled deck of playing cards as if someone had started a game and left. A couple of recliner armchairs surrounded the table. Two arcade games, along with a foosball and a pool table took up space along on the opposite side. And the most important equipment for men's survival? No TV. *Nada.*

"Who else lives here?"

"Two others. The kitchen's in there." He waved a

hand to his right. "Down the hallway are the bedrooms," he said, pointing left to the shadowy corridor, "and upstairs. We don't usually have guests, so most of the unused rooms are uninhabitable. My room is the second to last one down this hallway. Use it until I get something sorted out for you." He pivoted, then swung right back. "The other Guardians' rooms are off-limits. I'll see you later." Then he shimmered and just sort of faded like a ghost.

Really? That's it? She scowled at the spot he'd been moments ago. More rules, then he disappeared?

Damn man. But with exhaustion weighing her down, it wasn't like she could simply leave and go book a room at a hotel. No matter how beautiful this open mausoleum of a living room appeared, or inviting the leather recliner was, two other Guardians lived here. They could walk in anytime.

Resigned, she made her way down the dim corridor, warily avoiding the spidery cracks on the floor, and opened the door to Dagan's room. Empty. Cautiously, she stepped into his personal space.

Dust motes swirled in the light slanting in from the narrow, arched windows. Opposite, against the faded white wall, stood an enormous bed with a dark headboard. A steel and ebony chest took up space near the small, unlit fireplace. And above the mantel, several swords adorned the wall. Yup, this place appeared austere and rigid, just like him.

Shae got rid of her jacket, kicked off her boots, removed her socks, and flexed her sore feet. The cool stone floor soothed her soles. Fatigue felled her like a tree, and she slumped face-down on the bed.

The open windows let in a brisk breeze, but she was too drained to move and shut them. God, it had been a hellish night…

A splattering noise disturbed the quiet. Shae jerked awake. A little disorientated, it took her a moment to recall her whereabouts. Then everything that had happened crashed through her like a tidal wave.

Jesus, she shut her eyes, wishing the last six months were a really bad dream. Shifting a little, she snagged her jacket from the foot of the bed and retrieved her cell. Three hours had passed? It felt like mere minutes.

Yawning, she dropped her cell on the nightstand and shut her eyes. Sounds of rustling water seeped into her consciousness. She stirred enough to lift her head and look for the source. Her gaze settled on one of the two doors adjacent to the bed. The shower. Dagan?

Instantly, images of his sexy, naked body filled her mind, chasing away sleep. Warmth stirred low in her belly—ugh! Unable to nap now, she slid off the bed and wandered outside onto the rambling balcony. She passed the wooden table and chairs there and leaned her arms on the granite balustrade. Whoa, they were so freakin' high, the river snaking far below appeared like a silvery thread in the sunshine.

She couldn't stand enclosed spaces, but heights? She loved them. Enjoyed the freedom because it took her away from the bleakness of her life.

Closing her eyes, she lifted her face to the sun's warm rays. Something scuttled over her bare feet. A scream tore free. Shae jumped back, her hips hitting the table, her gaze fixed on a swarm of beady, black eyes. She scrambled onto a chair, her heart nearly flying over the balcony.

"Shae!" Dagan shot out through the door, a towel clutched to his man parts, and spun around, searching the place. His long, wet hair whipping around him, water spraying the windows and walls…and her. "What is it?"

"Ra—rats!" She gulped, pointing to several of them on the floor, gawking at her, their noses and whiskers twitching. "Chase them away—chase them away," she whimpered.

He straightened, then casually moved the towel to wrap it around his lean hips, the image of ripped abs and a semi-erect sex searing her mind. But her fear of the pestilences trapping her on a chair was too great to even admire his manly bits. Damn annoying vermin, spoiling her fun.

"This is their home, too."

At his droll words, fear morphed into irritation. "No way am I sharing anything with your pets!"

"They won't hurt you. They're quite er, tame." With that parting shot, he headed inside and then threw over his shoulder, "Are you coming?"

"No." She sulked, lowering to sit cross-legged on the table, and counted the rats. Five of them.

With a long, drawn-out sigh, as if she were wearing on his last thread of patience, he walked back, scattering the rodents, and swept her into his arms. She grabbed onto his neck.

"Make me carry you again, hellcat, and be prepared for the consequences." His arms banding around her like steel cables, he strode indoors.

Darn, but he smelled really good. He dumped her on the bed, and she bounced a few times. She stared up into his cool features and clashed with his searing eyes.

Did he really not like her?

Something inside her constricted at the knowledge. But then, neither did her mother, or even Ash when it came down to it.

Brutally, she squashed those thoughts and sat up. "It's not my choice to be in this rat-infested dump—"

"This *dump* and I are the only things keeping you safe. Let me refresh your cloudy memory, wildcat. Those assholes after you are not human. All they'd need is a hint of your psychic vibration to track you. So get rid of your opinionated thoughts. You are human, fragile, and too damn distracting."

The apology died in her throat. Is that what he thought?

His jaw rigid, he retrieved a pair of jeans from the closet, tossed the towel aside, and didn't seem to care that he was naked. He pulled the pants on, buttoned up, and then stalked out of the room barefoot and bare-chested, throwing over his shoulder, "Don't leave the room at night."

"Why not?" At night, she tended to raid the kitchen for food when she couldn't sleep.

He didn't look back. "Wait until I introduce you to the others, or they'll think you're a gift." With that delightful warning, he vanished.

Shae scowled. Well, she could take care of herself.

But Dagan's words echoed painfully in her head, *too fragile, too distracting, and too opinionated.* Was there anything about her he couldn't find fault with?

Her chest constricted. Feeling as if she'd suffocate if she remained in *his* room, Shae got off the bed and swayed as she stood. Damn. She reached for her jacket, searched for her Dextrose in the pocket and found just one left. Crap. The rest were still in her suitcase. She popped the candy into her mouth. It would hold her for a while, but she needed food.

Navigating the cracked corridor and the sunken living room, she found the kitchen easily enough.

Warmth surrounded her from the wood-burning stove someone had lit. An enormous fridge near the open window appeared to run off a generator, its drone drifting into the kitchen. A rustic table and six mismatched chairs finished off the décor. Two of the six were tucked under the table and appeared fairly new. The others, older ones, had boxes stacked on them and were aligned along the wall.

Shae ransacked the cupboards and found dishes but no food. The fridge, however, revealed loads of energy drinks, grapes, and some lifeless potatoes. She swiped a bunch of green grapes and ate several of them.

Scratching around in the freezer, she found steaks, took several, and dropped them in the sink. Then she hunted through the drawers for a knife, anything to peel the sad-looking spuds.

She didn't understand how the castle in Long Island appeared like a fairytale, and this one looked as if it belonged to a poor relative. But being men, they probably didn't care.

Dammit, where did they keep the knives? Did they even have any of those?

"I wish I had a blade. Heck, even the black one I fought with—" Something heavy appeared in her palm, glowing eerily. A muffled shriek caught in her throat, Shae jumped back, the obsidian dagger dropping onto the table with a loud clatter.

Holy shit! Where had that come from? It looked a lot like the one she'd found in Dagan's truck and threw away after the demon attack. Uneasily, she glanced up at the ceiling, but there was no porthole that it could have fallen through. A slack feeling in her gut, her gaze dropped to the dagger once more. Gingerly, she picked up the blade, but it didn't light up again.

Oh, man… She glanced at the door, hoping someone would miraculously appear—like the dagger had—and explain all this. But she remained alone.

Okay, Shae, in the past twenty-four hours, you've met people who hunt evil demons, you've teleported…heck, you even stepped through a portal! And the man whose room you now use is immortal, so why not a magical dagger appearing?

Ugh. She was going to give herself a headache. Right now, she needed to eat. She started peeling the potatoes. And what do you know? The dagger did a great job in the kitchen, too.

An hour later, the mouth-watering aroma of grilled meat permeated the place. She scooped out the freshly fried chips and drained them on a rack over a plate, then popped one into her mouth. As she chewed, she frowned at the small fried heap. Nope, those wouldn't be enough for a man Dagan's size or if the others turned up. Fetching several more potatoes, she pared again.

The sound of booted footsteps drew closer. The door opened, and Dagan entered. He'd put on a gray t-shirt, the fabric stretching over his wide chest. He crossed to the shelf opposite her.

Damn. His hair, like a sheet of black satin, did brush his sexy, jean-clad backside.

She looked up, and heat crawled across her face when she found him watching her. No point in pretending she wasn't eyeballing him. With her pale coloring, it was like a glowing bulb declaring her guilt. She cocked an eyebrow. "What?"

He didn't comment, merely uncorked the bottle of red wine he'd procured and poured some into a crystal goblet. Still silent, he leaned against the cupboard and took a sip. With his long, dark hair, ridiculously handsome face, and frightening charisma wrapping around her like a noose, her breath caught at just how easily he drew her.

Yep, just like her, to want what she couldn't have.

She lowered her gaze and started peeling again.

"Where the hell did you get that?"

At his sudden roar, Shae jumped. The dagger slipped from her hand onto the table. Scowling, she snapped, "The pantry. I'm hungry. There's no food."

He stalked closer, his eyes like molten fire, the orange sparks visible. "The blade, Shae, where did you get it? Did you go to the other warriors' rooms?" he demanded, suddenly looking like he'd swallowed a handful of broken glass.

"So what if I did? You have nothing in this place, no cutlery at all. I can't use my fingers to peel these."

"Where did you get the dagger?" he repeated. His tone held an edge now.

Sheesh, so much drama over a stupid blade. "If you must know, I couldn't find a paring knife, and I sort of wished I had something, even a dagger, and this thing just appeared in my hand. Ugh, I know, it's an implausible story, but it damn well happened," she ended defensively.

"Where did you first take it?" He sounded strangled as he set his goblet on the table.

What was with all the interrogation, as if she'd stolen the damn thing? "I didn't steal it, okay? The night those demons attacked us, I saw one just like this in your truck and used it, only I dropped it in the alley afterwards."

His color drained. Dagan lowered his head, his fists planted on the table, his hair cascading down to spill onto the wooden surface. She had to clench her fists to stop from reaching out and sliding her fingers through the black silk. Instead, she scooped the peelings onto a plate.

"What is that enticing smell?"

At the strange new voice, Shae glanced at the man sauntering into the kitchen wearing faded jeans. Tall, like all the other Guardians, he sported a buzz cut that left a brown shadow over his skull. An array of ink peeked out from beneath the neckline of his t-shirt, and more ran down his muscular arms. He sniffed appreciatively, his cool gaze settling on her. "Well, now, D-man, you didn't say we had a guest?"

Dagan didn't move, didn't answer the man, who then shrugged and said, "I go by Nik."

"Shae Ion. I'm grilling steaks. It's all you had here. Those and some sorry-looking potatoes."

He grinned, revealing a single sexy dimple on his left cheek, yet the smile didn't reach his pale green eyes, a startling contrast to his olive skin. While Dagan was a loner, appeared cold, and annoyed her like no one ever had, there was heat in him regardless. This guy, outside of his air of indifference, seemed to possess an innate coldness—a darkness—as if it seeped from his very soul.

"Right." Nik ran a hand over his buzz cut. "We have things here. Not so good in the cooking department. We usually throw meat on the burner. But there is food. I'll show you."

He strolled past her, the air suddenly so frosty it hurt to breathe. Her teeth clattered, and she rubbed the goosebumps on her arms.

"Cut the shit, Nik," Dagan muttered.

Instantly, the temperature rose, became bearable

Georgia Lyn Hunter

once more. More baffled than ever, Shae followed Nik. Obviously, he was another Guardian, because, amidst the myriad of inkwork, he too sported that familiar sword tattoo on his biceps.

Nik walked out through a side door into a back courtyard and over to a small building attached to the main one. A huge fridge and freezer took up space, along with shelves of unopened spices.

"I need vegetables."

Cold, green eyes looked up from the fridge he'd opened, his arm resting on the door top. "Yeah, we don't eat those, but you can get them in the village. There's more meat in here."

He snagged a soda, popped the tab, and took a swallow, revealing his tongue piercing. But that wasn't what caught her attention. He sported a snakehead tattoo right on his neck.

Uh, why would anyone want a creepy reptile inked on them?

"Fine." She stomped back to the kitchen. Dagan lifted his head, watching her with a strange glitter in his citrine eyes.

"I need to go to the village. Besides the veggies, I need my glucose."

Slowly, he straightened, like a panther unwinding after a long winter's sleep, his gaze never leaving hers. "Nik, save food for her. We'll be back."

"You could just take her out, you know, and leave all this for us," Nik retorted, munching a chip.

Dagan cut him a hard look. Nik lifted his hands in surrender. "Fine. Shae, maybe you can sweeten that mood of his? Three and a half thousand years is a mite too long to brood."

Dagan grasped her hand and tugged her through the

living room and out onto the courtyard. "Wait." She stopped him. "Maybe I should try and teleport again?"

"You won't. Not if you don't want those scourges tracking you."

"But how would they know? Even I had no idea what I was capable of until the demon attack."

His eyes narrowed. Perhaps it wasn't such a good idea to remind him of that.

"They know your scent—your power will always carry a hint of it. If they get a trace of your psychic vibe, they'll find you. You are not to use that ability until the threat to you is gone." When she said nothing, his grip tightened on her hand. "I need your promise."

"Fine, all right." *Unless we're in danger, then all bets are off.*

With a terse nod, he dematerialized them and reformed in a copse of trees moments later. When her heart settled into its regular rhythm, they walked out into a picturesque world. The afternoon sun cast a soft glow over the little village.

She squinted, examining the quaint stores with flower-filled windowsills lining the cobblestone streets that had actual streetlamps—dark, wrought-iron pillars with glass encasing the bulbs. "Oh, so pretty…"

She spun back to Dagan and found him slipping on dark sunshades. Her breath caught. Damn man was too irresistible for his own good. But she didn't like his eyes concealed because then she couldn't read him…well, when he let her see his emotions—which mostly appeared to be irritation at her.

Shutting away that thought, she asked, "Will you bring me back to look around?"

"We're not here on a sightseeing trip," he said, tone curt. "You forget, your life's in danger. If those after you do happen to trace you to this place, anyone who lives here could relay that they'd seen a new face around. This is a small village."

All she wanted was to forget her shitty life for a short while. Was that too much to ask? Still, she glanced warily around her. "There are demoniis here, too?"

"Occasionally, but in the city, yes. The poor slum areas are rife with them. But there are demons who dwell here."

The village was really charming, and it possessed a peace about it that she sorely needed. Since she couldn't explore, she stood there for a second, absorbing the tranquility.

"So, where exactly are we?" she asked. "I know you said Romania."

"At the foot of the Apuseni Mountains."

At his terse tone, she glanced back. Jesus, but the man appeared like a coiled spring about to snap. She couldn't resist. "So you brought me to Dracula's country—vamp territory?"

His mouth tightened. "Vampire's don't exist. Not on this realm anyway. Count Vlad Dracul was human and named The Impaler for his bloodthirsty habit of impaling his enemies on stakes in the ground and leaving them to die. Now, are you going to question me on the damn history of this place or go get your glucose?"

Chapter 7

The pleasure in her eyes dimmed at his words, but Dagan refused to retract them. The truth had to be laid out. Her life was far more important than a few damn hours of sightseeing. People remembered faces. Shae, with her distinct copper-red hair and scar, was quite memorable.

But when she just stood there, her chin angled in that stubborn tilt he was coming to recognize, it was hard to temper his growl. "What?"

"I would use my money or credit card, but someone dragged me out of New York with nothing but the clothes on my back. You see my problem?"

Without a word, he opened his palm and handed her his black card. "Get all you need."

"Handy trick that," she muttered. "Wish I had that ability." She whirled away and marched across to the greengrocer.

Dagan sagged against the wall and stared blankly at the store entrance Shae had vanished through, feeling as if he'd been clocked hard in the stomach. He pulled off his shades and rubbed his eyes.

Hell, when they—the protectors—were first sentenced to Tartarus for their failure to protect the Goddess of Life and the bloodshed and loss of innocent lives that resulted, even that disaster hadn't shaken him as much as what Shae had unintentionally revealed. He was already neck-deep in shit with his irrational attraction to her. But this?

"Dagan, how do we take this load back?"

He looked across to the greengrocer, and his gaze fixed on her beautiful face. When he'd tossed his obsidian dagger in the Ford months ago, he'd forgotten all about it. He could beckon the weapon anytime and from any place should he need it since it was intrinsically linked to him. In the kitchen, he'd summoned the thing until he was blue in his face and it hadn't even budged on the damn table.

"Hey, Dagan?"

"What?"

She tapped her booted foot like he was wasting her time. "The groceries, dude?"

Dude? He bit back the words that wanted to escape him. *I'm your godsdamn mate!*

"Just leave them there," he bit out. "I'll see they get delivered."

With a shrug, she disappeared into the store then stepped out a moment later. She threw him a dark look as she crossed the street in that too-damn-short skirt and steel-toed boots. "You're such a barbarian. There was no need to snarl."

Snarl—*snarl?* He wanted to gag her, preferably with his mouth. Instead, he clenched his jaw and watched as she marched into the pharmacy.

His mate.

Touch her, and he would seal her destiny with his dark curse. At the image of her throat torn out, and eyes unblinking in death, horror surged through him. He rubbed his eyes as if that would clear away the reality of his life.

Voices drifted to him. Shae stepped out of the store, a brown package in her hand, and the human pharmacist followed behind, too damn close.

"How long will you be in the area, Shae?" he asked.

Shae? Dagan narrowed his eyes and slowly straightened from the wall.

"I'm not sure," she murmured, pulling her gaze back from the looming mountain range surrounding the valley to look at the man. "Why?"

"If you want someone to show you around town, I'd be more than delighted to. Here..." He smiled, handing her a card. "My number."

She glanced at it, and the human's gaze tracked leisurely over her.

A slow burn, one of utter possessiveness, edged with irritation, took hold. Yeah, he didn't need his abilities or heightened senses to know what the dickhead wanted. Dagan strode across to her. "Let's go."

She threw him a cool glance, apparently not impressed by his bark, and turned to the fucker. "Nice meeting you, Vasile." She waved the card. "And thanks."

A low growl rumbled out his throat. Dagan cut the human a lethal stare—one promising a violent death. The man hastily retreated into the pharmacy.

"You're rude," she retorted, rubbing her palm down her skirt.

"And you're not a damn tourist making dates with

strangers when your life's in danger."

"Until that happens"—her eyes took on a feverish glitter—"which is unlikely, trapped in the most remote part of this back of the beyond, I need clothes."

Dagan went dead still, her hiking energy bashing at his psyche like a furious gale force. Before she drew all the demons in the areas with her dangerous vibe, he grasped her hand and jogged for the thicket edging the foothills.

"What the hell, Dagan?" She tugged at her hand. "Stop hauling me about."

Then he was running, forcing her to do the same because he couldn't dematerialize them from the street with the damn human still watching. They finally rounded the last building two streets away and hit the dense copse surrounding the village. Bits of debris rose off the ground and whipped past him.

"You need to reel in that power. Now. Do it, Shae!"

She yanked free. "Go away." She rubbed her face, panting hard. "I have to go buy clothes."

He pushed his shades onto his head and grabbed her by her upper arms, but her molecules were already shifting, fading. His hand passed right through her body. Shit. "Shae, look at me!"

Those blank, storm-gray eyes stared right through him, her entire body shimmering between solid and intangible.

No! Fear took hold, his gut twisting. The heavens knew where she'd turn up when she took form again—probably right in the enemy's lap.

In sheer desperation, he put his mouth on hers. It was like kissing a wisp of cotton then air. Godsdammit, she was his mate, she should feel *something*—some kind of connection to him, right?

C'mon, Shae, he begged, wanting her to kiss him back so he'd know she was still there.

A second passed, two…she began to take corporeal form and swayed into him. A tiny gasp escaped her, her body solid once more. A tentative touch of her tongue against his, and relief flowed. And then he lost what was left of his rational mind. So damn grateful he had her back, he deepened the kiss, sliding his tongue into her mouth.

Her lips moved against his, a soft moan escaping her and setting his senses alight. It was the most intense physical pleasure he'd ever experienced in his long life as she kissed him back. She tasted of warm female and the strawberry candy she'd eaten. Desire coiled through his body, and his erection kicked up uncomfortably behind his zipper. The rush of her blood in her veins a sweet lure… His fangs lengthened.

Fuuuuck! He leaped away, breathing hard, fighting to get himself under control. If he took her, it wouldn't be just her body he'd want.

"Dagan?" At her soft, husky voice, he spun around, ready to tell her that this couldn't ever occur again. She blinked and looked around her, rubbing her temples like she wanted to knead away a headache. "Where are we? We were at the store…"

She didn't remember? Not even the kiss that had shaken him to the depths of his bloodstained soul? One he realized would haunt him for the rest of his life.

Breathing in deeply through his nose, the taste of her on his tongue, wishing he could will away the aching tightness in his chest, he picked up her fallen package—

A tourist. Another notch for my bedpost, the man's thoughts seeped into Dagan's mind. His fingers clenched on the pharmacy packet. He would kill the bastard first.

"Dagan?" Her wary gaze searched his face. "What happened?"

It took him a moment before he could speak. "Your powers made an appearance."

Fear widened her eyes, chasing away the flush his kiss had brought to her beautiful face, leaving her pale once more.

"Oh, no." Hurriedly, she glanced around then back at him. "Did I hurt you?"

So many words burned in his soul, demanding release. *You're my mate—my other half.* Instead, he said, tone flat, "No. But we need to leave."

"Wait-wait."

His control hanging by a thread, he shook his head and drew her close. Trying not to breathe in her tempting scent, he dematerialized them.

Back in the monastery courtyard, he waited until she'd steadied herself before heading indoors.

"Dagan, wait." Her booted steps echoed off the granite floors as she raced after him into the living room. "What about my clothes?"

"Make a list, I'll see you get them."

Shae planted herself in his path, her chest heaving from her short sprint, her gaze searching his. "What is going on with you?"

Sidestepping her, he entered the kitchen and dropped her package and his shades on the table. He retrieved a loose cigar from his pocket, desperate to get his urge under control. Lit the thing and dragged in a lungful of narcotic smoke, hoping it would eliminate her scent, the feel of her luscious mouth on his.

"You've been snarlier than a rabid dog since you

barged into the kitchen earlier. Is it because I used the darn dagger to peel those potatoes?" Shae stomped across to him.

Aaand that thought got shot to hell. Biting off a curse, he blew a spiral of smoke away from her and dropped onto a chair near the wall.

She glared at him.

He wanted to pull her astride his lap and slide into her feminine warmth so it would take away the eons of emptiness. He breathed in her tantalizing fragrance, instead, and his body wound tighter than a fucking spring. The mating bond was a bitch when ignored. And kissing her had just made everything worse.

"Seriously, what's going on with you?"

Dagan stretched out his long legs, caging her between them, and eyed her lazily.

She scowled, her expression morphing from irritation to pissed. "What?"

Since he wasn't going to hide the truth about this, he nodded at the table piled with skins and unpeeled potatoes and the weapon there. "That's my dagger."

"So?" She stepped over his ankle and headed back to the half-cleaned vegetables then deliberately started paring another.

"So, it's intrinsically linked to me…because it's my *mate's* dagger."

She stiffened. Good, she knew what that meant. Just as fast, a short snort followed. "When you find her, I'll hand it over, along with my condolences. Until then, you're not getting it back. I need it for the kitchen. And it's nice and sharp."

For some reason, her comment amused him. But the threat tacked on wasn't lost on him. She could probably stake him, too. He'd seen how swiftly she'd

Georgia Lyn Hunter

taken out those demons.

He leaned forward, elbows on his knees, a thin tendril of smoke trailing from the burning tip of his cigar. His gaze pinned hers. "I couldn't take it from you even if I wanted to. It now belongs to you."

Chapter 8

Shae froze, knife poised against the potato in her hand.

Damn his mind games. She glowered at Dagan as he killed his half-smoked cigar on his heel. "Lie all you want, you're still not getting the blade back."

But his words rattled inside her skull: *It now belongs to you.* When he continued to simply stare at her, uneasiness took hold. "You're crazy."

Mate? As if.

He rose to his feet, pushed his cigar into his pocket, and crossed to her. Removing the dagger from her hand, he tossed it onto the table, grasped her wrist, and hauled her along with him like she'd forgotten how to walk. "Damn it, Dagan," she snapped, a little unsettled. "You could just ask instead of dragging me all over the place."

"Would you have come?"

"No."

"Then my way works." He stopped in the middle of the lounge and faced her, those yellow eyes searing her like a flame. "Summon the dagger. Use your mind."

"Why?"

"Because only *my* mate can do so."

"You're crazy. I'm not playing these games with you." She headed for the kitchen. But recalling how the thing had appeared in her hand earlier, a chill slid through her.

"Scared?"

At his softly uttered taunt, she spun back and met his challenging stare. "You're making up this drivel to drive me mad."

"Then let's find out. Summon the dagger, Shae."

Sheesh, he wasn't going to let this go. Besides, with that soft order, she had no other recourse. Fine, she'd do it, if only to give the lie to his stupid allegations.

In her mind's eye, she saw the weapon lying on the old, wooden table. Black. Harmless now. She willed it to her. The next instant, something cool took shape in her palm. Shae jumped back, the air vacating her lungs.

No. No way! This isn't happening.

She inhaled harshly, whispered, "I drew rats to me, it's the same thing."

"They probably saw you as one big pile of delectable human cheese."

Now he found his sense of humor? She cut him an annoyed glare. "Ha, ha—funny. We are not mates. I don't even like you."

For a second, his eyes blazed with an intense emotion. Then he shrugged like he didn't really care what she thought of him, wiping away that illusion.

"Good. Then this should be easy to do. You'll be fine as long as we don't mate and soul-join. So, little hellcat, refrain from provoking me, because every time you open your mouth, all I think of is stripping you naked and licking you from lips to toes before fucking you into surrender. But I'm sure you don't want the ties."

Her eyes widened. The erotic images so vivid in her mind, she swore she could actually feel his tongue slowly licking a trail down her tummy to between her…she inhaled sharply. Her face on fire, she retorted, "You're absolutely right, I don't. But thanks for the heads-up."

His lips took on a sardonic twist, like he knew something she didn't, which just irritated her more. She scowled. He smiled, revealing the tips of his…fangs?

What the hell? "What-what are you?"

The smile faded. "You're a clever girl, figure it out."

He definitely wasn't a demon. His irises didn't have that hint of red like Harvey's sometimes did…wait! The night outside The Tower, it hadn't been her imagination; she *did* see the tinge of red in his eyes.

Her gaze flew to his mouth, but his lengthened incisors were no longer visible. She pressed her hand to her neck. "You're a-a vamp…"

"…pire?" A dark eyebrow lifted. "If you want a tag, sure."

"B-but you walk in sunlight?"

"Yeah, I'm remarkable that way."

Ignoring his cynical retort, Shae glanced around, had no idea what she was looking for. Only knew deep down that she'd been prodding a really dangerous predator, one who could have torn her throat out in a heartbeat. She gulped.

"You're afraid of me."

Jesus, yes. But she never liked showing weakness. The thread of wariness dissipated like mist. "I'm not scared of you."

Georgia Lyn Hunter

Amusement lit his eyes as if he could see through her lie. Her gaze lowered back to his sensual mouth. Heck, she wanted to run her tongue along his lips, feel the tips of his fangs—ugh! This was entirely his fault for being so damn sexy that her mind kept sliding into the gutters.

Another image flowed into her mind. Intense yellow eyes locked with hers, a mouth on her neck, impossible desire heating her veins as he kissed…no…*sucked* her neck. And then she knew.

"You!" she sputtered. "*You* attacked me in the alley. You bit me and then took away my memories!" Furious, she hurled the dagger at him. His hand shot out and snatched the blade midair.

"I did not attack or *bite* you. If I had, trust me, you'd know. I had to get you to leave. It was a dangerous time. But you wouldn't. It seemed the best way."

That stopped her for a second. She'd been drawn to his pain and only wanted to help. But he hadn't denied taking her memories. "Don't ever do that again."

He ran his thumb carelessly over the sharp edge of the dagger. "I won't feed from you, if that's what's worrying you."

Then he did consume blood. *Jesus.* Of course, he did. All her questions vanished. Something inside her shifted and made her belly churn. So who exactly?

"Then who?" the words were out before she could stop them.

His expression closed off. "That's none of your business."

Unexplained irritation swept through her at his dismissive answer.

It's your fault. You told him you didn't like him.

Yes, she'd said that—a slip of her tongue. Truth was,

she did like him—hell, she'd been drawn to him from the moment she saw him in the club. His intensity and raw sexual magnetism wrapped around her like a silken web, tugging her closer and closer every time they were together.

Dagan strolled across to her, stopping only when a mere foot separated them. He smelled so good... sandalwood with a trace of cherry tobacco. His unreadable gaze drifted over her face and down to her collarbone. Frowning, he traced a fingertip gently over the scar running from her cheek to her neck.

"Your laptop accident?" he asked.

She nodded. Usually, the scar didn't bother her, yet instinctively, she covered it with her hand, her bracelets jangling against each other.

"Don't hide, Shae—" He grasped her wrist, then angled his head and studied the tattoo she had there. "What's this?"

She pulled free and stepped back from his disturbing presence. "Decorative ink—a bunch of knots. Got it 'cause it's so pretty."

At her tart response, his eyes narrowed, then he put the obsidian dagger in her palm and headed for the front door.

"Wait, where you are going?"

A hand on the doorjamb, he turned slightly. "To feed, of course. Unless you're offering? But with that comes fucking. You ready for that, wildcat?"

Her mouth snapped shut.

"Thought not." He walked out.

Shae stared at the empty doorway, his words ringing in her head, images crowding her mind of his mouth on her neck, his big body sliding over hers as his hardness moved inside her. Desire swept through her in a heat wave. God, she rubbed her face.

Restless, she wandered the length of the cracked corridor and back again. Blowing out a frustrated breath, she stopped at the coffee table and lowered on her knees to the cold floor. She collected the spilled cards and shuffled them, but her lone game of solitaire didn't take away the churning in her stomach.

He was going to feed, have sex with some nameless, faceless woman.

***

Dagan rematerialized in the village as dusk crept into the area. If he remained with Shae, chances were high that he'd end up taking her right where she stood.

His crude words had put distaste on her face. Better he showed her what a *barbarian* he was, then maybe *she* would stay away from him, because his resistance had all the strength of fraying cotton. If their paths hadn't crossed, he could have lived his empty existence.

The warriors all lived dangerous lives. Why the hell would Gaia do this to them?

When he'd first taken his oath to become a Guardian, she'd offered him an array of daggers.

Dagan had thought nothing of it, just picked one, and it had glowed. Hell, he'd been too steeped in a blood haze to care why. But a part of her words stayed with him: *Your dagger is the embodiment of your one weakness...* and something else, he couldn't recall.

Now he knew. His weakness would be his downfall. *And Shae is.*

Damn, he scrubbed a hand over his unshaven jaw in frustration then texted Hedori. *Send Shae's things over.*

A response came back instantly. *On it.*

Dagan made his way into Club Samhain and dropped

onto a barstool in the slowly filling bar. The bartender nodded and handed him his usual drink. Humans packed the place. Soon, the sounds of their heartbeats, the tempting rush of their blood flowing through their veins crowded his ears.

He drank deeply of his red wine, barely tasting the rich vintage, trying to shut off the sounds. His mind drifted back to his time in Tartarus.

One minute, he'd been fighting off vampiric vultures; the next, a whirlwind of impossible power had sucked him up and tossed him out into darkness— into this world, in the forest of the Tatra Mountains in Eastern Europe…and the horror that followed. Michael had finally found him after another bloody rampage, lying amidst the dead bodies and carnage…

"We will find a way out of this." A dark-haired male—no, an angel—squatted beside him, his shattered irises glowing an eerie silvery blue.

"No," Dagan rasped, his voice rusty from lack of use. "End this—end me. I cannot live like this."

With a wave of his hand, the angel incinerated the bodies instead. Then he went motionless, eyes narrowing. "Trouble."

The coppery scent of sweet nectar drifted to Dagan. The thirst, which never eased, stirred viciously again. His guilt forgotten, his fangs descended. He leaped up and took off like an arrow. The angel thundered after him.

Dagan faltered to a halt near a settlement, and froze at the massacre taking place.

Hysterical screams drenched the night air, along with guttural laughter. Human bodies were strewn on the blood-splattered ground. Except, he wasn't responsible this time. Demoniis.

Georgia Lyn Hunter

The angel dove into the melee. It barely registered that a few males in tattered clothes were already fighting evil. A demonii spun around, his eyes glowing like neon red orbs in the dark. "More food—immortal, too."

He grabbed Dagan, his blood-soaked mouth snapping open and revealing an orifice of stained teeth and fangs. Dagan punched the evil in the face and clamped his mouth onto the demonii's neck, his canines tearing through flesh and sinew. He gulped the thick plasma spilling free, and drank and drank. When the demonii stopped fighting and disintegrated into dust, he went after another...

His bloated stomach roiled. Bile rushed up his throat. Dagan stumbled through the forest, collapsing near a running stream. On his knees, he regurgitated all he'd drunk. Black blood.

He lowered his head to the flowing river and gulped water like an animal.

Vaguely, he recalled, demoniis were essentially dead, living off stolen human souls and blood. Then everything stilled, even the very air.

Dagan glanced to his side at the tall female standing on the riverbank. He blinked. Somewhere in the back of his mind, it registered that she had hair like the sun, skin darker than his, and eyes the color of leaves. But it was the intricate green patterns running from her eyebrow down to her cheeks that held his attention...they looked like crawling green serpents.

She stared at him for a long moment before she spoke. "Arise, fallen warrior from the godly realm."

There was a command behind those words, pushing through his dizzy mind. Dagan staggered to his feet as if he were inebriated. The angel with the broken eyes *appeared at his side.*

"I am Gaia. You've confronted the evil that has taken to pillaging my realm and, in your almost mortal state, you have vanquished them." Those glowing green eyes held his. "Become the realm's Guardian, and I will give you purpose. You will regain all powers. In time, you will find what you seek..."

Dagan stared at the wine warming between his palms. Sure, he'd regained his abilities and found a way to resist humans, but now he had to rely on Kaerys' *generosity* to feed and recharge. He drained his liquor.

At the itch bearing down his back, he looked up. A young, tattooed human seated across the counter cast him a sultry stare.

He shoved to his feet and stalked outside. The sun had set. Night cloaked the village.

"There you are..."

At the slurring voice, Dagan cut an impatient look over his shoulder. Lust and liquor wafted off the horny human who'd followed him out. "You sure you want me? You'll die."

"As long as your cock's inside me, I don't care."

Damn idiot was wasted, had no idea of the reality. Besides, he didn't roll that way.

Willing him gone, Dagan headed deeper into the rundown alley, his mood in the crapper.

There was only one person he wanted, longed for. Just thinking of her and his body coiled tight with arousal. He couldn't have her.

Hell, he was hurtling headlong toward a fatal collision, yet he couldn't seem to slow down any more than he could stop breathing.

***

Georgia Lyn Hunter

In the early hours of the morning, after a hunt in the nearby forest to satiate his hunger, Dagan took form in the monastery courtyard. As he made his way into the kitchen, Hedori turned from the fridge and shut the door. "I'm sorry about the delay, sire. I have left Shae's things at your door since she sleeps. Oh, I've two containers of pies and cookies in the fridge, they're ready to pop into the oven."

Dagan nodded his thanks grateful at the Empyrean's thoughtfulness.

"Wait," he called out as Hedori headed for the door. "I need someone to stay here for the duration Shae resides, to see to things and keep her safe when I'm out on patrol. Not Eron. The old fool spends most of his time in the village chasing after the females. Get Angelus."

"Certainly." Hedori hesitated, then asked, "Did you pick up anything else when you went back to The Tower?"

"I found the scourge who shot Shae. Got rid of him."

"That's good to hear. I meant about her mother."

Dagan frowned. "No…and Shae doesn't speak much about it," he said, taking the merlot from the shelf. "She only mentioned her mother had taken off a couple of months ago, wanted her own life."

"She did?" Hedori's brow creased in confusion. "It doesn't make sense or tie in with the sadness and despair I felt in the penthouse."

Dagan leaned against the counter and sipped his drink. "My thoughts, exactly. But I can't do anything about it until I get back."

"I can help out there. I'll make inquiries and watch The Tower, see what turns up." Hedori opened the outer door.

"Be careful."

The older Empyrean inclined his head, a hard smile on his face, reminding Dagan that he hadn't always been the amiable butler they saw daily—he'd been a protector. "Always am. You forget who's been under my care for millennia. As vast and dangerous as his powers are, he could never evade or kill me—a gift, courtesy of the mage of Empyrea for protecting that intractable Empyrean sovereign. Though I thought it a curse in those earlier days. Burnt clothes, singed hair…" He shook his head wryly.

Dagan found a rare moment of amusement filling him at Hedori's dry discourse about protecting a young Aethan. His smile faded. "If you find anything, call me. I don't want you caught in the middle if this turns bad."

Hedori's lips thinned briefly. "Very well, sire."

"And about that, it's Dagan, D-man, or whatever the hell the others call me these days."

"Barbarian?"

He scowled at the twinkle in the wiseass' odd, orange-green eyes. "No."

Laughing, Hedori walked out into the back courtyard when Dagan recalled something else he wanted to ask. He set the glass on the counter and hurried after him. "Hedori, wait." He found a twig, and on the dusty ground, he roughly drew the knots with the open end he'd seen on Shae's wrist. "Do you know what this symbol means?"

The Empyrean studied it. "I'm not sure, but I'll find out. I'll be in touch."

After Hedori had left, Dagan collected Shae's luggage and made his way to the last room. With a wave of his hand, he lit the taper on a dusty nightstand and set the case aside. The place was hardly habitable and covered with a layer of dust. Too tired to care, he shed his clothes, swiped the sheet off the bed, and dropped onto the mattress. The four tall bedposts loomed over him as if standing guard.

For as long as he could remember, his life had been that of a protector, first his mother and sister after his old man had taken off; then, when his sister became the Goddess of Life. And after being released from Tartarus, as Guardian of the human realm. Now, Shae.

At the thought, he threw his arm over his brow, a rough sigh escaping him. How the hell could he keep her safe from the worst danger she might face? She'd soon start to feel the pull of their mating bond, and it had tragedy written all over it.

A moan drifted to him…followed by clattering.

He lowered his arm. Frowning, Dagan pushed off the bed and, using the connecting door, entered his room. It was like stepping into an icebox. The windows stood open. With a thought, he shut them and crossed to the bed. Shae huddled beneath the thin cover, trembling. He never used anything when he slept, even in this high altitude and with the freezing temperatures at night. But she was human. Her teeth clacked together, forcing him to act.

He glanced down at himself. Naked would be asking for trouble. He got out sweats from his closet, pulled them on, then fed the dying embers in the fireplace more wood before heading to the bed. "Move over."

She peered out from beneath the covers. "I-I'm okay."

"Sure, you are." He lifted the thin sheet. She wore a black t-shirt and sweats…*his*. Damn, he should have gotten her clothes, some damn warm pajamas at least, and she wouldn't be freezing now. He got in and drew her close. She shuddered as her icy body slid alongside his. "You should have called me."

She didn't say anything, burrowing deeply into him as if searching for every bit of heat he possessed. He willed his warmth into her, stroking her back. As the shivering eased, her body loosened. Soon, a soft sigh caressed his skin as sleep took her over.

Or so he thought.

"Did you…feed?"

A sigh barreled out of him. "Go to sleep."

"Did you?"

"Yes."

Her entire body went taut. She rolled away and curled up on the other end of the mattress.

"How the hell will you get warm on that side?"

She remained silent. He reached for her.

"Don't." She flung out a hand, stopping him.

Dagan glared at the ceiling. He should just go back to the other room, get some sleep. Then it hit him—his taunting her earlier. Hell, she thought he'd fed and fucked another woman, then came to *her*?

Scowling, he leaped off the bed. Sure, he could be an asshole at times, but he did have a few ethics he abided by. One of which was, he didn't cheat, never had…unlike his old man.

He stalked around the bed and crouched at her side. A swathe of red hair covered her face. "If it eases your mind, I fed from an animal."

She appeared so still, he was sure she'd stopped breathing. After a second, maybe several, she said, "You don't have to explain. It's none of my business what you do."

"Then why ask?"

When she didn't answer, frustrated to his eyeballs,

he gritted out, "You're shivering, and I won't have you falling ill. It's been a long damn night, so move over."

When she stubbornly remained where she was, he picked her up, repositioned her, and lay down again. This time, he kept her locked at his side. She squirmed, trying to put space between them or probably wanting to leave and go find another bed. But her movements were having a serious effect on his body.

"For hellssake," he snapped. "I swear by every damn star in the sky, you wriggle again, I'll have you beneath me and my cock inside you in a heartbeat—is that what you want?"

She went utterly still.

Yeah, thought not.

Several minutes later, when she finally relaxed in sleep, her hand slid over his chest as if to keep him there. Yeah, right.

Dagan shut his eyes, his dick a throbbing ache between his thighs. Hell, he'd fucked-up spectacularly keeping her at a distance. He shouldn't have bothered with an explanation. She didn't believe him anyway.

Yet, in spite of what his brain theorized—it was safer this way—his heart overruled, wanting her.

The rhythmic thudding of her heart soon filled his ears, the gentle flow of blood in her veins a compelling lure. Fuck! He shut his eyes, trying to shut off the sounds as need wired his body to a razor's edge.

To stop the endless torture, he untangled himself from her seductive warmth. Since the kind of release he longed for wasn't going to happen, and he wasn't interested in a hand job, he'd settle for a brutal workout.

Satisfied that she was warm and the burning logs would last for several hours, he left the room and jogged upstairs to Nik's chamber. The warrior didn't sleep. Ever. He lay sprawled on his bed in a freezing room more barren than his own, and still in his patrolling gear. An arm flung over his eyes.

"Nik"—he nudged his shoulder—"let's go."

"Fuck, Dag-man," he grunted. "I just got in. Go annoy Race."

Race was worse than all of them when it came to his solitude. He completely shunned everyone and rarely stayed at the monastery, preferring his mountainous caves.

Dagan dematerialized to the summit some distance from the monastery, determined to haul him out of his hidey-hole. As he took form, the brisk winds slapping his bare chest barely registered. There, on the plateau, he found Race, still in his patrolling gear, minus a shirt.

Despite the dark sky, the cold, pale moonlight emphasized the warrior's flowing silver hair, broken only by the strip of black at the front. Brandishing curved twin blades, he moved with a deliberation that was as lethal as the steel of his dragon blades.

From the dying Lemurian pantheon, Eracier—aka Race—was one of the few of his kind left, and every bit as deadly as the black dragon warrior he'd been spawned from. He looked up and smirked. "Wanna play, Sumerian?"

Dagan didn't respond to the taunt, summoning one of his many swords.

Race's twin blades vanished, and a broadsword appeared in his left hand. He flew in the air, weapon swinging. Dagan lunged and countered. They spun around each other, slicing, blocking, and attacking.

"You're in a mood," Race grinned, revealing his own pointy canines. A deadly reminder that those fangs

Georgia Lyn Hunter

became a mouthful of deadly chompers when he shifted into his huge motherfucking alter ego.

"So…" An eyebrow cocked. "You found your mate, eh? I smell her on you."

Dagan said nothing, anger, longing, and frustration roiling through him.

"Human then," Race murmured. "Sure sucks. But let's work that fury outta you. I'm in a mood myself."

Dagan didn't ask why. There was only one thing that drove Race—drove them all—these centuries since their release from Tartarus.

Revenge.

Chapter 9

At the unearthly peace and warmth surrounding her, Shae's eyes opened in confusion. It took a moment to realize sunlight streamed in through the closed window and that the room was toasty warm. But Dagan was gone.

When she recalled her jealous outburst before she'd used him as her personal blanket, she grimaced and rubbed her burning face. But she was aware, too, she'd only fallen asleep *after* he told her he'd fed from an animal.

It's none of my business whom he fed from or slept with. Irritated at herself for stewing over it, she sat up, picked up her cell from the nightstand to call one of the two men who never let her down. She'd call Harvey later. Lem first, or he'd worry if she didn't check in. There was already a missed call from him. She hit speed dial.

He answered on the first ring. "Shae?"

"Uncle Lem—"

"Thank God! Are you all right? I called your cell,

you didn't answer. And the hotel you were registered at in Anchorage said you hadn't checked in."

Crap. She'd forgotten to cancel. "Because I'm not staying there. I'm er, camping out"—she winced at the lie—"and I was out of Wi-Fi range, but I'm fine. I just got into town and called so you wouldn't worry."

Silence. "I see… When are you coming back?"

Uneasiness stirred at his quiet tone. He didn't believe her? "As soon as I'm done. Uncle, I have a shot at working for *National Geographic*. I don't want to mess this up."

"I understand, child. Actually, I have some wonderful news. You remember those businessmen who approached me to run for mayor in the next election? Well, I've decided to do it."

"Really?" She grinned, tucking her long bangs behind her ear. "I'm so happy for you. I'll help you any way I can."

"I'll hold you to that. I'd like you to be there for my speech. It's next week."

"I will be. Do you want me to look over your notes?"

"That would be wonderful. When you get back, we can talk more. Goodbye, Shae. Go take some great pictures."

Darn. She rubbed her temple and stared at her silent phone, her guilt constricting her like a noose. While she was happy with the news of him running for mayor since it was something he'd wanted for as long as she could remember, how could she tell him the truth about the supernatural threat she faced? Demons who hunted humans with strong psychic abilities. Knowing Lem, he'd come after her, walk right into danger—and probably death. He was way too protective.

At a new unread message, she opened it. Harvey.

You didn't call? Are you postponing the summoning?

She chewed her lower lip then typed back. *Yes. Something came up. I'll call you later.*

As if he were waiting, a message instantly came back. *Okay. As long as you're all right. Saw you with HIM, was worried.*

She remembered Harvey saying something about saving his cousin from certain death, and now *he* was in trouble with that *cold Guardian bastard*—his words.

Since she'd met said Guardian, yeah, she understood. No way would Dagan have let that infraction go. Well, she wasn't letting any of them touch her friend.

Spying her luggage on the ebony chest, she breathed a sigh of relief. A half-hour later, showered and changed, Shae left the room, tying her hair into a ponytail.

Low, masculine humming coming from the kitchen had her frowning. Dagan would probably jump off this mountain before he'd hum, and she couldn't see Nik doing so either. But the delicious aroma of something baked scented the air, and her stomach kicked up a fuss.

Curious, she quickened her steps and stopped dead at the threshold.

A tall guy, about eighteen or so, was pulling out a tray of cookies from the wood-burning oven, but damn, the entire place was spotless. He sported skinny black pants and boots. His rich, mahogany-red hair was pulled into a low ponytail, a colorful contrast against the dark blue tunic he wore.

"Good morning," she called out. Sheesh, it was likely past midday.

He whipped around. His striking purplish eyes

widened, as did hers. Whoa! His ears—dammit, they were pointed!

"Good morn, my lady. I am Angelus." His voice pulled her out of her gawking. A smile lit his incredibly gorgeous face. Oh, man, he looked like an angel.

"Please, call me Shae. So, what are you?"

"The help. Hedori sent for me. I'm to take care of this place."

Laughing, she swiped an oatmeal cookie from the tray, took a bite, and chewed. "No, I mean, what *are* you? Angel, elf—"

"I'm fae. You are human."

"And she's not a collectible," her nemesis said, coming into the kitchen.

Shae wheeled around and nearly choked on the cookie she'd just taken another bite of. Heat suffused her face when she recalled cuddling up to him as if he were her own personal heater. "Collectible?" she asked.

"It's what faes do. They like to keep humans as possessions. They steal them and whisk them off to Exilum, a place just beyond the veils of this world."

Jeez. She arched an eyebrow at Angelus. "Really? Not happening."

He smiled and shrugged. "I know. You're important here and off-limits."

Rolling her eyes, she faced Dagan again, struggling not to blush. "Thanks for last night."

He stared at her for a second. Something dark flashed in those sun-bright irises and disappeared as fast. "Just make sure the windows are shut at night," he said, heading for the side door to the backyard.

She frowned. But she *had* shut them. Then shrugging off the thought, she hurried after him. "Dagan, wait."

He slowed. Those broad shoulders lifted then dropped as if in a weary sigh. She rounded to his front. "Will you teach me to fight?"

"No."

"Really? Just *no*? I'll have you know, Mr. I Am-the-Man, chauvinistic tendencies died last century, and I need to keep up my training."

He sidestepped her and continued around the building then jogged up the narrow, crudely mined granite steps. Undeterred by his rebuff, she followed, the chilly breeze barely soothing her heated face.

"Why are you being so difficult?" she wheezed when she finally reached the top, swiping her sweaty brow. Then Shae's jaw dropped. Her eyes widened. "Wow!" She spun around on the plateau-like surface of what must surely be the top of the world. Clouds hung so low, she reached up, and her fingers glided through the smoky miasma. "This is really awesome... And damp."

She wiped her fingers on her jeans then hurried to the edge some distance away and hastily leaped back. The forest appeared like a green smudge far, *far* down below. "Whoa! That's quite the drop. A slip-up, and I could end up splattered on the rocks."

"You won't."

Yeah, he'd probably leap after her with all his superpowers. She pivoted and nearly swallowed her tongue. He'd taken off his tee. Wearing only jeans, his muscle-packed chest bare, he was a mind-numbingly sexy distraction.

"What are you waiting for?" he asked, braiding his long hair into a single rope. The low clouds above appeared to rise higher.

She narrowed her eyes. "You were bringing me here to teach me?"

Georgia Lyn Hunter

"No, I'd planned to put in some hours in my workplace until you railroaded me."

"What?" She blinked. "You work?"

"Why the surprise? Did you think I just guard the realm?" He rolled those tough shoulders, thick with corded muscle. Before she could continue her questions, he said, "You want to fight, then let's."

The threat in his stance made her a little wary, but she wasn't backing off. "Let me change—"

"No. Trouble comes at any time. It doesn't wait for you to dress appropriately." He circled her. "C'mon, hellcat, what are you waiting for?"

The tag rankled. "I scratched you once, and you stick me with that annoying name."

"Once?" A dark eyebrow lifted. "If I didn't heal as fast as I do, I'd be pitted with trails of scars as proof of being hit, bitten, and let's not forget, having water bottles flung at me."

Heat scorched her face. She sniffed. "Yeah, well, you made me mad. Look, I don't want to fight you. You'll crush me with your huge size. I only need you to demonstrate your techniques. Besides, Harvey has already shown me just how fast you immortals move. He usually trains me."

"I see." His tone dropped to a worrying sub-zero. "Did it help?"

She eyed him cautiously. "Some. I think guns would be better."

What had changed? He'd been taunting and toying with her until she mentioned… Dammit! That reminded her. "I don't want you to touch, hurt, or kill Harvey. He was only protecting his foolish cousin."

Dagan continued as if he hadn't heard her. "Immortals can't die from gun wounds. If anything, getting shot will seriously piss them off."

"Maybe, but it will give me a chance to run if I need to. As long as I get them in places that hurt—*eeek*!" He came at her like a flash of lightning, grabbed her arm and spun her around—her heart beat so hard—hell, it was moments from crashing through her ribcage and hurtling to the gorge below. With her back plastered against his chest and her arms caught in a vise-like grip, she was…trapped. Dammit!

Shae glared at him over her shoulder. He lowered his head to her ear, his breath a warm caress on her nape. "And that's what can happen when you miss a shot or wound them—except your neck would probably be broken by now."

"How is this fair?" She shoved away from his disturbing warmth. "You didn't warn me."

"You think an enemy will?"

At his stinging words, she stifled a grimace. He was right.

"Here's the thing, Shae-cat, I won't allow harm to come to you in any form or manner. Yes, you need to be able to defend yourself. If it means using my *huge* size to get you used to fighting bigger opponents, then you will fight me. Weapons can get lost. And from what I've seen, you need to build up your strength and muscles."

He leaped at her. Shae ducked his grasp. Using the maneuvers Harvey had shown her, gathering power and speed, she spun around and lashed out a flying kick dead center to his chest. It didn't even move him.

He stepped back, his expression calm, but his eyes gleamed in amusement.

She scowled, and the next second, she went flying as he took her down. She hadn't seen him move. Bracing for a crushing impact, she squeezed her eyes tight, except he shifted at the last second, and she landed on top of him instead. The air flattened from her lungs. Too winded to care, she lay there panting, grateful she was still in one piece.

He was even faster than Harvey.

When she finally raised her head and met his deep stare, any words of gratitude she would have uttered got lost in the winds. She became aware of the warm, male body beneath hers. All hard angles and…rigid man parts pressed on her thigh.

"Very well, I won't touch your friend. For now." He wrapped her ponytail around his fist and brought her head down to him. His nose and lips grazed along her jaw and down her throat in a sensual glide, and without thought or reason in sight, she put her mouth on his.

It took her a moment to realize he wasn't kissing her back. Shae lifted her head. At the sight of his elongated canines digging into his lower lip—his glowing irises tracking her every move—she became aware of the deadly predator beneath her. Wariness overrode desire. Anxiety squeezed her chest and had her scrambling off him.

One minute, he was beside her, the next, he was standing at the edge of the plateau, the breeze whipping the loose strands of his hair. He didn't pace, just stood there. So still, watching her. His fangs still visible, his red-tinge eyes stark with a desire she felt, too, but his features were grim.

A little shaky, Shae swallowed and swiped at the bangs sticking to her damp brow. "Dagan…"

"No." He shook his head. "It's better Angelus sees to your training." He picked up his shirt and pulled it on. "C'mon."

Shae bit her lip and she pushed to her feet. *Perhaps it was better this way*, she told herself as she followed him. Too many complications. Yet it felt as if a hole had opened in her tummy.

In the kitchen, Dagan spoke to Angelus. She tuned them out, got a glass of water, and drank deeply. Exhaling a jagged breath, she set the tumbler down, but the stirring heat inside her amplified. She swiped her sweaty brow and pivoted to find only Angelus in the room with her.

"Are you all right?" he asked, pulling out steaks from the freezer for dinner.

No. "Yes." With shaky hands, she dug a piece of candy from her jeans pocket and sucked on it, but the energy continued to escalate. *No, no, not now!* Panic rising, she hurried from the kitchen only to bump into Nik about to step inside.

"Sorry." She jumped back. "Is there s-someplace I can run? This abbey…too confined."

At her faltering words, Nik's narrowed gaze swept over her face. *Please don't let him sense anything.* She shoved her trembling fingers into her jeans pockets.

"The foot of the mountain, along the creek. But you can't leave the monastery."

"I know, I know…must be safe. Angelus can come. He'll spring me back here if there's a need, right?"

Nik frowned and rubbed his palm over his shorn head. "I should check with Dagan."

"Why? You're a Guardian, can't you make a decision?" Dammit, she had to get outta here. Dagan in his black mood would never let her out of his sight.

Nik's pale green eyes became shards of ice. "Very well. Take Angelus. One hour. Or I'll personally bring you back. And that's a journey you won't enjoy."

What was with the threats with this lot? Too close to the edge to be annoyed, she spun for the bedroom in a feverish sprint. She far preferred the Guardians of New York. They were more civilized. Laidback. They didn't threaten and bully... She lost track of her frustrated thoughts, the heat inside her gathering momentum.

She changed and dashed out of the room. Angelus approached from down the corridor, a smile on his pretty face. "Ready?"

Moments later, they reformed at the foot of the mountains. The cold, earthy scent of soil and water nearly froze her. Despite the shivers flooding her skin, it did little to soothe the energy inside her. She let go of Angelus. "Wait here."

"Shae, I cannot. The sires, Nik and Dagan, would persecute me badly if anything happened to you."

"Ange, I need to run *alone*."

"I shall make myself invisible and accompany you."

Oh, great! She took off in a hard sprint, desperate to exert the energy swirling like a storm inside her. As she ran, the winds picked up speed, the trees raced past her like a movie on fast-forward. Her thoughts drifted away, as did time...

In some far-off place, she heard her name being called. Hands grabbed her, and she staggered to a stumbling halt. Worried purple eyes searched hers. "Hey, Ange," she panted.

"Are you okay?"

"What?" Then she nodded, her gaze skipping all around the place. "Why?"

"Your abilities surfaced."

Oh, no-no! She cast him a horrified look. "Did I—did I hurt you?"

He shook his head. "I'm fine. But your corporeal

body was fading, and you have a little blood here." He touched his nostril.

Breathing hard, she grabbed the bottom of her navy t-shirt and quickly wiped her nose, her heart pounding hard at the realization that she could have unknowingly teleported to some other place.

"It's okay. I-I'm okay—please don't tell the Guardians about this?" Especially not Dagan, he'd probably lock her in the monastery if he knew.

A pained expression crossed Angelus' features. "Shae—"

"You will allow the lad to become a pawn in your deceit?" Dagan strode up to her, his eyes spitting yellow fire. "I felt your distress from my workshop."

"Had to run—had to—" The words escaped in a staccato rush. "Couldn't do that up there—" She flung her hand at the mountains and swayed. Powerful arms caught her, and she sagged against his chest, breathing in his warm, soothing scent.

"Angelus, you can go."

After throwing her another worried look, Angelus shimmered and vanished.

"Is this why you wanted me to train with you earlier?" Dagan asked, stroking a hand down her back.

No, he never shouted or lost his temper. Whatever had happened earlier between them was probably a distant memory for him. But it only brought back the awareness that seemed to grow between them.

"I did want to train then…" She pushed away from him, retied her loosened hair, and faced the gurgling creek. "But, I need to expend the energy that suddenly overtakes me, and I don't know how. I used to run or do a rigorous gym workout when it first started…now, nothing helps."

He came up beside her. His warmth, his calm presence should be comforting, but now it only made her edgier and too aware. "Your abilities are growing stronger. You have to learn to shield them."

"You think I don't know that?" She shot him a frustrated look, feeling as if her entire being was fragmenting, and trying desperately to center herself. "I try, but I can't…"

Warm, callused hands engulfed both of hers. "Okay. Let's begin."

"What are you doing?" She stared at him in confusion.

"Seeing into your mind—"

"No!" She snatched her hands back and tucked her fists beneath her armpits.

"Shae," he said quietly, "I'm only interested in the events that led to this, but I have to touch you to do so before too much time passes, or I will miss the important details."

When she didn't move, his expression hardened. "You want to survive this? You need my help."

Her mouth opened and closed at his callous words. Damn him. With little choice, taking a deep breath, Shae straightened her spine and stuck out her hands. With no idea how to compartmentalize what she didn't want him to see, she gritted her teeth and waited.

His fingers wrapped around hers…a minute passed. At his sudden, fierce stare, her stomach cramped. "What?"

Had he seen her unrequited crush on Ash, seen the real reason why her mother had walked out on her? Or worse, had he seen her unexpected attraction to him?

She tried to snatch her hands back, but his grip tightened. "You don't learn to control this, it will not only wreak havoc on everything around you, it will also consume *you* whole."

"My life's on a fast track to disaster, and I have no idea how to stop it. Like you pointed out, I'm human, I didn't ask for this…" She pulled free. Her fury draining, her shaky knees gave way, and she sank to the ground and rubbed the aching scar on her cheek. "Why?" she whispered, despair sweeping through her. "All I wanted was to find my mother, but she doesn't want to be found. She can't stand me…"

Dagan lowered to his haunches beside her. "Whatever reasons she had for leaving, I'm sure it wasn't because she dislikes you—"

"You don't understand, *my* laptop exploded and sent her flying across the room—*I'm* responsible for her leaving."

"Shae, it was an accident. You couldn't have foreseen that… You're bleeding again."

Dammit. She swiped at her nose, and more blood smeared her fingers. Hurriedly, she looked up, met his burning gaze. At the hunger she saw there, apprehension swamped her.

"I'm not going to attack you because of a little blood," he said, his tone curt. He pulled off his shirt, tilted her chin up, and held the tee beneath her nose. A warm tingle flowed through her face. "This started because you were upset."

Not a question. And not one she'd willingly answer anyway. After several minutes, he lowered his hand, his mouth tightening. Yeah, he knew why she was upset. Because of what had occurred—or didn't occur—between them. He didn't comment, for which she was grateful.

"We need to strengthen your mental shields. It's the

Georgia Lyn Hunter

only way you will have any chance of controlling your power." He rose to his feet and helped her up. "Let's try this again. Now, go into your mind, to the place you instinctively use to shut out thoughts…"

Shae closed her eyes and let his words lead her into the space in her head where she felt the pull of her kinetic energy, the one that still hummed beneath her skin.

"Now, move it all back to where you feel it originating from. Lock it down, use a metal trunk, steel walls, whatever holds it…"

His shirt clenched in her hand, she grasped hold of the humming in her mind and fought to push it into a steel box. Perspiration beaded her brow…and the buzz spilled free. Dammit. Her eyelids snapped open, and she found him watching her.

"Again."

"I can't!" Her nerves stretched like a rubber band, she wheeled away and kicked a stone into the churning water. "Later—tomorrow, I'll try."

"No. Now is perfect. You're upset. It's when you need control the most." He cupped her elbows, making her look at him. "You can do it. This time, keep your eyes on me."

That was supposed to make it easier? Being this close to him, especially without his shirt on, wasn't helping. At all.

Mouth tight, she met his stare and let her mind take over. Only, she became aware of his warmth, his scent surrounding her. Her gaze lowered to his sensual lips. She wanted his mouth so badly on hers—

"It's not working," she bit out in frustration.

"You're not trying hard enough."

"Not trying?" she snapped. Every time she looked at

him, images of him kissing her crowded her mind. God, she had no idea why she was obsessing over a kiss that had never happened.

Her mouth pressed into a tight line, she shut her eyes and went back into her mind, found the thread of vibration humming through her body and stilled. Like déjà vu, a memory stirred…his mouth sliding over her lips, his tongue stroking hers. Her breath caught. Her eyes snapped open. "You—you kissed me."

"I did." There was no apology in his tone.

"Why?"

"I didn't want you to disappear. The afternoon in the village, we had an argument, and your abilities flared. Your corporeal body was becoming invisible. I had to anchor you. Seemed the best way to do it."

Of course. That's all she was to him. Work. Nothing else.

She rubbed her achy temple. Illogical it may be— considering he drove her crazy most of the time—but she wanted him to want her, to kiss her again. Wanted to be aware this time when his mouth was on hers, his tongue caressing hers—not trapped in her powers.

Earlier when she'd kissed him, he hadn't responded…

She lowered her hand. Despair taking hold, adding to her tangled emotions for this hard man. "It's gone. I don't feel the buzz anymore."

"Good. Whenever it slips free, go back and lock it up like you did today, until it becomes second nature."

She nodded, scratching the itch on her wrist.

Shae, we belong together, you and I. Soon…

What the—? She spun around and searched the wooded surroundings, an eerie sensation skating through her. A cascade of goosebumps flooded her skin at the faint voice in her mind.

"Shae?"

She shivered and shook her head. "It's nothing."

At the burn in her wrist, she frowned at the bloody welts marring her tattooed skin.

Dagan grasped her hand and pushed her bracelets aside, his eyes narrowing. "What happened?" He gently stroked the abrasions with his thumb, and a soothing warmth coalesced over the injury.

Tell him she was hearing voices now?

He'd lock her up for sure, and with her growing powers, she needed the open space.

"I guess I scratched too hard."

His mouth thinned. "If the damn thing irritates you, why don't you get it removed?"

Shae didn't respond. Her stomach taut with unease, she cast another look around her as he dematerialized them back to the monastery. It barely registered she had her face pressed against his naked chest, the unsettling words ringing in her head.

What had the voice meant...*soon*?

Chapter 10

Nightfall slipped in, casting shadows over the monastery as Shae pounded her fists into the punching bag Angelus had strung up from the thick branch of a tree in the backyard. Soft lights from the monastery wall reflected small circles on the ground.

Her biceps burned, and her fingers ached. She swiped her sweaty brow with her arm and blew out a frustrated breath, her concentration in knots. God! Two hellish days of training had passed. Angelus had worked her to the bone while Dagan helped her strengthen her shielding abilities. But there was a distance between them, which just battered at her.

She couldn't do this anymore—she needed a break or she was going to crack. She undid the laces on her glove with her teeth and pulled them free, all the while aware that Angelus sat on a wooden bench beneath the tree, watching her. Undoubtedly following Dagan's orders to keep an eye on her while he was gone on patrol.

The sensation of being trapped grew.

"You're finished?" he asked, smiling.

"Yes." She tossed the gloves on the bench near him and rubbed her sore knuckles. "Let's go to the village."

The smile faded. "Shae, I cannot. Dagan will be furious if I break his order."

"You won't. He said to stay with me, right? So, wherever I am? You. Stay. With. Me."

"I cannot." He rose and tied back his mahogany hair. A sword appeared in his hand, and he started a solo workout.

With the urge to keep moving growing, she trudged around the building to the front, stopping at the granite handrail enclosing the courtyard. There was nowhere else to go. She gripped the cold barrier, trying to center herself.

"Shae?" Angelus appeared at her side.

She didn't respond, cutting him a strained look instead. His dark eyes skimmed over her face, and he exhaled heavily. "Very well, but just an hour."

So sure she hadn't heard right, she blinked. At his wry smile, relief swept through her. "Thank you. Let me go change."

Ten minutes later, they took form in the dense trees surrounding the village, and as they headed toward the hub of the main street, Shae frowned at Angelus. He didn't have those stunning good looks she'd gotten used to, and his tapered ears appeared ordinary—like human ones. His usually vibrant hair was a dull shade of brown. "What did you do to yourself?"

"Glamour." A smile tipped his mouth. "So I could fit in here."

Shae didn't bother to tell him, even glammed down, he was still too pretty. Curious, she asked, "Don't you have wings?"

"I do. But while in the human realm, they are invisible. Humans see a fae's wings, and they become entranced. It is one of the laws that have to be adhered to before coming to this world."

Now she was prying, but who cared? "Do you know what Dagan is? I mean, you're fae. And him?"

"He's a Sumerian god. His grandsire, An, is the supreme high god."

She stopped dead in front of a closed bookstore, her jaw hitting the dirt. "No way!"

"He is." Angelus halted beside her. "As are all the Guardians, except for Aethan. He is an Empyrean, an angel, but not like the sire, Michael. He's *the* archangel."

Whoa. As far as otherworldly beings went, sure, she had a demon best friend and knew about them, demoniis, and Fallens, who gave up their wings to live a different life. Beyond that? She hadn't given much thought to what else lived in this world.

Dagan was a god—a Sumerian god.

Her heart skipped a beat when she recalled the difficult time she'd given him after he abducted her. And smiled. Heck, she wasn't even sorry. Most fun she'd had in a long time.

Shae continued walking. It all fit now, his enormous size, the height, his hair…the aloofness, and those hauntingly beautiful, inhuman, yellow eyes.

But he was a vampire, too.

How did that happen?

The noise and laughter from farther up the street drew her attention to a blinking red sign. *Club Samhain.* The thing was a beacon for party revelers. Hopefully, dancing and getting lost in the music would help ease this restlessness inside her.

Fees paid and wrists stamped, they walked inside. Heavy metal music rocked her eardrums. Perfume and liquor infused the cool air. Shae got a table in the back since it was still early. Drinks ordered from a passing waiter, she smiled at a wide-eyed Angelus. "So?"

"It is incredible. We have dances, but nothing like this."

"What?" She arched a teasing eyebrow at him. "No one jumps around like they're hooked to adrenaline?"

He laughed, his gaze still on the dancers. "Our music is different, too."

She could just imagine, people dancing daintily in circles around a ring of flowers, or was it mushrooms? The waiter set their drinks on the table.

"Want to give human-style dancing a shot?"

"It looks like fun. A moment—" He shifted on the chair and pulled out a cell phone from his pants pocket and read a message. Shae blinked. Heck, she didn't know he even possessed one. He looked up. "Dagan will be here."

Her mouth snapped shut, betrayal forming a hard lump in her tummy. "You told him? Why?"

"I had to." A red tinge washed his grave features. "You have dangerous foes after you, Shae. If anything happened on my watch, I'd never forgive myself."

Realizing she could do nothing, she drank some of her vodka tonic. Apparently, all immortals were single-minded when playing guard. At least, he hadn't mentioned she was a job. God, she was starting to hate the word.

Desperately needing a few minutes alone, she pushed to her feet. "I'm going to the restroom." The one place her guards couldn't trespass. She hoped.

Angelus rose. "Where is it?"

Hell, she had no idea. Lied. "Just past the bar. I won't be long." She spun away and cut through the thickening crowd.

"Shae?"

At the unfamiliar accented voice, she looked around and forced a smile as the friendly pharmacist detached himself from the bar.

"What a pleasure meeting you here," Vasile Petre said, stopping near her. "Are you alone?"

"No. I'm with a friend."

Cautiously, he looked around, no doubt recalling Dagan's aggressiveness the afternoon outside his store.

"I'm with friends, too." He stuck a thumb over his shoulder. "When you're free, call me, maybe we can have drinks?"

She doubted that would ever happen when she had babysitters twenty-four-seven.

Prickles of awareness skated over her skin like an electrical spark. She didn't have to look to know who it was. Still, it was impossible not to. She rubbed her arms and glanced across the club to the busy entrance. Being so tall, Dagan stood heads above the partygoers. Like magnets, their gazes connected, then his slid to her side. He went motionless, even the air around him stilled.

A hand touched her arm. "So you'll call me?"

She looked blankly at Vasile and must have nodded because he smiled and ambled off to his friends. But at the hard set of Dagan's jaw, she swallowed a sigh. People cleared out of his way as he strode to her. Yeah, he'd think the worst.

A woman in tight jeans and a halter-top stepped into his path, stopping him. He cut her a brief look. Though nothing showed on his face, Shae realized she couldn't even blame him. With a double dose of god and vampire magnetism, everyone was drawn to him. Even the damn rats.

How else could a predator tempt his prey to him?

But when the woman and held out a paper napkin, probably with a phone number, the abyss inside her deepened, knowing as far as *he* was concerned, there was nothing between them. He'd made that clear.

No matter the attraction, he was a Guardian, and she, his assignment. She was a fool to think otherwise or wish for more.

Desperate to get out of this suddenly airless place, and with no way to avoid him, Shae hurried past. Callused fingers snagged her wrist, halting her flight. "Let me go," she hissed at him. "I'm leaving."

"You are leaving." His cold expression morphed into hard anger. "With *me*."

The woman glowered daggers at Shae, still clutching the paper napkin.

Dagan hauled her to the exit, the crowd instantly parting, giving them way. He strode down the cobblestone street and into the shadowy thoroughfare just off the main road.

Angelus discreetly hung back.

Shae pulled free, rubbing her wrist. He stood there in front of her. Head lowered. Hands on his hips as if trying to get himself under control.

"Did you have to drag me again?"

Slowly, he lifted his head. "Drag you?" Ice edged his tone. "Your powers are escalating, your life's in danger, and you're in a club?"

Hurt flooded her that he refused to understand how hard this was on her. With her mother gone, the appearance of her new power, along with this impossible attraction to him, everything was caving in on her. She blinked back the burn in her eyes.

"I had to get out. I was suffocating on that mountaintop, doing nothing but train—for two full days—"

"Because you have to learn to shield. Your ability could have manifested, and the heavens know where you would've ended up with your shaky shields."

"I know what's at stake, and I'm not completely helpless," she snapped, anger sparking at his inflexible attitude. "If you think I'm such a damn liability, why the hell don't you lock me up?"

"Don't tempt me, Shae—" His nostrils flared. "I'm *this* close to losing—"

"What? Your temper? You wouldn't know how if it bit you in your—*oomph*!"

His mouth slammed down on hers in a searing explosion of fury. Her breath escaped in a rush of shock. His one arm banded around her waist, the other tangled in her hair. He may be kissing her in anger, but she couldn't deny that she savored the feeling of his mouth on hers. Dear God, it was like a drug to her senses. She slipped her hands around his neck and kissed him back.

"Gods, Shae…" A tortured groan escaped him, the sound impossibly seductive. "You drive me beyond sanity with that mouth—"

He deepened the kiss. Wild. Decadent. A dangerous kiss as his fangs brushed against her lips and tongue. And every nerve in her body flared alive with sensation, desire hijacking her thoughts. He kissed her deeper, drawing her tongue into his mouth, sucking on it, intensifying the exquisite ache pooling between her thighs.

Georgia Lyn Hunter

He picked her up and backed her against the building wall, not breaking their kiss. Her skirt slid up as she wrapped her legs around him. His rigid sex rubbed against her panty-covered core, creating a friction that had her body in flames, craving the release only he could give.

She could barely think straight. Yet, some deep part of her realized she'd pushed him because *she* wanted this—wanted his mouth on hers, wanted him to want *her*—not those other women.

He's a vampire; he's always going to seek them.

At the icy slap of reality, desire fizzled.

"No—" She tore her mouth free. "Let me go, I'm not one of those women you pick up every night."

"What?" His chest heaved, his brow furrowed in confusion.

Reeling with jealousy she had no right to feel, she shook her head. "Let me down."

A tic pounded in his jaw. He lowered his mouth to her ear, his erection pressing into her core. "If that asshole pharmacist touches you again, human or not, I *will* kill him."

She tried to push away from him, but the damn wall behind her, and his hold on her hips, kept her trapped against him. "No, you won't. Why do you care anyway? I'm just a job to you, remember?"

He stared silently at her for a long second. "You are my mate."

The word, so full of promise, pierced her in the heart like a dagger. Anger, fast and furious, exploded. "Whoa! You don't get to use the mate card when it suits you, you took *that* off the table the moment *you* realized the truth. As if I want to be tied to the most anal-retentive man—pardon—*immortal* ever."

With a growl, Dagan dropped her. Shae tripped, but he grabbed her arm. She shoved off his hold. "I hate you."

"No, you don't." He rubbed his unshaven jaw wearily. "It's why this is so damn hard." He pulled out a cigar from his pocket, struck a match on the wall, and lit it.

Her mouth opened then shut. She pivoted and stumbled out of the thoroughfare, bleakness sweeping through her at his words.

No, she didn't hate him. Somewhere in the last few days, she'd gone from being impossibly aggravated with him to wanting him. Yes, he desired her, but he refused to do anything about it because he didn't want a mate.

"Angelus?" Dagan's low voice drifted to her. "Take her back. Keep her safe."

"Of course, sire."

Blinking her burning eyes, she headed toward the copse of trees, wishing this emptiness inside her would somehow ease.

***

A sound pulled Shae out of her troubled dreams. Something hit the wall with a dull thud. Her eyelids cracked open. Cautiously, she peered around the dark bedroom. Faint light seeped from beneath the closed door to the next room.

He was back. Memories of what had happened earlier that night had her groaning. Normally, she was a get-up-and-face-the-world kinda girl, no matter the setbacks. Now, she buried her face in her pillow, wanting to hide in bed for the next several months.

At a low, harshly muttered expletive, she jerked upright, her heart thudding in apprehension. Was he hurt? With the kind of job he did, chances were he could be…and, no, *he* wouldn't seek help. He was as stubborn as the day was long.

She eyed the adjoining door warily—dammit, she couldn't *not* help if he was hurt.

Despising her weakness, she got off the bed and made her way across the room, her socks-clad feet silent on the granite floor, and opened the door. A dense gloom cloaked the room, but a short, fat candle burned on the nightstand, casting a pool of light over the man on the four-poster bed. She took another step inside and stumbled to a halt.

Dear sweet Jesus! Shirtless, Dagan rested against the headboard, eyes shut. His bronze pecs and biceps gleamed in the soft light. His one knee was raised, his leathers unzipped, and his big palm was wrapped around his cock as he stroked himself. It was the sexiest, most erotic thing she'd ever seen. He was so beautiful.

Held in the throes of the sensual spell, she swallowed hard.

His head turned, his movements slowed. Through half-mast eyelids, those molten yellow eyes fastened on her like a sleek predator's. He didn't speak.

Shae rushed into speech, her face on fire. "I heard a noise, and thought… never mind. I'm sorry—"

"Don't go."

His low words stopped her retreat.

"The moment you left me tonight, I couldn't get you out of my mind." His palm slowly worked his erection in mesmerizing strokes. Up. Down. Up. Down. "The way your body felt against me, your mouth on mine. I thought *this* would take away the impossible craving I have for you, but it's just a poor fucking substitute and doesn't even work…"

"Why? The woman in the club——"

He shook his head. "*I* don't want any of them." *He didn't?* "I tried to do the right thing and leave you alone, but I cannot. Come here, Shae."

Her heart stopped then started again, her fingers clenching her nightshirt. However, it was his stare—heavy with desire and edged with yearning—that trapped her. As if under hypnosis, her feet took the steps across the room toward him.

"Give me your underwear."

"W-what?"

"*Now.*"

The softly uttered word held an undercurrent of steel. And because she'd lost her ever-loving mind, and he was all she'd thought of since they'd stepped through the portal, she slipped her hands beneath her nightshirt and drew her panties off.

He took them from her shaky fingers and dropped them on the pillow beside him. "On the bed, opposite me."

Swallowing hard, she climbed up and pulled her nightshirt down, her knees pressed together.

A dark brow rose at her actions, but he didn't say anything. As his hand moved again, her focus lowered to his groin, and at the sight of him stroking his long, thick sex, heat licked through her veins.

His fingers slowed their pumping motion. Her gaze rushed to his. Those sun-bright eyes burned with carnal heat. He crawled over to her, spread his knees, and caged her—his leathers still undone. With slow, deliberate movements, he unclenched her ice-cold hand from the hem of her nightshirt, put her two fingers into his warm mouth, and leisurely sucked them.

Georgia Lyn Hunter

Her heart tripped. As if it were a direct line to her core, arousal flared as he lapped her fingers. Anxiety fled. Grasping her ankles, he put them over his thighs and pushed her nightdress up, opening her to his gaze. He brought her fingers down between her legs.

At the sensuality of him—of them both—stroking her most intimate flesh, her breath caught. She became aware then that his gaze wasn't between her thighs but on her face, watching her every expression. A flush scorched her cheeks.

"Don't think, just feel." He ran their fingers up her folds again, his thumb brushing her clit. Arousal grew. He let go of her hand and took over, his fingers stroking down her cleft and up again, slowly circling the bundle of nerves.

Dear. God. She closed her eyes, lust gripping her in a stranglehold, her fingers fighting for purchase on the bare mattress.

"No. Look at me, Shae."

She opened her eyes, it didn't occur to her not to, and met his piercing stare.

He leaned forward and sucked her lower lip, his thumb rolling her clit. Desire spread like a flame. Slowly, he dipped a finger, then two, inside her before adding another. She whimpered against his mouth, craving more of the incredible sensations building between her thighs. Her inner muscles quickened, her body tightened. She broke free from his sensual onslaught on her lip. "Dagan, please…"

"No." He withdrew his fingers, frustrating her, and then licked her wetness off them, shocking her. "I may not eat much"—his eyes blazed a brilliant yellow—"but this orgasm belongs on my tongue."

Before she could get her desire-laden mind to

connect, in that impossibly fast way of his, he shifted and slid his huge body down the bed, pulling her astride his face. Instantly, she braced her palms behind her on his chest, her knees spread wide. His warm, open mouth settled on her core.

Her thoughts fractured. He licked her as if she were the most decadent dessert before lapping at her clit; then he changed to hard, sharp flicks. Shae nearly came off him, but his grip on her hips kept her nightshirt up, and her exactly where he wanted. Another lick and with a whimper, she fell forward, her palms pressing down on the mattress above his head. His big hands squeezed her bottom before he eased a long, callused finger into her, then another. In and out, he began to thrust.

Ohhhh, God! At the combination of his pumping fingers and his mouth sucking her clit, Shae felt as if she'd been tossed into a whirlwind. She pushed harder into his mouth.

A low rumble of satisfaction reverberated against her. A hard tug on her flesh with teeth and lips, she cried out, her orgasm breaking, sweeping through her like a tidal wave...

Rough, warm palms caressed her hips as she struggled to find a way back from where he'd taken her.

Shae moved to get off his face. But Dagan pulled her down his body, to lie on him, his blue-black hair a tangle of silk on the mattress. Then he kissed her. Deeply. Sensually. She tasted herself in their kiss, his tongue licking inside her mouth before sucking hers. She shifted, and his thick, warm, *bare* sex pressed against her inner thigh. He was rock-hard.

Shae sat up, straddling him, and wrapped his heavy

erection with her fingers. The tip of him was seductively wet. As she stroked the soft, smooth skin over his rigid erection, his big body shuddered. With each harsh breath he inhaled, the play of muscles on his stomach rippled beneath his bronze skin like waves. God, he was magnificent in his aroused state. He shut his eyelids for a brief second, and then he was shaking his head. "No."

Despite the raw desire in his gaze, he removed her hands, put her aside, and leaped off the bed.

Hurt took hold. "Why not?"

He paced to the window like some caged animal. The skin over the bones of his handsome face stretched tightly as he tucked himself into his leathers and zipped up. His fangs had emerged. Longer. Lethal-looking. And they pierced into the flesh of his lower lip. He rasped through them, "I want you more than anything else in this godsforsaken life of mine, but my control is tenuous right now. When I come, and with you so close, I'll want your blood, too."

She swallowed in trepidation then straightened her spine. Okay, she could do this. "All right."

His gaze swiveled to her, searing in its intensity, a tinge of red streaking his irises. "No."

"What do you mean *no*?" She slid off the bed.

His chest heaving, he grabbed his shirt from the floor and pulled it on, his movements jerky. "Because you don't know what I'm capable of!" His words were thick with bitterness and fury. "And you don't go around offering your blood to anyone, especially not the likes of me!"

And then he was gone.

Chapter 11

Shae stared at the empty doorway, too shocked to move at Dagan's outburst. For the first time since she'd met him, she'd seen stark fear on his face. For her?

Was he afraid that if he fed from her, he wouldn't be able to stop, and would drink her dry like a demonii would?

Harvey had explained about demons who lost their dark souls after stealing a human spirit—and about their unending blood-thirst. But Dagan wasn't like a demonii…was he?

However, it was the pain she'd sensed in him that had her moving. Hurriedly, she pulled on her underwear, sprinted back to her room for her boots, dragged them on, then took off after him. She searched the living room and kitchen, but he wasn't there. She grabbed her outdoor jacket from the chair, hauled it on, and darted outside. Both courtyards were empty, too.

That left only one place.

With the moon her only source of light, she cut around the side, past the outbuilding, and ran up the steep, narrow steps. Panting hard, like she'd climbed a million of them, she finally reached the top and stumbled to a halt. The chilly winds echoed eerily around her, tugging at her clothes and hair.

Dagan stood at the edge of the plateau, gazing down into the gorge like a lonely statue of some long-forgotten god, a burning cigar in his hand. The silvery moon highlighted his hard, handsome features, the wind whipping at his unbound hair.

Shae darted across to him. "Dagan, talk to me. You can't say things like that and then just walk away. Do you think you'll kill me if you feed from me? Is that it?"

"Didn't you ever wonder why—*how* I became a Guardian of this realm?" he asked instead, appearing a little calmer, his fangs no longer evident.

She frowned at the change in conversation and grabbed onto her wind-tossed mane. "I assumed it was a job you applied for."

At his dark bark of laughter, she eyed him cautiously. "Then how?"

Killing his smoke, he tossed the stub away and removed a narrow black band from his wrist. Then, shocking her speechless, he gathered her tangled hair, and with a few twists, tied it back. "Because I, along with the other Guardians, was banished from the pantheons. We had nowhere else to go once we escaped imprisonment in Tartarus—"

"What?" She pulled back, shocked. "Why?"

His bleak gaze shifted away to stare into the distance again. "We failed in our duty as protectors to keep the Goddess of Life safe. During a bloody battle, the vilest evil out there snatched her. She was never seen again."

Dear sweet Jesus. No wonder he was so driven to

keep her hidden and safe. "What happened?"

His tone devoid of emotions, he told her about the attacks on the temple, then about the last protector arriving. "Unaware that it was Blaéz, a fight started. Hordes of demons appeared—demons shouldn't be able to enter the Realm of the Gods. While the battle took place, a narcissistic Fallen bastard used the distraction and abducted her."

"Fallen?"

"Lucifer." A tic worked his jaw. Shae knew Lucifer was one of the most beautiful and cunning of angels. "As punishment, we were judged and found guilty of blatant misconduct for allowing the denizens of the Dark Realm access to the sacred temple, which then caused the slaughter of Inara's handmaidens. Our powers and godhood were stripped, and we were imprisoned in Tartarus. Except, I wasn't with the others. I was in a different sector…"

As if unable to stay still, he paced several feet away, then back again, stopping to stare out at the dark horizon again. Silence lengthened.

"What happened?" she asked softly.

"When I came to, I found myself in a desert wasteland, surrounded by impossible heat but no sun. No night or day. No shelter, food, or water. And no death…"

At the dead look creeping over his chiseled features, uneasiness stirred. "Dagan?"

He blinked as if coming to himself. "Days—weeks passed, and my thirst and hunger grew. I must have fainted…" He told her the gruesome tale about waking up to huge, grisly, vulture-like birds tearing at his flesh. "I managed to grab one, but so badly weakened and unable to kill it, I bit its neck. Blood slid down my throat. I spat it out at first, but it was the only source of liquid I had…and I was so thirsty…" He rubbed a hand over his face. "It was the beginning, the catalyst to my change."

"Are you saying drinking from those birds made you…this way?" She stopped short of using the word *vampire*. She'd teased him the day at the penthouse. But dear God, this was so much worse.

A terse nod. "They weren't ordinary birds. They were vampiric ones that belonged to the dark goddess, Hel. Those avians were used to punish those sentenced to Reaper's Hell—it's what the demons call the place, I later found out. Five centuries of feeding off them would do that. When Michael finally freed us, it was too late. Blood is all I can handle as a food source, all that sustains me."

She rubbed her jacket-clad arms at the shivers wracking her.

He glanced at her. "You're cold. Let's get out of here."

She shook her head, her mind reeling from what he'd revealed. "I'm okay. Why do you think you'd kill me if you—"

"Later. You need to get warm." A hand on her back, he ushered her carefully down the shadowy granite steps to the monastery.

In the warm, brightly lit kitchen, he switched on the kettle. "You should have something hot…" He looked through the cupboards then exhaled roughly. "I'm afraid my skills are quite lacking in this area. Except for coffee…?"

"I'll make it." Since she wasn't a coffee drinker, Shae put milk to heat on the wood-burning stove, pulled out the cocoa from the cupboard and heaped two spoonfuls into a mug, along with some sugar.

He lowered onto the chair opposite her, resting one arm on the table, the other rubbing his unshaven jaw. She recalled the raspy feel of his face between her thighs, and desire pooled low in her belly again, warmth flooding her cheeks.

He lifted a questioning brow. She shook her head. "Do any of the other Guardians know about this? About you?" She brought the conversation back to where they'd left off.

A shrug rolled off a broad shoulder. "Michael. Nik…Hedori. The others, no. I rarely spend time with them…"

Shae stared at him. And at the rigid set of his features, she understood why. He probably thought they would condemn him because of what he'd become. Her heart hurt for him. Heck, the Guardians' main duty was to kill those soul-hunting, blood-sucking demoniis.

She got the pot of hot milk from the stove, added some to her mug, and stirred. "Is Nik your…close friend?"

A shadow flickered in his eyes. "Yeah."

Right. There was no getting around this. She smoothed her damp palms down her nightshirt and finally asked the one question she didn't want to know the answer to but needed. "The other day, you said something about sex when feeding…does that happen every time you have to eat?"

A sigh. "Shae—"

"Tell me."

He rubbed his nape as if uncomfortable talking about this. "Not always, but the female gets a high from my bite—it's the saliva that's produced, it's sort of an aphrodisiac to ease the donor's pain... So yeah, it happens."

Her stomach hurt like acid settled in there. Hell, he didn't need to seek out anyone with the way he looked with his immense height, tough body, and hard, handsome face. Throw in that sensual vampiric allure, and women would queue up for a roll with him.

"So you need a woman every night?"

"No, Shae, I don't seek out human females for anything. I've been feeding on animals more often than not for what seems like forever. It's less of a bother. Unfortunately, animal plasma only eases my hunger..." His gaze lowered to his hands clasped on the table. "Every few weeks, I need stronger blood."

Unease swept through her. Her grip tightened around her mug. "What are you saying?"

His shadowed stare met hers. "There's a goddess from my old pantheon...only immortal blood can strengthen my abilities."

It was the pause in his comments that had her gaze dropping to her untouched beverage. He'd had just *one* woman through the ages, and of his kind, too. One whom he'd obviously slept with and fed from. Pain burrowed deeper.

A chair dragged back on the granite floor. He rose. "Shae..."

She had to force the words out through a throat gone tight with anguish, "I...I braced myself for this, but it still hurts." Hurts? Christ. His admission was like a knife shredding her heart. Her hopes.

He crossed to her, but she stepped back, evading his hand.

His fingers clenched. "Shae, I hadn't been with her for weeks *before* I met you. Now, I couldn't—*wouldn't* hurt you in that way. You're far too important to me. You are all that matters."

Later…later she'd berate herself for this, for wanting to know everything despite being caught in this cyclone of pain. Because *hope*, that bitch, had cemented her feet to the ground at his admission.

"But without her blood, your powers weaken. And being a Guardian, you have to be at full strength, right?"

"I'm immortal. I'll be fine." He slipped his fists into his pants pockets and leaned against the table. "There's something you should know, why I can't—I won't ever feed from you."

Inhaling deeply, she braced herself.

"The change left me with a curse. An inexorable thirst when I consume human blood. It hikes my bloodlust, and I lose control," he said, tone flat as if reciting the addresses from a phonebook. "When I first came to this world, I killed many. I didn't know how to control this continuous hunger. Then I became a Guardian, and I couldn't. Harming mortals would break my sacred oath. Michael stepped in and suggested feeding from an immortal…"

He exhaled heavily. "But while on patrol, I needed help. We had another houseman in those early days, a fae named Izzeri, Angelus's kin. He makes those smokes for me. The plant's only found in Exilum—it's a place beyond this realm for exiled immortals and used by the vampires who live there. It blocks the scent of blood and eases me while on patrol. Humans can be quite careless when it comes to their penchant for violence, which more often than not leads to bloodshed. Mercifully, I have no contact with them except in the line of duty."

Georgia Lyn Hunter

"I'm so sorry."

"Don't be. I accepted what I am eons ago."

He may appear as if he needed no one, but she was starting to know this man. His weariness, and more, his self-loathing for what he'd done so long ago had left its mark on him. She set her cup down, stepped between his parted thighs, and hugged him.

He stiffened. But it didn't put her off. After years of being alone, isolated from everyone, she didn't expect him to go all cuddly-soft on her. He was hard, with so many rough edges. Life had made him what he was. But no one deserved the kind of horror he'd endured. And she'd do all she could to help make it better.

His chest heaved as if exhaling air—or secrets he'd kept locked for ages. And when his arms came around her and he buried his face in her nape, tears stung her eyes.

All too soon, he put her aside, stepping away. Strain lines etched the corners of his mouth. He was on edge again. "Is it hard if I'm close to you?"

He reached out, his fingers tracing her lips as if memorizing their shape. "I'm good." He dropped his hand. "C'mon, I'll see you to the room before I leave."

"I thought you were finished for the night?"

"Not exactly. After you left me, I couldn't focus on the job"—a wry smile—"so I cut short my patrol. But I need to do a quick run-through down at the village, then check in with Nik and Race."

In the bedroom, Dagan added several more logs to the dying embers from a crate near the fireplace. He crossed back to her and gently stroked her scarred cheek. "Get some sleep, I'll see you later."

After he'd left, Shae stopped at the window and stared outside. Even though she was happy the walls between them had lowered somewhat, what he'd revealed about his past had left a gaping hole inside her.

No matter what he said, he'd have to feed soon. Could she stay on the sidelines and watch him go to another for sustenance? At the thought of his mouth on some other woman, her entire being shut down. No, she couldn't. And it brought her right back to square one.

What the hell was she going to do when he was adamant about not feeding from her?

Chapter 12

*M*oonlight cast an eerie, pale light over the gloomy alley. In the shadows of a looming building, bodies moved. Shae's heart pounded hard, seconds from crashing through her ribs, then sun-bright eyes looked up, staring at her, his mouth fastened on a woman's neck.

Agony surged, a vise squeezing her chest. Dagan, no!

The dream distorted, reformed... *"You killed your father, it's all your fault he's gone—left me,"* her mother cried.

"Mom, please—" Shae reached out for her, but she dissipated into the night. Instead, darkness surrounded her.

There, in the gloomy corner of the empty parking lot, her father lay on the tarmac, amidst melted ice cream. "Daddy!" *Shae raced toward him. The dark shadow over him dissipated into the night, the lot lights flickering ominously.* "No—nooo!" *Blood seeped from several wounds, a dagger stuck out of his chest. Sobbing, she fell to her knees and wrenched the blade free—*

Hide, Shae, hide, his frantic voice echoed in her mind. *"Never..."*

Shae jackknifed up in bed, terror compressing her lungs. Gasping for breath, she sprang up and paced the bedroom, her arms wrapped around her body as more shudders wracked her.

After so many years, *now* she dreamed about his death? His unfinished sentence bounced in her head. *Never...* What? Let them find her?

Furiously, she dashed away her tears. Uncle Lem had said it was a robbery. She didn't believe it, not with her father's words echoing in her head. Something about his panicked voice resonated deeply within her. Terror...for *her*?

She stopped near the window. Did her mother's disappearance have anything to do with his death? Was that why she left? But nine years later?

God! Nothing made sense.

Shae scrubbed her damp cheeks, her fingers touching the scar on her face, wishing she knew what it all meant, and stilled.

There was one way to find out the truth.

Urgency had her moving. She changed, then retrieved the pewter dagger with the intricately carved hilt from her knapsack, one she kept close but never used, and pushed it into her boot. From her suitcase, she took the packet of salt and shoved it into her pocket then paused. She didn't want to bring Angelus into this, not after the debacle at the club. With Dagan still out on patrol, she didn't want to bother him either, or worse, fight him over this.

Shae stepped out onto the balcony and tried to recall how she'd teleported the night she killed those demons.

Her palms clammy, she closed her eyes and imagined herself at the place where Dagan had briefly trained with her. There was no spot safer than that.

She willed her abilities free. The air shifted around her. Moments later, she took form and landed with a hard thump on a granite surface. Pain jarred up her spine and rattled her teeth. Jesus!

A blast of freezing air stole her breath but did little to soothe her troubled mind. She pushed to her feet, wincing at the ache in her butt, and zipped up her jacket. Clouds hung low and ominous. She took off in a run, stopping some distance away from the spot where the warriors usually trained, and away from the monastery. The moonlight illuminated the stark, lonely stretch of rugged plateau in front of her.

Reclaiming the salt packet from her pocket, she marked a wide circle then placed the piece of paper with the name of the Edge demon and three X's around it in the center and then stepped out of the ring. "Shaximus, I summon you…"

***

His hunger temporarily satiated after feeding, exhaustion sawing through him, Dagan dematerialized back to the monastery. In the courtyard, he checked the wards protecting the place. All appeared intact. He went motionless, an unsettling sensation coasting over his psyche.

Shae! He flashed to his room. Empty. He scanned for her, but she was nowhere in the monastery. Fear clawed at his gut. He sprinted outside and scanned again. At the faint psychic vibration lingering in the air, he cursed a blue streak. What the hell had happened that she left the monastery alone?

Catching her lingering buzz, he dematerialized.

Seconds later, he reformed on the mountaintop some distance from the monastery.

An acrid odor burned his nose. His gaze clamped on the swirl of a thick, green, sulfuric cloud. A seven-foot-tall, black-skinned demon with glowing, pale eyes appeared—in front of Shae.

"What do you want, human?" the demon growled, arms folded over his enormous chest.

Shae stepped back. "To…find someone."

What the hell? A roar thundering in his head, Dagan dove for her, snatching her away from the demon. "There will be no deal brokered!"

"*No*—" Shae elbowed him, but he held her in a vise-like grip against his chest as the demon grew in stature, the swirling green mist becoming thicker.

"I should demand payment for time wasted, Guardian, but you will be a pain in my arse. Just this once, this is voided." In a swirl of violent green, the demon vanished.

"*Noooo!*" She thumped her fists on his chest. "What have you done?"

Still trapped in his fear, Dagan shook her, hard. "You summoned a fucking Edge demon. He would have demanded a payment that would tie you to him for life!"

"You don't know that." Her chin wobbled. Anguished, red-rimmed eyes speared him in the heart. "You've ruined everything—"

"I saved your damn hide!"

"I have money, I would have paid him."

"By the heavens—" Cursing in his language, he bit out, "Think, Shae. Think. They aren't human. They'd want your blood or your damn soul in reimbursement."

"Then I would have given him my blood," she

yelled. "At least it's good enough for him!"

At the low blow, his temper flared. "You ever do something this perilous again, so help me, I'll lock you up in one of those monk cells we have—"

"I don't care what you do. You destroyed my only chance of finding…" Her voice broke. Tears fell.

Frustration and helplessness tearing at him, he gentled his hold on her upper arms. "Look, when we get back to New York, I'll help you find your mother."

"It's not my mother," she whispered, her voice hoarse. She pulled out a dagger from her boot that looked a lot like his with the intricate etchings on the guards, except for the color and black stone on the hilt. "I want to know who used this last."

"You could have asked me," he snapped, temper rising again.

Her eyes widened. "I didn't know—you didn't tell me. I thought it was just with people."

Hell! It wasn't like he made a point of talking about his abilities. Furious at himself, Dagan took the damn blade, and his breath caught like he'd taken a blow to his belly. The sheer evil of the person who'd wielded the weapon twisted his gut. Images flashed through his mind…

Pain drenched him, the dagger plunging repeatedly into his chest. Blood flowed…a blurry face with dark hair appeared above his, cruel laughter echoed. "I will have what is mine…"

Dagan pushed harder, needing to hear the rest of the assailant's words…but it was all fuzzy.

"Do you see anything?"

Shae's voice hauled him out of the darkness in the blade, and the visions faded, but his own frustration escalated. He'd felt the victim's agony and had gotten a hazy visual of the attacker, but nothing else.

Meeting her hopeful, wet gaze, he hated having to keep this back, but he had to be sure before he said anything. "Vague images only. Where did you get this weapon?"

She wrapped her arms around her waist as if holding herself together. "I pulled it from my father's chest."

He frowned. "No one looked for it? The cops?"

"I don't recall. But I always had it. Uncle Lem said when they found me hiding in a nearby building, I was in a daze. I remembered nothing. The therapist I saw explained that I'd been too traumatized and had blocked my father's death from my mind. It was the only way I could cope with the trauma… Until now."

"What do you mean?"

"I was asleep…" She took a hiccupping breath. "I dreamt of my mother, then the next thing I knew, I was in a parking lot. Dad had taken me to buy ice cream. When he didn't return to the car, I went looking for him. He…he was lying there on the asphalt, blood and melted ice cream all around him. I pulled that blade out of his chest. Then I heard his voice in my head. He said I must hide from them. Who's *them*, Dagan?" she rasped, pressing a hand to her throat. "There was just a dark shadow surrounding him, and then it vanished, but no one was there. It's why I have to find out who used this blade to kill him—who would do something so evil. My father was a kind and gentle person. God, I hate that I ran and hid."

"You were just a child, Shae. You did what he asked." When she didn't respond, he said, "Let me keep the blade for a little longer, okay? I want to see if I can pick up anything else."

"Ok—" She winced.

Georgia Lyn Hunter

He reached out and gently stroked her pale throat, and the healing light flowed through his fingers, but the glow flickered a few times and died. His lips thinned. His restorative power wasn't as strong as it should be, and he knew why. He lowered his hand.

"Thank you—" She swallowed, her voice still husky. But at least she could speak clearer now. He drew her close and dematerialized them back to the monastery.

While she changed into her pajamas, he made a cup of tea, liberally laced it with honey, and headed back. He found her sitting on the edge of the bed.

"Get in." He pulled the covers back, and she climbed in, looking so beaten. He wanted to go and find the faceless bastard responsible for her anguish, show him the true meaning of pain. Instead, he put all of that on the backburner for now, sat beside her, and held out the tea. "Here."

"I'm not thirsty."

"Drink it." He pressed the cup into her hands. "The honey will help." Google had said so.

A shuddering breath escaping her, she sipped the steamy beverage. Dagan rose to his feet, mind-linking with Michael, wanting to speak to him, but hit a wall. Dammit. He got out his cell and shot off a message.

Once Shae was done, he took the cup from her and set it aside. Her shoulders drooped in fatigue as she lay down. He pulled the covers over her.

"Stay," she whispered, grasping his hand, her eyes like gray pools of desolation in her pale face. "I don't want to be alone."

With a nod, he undressed, pulled on sweats, and slid in beside her. Her eyes closed, her exhaustion sliding over him like a sheet of lead as she settled in the crook of his shoulder, a hand resting on his chest.

His heart surging with tenderness for his mate, he brushed his lips on her brow. She was so damn brave to have borne all this for so long. He'd make sure she got closure for her sire's death.

***

Late afternoon sunlight flooded his workshop. Dagan tossed the gouge he'd been using on the wooden gazelle onto the table and rubbed his jaw. He'd gotten up way before Shae had, deciding she should take it easy after her traumatic night. But she had other ideas once she'd awaken, insisting on keeping up her training.

His mind looped back to the Edge demon she'd summoned. Shit! His stomach still heaved in dread every time he thought of how close she'd come to being tied to one of those beings. It could only be that damn Harvey who had procured a name for her.

Unable to concentrate, he crossed to the window overlooking the backyard where she currently trained with Angelus.

The fae circled her with a broadsword. Instead of watching her counter moves, Dagan's gaze tracked down her body as she bounced back on her sneakered feet. A white tank top hugged her chest and black, knee-length tights revealed her long, sexy legs. She probably wore the attire for easier movement when training, but his body tightened at the sensual vision she presented.

His hands resting on the windowsill fisted when he recalled her sitting astride his face, his mouth on her——

"*Aieeeeee!*" Angelus's battle cry erupted, and he leaped at her. Dagan froze. Instead of using her sword to block, she countered with a solid kick to the fae's belly, sending him stumbling back.

Dagan growled, feeling as if his heart would escape its cage. Yeah, he would always feel way overprotective when it came to her. And that damn weapon she used was too heavy. He spun around to go and find her something more suitable when the air shimmered.

Michael took form, sporting his usual biker appearance in jeans and a faded black tee. He refastened his inky strands into a ponytail. "You called?"

Dagan snorted at the drawling tone. He picked up the dagger from the table and handed it over. Michael ran his thumb along the etching on the pewter-gray hilt. Tiny vertical lines creased the skin between his eyebrows. "I haven't seen one of these in ages." He studied the blade then sniffed the metal. "Where did you get it?"

"Shae. It's the one that killed her father. She pulled it out of him—doesn't remember much of the killing..." he told Michael what Shae had disclosed, and what he'd picked up when he touched the weapon.

Piercing, shattered blues met his. "It an angel's blade."

"I figured that from the design on the hilt."

"That's not what I meant. This dagger belongs to a rogue, and one I've been hunting for a while."

Rogues? Damn! This was worse than pursuing evil Fallens. To escape the gruesome punishment of losing their wings and powers in whitefire—the Celestial Realm's punishment for leaving the order—rogues went into hiding in this world. Problem was, they were very, very dangerous and a threat to mortals. "Any idea who?"

"A higher-order angel, judging from this blade."

Michael settled against the windowsill. "I'm surprised he hasn't searched for it yet. Fallen or not, celestial angels treasure their weapons. How long since Shae lost her father?"

Dagan frowned. "Nine years. Why?"

"About a decade ago, I was tracking Samael. I found him, but he escaped. If he's back in New York, we're neck-deep in shit. And there's one other, a throne. Bred for war, they're damn dangerous. If it's who I think it is, it's going to be a definite fuckfest. This dagger has just made finding the rogues top priority."

"If we come back, it will put Shae in danger."

"It would. I'll notify Nik about the change in duty. You and Race remain here for now." Those fractured irises met his. "Shae's abilities, any changes?"

"Her powers are growing stronger," he admitted. "She's still having trouble keeping her shields in place, but with a little more time, she should be good. Here's the thing, I still don't think she's psionic."

Michael set the blade on the table. "That can wait until you both get back to New York, unless her powers escalate. One other thing…"

Why did that pause feel like a tanker was about to fall on him?

"Is she your mate?"

Dagan didn't answer. Why bother when Michael already knew. He missed nothing.

"Make your decision soon. If she's psi, and no mating occurs, then she goes to the Celestial Realm. If she isn't, and you go back to New York without mating her, the Fallen after her will claim her—and they can, since the angelic laws no longer bind them. There'll be nothing you can do."

Dagan had to force himself to unclench his jaw to

speak. "I'll kill any who dare lay a finger on her."

Michael shook his head. "Why am I just learning now, after several millennia, what a bunch of stubborn bastards Gaia put me in charge of? Find a way, Dag. I didn't just send you back here for shits and fun. Nor can you keep her without claiming her. And be prepared for the Absolute Laws if she isn't psionic."

After that doozy of a warning, the archangel vanished in a silvery swirl of molecules.

With a savage swipe of his hand, Dagan swept the unfinished sculptures off the table, the wooden pieces and dust flying everywhere. He tunneled both of his hands through his unbound hair, pacing the wood-shaving-covered floor in frustration.

As if his vampire curse weren't enough, the Absolute Laws, which forbade mating between immortal and human, hung over their heads like a guillotine. It would mean instant death for both of them. And if he didn't mate Shae, then the asshole Fallen who was stalking her could lay claim to his woman. He was screwed from all sides.

A sudden pained cry shattered the haze in his mind. *Shae!*

Chapter 13

Shae rubbed her damp palm on her hip as she switched hands with her weapon and warily eyed Angelus circling her like a smirking hyena. Wielding a tree trunk would probably feel lighter than the darn sword.

You cannot hide forever, Shae. You are mine. At the ominous whisper in her head, she stumbled and blocked Angelus' attack a second too late. Pain lanced her chest, and she cried out, her sword clattering to the ground.

A roar erupted, and the tree shuddered, shedding more leaves, sending them scattering to the ground. Dagan materialized in front of her. He ripped open her tank top. Blood drenched her sports bra.

"Shae——" Angelus appeared at her side, his face pale. Dagan leaped at him. "You hurt her——you fucking hurt her!" His fist slammed into Angelus's jaw.

"Dagan, no——stop!" Shae grabbed his arm, trying to pull him off. A punch landed in her face. She went flying back, hitting her skull on the granite ground as she fell, unbelievable agony consuming her. She lay there, unable to breathe through, so sure her nose was broken. Darkness edged her vision.

"*No!* Shae, open your eyes. Look at me!"

At the raw terror in Dagan's voice, she forced her eyelids open. He knelt beside her, chest heaving, anguish engraved on his face.

Angelus squatted at her other side, sporting a bruise on his jaw. He laid one hand on her chest and the other over her nose. A warm tingle surrounded her injuries.

"My apologies, Shae," he said quietly, a pained look in his eyes. "Why weren't you paying attention?"

She barely heard him. Her gaze fixed on Dagan, his features gone a sickly shade of bronze, the tips of his fangs pressing into his lower lip. The moment she could speak, she whispered, "It's okay—*I'm* okay. It was an accident."

Dagan didn't respond, didn't even shake his head as he slowly rose to his feet. But the coldness seeping into his eyes terrified her.

The second Angelus lowered his hand, Dagan dematerialized.

"He's not going to forgive himself for hitting you," Angelus said, helping her up.

Shae sighed, holding the torn edges of her bloody top together. "It's my fault. I jumped in between you two. I have to speak with him."

She sprinted through the kitchen and skidded to a halt. Great! Go after him reeking of blood. Lips pressed together in frustration, she detoured for the bedroom.

After a quick wash and change, Shae hurried back to the living room, pulling on her jacket to find Nik coming out of the kitchen. She skated to a stop. "Have you seen Dagan?"

He shrugged. "If he's not here, he must have already left for patrol." He headed for the door.

No—dammit! Her gaze rushed to the arched windows. Dusk had already settled along the mountains, casting looming shadows over the room.

"Nik, wait." Shae rushed after the warrior.

He stopped, pinning those impossibly cold, pale green eyes on her. The terrifyingly realistic serpent head tattooed on his neck appeared to watch her, too. Ugh. "I have to talk to him. It's urgent. Would you take me to him?"

"Can't it wait until he gets back in the morning?" Nik glanced at the exit again, as if he wanted to be gone.

"No, please. It's really important." She needed Nik to understand. And not wanting to get into the entire thing, she simply said, "I got hurt. He's upset. I have to talk to him."

The warrior's gaze snapped back to her. "Hurt as in bleeding?"

Lips pressed together, she nodded.

"You do know why he won't come near you, right?"

"Yes, he told me. But I'm his mate, he wouldn't—at least he *shouldn't*—harm me."

"Mate?"

She nodded again. He went quiet, *really* quiet, as if he were taken back to a terrible or painful time.

"Nik?"

His expression smoothed over. "Very well. Let's go." He headed outside.

The moment he touched her hand, her breath froze, an icy draft enclosing her entire body. But just as fast, the cold disappeared, like he'd drawn his shields up again.

Georgia Lyn Hunter

Without a word, he dematerialized them.

They reappeared in the forest bordering the village. Shae quickened her steps to keep up with Nik's long strides as they headed toward the busy main street. People hurried from their jobs, and others made their way to the bar. Her stomach in a knot, Shae searched the busy place. Several women watched them—or rather Nik—with carnal interest. She knew exactly what they were reacting to—the bucket-load of magnetism these Guardians possessed in spades.

"I found him," Nik said. "Go wait in there—"

"I'm coming with you."

"No." His hard expression allowed no argument. "It's dangerous, I sense him in a fight. Stay in the café, it's safer among the crowds."

Exhaling in frustration, she glanced at the café-slash-bar he'd pointed to, one of those places with wooden tables and chairs spilling out onto the sidewalk. A lively crowd gathered, and much laughter flowed.

She didn't want to make things worse, so she nodded and then quickly said, "Er, Nik, before you go…" She chewed her lip. Darn it, he was the only one who could help her with this, so she forged on. "Can I speak to you about something else?"

He stepped back, avoiding the three older women passing them, his ice-green eyes narrowed.

Taking a deep breath, she said, "It's about Dagan and me—and his feeding."

Expecting Nik to walk off, he merely folded his arms and waited for her to continue. Encouraged, she told him the rest. When she finished, he rubbed a hand over his jaw, his brow lowered in a frown. "I'll have to think about it. Wait in the café. I'll send him to you."

Rubbing her cold palms down her jeans, she headed

across to the café and chose an outside table, wanting to see Dagan when he arrived.

He was fighting. *Christ.* She leaned her elbows on the table and rubbed her scar. As a Guardian, she understood it was his job, but still, her fear wouldn't leave.

Shae anxiously searched the street then spied a familiar, lanky figure heading toward the bar.

"No, not now," she groaned, not when Dagan would be by anytime.

***

A fist plowed into his face. Dagan stumbled back, hitting the building wall in the darkened alley. He leaped through the air and kicked the demonii in the chest, sending him crashing into a dumpster. Breathing hard, he eyed the other two circling him like he was prey—the shitheads!

So damn glad he'd come across these three scourges shadowing a lone female.

But with self-loathing churning through him, he hoped this fight would give him what he needed. But nothing could wipe Shae's agonized cry from his mind. He'd hurt her—he'd fucking hurt her.

Hell, he finally understood Blaéz's need for pain all those centuries before he met his mate—it blurred his guilt and forced his screwed-up mind to focus.

The blond demonii grinned and hurled a hissing, red hellbolt. Dagan ducked, the thing nearly swiping off the left side of his face. He didn't bother to summon his sword. He craved the physical fight—except his fun was cut short as three black ice lances pierced the demoniis' chest. Within seconds, the spears transformed, and ice encased their entire bodies, freezing them.

Georgia Lyn Hunter

"Stop playing with the fuckers, D-man," Nik barked from behind him.

Reining in his frustration, Dagan flung himself into the air and, with a flying kick, shattered the demonii ice-sculptures. The pieces fell to the asphalt in a loud crunch before dissipating.

With nothing else to take his mind off his remorse, he fumbled a cigar out of his pocket and lit the thing with unsteady hands, deeply inhaling the sedative smoke—nothing helped. He could still see the blood seeping from her nose...her chest. Gods! He shut his eyes.

An odd sulfuric stench marred the air. Dagan's eyes snapped open. Before whatever evil lurking in the shadows emerged, Nik moved like lightning, swinging his obsidian dagger, the blade a deadly black gleam in the cold moonlight. A raucous squawk erupted as the smoke vanished into the chilly night air.

Dagan didn't ask, he'd seen the shadows follow Nik a time or two through the centuries.

He flipped his dagger into the air and caught it. "Shae's looking for you."

Dagan shook his head, unable to face her.

"Says it's urgent."

"It can wait." Exhaling a rough, smoky breath, he did a psychic scan of the village. Picked up no malicious demonii strains. "Place is clean for now. Let's head to the city."

"You could do that. But she's waiting for you at the Korner Pub."

The Korner-fucking-Pub? That was on the same street as the damn pharmacy! "You left her there alone?" he snarled.

"It's the safest place for her. Amidst humans, while I

hunted down your surly ass. Besides, if I hadn't brought her, she would have asked Angelus. The lad's smitten enough to walk on water for her. I saw no reason to get him in trouble with you. You and I can have it out later." Nik's dark eyebrow cocked. "Well, are you gonna stand there and eyeball me, or go get her?"

"Stay the hell out of this."

"Believe me, it's my wish. But she asked…" A shrug. "Right, then. My job here is done. Go get your mate."

His gaze snapped to Nik.

"What? You're like a rabid dog around her. Besides, she told me." With another toss of his blade in the air, the warrior and his weapon vanished from the alley.

Dammit! Dagan flicked the dead stub into a nearby dumpster and took off up the main street. Seconds later, he slowed down, struggling to keep his anger checked, not surprised to find the pharmacist already on the prowl. He stood near Shae, who sat at one of those outside tables, his hand on the backrest of her chair as if staking his claim.

Can't kill a human—can't kill a human! Shae would never forgive him if he hurt the fucker.

Dagan stalked over. She looked up and shot to her feet when she saw him, seeming to forget her admirer. It eased some of his annoyance.

The asshole touched her arm.

For the second time, Dagan lost his shit. Fury zipped through his veins and thundered in his ears. He shot across the road faster than human eyes could track, and with his mind, hauled the male away and shoved him against a pillar. To the customers, they appeared to be having a friendly little conversation, thanks to his mind tampering skills.

His fists pushed into his jeans pockets, tone low and very, very deadly, Dagan said, "Touch her again—or even seek her out—and I will break every bone in your pitiful body."

"I meant no harm, she-she's just a friend," the human whimpered, fighting to break through the invisible bands keeping him restrained.

"Really?" he drawled, forcing his rage deep into his gut. "That's not what I've seen."

"Dagan—" Shae hissed, clutching his arm. "Don't do this."

It didn't move him. *I know your thoughts,* he telepathed into the human's mind, letting the tips of his fangs show. The man turned sickly pale and started struggling frantically. *I'll enjoy drinking you.*

"Dagan, stop it!" Shae yanked harder at his forearm, panic etched on her beautiful face. "Let him go."

Thank your lucky stars for her intervention, human. Now fuck the hell off. He dropped his hold on the fool, grasped Shae's hand, and strode out.

In the shadows of a copse of trees, she spun to him. "What is wrong with you? You scared Vasile half to death grabbing him like that."

An icy smile touched his mouth. "I would have done worse, but you would have been mad. You're still an innocent when it comes to the male species."

Her eyes grew dark and stormy. "Whatever his plans were, I can take care of myself."

Dagan studied the empty side street through the trees. Yes, she could. Still, no damn fucker would have those filthy thoughts about her. She was his. *His!*

She stepped in front of him, her anxious gaze searching his face. "Are you okay? I was so worried."

"Do I look injured?" Anger resurged. "You were hurt, and you recklessly jumped between two fighting warriors. You could have died!"

She rolled her eyes like *he* was overreacting. "Look, I'm fine. I know what to expect. I trained with Harvey. Yes, it hurts like crazy, but it's just one of those things."

His mate had a way of fanning his temper. "Well, I'm not. I not only fractured your nose, I could have had my fangs in your carotid. This could have ended in tragedy!"

"Dagan, stop. If you're trying to scare me, it won't work. You won't hurt me—not deliberately anyway," she quickly added before he opened his mouth.

By the stars! He wanted to shake her at her misplaced faith. Instead, he cut her a hard look. "I may be a Guardian, but beneath it, I'm a damn predator. In the animal kingdom, gazelles would flee from me."

"Not this gazelle. I have some dangerous moves of my own."

"Dammit, Shae—"

"No, you listen to me." She coolly held his glare. "Yes, you could have overpowered Angelus and drank me dry. *But. You. Didn't.* And I'm all right, see?"

She undid the top three buttons of her dark green sweater before he could stop her, revealing the smooth, pale curve of her breast. Unable to stop himself, he cupped her face and kissed her nose, then lowered his head and pressed his lips to her warm, silky skin, running his tongue over where the cut had been.

"Dagan…" Her fingers tangled in his hair, her husky voice filling his ears.

His resistance shattering, he pulled her bra down and sealed his lips over her tight nipple. She moaned as he

Georgia Lyn Hunter

suckled the tempting bud. A growl rumbled from deep in his throat, and he squeezed her breast. Desire coiled through him, his cock a throbbing ache. His other hand slid under her sweater, caressing her warm back. A sudden sharp sulfuric stink overrode Shae's seductive scent and crowded his nose.

Biting back a curse, he quickly buttoned her top while mentally tracking for the source. Faint voices reached him. "I saw her with *him* in the pub moments ago, they must be close. We can't lose her…"

"Dagan?" Shae clutched his shirt. Her slumberous eyes more gold than gray were edged with anxiety. "What's wrong?"

It was hard to keep a lid on his temper at his mate being hunted like she was fucking game.

"Demons. We have to get out of here." He held her close and dematerialized.

***

They took form, not in the monastery as Shae had expected, but on the shadowy side of a looming building with tall spires, its pale facade gleaming in the moonlight. A church.

Dagan hurried her around to the front, up a few steps, and through the massive doors that opened at a touch. He ushered her into a gloomy vestibule. The doors shutting behind him, he crossed to the window and searched the streets again.

She hurried to his side but could see nothing in the dark night. Guilt and worry overrode the desire still coursing through her. "I'm so sorry."

"For what?" His gaze cut back to her.

"They must have gotten a trace of my abilities when I teleported last night and followed me here."

"I don't think so. We've been extra vigilant since

you first lost control of your powers, and even last night, we didn't pick up anything. Besides, the Fallens would know we have another base in Romania but not where we actually live. Shae—" He angled her face to him when she kept her focus glued to the silent street, his fingers warm on her chin. "This is not your fault. The monastery's warded against demons, immortals, and humans finding it. I brought us here because I don't want to take a chance and lead them there."

Perhaps, but unease churned her stomach. She moved away from him, needing to think. Michael had said evil demons would be after her because she was psychic. The latter she still didn't get. "I don't understand why demons would want my abilities when they have their own?"

"Because you could be a psionic."

She paused in her restless roaming of the vestibule. "A psi what?"

Dagan leaned against the low windowsill, hands resting on the ledge. "I meant to talk to you about that, but things got in the way…"

Like their unexpected attraction...and finding out they were destined mates? Shae didn't say anything. Waited.

"It's about the Watchers. You know those biblical angels who watched over early mankind?"

"Some…" Shae nodded, recalling something she'd read about them years ago when she first became aware of Fallens living in this world. "They fell for mortal women and were all killed."

"Yes. They broke a sacrosanct law. It's why they were annihilated."

"That's a horrible thing to do—you can't help who you fall for." When he didn't respond but watched her quietly, she whispered, "What's going on, Dagan? Why the history lesson?"

"Because you could be one of their descendants."

She stared perplexedly at him for a second, then burst out laughing. "No way. I'm not."

"Yes, Shae, everything points to you being one. Even if your aura's not revealing much right now. In time, it will."

At his serious expression, wariness knotted her stomach at how ominous that sounded, like it was a death knell or something. Dagan continued, "Zarias was the leader of the Watchers and the last to fall. Angry at the injustice of their sentence, he cast an ancient spell to protect his bloodline. His dying words became this prophecy—"

"Just his bloodline?" she asked trying to get her reeling mind to focus.

He frowned. "I don't think it's meant to be taken as singular since all the Watchers were brethren. He foretold that *females* would rise again, and the very ones who'd destroyed them would be responsible for protecting them…"

Dagan glanced out through the window again, his hair shifting like silky, blue-black whips down his back. "We had to find the first one—the Healer of the Veils—and protect her. If she died, then Zarias' prophecy would come to pass, and that can't happen. Chaos unlike any other will overrun this world, and with mortals possessing the abilities of gods and angels, demons and every other evil out there will be after them—"

"Not all demons are evil," she interrupted, thinking of Harvey.

Even though his tone remained quiet as he spoke, a

tic worked in his jaw. "Last fall, we found the first one. Echo. But with a demon after her abilities, during her retrieval, it didn't end well. She died—"

"Wait a minute, you're talking about the woman with the spiky hair from the castle?"

He nodded.

"But how can that be? She's alive."

"Aethan brought her back, a gift he has. Anyway, because she died, the prophecy came to pass. Other psionics will awaken, we just don't know when. And those with powerful abilities like Echo's have to be protected. They cannot survive on their own otherwise."

"Protected how?"

"We find them and hand them over to Michael. If the seraphim can, they will bind their abilities and the mortal will live a safe, normal life. Those who wield unnatural powers that can't be bound will traverse to the Celestial Realm to live out their human lives. If they refuse, they die—it's the same with nephilim offspring. But they are rare..." He broke off, his entire manner changing, remolding into the cold, hard lines of the man she'd first met.

A hand on her lower back, he opened the main doors to the church and ushered her inside. "Stay here. Demons can't enter a holy place. It will shield you."

A glow emitted from the sword tattooed on his biceps. The next second, it vanished, and took form in his hand in a smoky haze. Whoa! "That weapon's real?"

"Yeah." He glanced through the elongated window.

She drew closer and examined his now unmarred biceps in the faint moonlight slanting through the glass pane, gently touching the place where the obsidian sword usually resided. "How?"

"When I—we became Guardians, Gaia, the ancient goddess who watches over this realm, bestowed this and the dagger to us so we're always armed."

"Wait, I thought Michael was your leader."

"He is, but Gaia is boss." He headed for the door. "I'll explain later. Don't move from here until I come for you. And stay away from the windows."

"I can fight, too, you know."

He turned. There was utter lethalness in his stillness. "Not for this." Then he was gone.

Her mind in complete chaos, Shae rubbed her face, her fingers slowing on the bumpy scar there. A psionic? Jeez, she still couldn't wrap her head around that. And really hoped she wasn't one. She didn't want to leave this world, leave her mother, Uncle Lem…or Dagan.

With everything finally going the way she wanted—yes, he was stubborn, with a will of iron, and could be utterly frustrating, but he cared, too. And she wanted a chance with him.

Shae remained in the shadows but peered out an elongated side window, listening for trouble. Nothing. All appeared quiet. Frowning, she looked around the gloomy place, the faint scent of incense and wood wax teasing her nose.

The sudden unmistakable cacophony of fighting yanked her head around. Not in the street, but the side of the church. She darted between the pews, banging her ankle on a wooden corner.

"Fuckity-fuck!" the curse flew out of her mouth. It took several moments to breathe through the pain. "Sorry, God." Hopping on one foot, teeth clenched, she hobbled to the window.

Holy mother—! Pain forgotten, she gaped at the parking lot.

A horde of demons scuttled about like black beetles, attacking a central figure.

Her gut cramped in fear for Dagan. Then a familiar glimmer and another sword appeared amidst the violent chaos. Nik? Shae searched the horde but still couldn't see them. The frenzy grew, bodies flying through the air from the center.

Movement in her peripheral vision caught her attention. There, at the edge of the parking lot, a tall man with silvery hair appeared. He watched the fight for a second and then leaped into the air and flung himself into the vicious battle.

She had no idea who he was, but she was darn grateful Dagan and Nik had help.

Screeches and grunts grew. Body parts soared and disintegrated in the air. Yet the chaos didn't diminish as time passed.

Her fingers dug into the cold stone sills, her stomach queasy. *Please, let him be all right.*

The entrance door slammed open. She spun around, her heart racing to her throat.

"Shae!"

Relief flowing, she darted through the pews and sprinted back to the vestibule. "I'm here." Her gaze rushed between him and Nik. "What happened?"

His expression harsh, lines bracketed his mouth as if in pain, he hauled her close. "We have to get the hell out of here."

"Wait, wait, are you hur—"

A flare brightened up the inside of the church like the Fourth of July, distracting her. Shrieks of terror echoed through the night. She looked back through the

Georgia Lyn Hunter

windows. A spray of fire rained down.

"Dear Lord, what is that?"

"Race," Nik's voice was a disembodied echo as he disappeared.

The raging fire was Race? An enormous black silhouette with flapping wings hovered above the fleeing demons, more flames streaming out of its mouth. Crap, it looked like a—a—no way!

Heck, if demons, gods, and vampires existed, why not...dragons?

She tightened her arms around Dagan, and he dematerialized them. As her molecules dispersed, so did the brief sight of the dragon Guardian she hadn't yet met.

Chapter 14

The instant they took form on the gloomy balcony, Dagan let her go.

Shae grabbed the wooden chair, steadying herself. He and Nik had already disappeared indoors. Forgetting her awe at seeing a live dragon, she hurried into the bedroom and slowed when she found Nik standing just inside Dagan's bathroom entrance, his arms folded, his stance ready for a faceoff.

Frowning, she angled past him into the smallish space that held a glass-paneled shower stall, toilet, and basin. Dagan lowered an opaque brown bottle he'd obviously drunk something from.

"What is that?" she asked as he screwed the top back on.

"A potion," Nik answered. "It helps restore our strength and takes away the weakness when we're hurt from a demon bolt. That shit's just brutal—"

"Dammit, Nik!"

"What?" Dread surged, and Shae's gaze darted over Dagan, but with his black shirt, it was impossible to see where he was hurt. "Dagan?"

"It's nothing. I'll be fine," he said, nailing Nik with a dark glare. And as he shifted, setting the bottle back in the cupboard above the basin, there, on his side, she saw the scorched slash on the dark material. She touched the glossy, wet patch and came away with fingers smeared crimson. He pivoted and scowled. Too worried to care, she grabbed the hem of his shirt. He snagged both of her wrists. "I said I'm okay."

"Yeah? Then take off your shirt and show me the *nothing* you have on your side."

Nik coughed as if trying not to laugh. Dagan shot him a killing look.

Christ, he made her so mad with his obstinate, I'm-the-big-strong-warrior attitude. "Dammit, Dagan, let me help you."

Mouth tight, he yanked off his shirt and flung it aside. "Happy now?"

"Heaps," she muttered, until she saw the wound. Her tummy lurched. It appeared as if a red-hot poker had singed the flesh of his side in a six-inch-long gash. The wound continued to bleed. Fear chased away her irritation. "Why aren't you healing? You're immortal, you're supposed to have quick healing abilities."

"Harvey," he muttered.

"What?" Shae looked up, and at his rigid features…yeah, she'd probably have better luck getting the walls to answer. "Nik, do you have a first-aid kit?"

"No need." Dagan put her aside like she weighed about as much as a feather, opened the cupboard beneath the sink, and got out a box. He grabbed a couple of dressings and a small jar and set them on the counter. Unscrewing the container, the musty odor of old moss and roots drenched the bathroom. He scooped out a blob of the greenish-colored ointment, angled his body, and smeared it over the burn, then slapped a layer of gauze over the wound and taped it down.

Yeah, he was all done. Darn man!

"He needs to feed."

"Godsdammit, Nik," he snapped. "Just get the hell out."

"Nik, stay," she countered.

At his indiscernible nod, her heart tripped. She realized he'd agreed to help her with her plan. This was it.

"What the hell's going on?"

So Dagan had caught their little exchange? No matter. She may not be a goddess, but she was his mate, *and* she possessed kinetic powers. It should make her blood stronger, right?

One thing she did know, she didn't want him putting his mouth on another woman. At the thought, her entire being rebelled. She pulled off her jacket, tossing it aside

"I'm your mate." She pinned him with a determined stare. "You're afraid you'll get caught up in bloodlust and won't be able to stop if you ever take my blood. No matter how shitty my life is right now, I don't want to die. So, Nik's here to make sure that doesn't happen."

A vein throbbed furiously on his brow, his tone lowered in warning. "Don't even think about it."

"Then you leave me with little choice." Before he could figure out what she planned, Shae snatched the scissors from the first-aid kit and swiped the lethal side against her wrist. *Shit!* Pain spread like a flood up her arm. *That freakin' hurt!*

"No!" Dagan's snarl thundered off the walls. He

lunged for the scissors and flung them aside. The thin, red line on her wrist gave way, blood seeping in a steady flow. He leaped away from her, his fangs out. *"Are you both fucking crazy?"*

"You need to feed…" She held out her wrist, and he pushed farther into the wall as if the thing would open up so he could crawl inside. "Dagan, you have to."

"Dammit, D-man, what the hell are you waiting for? Eat."

Dagan didn't move, didn't blink, appeared nailed to the wall.

Despair took hold. At the sight of her blood flowing from her wrist and spilling onto the floor, her knees gave way, and she swayed.

Cursing, Nik caught her, and snarled at Dagan. "You're a damn idiot! Shae, I cannot let you bleed out for nothing…" Nik put his mouth on her wrist and licked her wound.

She shut her eyes as the burn faded, feeling as if someone had stomped on her heart. Pain flowed. A deadly roar filled the small bathroom like a wild animal had been let loose. Her eyelids snapped open just as Dagan flung Nik away. He snatched her before she hit the floor.

"I will kill you for this," he promised Nik, sweeping her into his arms and carrying her into the bedroom.

Wiping the red smears from his mouth with the back of his hand, Nik shrugged and followed. "Get in line."

"You knew what she planned, and you didn't tell me?"

"Stop," she whispered, trying to will away the dizziness. "It's not Nik's fault. I asked him for help."

"I don't know what the hell's going on with you, man. You won't even try. You've struggled through the centuries because of that—" Nik broke off and cursed. "Maybe you like being tormented by that sadistic— Shit, just forget it."

Why did she get the feeling that Nik would have tacked on "bitch" to his comment? The goddess?

His features set in stone, Dagan settled her on the bed. "Stay there."

"Would you stop treating me like an invalid?" She pushed him away and sat up. Dug into her jean's pocket for a candy and put one into her mouth. "I felt faint because I haven't eaten anything since lunch except for the soda at the pub—"

"Because you were busy planning this shit."

"Call it what you want." She tipped her chin in determination. "We're going to do this again tomorrow and every day after that. Nik will be there to make sure nothing happens."

"You are mortal. *You* cannot give me what I need." His tone was pure ice. "Your blood will only bring on the bloodlust."

"You don't know that—"

He grabbed her by her upper arms and yanked her up, his nose almost touching hers, his eyes scalding her. "I drank from humans—hundreds of them. *I*. Killed. Every. One."

Wariness crept through her. That may have been true once, but she didn't believe that now. Frustrated with his inflexible attitude, she taunted, "You're telling me, *you*, a big, bad warrior, still has no control after so many millennia?"

"This discussion is over." He dropped her, and she bounced down on the mattress.

Nik simply shook his head and headed for the door.

"We're not done," Dagan snapped at the warrior, his

tone like razors.

"Then I'll meet you on the mountaintop with swords." Nik threw over his shoulder. "Take your best shot, maybe you'll get lucky."

"Angelus?" Dagan barked. "Get food in here. Fast." Then he pinned her with those lethal yellow eyes. "You ever do something that reckless again—"

"You'll, what? Leave? Pawn me off on Nik or someone else?" Anguish constricted her chest, making it hard to breathe. No matter the attraction between them or that she was his mate, he didn't want her help—didn't want anything from her. He couldn't have made it any clearer while she was bleeding all over the floor. She would never be enough.

No longer. She knew when to cut her losses. Only an idiot would put herself through more misery. Unable to stifle her pain, needing to be in motion, she got off the bed. Wavered. He was there, reaching for her.

"Don't!" She flung out a hand, her cold tone stopping him dead. "My personal well-being is not your responsibility. You made it quite clear you want nothing from me. So this is me, giving you what you want."

His nostrils flared, jaw hardened. "This is not over."

For her it was. Struggling not to let her devastation show, her hope of a relationship with him shattering like glass, she shuffled from the room, praying she wouldn't fall flat on her face. All those sensual touches and kisses meant nothing.

She rubbed the throbbing scar on her cheek as she entered the kitchen. Angelus looked up from setting the tray, his troubled gaze skimming over her. "I was about to bring you food. Are you all right?"

No, I'm not. I just made a complete fool of myself

with a man who will never see me as more than a liability.

"I'm fine, Ange." She took the soda from the tray, popped the tab, and swallowed some to ease the constriction in her throat.

The door swung open, and Dagan stalked inside wearing a fresh t-shirt, still looking like a thundercloud about to erupt. She marched around to the opposite side, putting the table between them. His mouth tightened.

Angelus got a drink from the fridge and gave her an encouraging smile before hoofing it out of there and leaving her alone with Dagan again.

Her cell rang. Thankful for the distraction, she pulled out her phone from her jeans pocket and lowered to the chair. When she saw her friend's name, for some idiotic reason—maybe because she'd never felt so low in her life—a tearful knot formed in her throat. "Hey, Harvey."

"You didn't call. I was afraid something had happened."

"I'm fine, really."

A short silence. Then, "What's wrong? You sound…upset."

"No, all's good…I miss you."

"Hey, I miss you, too. I don't get to see your gorgeous face every morning. It's all gloom and doom here."

A shaky smile tugging at her lips, she traced the blue writing on the soda can, finding it hard to keep her gaze off the glowering immortal opposite her. "I'm sure it's not that bad—"

"Actually, I'm calling because of your uncle's biz man, Aza. He's been on my back about you."

She stiffened. "Why?"

"He knows we're friends…" Harvey lowered his voice. "That Fallen wants you real bad. The whisper among my kind is that you belong to him and are to be his mate."

"*What?*"

"Yeah, I know. Delusional ass."

As chilling as that sounded, and God knew she was shaken, a hollow laugh escaped her. One immortal wanted her, and the one she wanted didn't. The story of her life.

"Shae, with you suddenly gone AWOL, I'm concerned. No, don't tell me where you are—I don't want those bastards crawling around inside my head and getting the truth."

"I'm sorry, Harvey."

"Don't be. Most fun I've had in a long time. Hailing cabs and opening doors gets old real quick," he drawled, making her smile. "Stay safe. I'll call you."

After he'd rung off, she rose and slipped her phone into her pocket.

"What did he want?"

At Dagan's abrupt voice, she looked up. He had to have heard every word, so why ask?

Stiffening her spine, not wanting him to see how she was hurting, she said coolly, "Seems my uncle's business partner is looking for me. Apparently, I'm his mate. Now there's a word I'm really starting to hate. Another immortal who wants me. No, correction, just Aza. He has people looking for me, probably so the mating can take place."

Hoping her words struck him in the balls, or wherever the hell his heart lay, she walked out.

Tears burned her eyes. Well, she didn't expect a

declaration of anything from him.

Something crashed in the kitchen, making her jump. Inhaling sharply, she didn't turn back, but headed straight for the bedroom.

***

Dagan slammed his palms on the table, glaring at the broken shards of what was once a chair, struggling to contain his temper. She'd put her damn life on the line to feed him, and now, she totally cut him out, like he didn't exist, talking to bloody Harvey—whom she'd missed. And that fucker Aza was still after her.

Nik walked in through the back door, glanced at the mess on the floor, and arched a dark brow as he stepped over it. "What did the chair do?"

Anger flashed through him, white and hot like a fireball when he recalled Nik's mouth on Shae's wrist. Even though he understood Nik had healed her the only way he could, with his saliva, it was a struggle not to rip his friend apart.

"You're an asshole. Be grateful it's Shae who has my ire." He straightened—fuck! He gritted his teeth, pressing a hand on his throbbing injury.

"That thing's not going to heal. We're low on the healing salve, and you've finished the last of the brew from Lila," Nik informed him, like he'd lost his brain cells, too.

While they could self-heal most wounds, a direct hit from a hellfire bolt, not so much. It was why the Oracle's healing ointment and potion were much needed. And since his restorative abilities had all but flat-lined, he would rely on them more.

He dropped his hand. "Text Hedori for a restock."

"Already done." Those pale green eyes trained on him, narrowed. "I didn't want to say this in front of

Shae, but you have no other option, Dag. You need to feed. Summon the goddess."

Call Kaerys? His entire being revolted. "No."

"Don't be a dick, you can't go out on patrol while injured. The hellfire wound will be a beacon for every evil thing out there tracking us—"

"I damn well know that."

Nik leaned against the counter, eyeing him thoughtfully. "So then you're going to be off patrol until you're healed?"

"Don't fucking push this, Nik." Dagan raked his fingers through his hair in frustration, but they caught in his many braids. "The wound's a shallow one, I'll be fine."

"Right," Nik grunted. "So what are you going to do about Shae?

"What I planned to do before you waylaid me, you pain in the ass!"

"About time," Nik smirked. Dagan growled, pivoting for the door. Then Nik drawled, "You're lucky she didn't fall for Angelus' pretty face."

Damn bastard, screwing with his head when it was already fucked-up. Later, he was going to kill the motherfucker.

Chapter 15

Shae paced the length of the dimly lit balcony, the cold night air barely calming her. Wearily, she rubbed her heated face then dashed away her foolish tears, wishing she could teleport out of there to someplace where she could lick her wounds in private.

Callused fingers grasped her wrist. She whipped around and tugged her hand, but Dagan's grip tightened. "What do you want?"

Without a word, he pulled her into the bedroom and shut the door behind them, the fire from the hearth shedding a warm glow over everything. He let her go. She stepped back, rubbing her wrist. He removed a cigar from his pocket and lit it, inhaling deeply.

She breathed in the whiff of the cherry tobacco drifting through the room.

Oh, man. Of course! "If that's to make a point, no need. I'll be out of your room in a moment. Angelus is going to help me tidy up one of the unused bedrooms."

Still silent, he strode across to the bed and set the burning smoke on the edge of the nightstand. Then, like the panther she often thought him, all lean, sinuous muscles rippling beneath the stretched tee, he moved toward her. Hastily, she widened the distance until her back hit the opposite wall, the windowsill digging into her spine.

"Do you want this, Shae? Want *me*, knowing what I am?" he asked softly, stopping an inch from her.

How could he? Not moments ago, he'd rejected her, and now he was back to tormenting her. "What difference does it make? You made it clear I'm the last person *you* want."

In response, he brushed his knuckles along her jaw, and a tremor of desire skittered through her traitorous body. God, not now! She pushed his hand away. Glared. "Why are you doing this?"

"Because I must. You are human. Free will's your right. You say yes, I'll never let you go, bond or not…"

He gently traced the damp skin beneath her eyes. Remorse flickered in those sun-bright irises. Then his warm lips took the place of his fingertip, and her heart nearly stopped.

"I'm sorry I hurt you and made you cry." He pressed his mouth beneath her other eye. "It was never my intention. I only wanted to keep you safe from the violent side of my nature. Gods, Shae, you take over my thoughts awake or asleep. When you're not with me, my mind's a fucking mess—"

Her heart filled with longing, but she refused to let hope bloom only to be crushed again. She'd been hurt too many times. "You blame me for this?"

"Hell, no! The fault's all mine. Nik, the bastard, licked your wound better…" He picked up her left hand and gently pressed his lips to the newly healed lesion where she'd cut herself. "Angelus worships the ground you walk on, and bloody Harvey teaches you to fight. *You* like them."

"I do." At his dark look, she finally relented, said softly, "But they aren't you. Mad as I get, and God knows at times I want to stake you with your own damn sword, I only want you. I feel it so deeply inside here…" She took his hand and placed it over her heart. Naturally, that hand cupped her breast and squeezed, his thumb lightly flicking her nipple.

He lowered his head and ran his lips over the jagged scar on her cheek. "I don't deserve you, but I need you…" A whisper of aching need.

Her chest tightened. She swallowed, and then asked him about the one thing that stood between them like a canyon. "What about your feeding?"

His big body went motionless for an endless second, before his shoulder lifted in a shrug. "I'll have to use that iron will you often think I have when it comes to you to not go feral when we make love."

"That's not what I meant—"

"I know." He kissed the corner of her mouth as he unbuttoned her top. The next moment, it disappeared, along with her bra. "I'll be fine. Animal blood will do."

"Dagan—"

"Later." He palmed her breasts, squeezing the mounds. Lowering his head, he ran his tongue around her areola, and she shuddered. Then he sucked the hard, aching nipple into his mouth, and Shae forgot her concerns, a wave of pleasure sweeping through her body like liquid heat to settle in her core. Her fingers tangled in his hair as he bent her backward over his arm, the hard bulge in his pants rubbing against her jeans-covered core.

"Dagan…" A whimper escaped her.

Georgia Lyn Hunter

"I'll give you what you need—we both need soon, Shae-cat. First..." He turned his attention to her other breast, sucking her aching nub with even deeper pulls.

Oh. She squirmed. There was no way she could endure this sensual assault.

Letting go of her nipple, he pulled her upright and lowered to his haunches. She grabbed his shoulders as he unlaced and removed her boots, followed by her jeans and underwear. He peeled off her socks and paused, his stare tracking slowly up her naked body to linger on her damp, brightly flushed nipples. He lifted those searing yellow eyes to hers. At the hunger there, her heart thudded in anticipation.

"You're beautiful, Shae-cat." He pressed his lips to her lower belly then rose to his feet. He put his mouth on hers, claiming her in an all-consuming kiss. A low growl of satisfaction rumbled deep in his throat when she kissed him back.

Shae drowned in the sensation of his tongue, licking and caressing hers, his hands stroking her body to squeeze her backside.

Panting for breath, she broke free of his kiss. Needing to touch him, she pushed her hand between their bodies to the waist of his jeans and stroked his sex. But his rigid erection made the task of unbuttoning his jeans difficult—suddenly, the fastenings popped open. Thank God for his telekinesis.

The fly parted. His impressive cock sprang free. Slowly, reverently, she wrapped her fingers around his rock-hard sex. He was smooth and hard...satin over steel. Tightening her grip, she moved her palm over his rigid length.

"Fuck," he groaned, the sound raw, sensual, and incredibly masculine. She looked up. His eyes were shut. His head kicked back, the veins on his neck straining with his desire. Christ, the vision he presented was utterly consuming and so mind-numbingly sexy. And she wanted him with every fiber of her being. More, she wanted to watch him come. She worked his cock harder, but he had other ideas.

With a growl, he pulled her to her feet, dislodging her hand from his shaft. He picked her up, and she anchored her legs around his hips, the searing length of his sex pushing between her folds.

Then he was moving, walking across to the bed, his erection sliding in her wetness and rubbing against her clit. Pleasure escalated. His mouth came back on hers, his kiss raw. Insatiable. The dangerous tips of his fangs scraped against her tongue, hiking her arousal. Desire stormed through her with the strength of a gale force.

He put her on the bed. Instantly, she pushed up to her elbows. He ran his gaze down her body. "I haven't eaten for thousands of years, but you are an absolute feast, my wildcat... Spread your legs for me."

Her body strung taut with need, she parted them.

He hauled off his t-shirt, tossing it aside. Muscles rippling beneath his skin, he settled between her legs. It was the sexiest, hottest thing ever, seeing this hard, dangerous man between her thighs.

His mouth came down on her core. "*Ohhhh...*" She grabbed his hair, her legs sliding over his broad shoulders. He licked down her folds then up again, lightly flicking his tongue over her aching clit. Shae nearly came off the bed. With a hand on her stomach, he held her down. His mouth tormenting her cleft with feather-light kisses, he pushed a callused finger into her, then added another, stretching her.

Oh...*God*! She moaned, pushing into his mouth,

seeking release.

His burning gaze held her as he thrust slow and deliberate as if to drive her out of her mind. Her body a vortex of sensation, he hauled her higher and higher. Shae could do nothing but hold onto to him. Pressure built. Agonizing pleasure grew, coalescing between her thighs. She grabbed his hair. Then his mouth closed around her clit and he sucked on the throbbing flesh firm pulls. A cry tearing free, her body bowed, an orgasm shattering her mind...

Shae came back to herself some moments later and met his intense gaze. The rigid lines of his jaw revealed just how hard he held onto his control. Still, he placed a kiss on her tummy before moving off her. Her gaze shifted to the gauze on his side, but he didn't seem to be bothered by it.

As he reached for his pants, she sat up. "Let me."

***

His body wired like a spring, Dagan lowered his hands. Shae slid off the bed and dropped to her knees in front of him. She didn't pull off his boots or tug his jeans down like he expected, but instead wrapped her fingers around his painfully stiff shaft and stroked him. Then her grip tightened like a vise. *Fuck*, he groaned. It felt so damn good. He smoothed back her tangled hair from her face.

She looked up. "I wanted to do this the other night. But you wouldn't let me."

"Cause I'm a damn idiot—" He hissed as her warm tongue licked the head of his sex. Gray-gold eyes met his, then she took his cock into her mouth and tightened her lips around him, her fingers encircling the extra inches she couldn't quite reach.

Desire pounded in his blood and thundered to his

head, need gripping him by the balls as she worked him with her lips and tongue. Eyes squeezed shut, he flung his head back. Release hovered. Fuck, he didn't want to come in her mouth the first time.

He grasped her arms and pulled her up, shaking his head. "In. You."

Kissing her deeply, he tasted himself, but it was *her* he wanted to savor, to taste. Desperate now, he picked her up, and those long legs he adored wrapped around his waist. He braced her against the nearest wall, ran a finger down her folds—she was deliciously wet—and in one thrust, he was sheathed straight into the heaven of her body, her feminine muscles closing around him like a glove. She stiffened at the invasion. Her face buried in his nape, her gasp filling his ears, he waited for her to adjust to him.

"You okay?" he rasped. He had to have her—all of her. He'd waited an eternity for her.

She looked up and smiled, her eyes almost gold in her passion. Tenderness flooded him for this incredible female who was his mate, he kissed her deeply as he pulled out and thrust back into her. Then he lowered his head to her shoulder. Harder, faster he drove, the slap of flesh on flesh echoing in the softly lit bedroom. Everything in him focused on her. Pressure built along his spine with each desperate thrust. The urge to possess coursed through him. He wanted her etched on his soul. She was his.

Today. Tomorrow. And in every other lifetime.

As if attuned to his thoughts, the mystical light hovering inside him rose. Light as gossamer wings, it emerged from the deepest part of his soul. It grew stronger, burned brighter, and spread in a wave.

Her body shuddered, clenching him as he thrust into

Georgia Lyn Hunter

her, the heels of her feet digging into his backside. He sucked her neck, and another, darker need slithered awake. His incisors lengthened, and he scraped them over the skin of her carotid. The desperate urge to sink his fangs into her neck took hold—

"Do it," she whispered.

Yes, do it—it's what you hunger for—human blood, the insidious voice rose in a cacophony.

Fuuuck. He bit into his lip instead, shutting off the damn taunts. Tasted blood.

His body tensed, and release ripped down his spine in a tidal wave, squeezing his balls in excruciating pleasure. He lowered his hand between their bodies and found her clit. A firm tug gave her that final push.

"Dagan!" Her cry echoed in his ears, her orgasm sending her over the edge. It triggered his own release. A harsh groan lodged in his throat, he spilled himself into her. Panting like he'd run a thousand miles, he dropped his head to her nape and held onto her as the white light swept through him and into her.

When he could breathe again, and his limbs hopefully functioned, he lifted his head. She smiled, and everything felt right in his world. She pressed her mouth to his, and his heart stuttered…in happiness?

He'd forgotten what that felt like—no, he realized, he'd never experienced that emotion. Since he was a boy, his life's purpose had always been to defend. With a mother and sister who relied heavily on him, and a whoring sire they wanted to avoid.

Still intimately joined, Dagan walked to the bed and sat down with Shae in his arms. Desperate to savor this transcendent moment—the unexpected peace he'd found in her—because he realized it was transient.

Shae eased back on his lap. Her gaze dropped to his

lengthened incisors and skipped back to his eyes. He knew what the look was about, but he didn't want to go there just yet. He shook his head when she opened her mouth to speak. "Later, we'll talk. I just want to hold you. I need this."

She nodded. Sliding her arms around his neck, she hugged him tightly, and his heart clipped painfully. Then she eased off him. He didn't hold her back. Although he regretted the loss of her warmth, he knew he had to get this damn thirst under control. Clamping down on his molars, he picked up the remaining inch of the still burning cigar from the nightstand.

"Dagan?"

"Yeah?" He inhaled deeply of his smoke then stared at the trailing wisps. He'd hoped this narcotic shit burning in the room would keep the urge at bay. No such luck.

"Are you okay?"

He glanced sideways at her, sitting naked on the bed beside him, her arms wrapped around her bent knees, her red hair a seductive mess—and he wanted her again.

"I'm fine," he said instead. "Let me finish this first." He indicated the cigar between his fingers. Pushing to his feet, he crossed to the window and opened it.

As he inhaled the sedative smoke, he rubbed a palm down his side and bit back a vicious curse. He hadn't given two craps about his injury while making love to Shae, but now the fucking thing hurt like hell. And it was seeping again. Shit.

Before she saw it, he strode to the bathroom, put his cigar between his lips, and ripped off the dressing. Grabbing more gauze from the cabinet, he wiped away the blood, slapped on more healing salve, then taped on

Georgia Lyn Hunter

a fresh bandage.

With his thirst blocked for now, he killed the end bit of his smoke and tossed it into the toilet. He removed his boots, pulled off his jeans, and dropped them into the laundry basket. A wave of his hand, and his ropey braids slipped free.

He walked into the bedroom. Shae turned, her gaze roaming down his naked body and up again. Stopping in front of her, he cocked a brow in amusement. "What?"

She reached out and touched his stomach, and his muscles clenched in response. He breathed in deeply through his nose, trying to get his damn body to calm down. He'd never experienced a carnal hunger like this before.

"You're beautiful, you know that? Your hair, this body—this…" Her fingers lightly stroked his semi-erect sex, pulling a groan from him. Sighing, she removed her hand and slid off the bed. "I'll be right back."

"Hold it." He grabbed her, his arms banding around her waist. "You don't get to tease me then decide to leave."

"Dagan—" Laughter fell out of her as she tried to free herself, then she lightly traced the tattooed sword on his biceps with a fingertip. "I'm glad the goddess Gaia was there and looking out for you through the centuries."

Frowning, he glanced at his mystical ink. "Yes…she gave us purpose in our lives again after escaping Tartarus. Once we pledged our oath to her to be Guardians, she gave us our powers back, and gifted us with these tattooed swords and the obsidian daggers…"

As he explained about the day Gaia had approached

them, Shae didn't even blink while she listened. But he was all too aware of her warm, sexy body aligned with his. His blood fired up, and he was rock-hard again.

He picked her up and dropped her on the bed. A startled squeak escaped her. He settled between her parted thighs and continued speaking as if he weren't the least bit affected. "But then we were a rabid bunch, and with five hundred years of barely suppressed anger from being imprisoned in that hellhole pressing down on us, we needed an outlet. It had to be why she took us on, so we had something to direct it at. Now, I need to work off *that* energy."

"What?"

He shifted his hips, letting her feel what he meant.

Her face reddened. She smacked his arm and rolled her eyes. "We just made love—" She tried to push him off her. He didn't budge. Amusement and tenderness crowded him for his mate. His life had been a violent one—even sex, until now. Shae didn't use him. She gave.

"Dagan," she sighed. "I'm hungry."

Dammit, how could he let something so important slip his mind?

"I'm sorry, Shae-cat, I should have remembered." He rolled off her. "You stay. I'll go get food." He headed for the door.

"Wait-wait. You aren't going out there without any clothes on, are you?"

He glanced back. "It's just Angelus and Nik. They won't care. But if they look at me the way you do, I'll castrate them."

She laughed, but her discomfort had her flush deepening. "They'll know that we—that we…"

He shook his head. "Shae, I don't care if the entire

world heard us when I made love to and claimed you. You are mine. Stay here and don't move. I'll be right back."

***

Shae sighed as Dagan walked out of the room, his inky hair swaying down his very naked, very sexy backside. The man was shameless. Hell, if she had that kind of body, she'd probably walk around bare-assed, too. No, not really.

She slid off the bed and hurried to the bathroom. A quick shower later, she walked out, but Dagan wasn't back yet. She got a t-shirt from his closet, pulled it on, and wandered out onto the balcony. Even though the night had a crisp bite, she didn't feel the cold with the higher temperature she now seemed to possess.

She leaned her arms on the railing and inhaled another lungful of cool air. Down below, the forest appeared like a darkened blur.

A scuttling sound and faint squeaks drifted to her. Rats? Ugh. Hastily, she sat down on the wooden chair, pulled her feet up, and wrapped her arms around her knees. Content, she stared at the stars littering the dark sky. More, there was this faint spark of light inside her, one she sensed was all Dagan, and she sighed in pleasure. She didn't know why, but she'd expected a more incandescent…transcendent moment at their soul-joining.

Still, in his arms, she'd found her safe place–her safe haven.

Now, just one more hurdle to cross, and that brought her happiness down several notches.

Soft footsteps sounded. "Shae?"

"Balcony."

He appeared in the doorway, carrying a tray, a frown

on his gorgeous face. "What are you doing out here?"

"Everything's so peaceful," she breathed, turning to stare into the night again. "I like it up here."

"Good thing since I tend to live here more than any of our other houses. Don't worry, I'll get this place done up better." A clatter of dishes echoed as he set the tray on the table and scooped her up. She yelped, her arms flying to grip him around his neck.

Without a word, he claimed her seat, shifted her knees, and had her straddling him. Her eyes widened in disbelief as he eased that hard, thick length into her. "What-what are you doing?"

"Getting what I want while you partake of what you need." He nodded to the tray behind her.

Her mouth opened, but no words came out. When she made no move to take the food he'd brought, he asked, "Aren't you going to eat?"

"How can I? When you—with you—"

"Me what?" A dark brow lifted.

Was he kidding her? He carried on like they were dining at a five-star restaurant—all polite, considerate, and everything, as if he didn't have his cock inside her.

"Let me sit on the other chair so I can eat."

"No." He shifted and reached for something behind her, his erection pushing deeper—oh, shit! She bit her lip when he eased back and held the sandwich to her mouth. "Eat."

God, she was literally nailed in place by his cock. She inhaled a shaky breath. With those sun-bright eyes watching her, and his one hand on her hip keeping her there, she had little choice.

Shae reached for the sandwich he held, but he shook his head. "I'll feed you."

Heat streaking her face, she bit into the rye bread and

roast beef and tasted a hint of mustard as she chewed.

It was the longest, weirdest meal ever. Once she'd finished the sandwich, he held out a chicken drumstick. As she chewed the succulent flesh, his gaze tracked her every movement. Then she recalled everything he'd lost when he was changed, and her heart faltered in compassion.

"Don't," he said quietly. "I find I enjoy watching you eat."

"Do you miss it?"

He frowned, then said slowly, "I did in the beginning when I was first trapped in that arid wasteland, but it has been millennia, so no."

He dropped the bone on the tray and wiped his fingers on a napkin before he reached for something else on the tray. Every time he moved, his sex twitched inside her.

Lord! She bit back a moan, desire flooding her like a breaking dam. His gaze shifted to hers.

Ack. With his heightened hearing, he probably—no, he *definitely* heard her whimper. He didn't ask what was wrong, not with her face probably brighter than the strawberries in the bowl. He handed her the water bottle.

Shae gulped the cold liquid, hoping it would cool her—nope, it didn't work. She thrust it back at him since she couldn't very well turn around and set it on the table, not when he had her pinned—

A slice of melon touched her lips. His hand slid beneath the tee she wore, and his fingers stroked her bottom.

Damn. Well, then, if he could sit there so calm and unaffected, so could she. She took the fruit and deliberately sucked his finger. His eyes narrowed. Still, he said nothing, but he leaned closer, his bare chest brushing her t-shirt-clad breasts. Her nipples protested the taunt, wanting his hands or his mouth on them. But, apparently, he was more interested in choosing her next selection of food.

A strawberry.

With his body flush against hers, and being so intimately joined, her breathing became ragged. She shook her head, her brilliant plan to unsettle him falling flat like a pancake.

"Had enough?"

Of making love? God, no—wait, he probably meant the food. "Yes."

He lifted her off his lap and, instantly, she felt empty as he set her on the table in front of him. Shae watched him warily. Because Dagan, she was coming to understand, always had some diabolical card waiting to be played when it came to her.

Still silent, he reached for the red wine on the tray, leaned back against the chair, and took a sip from the glass. His gaze drifted over her, then back up to her face. "Go ahead."

"What?"

He fingered the hem of the t-shirt she wore. "Take this off so I can feast on *my* banquet."

"It's cold." The words tripped out.

"I'll keep you warm."

Oh, man. She shouldn't feel shy. Heck, he'd seen every part of her. Still…

"I'm waiting."

Slowly, she drew the shirt over her head and dropped it on the table beside her. Drink forgotten, he reached out and rolled her nipple, and she shuddered.

"My beautiful wildcat," he murmured, his tone low,

rough. Setting the glass aside, he dragged her to the edge of the table. With a palm on her chest, he pushed her down to the wooden surface and put his mouth between her thighs again. She grabbed his hair as his tongue teased and tormented her, impossible desire spiraling through her.

He sat down and brought her onto his lap again, and at the thick, hard flesh pushing into her, stretching her, a moan broke out.

A rough whisper of need, of longing drifted into the night air. "Ride me, my Shae-cat…"

Chapter 16

Curled up against Dagan's warm body, his even breathing and heartbeat soothing sounds, Shae stared drowsily through the night-dark windows, her heart expanding with happiness. Dagan was finally hers.

A light flickered past the window like a… A falling star? She wondered as sleep hovered…

The smell of wood and ash crowded her nose. Shae frowned, looking around the room—a workshop of sorts. Shelves lined the walls, but the tall, dark-haired man standing near the window caught her attention. Lines of strain etched the corners of his hard mouth. Those yellow eyes she adored, burned with such harsh intensity, her stomach knotted in worry.

"Dagan?" she whispered. *He didn't appear to hear her.*

Another figure wandered into her line of view, a tall, striking woman with honey-gold skin and a thick swathe of cinnamon-hued hair. She circled the worktable and picked up a half-finished, ten-inch, wooden wolf.

Georgia Lyn Hunter

"I don't understand how you can stand drinking from these stinky creatures." With a little moue of disgust, she tossed the wolf aside and selected a gouge, stroking the edge of the blade.

"Oh, would you look at that? I nicked my finger." She dropped the tool onto the table as blood pooled on her fingertip and dripped to the floor.

Dagan stiffened. His fangs lengthened, piercing into the flesh of his lower lip. A nerve pulsed furiously on his jaw. "Kaerys..."

She looked up, her gaze cool. "I'm not in the mood. Go find a mortal female to feed you."

He squeezed his eyelids tight and choked back an agonized groan. "You win."

A gleam of excitement lit her face as she leaned against the table. "You know what I want. Give me all, *Dagan. And you can take whatever you need."*

A growl emitted from him. The woman laughed as he slammed her on top of the worktable, his fangs sinking into her neck. He gulped on her blood like a starving, wild animal...

Nooo! Shae bolted upright, breaking through the lethargy trapping her, anguish ripping her chest open. She grabbed her head, trying to shut off the images pinging inside her skull.

"Shae?" Dagan jackknifed up at her side, the covers bunching around his lean hips. "What's wrong?"

Inhaling harshly, her emotions running too high, she pressed her cheek against his cool chest instead, trying to will away the pain.

"It's okay." He tenderly stroked her hair back from her heated face. "I will find the one who killed your sire, I promise."

She held him tightly. How could that horrible

woman have done that to him? Despite Dagan's cold appearance and solitary preference, one she now understood, he had a heart that cared.

A shuddering breath escaped her. Why couldn't *her* blood sustain him, why couldn't *she* be what he needed? Then she could spare him the humiliation he'd endured at the hands of that conniving goddess.

He lay down again, pulled her close, his arm wrapping around her. "Everything will be okay."

Will it? She needed a damn miracle. But she was running short of those.

***

Late-morning sunlight streamed into the room. Shae awoke alone in bed. She groaned and rolled over, wishing she could pretend that the horrible dream hadn't happened, but the heaviness inside her said otherwise.

With a sigh, she climbed out of bed, and after a quick shower, she changed and took the excavated steps to the upper level, needing to see Dagan—see that he was okay.

As soon as she opened the first door in the dim corridor, the smell of wood, sawdust, and a hint of cherry tobacco teased her nose. But he wasn't there.

A sense of déjà vu settled over her as she stepped inside his workspace.

Shelves lined one wall with completed animal sculptures of various sizes. Larger ones were pushed in the corner. Reverently, she ran her finger over a pouncing cheetah. The brilliant craftsmanship of each creature stunned her. Several pieces of furniture made of different woods were stacked near the wall.

Now she understood the mismatched furniture in the kitchen.

A familiar scarred worktable in the center held a few unfinished works. She picked up a half-finished gazelle from the table and traced the fluid lines of the carved figurine. Frowning, she put it down on the wooden surface then yanked back her hand as the truth hit her like a punch in her chest.

Oh, God! Bile rushed to her throat. Her stomach heaved. This was the table from her nightmare—

"Shae?"

She spun around. Dagan stepped into the room. "I was looking for you."

"And you found me."

Amusement brightened his eyes at her comment. He strode across, put his mouth on hers, and kissed her. But her heart was too heavy to enjoy it. He eased back, his gaze searching hers. "What's wrong?"

Tell him she'd *seen* his encounter with that horrible goddess? Everything inside her rebelled at that thought, but she had to. If she didn't, it would fester inside her and cause a rift between them. And they already had one thing that hung like a black cloud between them.

She pushed away from him and wandered to the window overlooking the back courtyard, rubbing the chills spreading over her arms. "Last night, my dream..." After an emotion-laden pause, she faced him. "It wasn't about my dad. I saw you with *her*. With Kaerys. In *this* room."

Instantly, his expression shut down. "What else?"

Shae bit her lip, hating to reveal what she'd seen, more, loathing that he'd been with the goddess in *that* way for so many centuries. It took everything in her not to rub the piercing ache in her heart. "She said you knew what she wanted, and if you gave her everything, then you could have what you needed."

A nerve jumped on his rigid jaw. He leaned against the table, gaze lowered to his sneakers. But she'd seen the anger in his eyes.

"She wouldn't let you feed because you wouldn't sleep with her?"

"I'm sorry you had to see that."

He was apologizing? "You didn't ask for any of that to happen to you."

Silence lengthened dark and heavy. Just when she thought he wouldn't speak, his gaze lifted to hers. The shame there—God, to see her big, brave warrior so utterly humiliated stole her breath.

"When I finally realized I could only feed from immortal females without killing, Michael arranged for a few to be donors. But they wouldn't come. Only Kaerys did. She refused any monetary payment—"

"Because she wanted you."

He nodded. "I thought it a small price to pay until she started using it to control me…"

"Why would she do that?"

His mouth tightened briefly. "Resentment because I ended our betrothal."

They'd been engaged? Shock held her immobile. Of course, he would have had someone. *He's centuries old for Christ's sake.* But that his ex was still in the picture…the hole in her stomach deepened.

"My grandsire, An, is the ruling god of the Sumerian pantheon," he said then. "It was an unpardonable thing I did."

Her eyes widened. "You're…like royalty?

A terse nod. "I was with Kaerys for a while. She wanted a commitment, so I agreed to the betrothal. Except my sister, Inara, became the Goddess of Life, and I her protector. Away from home, I realized my life

Georgia Lyn Hunter

would never be my own, so I broke off the arrangement, wanted her to find a male more suited."

"But she didn't want that. She wanted you and what you represented."

"Perhaps." He exhaled heavily. "I realize now, had I mated her, I would have missed out on finding my destined mate. Despite the dark path my life took, it led me to you. For that—hell, I never thought I'd be grateful to the damn Fates for anything."

Her eyes misted at his words. "And your obsidian dagger stayed with me when I first used it."

"Yes. Only the Guardians possess those blades, a gift from Gaia. We had no idea what it meant then, thought it just another weapon to aid us. Her cryptic words didn't help much either."

"What do you mean?"

His gaze drifted over her face. "Gaia called it, the *embodiment of my one weakness.*"

She was his weakness? Her smile trembled, and her heart expanded at his words, then dipped. She didn't want to be his weakness. If anything, she longed to be his strength.

Straightening her backbone, she crossed to him, stopping an inch from his foot. "Dagan… Feed from me. Please."

"Shae—"

At his refusal, she hurriedly pushed on. "How will you know what will happen if you don't try? With us being soul-joined, surely you'd sense if I was dying?"

"No." Steel edged his quiet voice. "When I'm in the throes of bloodlust, I lose cognizance. I am aware of nothing except feeding the hunger that never ends. You'd never survive me, and I refuse to take that chance. I won't lose you."

Her gaze dropped, dejection settling over her like a thick black cloud.

He drew her into his arms. "I'll find another way."

Another way? He meant someone else. Another *immortal* woman.

Pain flowed, and she buried her face against his neck. She would always have to share him with someone. At the thought, her stomach hurt so much, and she had no idea what to do. She looked over his shoulder, her gaze settling on the scarred table they rested against. Images from last night broke free. *Jesus!* Despite knowing that none of this was his fault, she pushed away from him, needing distance so she could breathe again.

"Shae?"

She simply shook her head. "I-I have to go. I haven't eaten yet."

"Dammit, Shae—" He grasped her arm when she would have walked away. "Don't lie to me. I feel you inside here"—he slapped his chest—"and sense your pain. Tell me what's wrong?"

She cast him a distressed look. "I hate that I've seen you with her, and even though I understand why, but every time I look at your table…" She pressed her lip together, trying to stop them from trembling.

Instantly, Dagan straightened. The next second, the wooden sculptures and tools clattered to the floor, the table compacted into itself and rained down in a shower of splinters. Her shocked gaze rushed to his grim ones. "I won't have you hurting. And that damn thing was upsetting you."

With a wave of his hand, the shards of wood rose and landed in the small fireplace. He struck a match on the granite surface and tossed it on the wood. Seconds later, fire crackled and roared to life, brightening the room. A hand resting on the mantel, he stood there, staring into the leaping flames.

Shae hurried across and slid her arms around his waist. Yes, her family and Harvey cared about her. But, Dagan, no matter their unorthodox meeting, he made everything right, better.

"Shae…." His lips brushed her brow in a soft kiss. "I've lived millennia. And after what I became, I never thought I would ever find my mate, let alone be happy. Then you stumbled into my path"— a smile—"greeted me with a punch that made me reel."

She leaned back as far as his arms would allow, wrinkling her nose. "Yes, well, I was pissed at you."

"I know." His gaze softened. "I never expected you, and now that you're here, I will remind you often that you and I were meant to be."

Chapter 17

The sounds of swords clashing echoed over the mountaintop. A deadly katana winged in the air—*shit*! Dagan jumped back before half his face landed at Nik's feet.

Chest heaving, he held up a hand and called a halt to the training, his mind still on how Shae had found out about him and Kaerys. With her penchant for causing trouble, he wouldn't put it past Kaerys to induce the fucking *dream* Shae had.

Frustration gnawing at him, he pulled out his cell and messaged Angelus.

"Just an hour and you're quitting?" Nik drawled, dropping his sword to the ground. He picked up his t-shirt and pulled it on, covering the myriad of tatts on his body and his nipple piercings.

"Angelus can take my place." He hauled off his shirt, wiping the sweat off his face and chest, then gingerly pressed a hand on his stinging wound. It was probably bleeding again. "I gotta go."

Showered and changed, Dagan headed to the kitchen

where he sensed Shae. Her back to him, she appeared to be staring at several grocery items on the table.

He slipped his arms around her and pressed his lips to her nape. Just holding her eased the upheaval inside him. "What are you doing?"

She turned in his arms, a smile brightening her pale face. "Baking. I thought you'd be hours with Nik."

He shrugged. "I'll make it up later. I needed you more." He lowered his head to kiss her but cupped her chin instead, eyes narrowing. Despite the gold specks warming her stormy gray irises, pain edged them. "What's wrong? Is this about…Kaerys?"

She shook her head. Her throat worked as she swallowed and waved a hand at the table and the things she had there. "Mom used to make this stacked applesauce cake my dad and I loved…"

"I'll make everything right for you, Shae. Just give me a little time."

She didn't say anything for a second. Then she stepped back and frowned, sending her gaze down his torso and up again. Everything inside him went into slow burn. He'd made love to her twice last night— didn't dare risk anything more until he got his damn thirst locked down. Now, he hungered for her again.

"Are you going out?"

Her voice pulled him back to sanity, and the work he'd elected to do. "For a short while. I want to check out the church's parking lot after the fight last night. Why don't you come with me? Afterwards, we can stop in at one of those little sidewalk cafés you like."

"Really?" Her eyes sparkled in excitement, then faded. "But you don't eat."

"Solids, no. I can consume liquids. All right, let's get all the fallacy about me out of the way. I won't burst into flames in sunlight, but it tends to weaken me. My eyes are extra sensitive to it, so dark shades help. Liquor doesn't inebriate me with my quick metabolism. A stake in the heart won't kill me, but beheading? Yeah, that shit will probably kill anyone. However, *we* have never been caught in *that* situation, so it remains to be seen. But certain angel weapons and our Gaian ones *can* kill an immortal."

"Silver? Crosses? Holy water?" she threw in fast like there was a time limit to him answering.

He cut her a sardonic look. "Only if you're the undead. I still have a heartbeat. I didn't die, Shae. My DNA simply changed over time."

"Just checking," she countered, putting the cake things away. "Because I don't want anything to happen to you."

Shaking his head, he crossed to a drawer near the wine shelf, then got out paper and a pen and jotted a message on it. He set the note on the microwave and continued, "Bodily functions? Sure, I can take a piss, but that's about it. And yes, I get a fucking erection every time I see you. Can I sire children? I don't know."

Shae stared at him for a moment then she smiled. "We can deal with everything else as it occurs. For now, I'm happy I have you. Let me change my slippers and get a jacket." She hurried to the kitchen door, skated to a halt, and spun back. "I'm really, really glad you still have a heartbeat, and you aren't like the vampires movies and books depict—the ones who don't breathe and drop into a dead sleep at sunrise—that would be scary as hell."

"And you think I'm not?"

"Oh, I know you are."

"Good." He cut her a serious look. "Never forget, Shae, I'm a predator first and foremost."

***

Honestly, she didn't care how threatening Dagan appeared, he was whom she wanted. This attraction had taken root that night outside the club when he'd abducted her, though she hadn't appreciated it at the time.

In the bedroom, she traded her warm, fuzzy slippers for boots. The long-sleeved, maroon knit-dress would do. She grabbed her leather jacket and sprinted to the front courtyard where she sensed him waiting.

He turned from staring into the gorge below, the light breeze playing with his unbound hair. At the darkness in his expression, her steps faltered. "Dagan?"

He shook his head. Was he thinking about his past? When she recalled his awful confinement trapped in the wasteland of Tartarus with nothing—no one to talk to for five centuries—her chest hurt. Maybe, in time, she could ease some of those nightmares. Replace them with better ones.

"What was the note you left in the kitchen?" she asked instead, pulling on her jacket.

"I requested Angelus to make you an apple cake."

"You did?" Her gaze widened, then she smiled. "It's okay, I like baking. I wasn't born into wealth, you know. My father was a farmer. Apples."

"Where?"

"Stone Ridge, Upstate New York. I really loved it there…" A wistfulness entered her tone. "It was so peaceful."

"I like apples, too…"

"What?" She blinked. "But you don't…"

His gaze lowered to her chest. "They're round, firm,

and really delicious. I can eat them all day, every day."

She burst out laughing. His lips twitched in amusement. Only he could do that, make her smile when her heart was filled with sorrow.

"C'mon, my wildcat, let's go." He drew her close, and she put her arms around his waist. But at the tempting bulge nudging her, she couldn't resist, and she slowly rubbed her hips against his groin.

He went utterly still, and without a word, he dematerialized them. The moment they took form on the shadowy side of the church, he slammed her against the wall, his mouth crashing onto hers. He kissed her deeply and, just as suddenly, pulled back, leaving her panting. His gaze heated to a brilliant yellow, he dropped to his heels and reached beneath the hem of her short dress.

"Wait, wait!" She grabbed his thick wrists. "What are you doing?"

He pulled off her underwear. Like a man possessed, he pushed her legs apart and put his mouth on her. She grabbed his head, pleasure igniting as his tongue parted her and he licked up her cleft and over her clit. A moan rushed free. "God! Dagan, we're in a church."

"Outside," he corrected against her flesh and deliberately hooked one of her thighs over his shoulder. With teeth, tongue, and lips, he sucked and nibbled, and she whimpered. He appeared determined to make her lose her mind. She'd had no idea her teasing would take such a sensual turn. Desire coalesced, her every sense focused on one part of her body. Her fingers tightened in his hair. Shae no longer cared that they were in the open as he tormented her with lazy licks. "Dagan," she moaned, she was so close.

A sharp tug on her clit and she cried out, her orgasm

hauling her up as she broke apart. Birds roosting on the small shrubs nearby took flight in a rustle of wings. Arms steadied her.

Breathing hard, she came back to her senses and found him watching her with an emotion she couldn't decipher, one that made her heart race. He straightened her clothes and rose. "Tease me that way again, Shae-cat, and you pay."

She wanted to glare at him. Instead, she panted. "I can't believe you did that against a church building."

A dark eyebrow arched. "And you're complaining because?"

"Anyone could have seen us."

"But the danger made you hot, admit it." His tone lowered. "I love mouth-fucking you, but I really wished my cock had been inside you when you came—"

"Oh, God." She slapped a hand over his mouth, halting the sinfully erotic words, so sure her face must be brighter than her hair. But deep down, she wished the same. "Stop that."

He kissed her palm, then lowered it. "Why? I find I like my mouth on you, so fair warning, my sweet cat, I'll continue to do so whenever I can—wherever I want. Ready?"

"My legs feel like jelly. I don't think I can walk," she grumbled, fighting to focus on why they'd come here and not on tackling him to the ground for more sexy fun. "My underwear?"

A hint of a smile, he handed it over. "Okay, wait here while I do a recon of the area."

Shae pulled on her underwear and slumped against the wall, her breath choppy, and her legs still wobbly from the unexpected sensual encounter—and in broad daylight, too.

Dagan slipped on his shades and stepped out from the building's cool shadows. The weak, noonday sun gleamed off his blue-black hair as he strode across to the parking lot. With a wave of his hand over his loose tresses, like several invisible fingers working at once, the strands parted and wove into numerous warrior braids. He glanced about the place, appearing to study the air around them.

Her legs functioning once more, Shae wandered over. "What are you doing?"

"I'm trying to find a tear. It's the only way all those demons appeared so suddenly last night when only four followed us."

"What tear?"

"It forms in the mystical veils that separate the realms, and it keeps this world safe from supernatural evil." He frowned, his attention back on the gravelly surface. He hunkered down and put his open palm on the dirt-packed ground. "If there's a crack in the veils, they'll use it to enter this world, and we can't allow that to happen."

Warily, Shae looked about her then crouched beside him. "Is there one?"

"No. They must have accessed a portal." His moving hand stilled. "I feel the lingering vibration...the entryway was through here."

"But the other Guardian, Race, he would have killed them all, right? I mean, those flames last night were pretty scary."

"Yeah, he would have taken them out..."

Still, her stomach knotted at the hard set of his jaw as he glanced in the direction of the village. "What's wrong? Oh, no, do you think there could be more of them still lurking about?"

His gaze came back to hers. Softened. "I won't let anything happen to you." He helped her to her feet. "I'm sorry, Shae-cat, but a rain check on the café? I need to make sure none of them are around."

Blowing out a rough breath, she nodded. Her cell rang. She retrieved the device from her jacket pocket and answered.

"Shae?" Harvey's harried tone cut through her worry. "I found out something I think you should know. It's about your mother—"

"What is it?"

"I was in a club last night and overheard a demon bragging to a few of his pals about something big going down soon, then I heard the name Jenna mentioned. I know it's your mom's—"

"What did they say," she demanded, feeling as if someone had sucker-punched her.

"Asshole wouldn't say anything when I pushed for more. But it sounded like they knew where she is."

Her fingers clenched around her cell in frustration. "Where can we find this demon?"

"He usually hangs around at Club Anarchy. I'll keep pushing, see if I can get more information from him."

"I'm coming back. I want to talk to him." She ended the call before he could protest and lifted her determined gaze to Dagan's shaded one. "I have to do this. I've looked for her for so long. If there's a chance it might be her and they know where she is—" She bit her lip, unable to stop the tremble or the fear seeping through her.

"Shae…" He pushed his sunglasses to his brow and pinched the bridge of his nose. "I'd ask you to let me handle this—"

"Dagan—"

"But since I know you won't," he cut her off, "we'll do it together—unless I deem it too dangerous." He squinted in the sunlight, but his features were hard. Forbidding. "And you aren't doing anything on your own with that Fallen after you. I need your word on this."

She sighed. "Fine."

"C'mon, let's head back. Besides, I don't think it matters much now which place we're at since they know you're here. I still can't figure out how the hell the bastard tracked you here so fast."

Shae knew whom Dagan meant. Aza.

Chapter 18

They stepped through the portal onto the Guardians' island on Manhasset Bay, leaving behind the Romanian sunshine. Dusk and a chill enclosed them, night insects hummed in disharmony. The castle was ablaze with lights as if in welcome. Despite the warm feeling it gave her, her stomach remained in a knot after Harvey's call.

"Remember, you can't go back to the penthouse, Shae, not until we know what's going on," Dagan said as they headed toward the castle.

Like she wanted to bump into Aza. A few dates, and now the delusional Fallen believed she was his mate. *God.* She rubbed her cheek. Could this day get any worse?

"Dagan, wait. I have to call Uncle Lem, let him know I'm okay. What do I say about why I'm not at home yet?"

His brow furrowed. "Text him that you're delayed because of work, it should give us a few days leeway. We'll go see him together, then you can tell him about us."

"He'll freak out."

"Then I'll just have to make sure he doesn't."

Shae stopped in the shrub-lined pathway and shot off a text to Lem, praying that Harvey had found something they could use to locate the woman who might be her mother. If the lead didn't pan out, then it meant her mom did hate her and had simply left. Much as it pained her, Shae preferred the latter. She didn't want some evil demon holding her mother captive…hurting her—*Christ!* Bile burned her throat at the thought.

Dagan stroked her cheek with his knuckles. "It's going to be okay."

She looked into those bright eyes—so calm and steady—inhaled a deep breath, and nodded.

As they neared a terrace with a wrought-iron table and chairs, he put his hand on her waist and ushered her through the open French doors and into an enormous rec room. A flat-screen TV took up space on one side with leather recliners facing it. Adjacent to it stood arcade games and a foosball table.

The blue-haired warrior, Aethan, looked up from the pool table, so did the one with the cropped black hair. Blaéz. He smirked. "And another one bites the dust."

Snorting, Dagan crossed to the inner door then asked, "Is there a meeting this evening?"

"Yeah," Aethan answered.

"Right. I'll see you there, then."

The door shut behind them. Dagan led her down the softly lit passageway lined sporadically with paintings by old masters, along with rather authentic body armors from medieval times that sported dents and slashes. "I'll show you to our quarters, then we can get an update from Hedori."

"Hedori?" She frowned. "Shouldn't we be talking to Harvey?"

Dagan didn't answer as a tall, dark figure stepped out of the kitchen, chugging down a soda.

"Hey, Nik," she called out, happy to see a familiar face. "When did you get here?"

His gaze shifted to Dagan then back to her. "Moments before you two did. You okay?"

She smiled. "I am."

Dagan remained silent, and Nik cut him an amused smirk that did little to warm the coldness in his eyes. "And the other?" he asked.

Her smile dimmed. There was still one treacherous ravine to cross. With Dagan as unbending as a steel arrow, she had no idea how to get him to change his mind about feeding from her.

Ignoring Nik, Dagan tightened his grip on her hand and headed for the grand staircase in the front. Shae had to hurry to keep up. "He cares about you, you know that, right?"

"Yeah, it's what saved his neck from my sword with what he let you do."

Sighing, she let it go for now.

As they took the stairs up, the blond warrior who looked like the heavens had been having a seriously good day when he was created loped down. He slowed. Dagan didn't even glance his way.

Shae had no idea what was going on between them. Still, she couldn't ignore him. "Hello."

Sexy, masculine dimples appeared briefly, even though the warrior's smile didn't reach his toffee-brown eyes. "Shae." And then he was gone.

A tic pulsed hard on Dagan's jaw as they headed for

the third floor. He pointed across the landing and said something about the other wing belonging to Aethan and Echo. She barely heard him, her mind on the obvious friction between the two men. "You and Týr don't talk?"

"It's not important."

"I think it is." She eyed his rigid expression thoughtfully. "I once asked you about who you consider a friend, and even though you said Nik, I always thought you meant to say another name. It was him—it was Týr, wasn't it?"

He finally looked at her. Those beautiful, inhuman eyes were haunted and filled with desolation. "He was my sister's protector. He failed her."

"What?" Shae halted in front of an intricately carved, wooden door. It was the last thing she'd expected to hear. "How—why?"

"It doesn't matter how or why. We have things to do."

"Tell me." She stepped in front of him when he would have opened the door.

His expression tightened. "Inara was not yet eighteen and far too young when she became the Goddess of Life—her safety had to be absolute…" He told her what had happened the last day in the Sumerian temple—about Lucifer's attack. "Týr was her guard that day. And I trusted him."

Shae didn't know what to say, but the anger behind his flat words troubled her. More, she'd seen the shadow of torment in Týr's eyes, too. "Did you speak to him? Find out what happened?"

Silence. It wrapped around her like barbed wire.

He opened the door into a massive bedroom and stood aside. "That's not important right now. You are."

Knowing it was a painful subject for him, she didn't push. She stepped past him, and her eyes widened. Gorgeous, vaulted ceilings rose high above her, and two doors flanked a massive fireplace accented by a beautiful, earth-toned Aubusson carpet. Above the mantel, several old-looking swords were mounted.

"Oh, how lovely." She wandered to the wall of windows with undrawn, champagne-colored drapes and retracted blinds and looked out into rolling gardens as dusk encroached.

Her worried mind slipped back to her mother. She pivoted to him. "What did you mean when you said we needed to speak to Hedori? What does he have to do with my mom?"

"About that..." He shut the door behind him. "Hedori's been checking things out for me while we were in Romania. We don't believe your mother ran off."

Unease prickled her skin as he made his way to her. "What do you mean?"

"The last time we were at the penthouse, Hedori picked up on anguish and despair. Not yours, but definitely female. It didn't connect with a woman who'd want to take off and live her own life. Now, with your demon friend's news, it increases my suspicions."

Anger swelled. "We were in Romania for several days, and you didn't say a word?"

"You're too emotional when it comes to your parents. You'd have dashed back to New York and into danger the moment you knew. And with your growing power, you'd have every evil thing out there after you."

Even though he was right, betrayal still cut deep. "You should have told me, should have given me a choice, not made it for me. For so long, I thought…" Tears and frustration formed a hard knot in her throat. "I thought she took off because she couldn't stand to look at me, that she hated me for what I'd done, for hurting her when my laptop exploded. And you kept quiet about something so important?"

"I couldn't take a chance."

"You didn't trust me!"

"And you just proved my point when your friend called."

God! She inhaled a shaky breath and pivoted to the window. Getting upset wasn't helping. Maybe he had a point, but she was used to doing things on her own. She was all her mother had left after her father died.

"Shae." He came up behind her, his hands settling on her waist. "I only have your best interests at heart."

"How can I believe you when you keep things from me?" She swiped the perspiration beading on her brow.

"You are my mate. And human. I'll do whatever it takes to keep you safe, even if I have to bear the brunt of your anger."

The heat inside her hiking, she broke away, opened the door, and stepped onto a small balcony overlooking the trimmed lawn at the back of the castle. The cold night air swept over her, cooling her damp face. She inhaled deeply, making sure her psychic shields were locked in place, then got out a dextrose from her pocket and chewed it.

Dagan stepped up behind her. "All my life, I've failed the people who mattered most to me, those whom I'm supposed to protect. I will not lose you, too."

At the raw pain in his voice, she pivoted. She had a feeling he wasn't only talking about his sister. "Who?"

The grief on his chiseled features morphed into stone. "Enki, my sire, was a whoring son of a bitch despite being soul-joined to my mother. After one of his many indiscretions, he was killed—"

"Wait, I thought once soul-joined, you never strayed?"

"You usually don't." He stared into the night as if lost in the past. "Finding one's bonded mate is rare among the gods, and treasured. Many want it, very few find it. *He* hated the Fates tying him to one female and was determined to do as he pleased. Being the progeny of the ruling god An, no one dared stop him. Even in death, he had the last laugh, sealing my mother's fate."

"What do you mean?"

A vein throbbed on Dagan's brow. "Once soul-joined, if one mate dies, so does the other. Before she succumbed, she begged me to keep Inara safe. And I failed her. I godsdamn failed them both!" He slammed his palms on the metal balustrade, and the thing shuddered.

"Dagan!" Shae grabbed his arm.

He pivoted. "It's why I won't let harm come to you. You are my mate, Shae. Maybe I should have told you about my suspicions regarding your mother, but I didn't want to worry you or get your hopes up if I was wrong. I made you two promises. I'll find Jenna, and the one who wielded that dagger."

A thought struck her then. "Wait. You can see a person's thoughts when you touch an item of theirs, right? If I gave you something of Mom's, would you know why she left?"

"Depends on what she touched last. You have anything here?"

Her heart slid to her feet in disappointment. "No, but

at the penthouse…"

He shook his head. "We can't draw undue attention to ourselves, not with a Fallen having access to your kin's place and possibly waiting for you." He pressed his lips to her brow. "We'll find another way. Come. Let's go down and see if Hedori found out anything else."

***

Shae sat at the giant oak dining table in the kitchen, her anxiety growing while Hedori reiterated all that Dagan had revealed. She forced herself to eat one of the two sandwiches he'd made for her.

The last bite sticking in her throat, she pushed her plate away and picked up her cell from the table. "I have to call Harvey."

Dagan nodded and leaned a shoulder on the jamb of the French doors leading out to the small, herb-scented terrace.

Harvey answered after a few seconds. "Hey, Shae."

"Any news on my mom?" She put her cell on speaker and set it on the table.

"No, nothing yet. But the demon I told you about goes by Luka. He's as tight-lipped as a closed porthole with his cronies around. I tried following him a short while ago, but the bastard took me on a wild goose chase. He was highly amused when he cornered me, and I had to freakin' pretend I had an itch for him." His surly tone made her smile. "Said I ruined his fun. The butthead was trailing after some human girl he had the hots for—"

"Wait—" Hedori stepped closer to the phone. "This Luka, is he a little on the thin side? Dark hair, average height, with an eight-point star tattoo on the side of his neck that goes up to his jaw?"

At the silence coming down the line, Shae hastily said, "Sorry, Harvey, I should have told you, the Guardian, Dagan, and Hedori are here." She'd tell her friend the truth about her and Dagan later. "They're helping me with this, too."

"Okay," Harvey muttered. "Yeah, it's the same asshole."

Hedori nodded at Dagan. "I trailed him to the Bronx last night, but then he did a turnabout and vanished. Probably sensed he was being followed."

A light, ocean-scented breeze with a hint of amber swept through the kitchen from the open French doors. Frowning, Shae looked up as Michael took form on the night-darkened terrace and strode into the kitchen, his shaded gaze sweeping over them.

"I'm assuming there's been a change in your situation and you're not here for the briefing before patrol?" he drawled at Dagan.

"As if there were any doubt," he countered.

"Harv, I'll call you back." Shae hurriedly ended the call. She had no idea what they were talking about, but she had the distinct impression that Michael was amused.

He pushed his shades to his brow, revealing eyes like shattered blue gems. Shae gaped. The silvery light seeping out of his cracked irises gave him an otherworldly appearance. No wonder he wore dark shades all the time.

A moment of surrealism hit her square in the face. Hell, she was in the presence of a being most humans thought a myth—*the* leader of all the archangels. Her gaze skipped back to her own immortal.

Dagan lifted a brow in question. She shook her head and slid her cell into her jacket pocket.

The kitchen door opened, and Týr and Aethan entered.

"Nik and Blaéz took off to check out a disturbance in the Bowery," Týr said, dropping onto a chair at the end of the long table. Aethan took the one opposite him.

Michael nodded. Then Dagan filled them in. "We may have a lead on Shae's mother. If it pans out, then the demons have her."

Unable to sit still, Shae jerked to her feet and paced the short side of the table. "Why would they take her? She's one of the gentlest people I know."

"We'll find her, Shae—" Dagan broke off, tiny vertical lines creasing between his eyebrows. "Damn, I should have asked you this. Is your mother psychic?"

She slowed to a halt. "Yes. She has flashes of precognition, and she senses Others like I do."

At the sudden stillness in the room, she glanced at the silent men. Her gaze darted back to Dagan. "What? What aren't you telling me?"

"It's about those murdered men I first asked you about." He explained about the psychic killer he'd been tracking for several months who'd left a trail of Fallen and human bodies. "Whoever's killing them, is doing it by turning their insides to liquid. We thought at first a demon or Fallen could be using *you* to do that, but your powers aren't like those of the killer."

"You thought *I* was the killer?" she whispered, feeling as if he'd slapped her.

"Shae—"

"No." Then shook her head. "It doesn't matter—"

"It does to me." He dropped his hand, his irises flaring in frustration. "Nothing like this has ever occurred before. Fallens don't possess those kinds of powers after they fall, but the rising psionics would."

Georgia Lyn Hunter

She understood their caution. Heck, she was aware she could destroy them, too, with her new ability, and she *had* killed. But illogical as it might be, the fact that he'd thought, even for a second, that she could deliberately harm anyone…it hurt her. "My mother is what matters. I have to find her."

"I'm going to meet Shae's demon friend," Dagan told the others, his tone flat. "And get a location on this Luka."

"He's not going to say a word to you," she countered.

His hard gaze met hers—yeah, he was still upset. "I have my ways."

"Yes, bloodshed always solves everything. Dagan, he dies, we have nothing. But I know a sure way to find out where she is."

He folded his arms over his chest. Waited.

That stance didn't bode well at all. It didn't deter her, though. Ignoring the stares of the silent warriors—damn, they'd most likely be of the same mind as Dagan—she said, "I'll be bait."

"Absolutely not!"

At his unequivocal veto, she pressed on. "How can you say no? It makes perfect sense."

"I won't heedlessly put you in danger, even if you can't see straight in this regard," he bit out. "And especially not with that Fallen after you."

"Dammit, Dagan—"

"I don't think they'll readily spill their secrets," Hedori said quietly, glancing between her and Dagan. "At least not without some incentive."

"No, they won't," she agreed. "Not to you guys, anyway. But to a woman they wanted to impress or hook up with? Why not?"

"It's not happening!" Dagan's eyes burned with suppressed fury. "You aren't placing yourself in danger."

She notched up her chin. "You know it's the best way."

"Hold on a sec…" Michael slowly rubbed his chin. "Perhaps another female."

"Ely," Aethan added, leaning back in his chair. "We should call her in for this meeting."

Shae had no clue who this Ely was, but she detested the idea. For months, she'd been in several dangerous places, underground clubs, following leads on her mother. Now, when she was so close, Dagan would deny her this?

"No, Ely won't work," Týr said, tipping his chair back on its two back legs. "Those demons will know she's immortal—and a Guardian to boot since she already took her pledge. They'll sense a trap, and if they do have Shae's mother, well, they could disappear with her for a really long time."

Much as elation coursed through her, dread followed sharply on its heels. She glanced at Dagan, her biggest obstacle, and held his gaze. "That leaves only me."

The twitch was back in his jaw. "We might be going into a place that could just be a cover-up and drop us straight into Hell."

Did he enjoy scaring her? But at the thought of her mother being held in such a place, she straightened her backbone and met her mate's frustrated gaze dead-on. "Dagan, I've done this enough times while searching for my mother, playing bait. Besides, you know if trouble comes, I *can* take care of myself."

He shoved away from the door crossed the short distance to her, hand fisted as if trying to keep from dragging her off and locking her up. He slowed. Expression flat, eyes hardening. "On one condition only."

He agreed? Shocked, she nodded. "Anything."

"When we get the information we need, you will remain behind and let me handle the rest."

Remain behind? Ugh, she didn't care for his terms one bit, but he'd agreed, and that was all that mattered. She'd find a way around his codicil when the time came.

"Call the demon back and arrange this for tomorrow night," he said.

She nodded. Much as she wanted to march out there now, she didn't want to risk antagonizing him further and have him change his mind. Besides, knowing Dagan, he'd probably want to stake out everything first.

As Shae left the kitchen, the other warriors rose. Týr's voice drifted to her. "Ely's ready for her duties, Arc. She fights with more power and skill than we expected. Hell, she dropped me on my ass a couple of times. Don't you think she's ready to go out on patrol with us?"

"She's still ruled by emotions. And that can be deadly for her—"

The door shut on the rest of Michael's response. She stood there for a second, inhaling deeply. The door opened again.

"Shae?"

She turned to find Dagan behind her. The words burst out, "Did you honestly think I was the psychic killer?"

"Not even for a minute, but it's my job to check out everything, no matter what." He tucked a strand of hair behind her ear. And the churning inside her eased. "I'm going out on patrol. I'll see you in the morning. You need me for anything, I don't care how small, even if your abilities take hold, call me."

At his grim demeanor, she sighed. "You're still upset that I want to do this?"

"How can I not be? Shae, you are my mate, I just found you. Now, you're planning to go out there, alone—"

"I'll be fine." She caressed his chest, trying to win him over. "Besides, I'll have my big, bad warrior close."

His expression didn't change. "I'll be invisible *and* with you."

Invisible? Well, she didn't know about that ability.

Not liking this distance between them and needing the comfort of his touch, she grasped a handful of his shirt and pulled him down—God, she loved that he was taller than her—and put her lips on his. A groan escaped him, he deepened the kiss. His tongue licked inside her mouth, his arm banding around her waist, every inch of his hard, delicious body aligned with hers. The tips of his fangs grazed her lips—a perilous kiss—one she relished. Desire coiled low in her stomach. Moaning, she ran her tongue over his *extended* incisors.

He jerked back as if burned.

"Dagan?"

Breathing hard, lips tight, he paced a few feet away from her. Her heart sank, realizing she hadn't imagined it. "You made love to me last night, you kissed me, but not in the way you first did outside the club in Romania," she whispered. "Even outside the church today."

He scrubbed a hand over his shadowed jaw and pivoted to her. His gaze burned fiercely, his fangs still visible, revealing just how close to the edge he was. "Yes, I was careful with you. I'm always careful with you. You know this."

Right. Struggling to stop the widening pit inside her, she countered, "Then I guess I'll have to expect less than I thought I'd get in a committed relationship."

He growled. "I give you everything—"

"But one!" she cried. "Even though Nik promised he'd be close to stop you if things went wrong, you refused. But then you have *her*, right? You don't really need me."

He stiffened. "That's a low blow, Shae, and you know it. I have to go. We'll talk when I get back."

Emptiness seeped through her. She cast her gaze down the long corridor, knowing he wouldn't change his mind. "Do you know where Echo is?"

"Library. I'll show you—"

"I'll find it." She walked away, feeling as if she were plummeting into an abyss with nothing to break her fall.

After several minutes of wallowing, she slowed to a halt and dashed the blurriness from her eyes. She wasn't going to let this pull her down, finding her mother was all that mattered.

Shae looked around at the elegant but unfamiliar corridor with abstract paintings on the walls. Okay, she was lost. Besides, if Echo were this all-powerful Healer, then she'd pick up on Shae's distress.

How could she explain her messed-up life? Explain she was mated to a man she was half in love with, but she wasn't what he needed. No, she couldn't bear anyone's pity. She pivoted to head back the way she'd come when laughter reached her.

Feminine laughter.

Like a hypnotic pull, it lured her. She pushed open a huge, black door and stopped short, just inside the entrance of what appeared to be an enormous, two-level library with countless towering bookshelves and a stunning ceiling mural.

Four women were in the seating area, each going through a magazine. Two reclined on the couch in front of the huge, lit fireplace, and one lounged in an armchair. Echo sat on the floor near the coffee table that held a tray with an assortment of cookies and cake, and a few more magazines.

"Darci, everything in here looks so wonderful," the redhead sporting a headful of skinny braids, a glimmer of gold flickering through her hair murmured. "Did you decide on the flowers and cake yet? What about a venue?"

The curvy brunette sighed and pushed back her curly bangs. "No. Blaéz gave me two weeks to get everything organized. *Two*! Now, all I see is a huge number two, and no time to pull off anything."

"Don't worry," Echo said, flipping a page, "we'll help any way we can—" She glanced up and her gaze flickered toward the doorway. "You're back!" Her smile widened, and she jumped up.

All eyes turned to Shae. Echo waved excitedly, beckoning her inside. "Come. Meet the rest of the gang. You guys, this is Shae Ion. She could be like me, but I can't read her aura yet, so we wait…"

Shae slowly crossed to them, pulling her shields tighter around her, not wanting to reveal even an inch of her despair to anyone.

"Shae, that's Darci." Echo pointed to the tall, curvy

brunette with the pale caramel skin and long, curly, honey-brown hair seated on the couch. Her eyes reminded Shae of sunflowers. "She's mated to Blaéz. They're getting married soon."

Now the bridal magazines made sense. "That's wonderful. Congratulations."

"Thank you." Darci smiled.

"And that's Elytani, another Guardian." Echo pointed to the slender, six-foot, blonde goddess next to Darci—because, really, there was no other way to describe just how beautiful she was with her lightly tan skin and pale, moonlit hair, which she'd pulled back in a high ponytail.

"A Guardian?" Right. Aethan had mentioned her.

Echo laughed. "Yup. We lowly humans aren't strong enough."

Elytani rolled her bright, copper-hued eyes and snorted. "Yes. It's why I'm still stuck at the castle and not out on the streets yet. Shae, lovely to meet you."

"Oh, stop complaining, you know the big guy wants you safe." The redhead shot Shae a grin. "I'm Kira, by the way." She jumped off the armchair, her movements making the black beads on the ends of her multiple braids jangle. Her hazel eyes sparkling in delight, she grabbed a plate piled high with mouthwatering, chocolate-coated biscuits off the coffee table. "Have a cookie. And welcome to this dangerous world."

Feeling a little overwhelmed, Shae selected one, aware she hadn't eaten anything for a while and took a bite. She didn't understand Echo's sympathetic look. She chewed and almost choked at the dry, cardboardy taste that not even the chocolate could save.

"Sorry," Echo mouthed, handing her a soda. Shae quickly popped the Fanta and gulped some, washing away the awful taste.

"It's good, huh?" Kira asked, setting the plate down and plopped back on the couch. "I made them—it's a new recipe."

"Er, yes, love the chocolaty taste," she croaked, consuming more soda.

"Did you find whom you were looking for?" Elytani asked softly, dragging Shae's attention back to her.

She frowned. "What?"

"I'm sorry, I didn't mean to eavesdrop, but I heard you when I walked past the kitchen earlier."

And that brought her right back to the friction between her and Dagan. The knot in her stomach tightened further. She briefly told the women about her missing mother and the plans for tomorrow night.

"And they agreed you can be bait?" Echo asked, her bi-colored eyes bright with shock.

Shae grimaced. "I didn't give them much choice."

"Had you been mated to one of them…nope, you wouldn't be doing it because you'd be locked up for sure by now," Kira drawled.

"I second that." Echo grimaced.

Before Shae could tell them the truth about her and Dagan, Darci asked, "Have you decided on what to wear?"

"From what I've seen in nightclubs, lots of skin is best," she said dryly, thankful Dagan had sent her things over with Angelus.

The girls laughed.

"Come on, let's go help you look for something sexy." Kira leaped up. The others glided to their feet and ushered her out. Farther down the corridor, they stopped near a wood-paneled door. Kira stabbed the button to summon the elevator.

Her fingers clenching, Shae eyed the door as it slid open. "Er, do you mind if we take the stairs? Enclosed spaces and I don't go so well together."

"No problem." Darci gestured to the way they'd come. "We'll take the back stairs. It's closer."

Echo led the way up the narrow, spiraling staircase, and stepped onto the first level, probably for the guest room Shae'd first used. "Not here," she said. "Actually, I'm on the third floor."

All eyes turned to her, frowns followed.

"But that's where my and Aethan's quarters are," Echo said, then slowly added, "and Dagan's."

Heat flooding her face, Shae nodded. "I know."

"Say what now?" Kira gasped, her mouth hanging open. "You and the ultimate hardass. Wow! He never speaks to any of us."

Shae didn't say anything. She, more than anyone, now understood why.

"That's wonderful," Echo said. "I had wondered when I first saw you two together—the tension and sparks flying. I'm so happy for you."

"And that man's hair," Kira continued, seeming to enjoy herself, "does it touch his ass when loose?"

Shae smiled as they started up the stairs again. "It does."

"I can't believe he's actually letting you do this—be bait," Elytani, the voice of reason said. "I know my kind. When they find their mates, they can be a tad protective—"

"*Tad*? You're kidding, right?" Darci laughed as they spilled out of the narrow staircase into the softly lit landing on the third floor. "But you're excused since you just got back from another realm and training and have no idea how bullheaded they can be about keeping us *safe*. When you find your mate, you'll see. There'll be constant complaints about you going out and putting yourself in danger, even if it's just shopping. So, enjoy this freedom while you can."

Though Ely smiled, Shae caught a hint of wistfulness in her gaze. It disappeared the next second. "I don't plan on being mated to anyone. And, before you ask," she told Kira, "no, I'll not even consider any of the unmated Guardians, too much intractability for my liking. But, in the unlikely event I do think of taking a mate, not only will he have to accept my job, it will also have to be a soul-joining—like you all have. I won't settle for less."

"Yes, that is the best type," Echo and Darci agreed in unison, sharing a smile.

Shae inhaled a shaky breath. She and Dagan might be soul-joined, but it hurt more, knowing she could never have the intimacy these women obviously enjoyed. There would always be that one barrier between her and him.

"When are you going out on patrol?" Echo glanced at the blonde as they traipsed the wide corridor.

Elytani sighed. "Michael said two months in-house training with the Guardians first. I've been here for almost that length of time, so hopefully soon."

"Maybe we can train when you have time?" Shae asked her.

Surprised brightened her coppery eyes. "You fight?"

"I'm a lot stronger than I look. My best friend is a demon, he helps me train."

"That's wonderful," Echo chipped in. "Now, I have another sparring partner. I adore Hedori, but I like having different people to train with." Then she scowled. "Aethan is still hanging back in fear he'll hurt me."

Feeling a lot more at ease now, Shae glanced at Darci.

"Oh, no, don't look at me," she protested. "I'll do the treadmill if need be, but you guys are quite welcome to slice and dice each other."

"I'm right there with ya." Kira slung an arm through Darci's. "All that bloodshed—ack, not for me."

As their friendly banter and laughter continued, Shae entered her and Dagan's quarters, her mind slipping back to him, her heart heavy at the conflict between them.

Chapter 19

Unable to sleep, Shae twisted beneath the duvet and stared through the undraped windows into the dark night. Her thoughts were in chaos, the hollowness in her tummy deepening.

The door to the bedroom opened. Footsteps sounded. Dagan entered the dressing room, the lights from the bathroom silhouetting him. Then he just stood there, head lowered, hands on his hips. His shoulders heaved as if in weariness. He unbuttoned and shrugged off his shirt, his muscles rippling with his movements. At the sight of the bloody dressing on his side, she jerked upright, worry surging.

Dagan yanked off the gauze from his wound with a vicious tug and stalked into the bathroom. The shower came on in a harsh rustle.

Helplessness sweeping through her, Shae slumped back on her pillow. *Christ*. She squeezed her eyes tightly. How were they going to fix this? He needed blood. And she couldn't deny him that.

Feeling as if her stomach would escape her, she

Georgia Lyn Hunter

buried her face in her pillow…

The bed covers lifted. His cool, very naked body slid alongside her t-shirt-covered one.

"Shae?" He swiped her hair aside and pressed his lips to her nape. Her breath hitched. "I know you're not asleep." A heavy sigh barreled out of him. "I hate hurting you this way. I wish things could be different, but I am what I am."

"No, don't." She twisted to face him. "I'm sorry for what I said. I don't want you to be different, I just—"

"Shae—"

She put her fingers on his lips. "You're healing too slowly, I saw your dressing, Dagan. Animal blood can't give you what you need, and that leaves you vulnerable." This close to him, she could see the tense lines around his eyes and mouth. Not having a true feeding was taking a toll on him. Much as it hurt her, she couldn't force him. And he would never risk her. "You're probably right. I am human—"

"And mine. You give me all I need, my wildcat. Yes, my wounds will take longer to heal this way, but I just have to be careful."

She lowered her hand to his abs, and the muscles there tensed at her touch. Lightly, she traced the edges of the new dressing on his side. "The way you worry about me, I feel the same about you. You put yourself out in deadly situations daily. Maybe if…" God, it was so hard to say it. "If it was just the goddess' blood, I could accept you feeding from another…"

The hand caressing her hip stilled. He stared at her as if she'd said the sun was pink. Then he hauled her close and wrapped her in a bone-crushing hug. "I couldn't. You are all that is right in my life, and I won't dishonor you or defile my mating bond in any way. Animal blood is fine."

"But for how long?"

He shrugged. "Humans get hurt, heal, they move on. It's the same thing. I just have to give this wound a chance to mend and I'll be okay."

She shouldn't be relieved, but she was. He was hers.

"I checked this Luka out through my sources while on patrol," he said, distracting her, his tone hard. "He's a dangerous bastard with deprived needs. Women usually don't make it out alive once he has them."

"Then that's all the more reason to stop him."

Dagan glared up at the ceiling.

"You know I'm right." Shae pushed to her elbows and waited until those frustrated yellow eyes met hers. She kissed him.

Growling, he nipped her lower lip, his fingers tangling in her hair. Slow and decadently, he sucked the sting away. Amazing how he could bite her without breaking her skin…her thoughts scattered as he trailed sensual little kisses along her jaw before he pounced. Like a huge cat, he had her under him, his eyes dark and intense. "You are mine, Shae. *Mine.*"

His mouth covered hers. Her heart skipped at how tenderly he kissed her, and she realized he did give her his all when he made love to her. It was right there in his kiss. But, still, she longed to be the one who could fill his other need…

***

It was long past noon when they got up. While she had breakfast, Dagan left for a run on the estate. Now secluded in the turret TV room, she worked on the editorial for her Nightlife series while she waited for him.

The door opened. Dagan walked in with Hedori. His

gaze touched hers briefly. No smile, just that look he had for her alone. He said something about clearing out his workshop and turning it into a study/living room before disappearing into his workspace.

"Wait." Shae set her laptop aside, jumped up and followed them. "What about your sculpturing?"

"This is a castle, Shae. We have space."

"Yes, we do," Hedori agreed. "There's an unused storage room in the basement."

"Perfect." He strolled closer. "Don't worry, Shae-cat, I'm not one of those vamps who like dark, gloomy places." His lips twitching, he gave her a heated stare. "Besides you, I enjoy woodwork. It keeps me pleasantly occupied."

Warmth rushed to her face.

Amusement crinkled the corners of his eyes. "I want a place for us to relax and be away from everything. I'll help Hedori sort this out. It's better you work in the library for now."

"Okay." She grinned and then told him the news. "*National Geographic* wants the series I did on Nightlife."

"That's good... Damn." He rubbed a hand over his stubbled jaw. "I hate doing this when I see how excited you are about your work, but being my mate, it will be dangerous for you to continue. We have deadly enemies."

She chewed her lip and looked around the workroom covered in sawdust and wooden sculptures. Yes, she'd known that after her conversation with the other women. Mostly, her job was a way to move around the country while she looked for her mother.

"I know." A thought took hold. She smiled. "Since I can't be idle, I'll work for you and design a catalogue selling your sculptures online. It's sacrilege that you use them as firewood."

He stilled, but his eyes gleamed with an emotion that made her heart trip. In one stride, he crossed to her and pressed his lips to hers in a soft kiss. "We are meant to be."

***

Dagan parked the Ford deep in a dingy alley downtown, and Shae warily took in the gloomy surroundings. Nothing moved in the still night, except for up the street where a noisy crowd gathered near Club Anarchy.

He leaped from the vehicle and rounded the hood to her side. She swiped back her wavy bangs with cold fingers as he opened the door, and got briefly distracted by him. Leathers hugged his muscular thighs and a black Henley covered his wide chest. Despite the chilly weather, he hadn't bothered with a coat tonight.

"Stick to the plan," he repeated, grasping her waist and helping her down. But the intractable jut to his jaw spoke volumes. No, he wasn't happy about any of this. Still, even he couldn't argue with the logic of how fail-proof her plan was.

"I got this. Stop worrying." She patted his chest.

"Not worry when *you're* putting yourself in harm's way?"

"Dagan—" She sighed. "You know it's faster this way. Besides, what they don't know is that I'm no longer what I once was. If anything goes wrong, you'll be close and can kick their asses."

He gave her an unamused look. "Nice try, but you aren't leaving my sight, not even for a second. If you sense an inkling of danger, call me, use your telepathic link."

She rolled her eyes. "I can teleport, not telepath."

Yes, you can. He pulled off one of the several black bands from his wrist and tied his ropey hair into a ponytail. *Just think your message to me, like I'm doing now. Use your mind. When we soul-joined, it opened our mental pathway.*

At the faint sound of his voice in her head, her mouth dropped open. Well, *that* she didn't know. She nodded. *Okay.*

Laughter at the entrance to the busy club up the alley drew her attention. Her cell beeped with a message. She pulled her phone from her coat pocket. *He's here. I'll hang around in case you need me.*

"It's Harvey. Luka's here." Right. Time to get the show on the road. No use putting off the inevitable—the moment she'd been dreading since their arrival. "Let's get this done. You should make yourself invisible."

When he didn't move, she reminded him, "It's the only way you can be close enough to keep watch."

She unbuttoned her long coat, and his gaze lowered to the dipping neckline of her dress, revealing the curves of her breasts. A tic started on his jaw, but he remained silent. She shrugged off her outer garment, and as she turned to leave it in the truck, a furious snarl erupted behind her.

"No. Fucking. Way!"

She winced. Taking a deep breath, Shae pivoted, keeping her expression calm. "What?"

"Don't play the innocent game with me, Shae-cat, you won't win." His eyes narrowed dangerously. "Is that why you dressed *before* I came up to change for work? So I wouldn't see this…this underwear you call a dress?"

She grimaced. True. Still, she'd thought the mid-thigh-length, silky, black dress sexy. But seen through *his* eyes with its backless style dipping low to her hips and almost non-existent straps—yeah, it probably showed too much skin.

"You've seen me in short skirts before, how is this any different? Besides, men are visual creatures, so this slip dress is perfect."

"You are *my* mate! *Mine*. Only I get to see you this way!"

At the utter possessiveness rolling off him, Kira's comment from last night ricocheted in Shae's head, *The hardass is gonna go crazy seeing you like this.*

Before he could flash her back to the castle to change—and he was quite capable of doing so—she hastily added, "Dagan, I have to draw his attention. Fast. This is the only way…unless you want me to throw myself at him?"

Those sun-bright eyes scalded her.

Blowing out an unsteady breath, she stepped around him, out from the shadows, and headed toward Club Anarchy. The heels of her blood-red stilettos clicked on the asphalt, and the slightly flared hemline of her dress fluttered around her thighs. She smoothed her cold, damp hands down her hips when the warm, woodsy smell of sandalwood with a hint of cherry tobacco surrounded her. And she sighed in relief.

In his invisible form, his presence felt like a soft caress against her skin, as if he'd put his arm around her shoulder. He probably had.

Shae shivered, not because of the chill in the air, but because a tingle of desire flowed through her. Yes, he could do that with simply a touch, a look, and now, his concealed presence.

Aware that Dagan would get her inside the club easily, she glided past the line of people waiting on the sidewalk, her mind back on the plan. She'd called Harvey to lay out the strategy that morning. He hadn't been happy either, but had agreed to the plan as long as she had backup in place.

These weren't the local demons she was going up against, but ones from the Dark Realm. So having heavy Guardian artillery close by was good.

As she approached the busy entrance, the bouncer gave her the once-over, his gaze lingering on her chest. Then he started to choke, coughing violently, gasping for breath. Red in the face, the bouncer waved her inside.

Darn it, Dagan, she sighed through their mind-link.

Then it's best they keep their eyes and thoughts to themselves, his cool tone flickered through her mind. *Or they'll lose far more than limbs.*

Really? You'll give us away with that possessive display.

At his silence, she rolled her eyes and pushed open the heavy door into the club. Strobe lights whizzed around, almost blinding her. Heavy Goth rock ricocheted off the walls as she headed down the stairs, past the crowded dance floor, and made for the bar.

Stick to the plan, Dagan reminded her again. *Don't question him about your mother, just get him outside.*

I know.

His presence faded, leaving her a little wary. A survey of the packed counter and she found the demon who matched Harvey's description; tall, olive skin, built like a swimmer. He'd pulled his dark brown hair into a ponytail, revealing the telltale star tattoo on his neck that rose to his jaw. He appeared young, harmless, like some college boy. But she knew better.

With a sway of her hips, Shae headed for the bar. As she neared Luka, a guy a few seats down from him got up and left. Luka glanced her way.

Amazing how fast her psychic vibe drew those of his ilk despite so many good-looking girls around. None seemed to care about her scarred face, unlike human men.

She claimed the seat and ordered her margarita, keeping Luka in her peripheral view. He spoke to two other demons.

As the bartender set her drink in front of her, a voice said from behind her. "That's on me."

The bartender nodded. A hint of the demon's power brushed against Shae's senses. The tiny hairs on her arms rose. He was testing the strength of her abilities. Thank God, she'd learned how to shield, but she let a little of her power stream out to keep him interested.

She cut him a cool look. "I can pay for my own drink, thanks."

And judging by his confident swagger, he had no idea that she knew who or what he was, but her refusal certainly piqued his interest. "Yes you can, however, this way I get to talk to a pretty girl."

Smooth. He probably had women falling over themselves when he worked the charm. She needed to get him outside, but she'd ruined that with playing hard to get—damn! It was just habit and wariness. If Dagan knew, he'd be pissed.

Get him out of the club, now! Dagan's terse telepathic message held a cold bite.

Crap. *Can't. Need a few more minutes.*

She drank more of her liquor. The guy seated next to her suddenly rose and left. Luka had to be using mind control. Before he tried that shit on her, thinking fast, she gulped down the rest of her drink. "Wow, needed that."

"Tough day?" he enquired politely as if he weren't an evil asshole who hurt women.

Shae scrunched her nose and said with a rueful smile, "The worst." Pretending to be tipsier than she actually was, she angled her head at him. "What's your name?"

A satisfied smile stretched his mouth. "I'm Luka." He clicked his fingers, nodded, and another margarita appeared. "And you are?"

She picked up the frosty glass and slowly licked the salty rim. "Shae."

"Ah, beauteous, just like you." Dark, lust-filled eyes barely lingered on her damaged cheek but stayed on her mouth for a bit before they roamed down her body, undressing her in their descent. "Want to talk about this bad day?"

Right, as if he were really interested.

He stroked a finger along her forearm resting on the counter. Her first instinct was to snatch her hand away. Instead, she leaned forward, giving him an eyeful of her cleavage. "There's this asshole at work who comes on to me every day, and he's here tonight."

"Good thing I'm here, then." His fingers drifted to her hair and down her shoulders, his power like sharp pinpricks against her skin, stronger now. His irises took on a creepy, reddish glow.

Hurriedly, Shae blocked him before he did his mumbo-jumbo on her. "Whew! I'm hot." She brushed the wavy strands away from her face.

His eyes narrowed, he didn't respond. In a flash, he cupped her neck with one hand and kissed her.

Shae froze. He swept his rough tongue over her lower lip before pulling back. Bile rushed up her throat in revulsion.

Fuuuck! *That* she didn't expect.

He smiled. And then she knew. Bastard! He'd been testing her, checking if her abilities had obstructed his mind control. Christ, she longed to scrub her mouth and smash her fist into his face.

"You wanna get out here?" he drawled.

She nodded, smiling happily. Gah!

"Come on, human," he murmured. Secure in the knowledge that her mind was his, he let his true nature free. Asshole.

Shae stumbled off the stool. He slung an arm around her shoulders and gave a slight incline of his head. "I have something you're really going to enjoy." He licked her ear. Her fists clenched. "My cock. Then I'll gift your blood to my two minions. See, I promised them payment for a job they did. And, little psychic, you're perfect."

That's what he thought.

Shae gritted back a retort. God knew how many other innocent women had fallen into their trap and died. But this bastard allegedly knew where her mother was. So she clamped her teeth down, bore his touch, and couldn't wait until they got outside.

He led her through the congested nightclub and down a dim passage. Moments later, she stepped into the cooler night and furtively cast her gaze around for Dagan but couldn't sense him. Except for his curt order earlier, there had been radio silence from his end. It didn't take a genius to figure out why.

In a fast trot, Luka steered her into a stinky backstreet where he cornered her against the wall.

"Come on, beauty, let me get a taste of you before I see what you have hidden beneath that dress."

"Wait, wait." She turned her head, avoiding his mouth. Thinking fast, she said, "Let's go to your place—"

"No, here." He slipped his hands to her thighs. Shit. About to summon her obsidian dagger, suddenly, Luka was hauled away from her and rammed into the wall.

"What the fuck? I said after I'm done with her!" Luka spat then cursed. "Dammit, not *you* fuckers."

Relief surged through her when she laid eyes on Dagan's tall form.

"What are you up to, demon?" he asked coolly as if he'd just stumbled into them. No sign whether he'd seen Luka touching her.

"Just having some fun."

"Right." Cold, yellow eyes flickered dispassionately to where she stood a few feet away. "You here of your own free will, *human*?"

What the—? Shae scowled, wanting to hit him at the tag. "Yes," she shot back.

A nerve jumped on his jaw.

"You heard her, now get lost," Luka drawled, brave once again.

In response, Dagan grabbed the demon by his shirtfront.

"What the hell?" Luka snapped. "Why are you all over me? I just wanted some action with this hot piece. I don't know why you're harassing me. I'm not breaking any laws."

"Would you give us some space, Shae?" He cut her a cool look. "I don't want to get blood on your little dress."

Little? Uh-oh. Uneasy, she stepped back. He was

pissed as hell.

"I haven't done anything," Luka protested, struggling to free himself from Dagan's grip.

"Haven't you now?" Dagan asked, tone dangerously pleasant. "We can do this the easy way. Or the hard… I'm really hoping you'll choose the latter. Tell me about the female, Jenna. Where is she?"

"I don't know what—" Luka's dark gaze flashed to Shae and glowed red in understanding. "You fucking whore—"

Dagan punched him in the face. Bones crunched. Blood flowed. "Never speak to my mate that way again."

Luka roared, clutching his nose. A wave of his hand, and his face healed. A flash of metal reflected in the moonlight. He leaped at Dagan, who didn't even attempt to evade the attack.

Nooo! Shae darted to him.

"Don't." He flung out his hand, stopping her, jaw tight as Luka slashed at him. She bounced against the invisible barrier that had sprung up between them.

Dagan trapped Luka with invisible restraints against the wall. The demon squirmed, scratching at his throat with one hand, trying to break free of the psychic hold, his skin taking on a red, leathery appearance, before morphing back to the frat boy. His eyes bulged from their sockets as if he were choking. He rasped, "You don't know whom you're dealing with."

"And you, it seems, want to learn the many ways I can make you scream without touching you."

The dagger in Luka's hand rose and pressed against his neck. Slowly, it started digging into his flesh. A raucous growl erupted as blood seeped from the hole.

"Where. Is. Jenna. Ion?"

"Fuck off."

The blade sank deeper. A cry rattled out of the demon as if his larynx were damaged.

"You don't talk, you'll kill yourself."

More blood spurted from his deepening wound. Perhaps finally realizing just how precarious his situation was and whom he was dealing with, Luka choked out, "Let me go, and I'll tell you where she is."

Dagan folded his arms and waited. Shae was aware that he could simply kill the demon and get his last memories off the blade he held, so why was he torturing him?

"She's in a warehouse in the Bronx. You won't get in, she's heavily guarded."

"Address?"

After some stuttering and gurgles, and with the blade pushing deeper, the demon gasped out the answer. And the dagger sliced him clean across the carotid. Blood gushed. He slumped to the ground. Seconds later, his body shimmered and crumpled into ash before vanishing. Not even a spot of blood remained. The blade on the ground melted into a lump of steel, and with a wave of his hand, Dagan flung it into a nearby dumpster.

Shae stood there, frozen to the spot. She knew he was lethal, but to see him kill so coldly and without any bodily contact shocked her. "Why?"

He cut her a flat look. A tick pulsed hard on his jaw. "He and the rest of those assholes have had your mother imprisoned for six months."

They did. God. She rubbed her cheek, unable to bear the thought. "Wait, there were two other demons with him."

"Both dead." At the chilly tone behind her, Shae

wheeled around. Hedori stood a foot back, his expression scarier than Dagan's icy one.

"I'll be back," Dagan told Hedori, grasping her hand. "I'll see Shae to the castle."

Uneasiness twisting her stomach, she shut her eyes and held on tight as he dematerialized them. They took form again at the castle portico. He ushered her into the brightly lit foyer and, without a word, turned to leave.

"Wait." She grasped his arm. His muscles tensed beneath her fingers. "I'm coming with you, I want to be there when you find her."

"Don't push me, Shae," he said in a dangerously low tone. "Don't make me do something we'll both regret."

"What? You'll lock me up in the basement again?"

"Are you really going to start an argument you won't win while your mother's held captive?" His bright eyes burned with suppressed anger. "The deal when I agreed to that asinine plan of yours was that once we got the address, you'd let me handle the rest—"

"Asinine?" she retorted. "We got a location, didn't we?"

"I could have gotten it regardless—and with less fuss. I only agreed so *you* wouldn't insist on going with me to find your mother."

"Damn you, Dagan," she bit out in frustration. Why had she thought she could change his mind? The man was like a damn rock.

Those cold eyes held hers. "I'm already damned, Shae. Don't you know that? And very easily since you are my mate. Your part's done. You will keep your promise and remain behind."

Then he vanished.

Chapter 20

Dagan took form in a derelict backstreet in the Bronx near a looming building. A dog barked in the distance, the sound cutting eerily through the far too quiet area. The brackish odor of the East River drifted to him, merging with the reek of piss and other nasty things stung his nose.

It took several moments before he managed to get his mind focused on the job.

"The building's guarded and warded," Hedori said, detaching from the shadows nearby while he remained hidden in gloom.

Still silent, Dagan scanned the warehouse situated near the river. Several figures roamed inside. Demons or humans, he wasn't sure—didn't care. They'd all pay, except he couldn't kill the human fuckers.

"But I can," Hedori muttered as if reading his thoughts. "I will end those responsible for this crime, human or not. I'm not bound by Guardian law."

Perfect.

To conserve his psychic energy since he'd used

plenty killing that asshole Luka, Dagan summoned an iron dagger. Besides, he was wired too hard and needed the fight. Letting his form blend with the shadows, he headed for the front entrance while Hedori quietly made his way to the back.

Dagan bypassed the stacks of decaying wooden crates leaned against the grimy wall. He came up behind the first demon guard, slit his throat, then rammed the blade into the other one's heart before a word had even left their mouths. As they crumbled to dust and vanished, Hedori reappeared, stopping at the front entrance. He immediately set about unscrambling the protection wards, then opened the door and glided inside like a shadow.

Dagan followed. Hedori flashed in a dark glimmer. A sword appeared in his hand, and he tackled the three humans, his movements swift. Deadly. Bodies fell with thuds. They lay still on the ground, blood seeping profusely from the wounds in their chests—and *fuuuck*! The decadent scent of blood crowded his senses, his incisors throbbed. Hunger rose. It took all his control not to tear into those still-warm bodies.

The other Guardians appeared at his side as if to witness his hideous nature. His teeth clenched. It was why he preferred patrolling alone.

A ball of flame shot past him, incinerating the bodies within seconds and eliminating the temptation. He knew exactly who it was. Smaller flickers of flames still licked over Týr's palm as his fingers fisted, shutting off the fire.

He cut Dagan a quick glance as if in understanding.

Jaw tight, Dagan looked away. Aethan and Blaéz nodded at him.

"Hedori filled us in," Aethan said then. "We've got

your back."

Shit. Of course they knew.

As they searched the massive chop-shop warehouse and its adjoining buildings that fronted as a garage, Dagan prowled between vehicles in various stages of stripping.

He had a bad feeling about this. It was why he hadn't wanted Shae involved in the rescue. His blood went into a slow boil when he recalled that fucking demon kissing her. Teeth clenched, he shut off the thought, or he'd lose his shit. Right here. And that wouldn't help anyone, so he focused his attention on the only thing important—saving her mother.

He inhaled deeply, separating the odors of metal, grease, and lube, and finally hit on one—a faint thread of sweet fruit with a hint of spice. A tingle brushed his psyche. Eyes narrowing, he trailed his palm over the length of the floor then stopped at the center, placing his hand on the grimy surface. "She was here. I feel her, but I can't make out her thoughts. Everything's too hazy…"

"The basement's empty," Týr said, coming up the stairs.

Frowning, Blaéz lowered opposite Dagan. Lines marred his brow, then his eyes did that eerie swirly thing when his precog kicked in. The others crowded around him. For several seconds, he remained silent. Then, "She's below, but not in a basement..."

No one said a word while they waited. It would be pointless since Blaéz wouldn't hear them. He blinked, coming back to himself.

"What do you mean she's below but not in the basement?" Aethan asked.

"He means the Dark Realm." Once more, Dagan

trailed his palm over the spot where he'd sensed Jenna's essence.

"I imagine this must be an entrance to a portal then." Blaéz rose to his feet. "A soft spot to traverse either way."

"So, what are we waiting for?" Týr drawled. "Life just got fucking interesting. Going back to the place we abhor."

Nik snorted. "Only you would see this as fun."

"Killing those damn bastards? You bet ya ass." Shooting Nik a nasty grin, Týr waved his hand. The air above the ground shimmered, and the gateway slid open in a hiss. A churning, gray smog rolled out through the dark portal. *What the—?*

A pale-skinned demon appeared, flashes of lightning shooting out of him, sending the Guardians flying back. One streak slammed Dagan in the chest, knocking him several feet away. His teeth ground down, impossible pain zipping through his body; so sure his lungs were bashed out of his ribcage. Fury igniting his adrenaline, he jumped the scourge and pounded him in the face. The demon stumbled back and didn't attack, his red-rimmed eyes staring blankly at Dagan. Only then did he become aware that Blaéz held the fucker immobile with his mind.

"Much as you want to hammer him into a pulp"—the Celt grimaced, rubbing his chest, his tee sporting a charred hole—"you're gonna need the motherfucker. Seems he was guarding the entryway into this world."

Whoever was behind Jenna's abduction would have his bases covered.

Dagan grabbed the scourge by his shirt and hauled him back toward the shimmering gateway, throwing over his shoulder, "You all should remain here. If things turn ugly—"

"I've been on this from the onset." Hedori strode past and stepped through the portal. Dagan grunted, shoving the demon forward. "Okay, then, guess I'm having company."

"I'll tag along, too. You'll need me," Aethan said. "Týr, Nik, and Blaéz can keep watch up here."

The others nodded. Yeah, someone had to be in this realm if trouble appeared and shit started flying.

As Dagan stepped through the portal, impossible heat surrounded him, along with an acrid, moldy odor. A trace of sulfur stung his nose. The sky appeared an endless, deepening gray. It had to be another level of the Dark Realm. Which part, Dagan had no idea, or cared. He'd get Jenna and leave.

He hauled the demon up to his toes. "Take us to the holding cells where you have the human female, and we'll make sure death comes quick. If not, you will have eternity to wish you'd made the right decision."

"Fuck you!" The demon yanked free.

"Guess they all speak the same language," Aethan muttered, grabbing the demon before he flashed. Whatever he did next, the demon lit up like a bulb, his tortured screams echoing in the dark. Blood streamed out of his eyes and nose. Voice lost, he fell to his knees and doubled over, pointing a quivering finger to his left. "M-must flash to-to get there. C-can't now..."

"And you're wasting my time," Aethan snapped in annoyance and held out his hand. As he healed the demon, Dagan took in the vast emptiness. The desolate place reminded him too much of his time in Tartarus. The sounds of whimpering faded. The healed demon lurched to his feet and eyed them cautiously.

"Just so you know," Dagan said, his tone as flat as

the vast plains surrounding them, "you try to escape, even in molecular form, and *will* find and kill you."

The demon's mouth thinned, his eyes glowed red, but he remained silent. His body shimmered into a dark cloud and dissipated into the air.

Dagan dematerialized and followed him. Several seconds later, they took form. The sky in this place appeared a deep purple-gray. Dense, black clouds hung low. A hot wind blew around them. Sweat beaded on his brow and dripped down his back.

He scanned the structure built between the looming trees with leaves dark and impenetrable. It appeared as if soot covered everything. Pushing away a branch blocking his view, Dagan studied the building. Something about the place had all his alarm bells ringing. Nothing in the hellhole gave off a natural vibe. Everything appeared demon-made or spell-formed. The damn incantations used scoured his psyche like a steel brush.

"You feel that?" he asked Aethan quietly.

A terse nod. "Someone with vast powers did this. Let's end the bastards, and get the female outta here."

The Gaian sword tattooed on his biceps had gone quiet. It didn't matter much to Dagan. It was probably why their lady-boss hadn't wanted them coming to this realm and seeking vengeance for their horrific imprisonment. But then he'd had no real enemy to blame. He had turned himself into the creature he was.

No use worrying about what couldn't be changed. With his mind, he grasped all the figures inside the dwelling and held them still. "We're clear," he said, striding toward the building. "Let's get the fuckers—shit, it's warded."

"I've got this." Hedori stepped past him, studying

Georgia Lyn Hunter

the doorway. As he set about unscrambling the wards, he said, "These feel dark...deadly."

Good thing he'd come with them then. The minutes rushed past, too much time wasted. Dagan's telekinetic ability was starting to waver. "How much longer?" he grunted.

"Almost there..." Hedori mumbled, his hands weaving furiously, unscrambling the spell. "And... Done."

Aethan kicked open the door, revealing the demons floating above them in the dimly lit room. He cut Dagan a quick look and shook his head.

Hedori disappeared through a door at the far back. A faint cry sounded. Dagan moved with preternatural speed, still holding the bastards with his mind. At the sight of the female clad in a thin, underwear-like dress, her one ankle shackled with a steel cuff and chained to the bedframe, anger scored his gut like acid at the fuck who'd done this to a helpless human female. The stringent odor of pain, despair, and sex thickened the sulfuric air.

"No," a terrified moan escaped her. She yanked at her manacle.

Damn. They probably looked scarier than the evil asshole who'd trapped her here. Not much they could do about that.

"We're not going to hurt you," Hedori said, his tone soothing as he unchained her. "We're here to save you."

Her gray eyes stark with fear darted between them. The moment she was free, she scampered to the corner of the room and huddled there. Knees drawn up, her auburn hair limp, she watched them.

Not wanting to terrify her with his immense height,

Dagan crouched, keeping a little distance between them, his forearms resting on his thighs. "Don't you want to see your daughter?"

She lifted her gaze. Those eyes, so much like his mate's, brimmed with tears and tugged at his soul.

"Shae?" she whispered.

"She awaits you. She never stopped searching after you vanished," he said quietly.

"Who—who are you?" Her voice held a raucous edge as if she hadn't used it much.

"I'm Dagan, a Guardian of Earth. Shae's my... She's under my protection," he said instead.

She didn't move, her wary gaze fixed on them. "You...you're one of them. He said you're all wicked...amoral, and corrupt...you plan to ruin our world."

"Who?"

She blinked, and a dazed expression stole over her face. She rubbed her brow. "I don't know."

Dagan wasn't surprised. The bastard had probably used mind control with trigger words in place.

Hedori grabbed the thin sheet off the bed and wrapped it around her, but she shied away. "No." She pointed to something behind Dagan. "Coat."

Frowning, he glanced back at the wall, then rose and headed across. He ran his palms over the rugged surface. A click sounded, and it slid open. Clothes filled what appeared to be a closet. A familiar fruity scent...with a hint of spice. A rush of rage brushed his senses.

Oh. Shit! His gut constricting at his discovery, Dagan touched a black coat—and night flickered in his mind as a vision emerged, revealing a dark alley.

"Don't—don't do it..." the Fallen pleaded as he

rose in the air.

"Go on, Jenna, you know what I want," a male voice said. "And what I'll do to your precious Shae if you do not."

Ah, hell. Dagan shut off his ability. He didn't need any more evidence. He'd seen this all before.

He glanced back at the cowering woman as he moved his hands over the clothing. She shook her head until he found what appeared to be an older, dark blue coat, and she nodded. He let his senses flow over the fabric… No, this didn't have rage attached to it. It was hers. He gave the garment to Hedori and headed back into the other room, his mind churning like a geyser about to explode.

"You dare come in here and steal our Lord Samael's property? He will kill you," one of them snarled. Fury pinging like spears inside him, Dagan grabbed a fallen sword and sliced the scourge's head off.

Seconds later, Hedori appeared with the female cradled to his chest and strode outside.

"Let's deal with these assholes."

Dagan barely heard Aethan. With a flash of his mind, he removed all their weapons and let the daggers slice brutally across their jugulars. Blood sprayed like a waterfall, drenching them. Heads rolled, and the demons fell. Aethan cocked a brow at him. "You're one terrifying bastard."

Dagan grunted, watching the disintegrating corpses. "Am I? I've seen you."

A wry bark of laughter left Aethan. "My scariness is known by all. But witnessing yours? Man, it sure is something to behold."

"Never had reason to use it before."

"True." The warrior nodded. "I guess having mates

changes our perspective on life. Everything is about them, isn't it? Why we hone our abilities whenever we can, so they're safe."

He didn't respond to the truth of Aethan's words. Because one thing he knew, no matter the rough road ahead of them, he'd do anything to protect Shae. "I'd lay down my life for her. She probably doesn't need me to keep her safe, but I'll do it anyway."

But with the damn dark cloud of his need for stronger blood hanging between them, the outlook wasn't promising. At all.

"Shit!" Dagan cursed as what the demon had said clicked. "Samael! He's not Fallen, he's rogue."

Aethan frowned. "Why the hell would he want Jenna? He still has his own abilities."

"Who knows with these fuckers? It's probably not to draw Michael's attention. What better way than to use a psi to get what he wanted done."

"We're in for one helluva shit-show now," Aethan muttered. "Let's get outta here and destroy the damn place. Maybe we'll get lucky, Samael will show his face sooner and we can end the scourge."

Dagan headed outside, the odor of sulfur burning his gut. "There's something else. Jenna is whom I've been tracking these past months. She's the psychic killer. The scent, the images I picked up from her clothes, everything matches."

Aethan's eerie, gray eyes took on hints of his whitefire power and shifted to Dagan. "Sorry, man. That sure sucks."

Yes. Shae would be devastated to learn the truth. A death sentence now hung over her mother.

As he stepped through the shimmering portal, Aethan's deadly power streamed out of him like a wave of lightning and consumed the building, turning everything to ash.

***

Night shrouded the castle as Dagan took form on the portico. He gratefully breathed in the fresh air, expelling the acrid stench of sulfur from his lungs. It took a little while to get his equilibrium back and the burning sensation on his skin to ease.

He pressed a hand to the throbbing wound on his side and grimaced as hunger clawed at him.

First, he had to see Shae. They hadn't parted on a good note. He scanned and found her in the gym, so he made his way to the basement.

He entered, half expecting a bottle of water to come flying at his head. Instead, Shae pounded the treadmill in a hard run, wearing knee-length black tights. Sweat dripped off her face and chest, dampening her dark-green tank. She looked incredibly delicious. By the stars, he'd missed her.

She looked up and stopped the machine. Gray-gold eyes stark with worry. "You were gone so long. Almost twenty-four hours! And it's night again."

He crossed to her. "I'm sorry, I forgot that time moves differently in the Dark Realm. We were gone three hours at most for us. We have her."

She faltered on the slowing belt. "Mom's here?"

He nodded, helping her down. Reaching out, he released a coppery strand of hair stuck to her damp face. "She wasn't in the Bronx. They used the warehouse there as a front to open a portal into the Dark Realm."

"What?" Shock leeched the flush running had installed in her cheeks, leaving her ashen. "Who would do such a thing?"

"A rogue angel named Samael."

Her mouth opened then shut.

How the hell did he tell her that the mother she'd just gotten back was the killer he'd been tracking for months. That she could die? No need to add to the shitload of pain that was about to come crashing down on her. At least he could let her have this time with her mother. "C'mon."

She grabbed her hoodie from the bench press and followed. On the ground floor, when she would have headed for the stairs going up, he turned her toward the short hallway leading to Hedori's quarters. "She's there, in the guest room." He grasped her hand before she could leave. "Shae, your mother doesn't remember things from before or what happened to her. Except for you."

Her eyes swam with unshed tears. "They took away her memories?"

"Yes. We will find him," he said quietly. "He will pay for what he did."

Her delicate jaw firm, she nodded then sprinted to the doorway and grabbed the doorjamb as if needing the support. Dagan followed.

"Mom," she whispered and darted inside to where her mother sat on a couch, still wrapped in the blue coat.

He waited at the entrance as Shae dropped to her knees and put her arms around Jenna's waist. Her tears fell like rain.

His chest tightened, her anguish squeezing his lungs like a damn vise. For all the pain she'd suffered, he couldn't wait to get his hands on the bastard Samael.

He telepathed Michael, *Found Jenna. Samael had her. She's too traumatized. Memories blocked.*

I'm not surprised. All right. Let her rest for now. I'll be there tomorrow.

Until Michael met Jenna and gave the go-ahead, Dagan couldn't tell Shae anything. And that wasn't something he looked forward to, revealing the truth about her mother.

***

Shae bolted awake. Sunlight streamed into the room. Darn, she hadn't meant to sleep so late. But with all that had occurred and Dagan finding her mother, exhaustion had her crashing in the early hours of the morning. Dagan must have put her to bed, but he wasn't around.

Shae hurried through her shower, changed, and was pulling on a tawny sweater when she realized she wasn't alone. She looked up and found Dagan at entrance, wearing sweats and a t-shirt.

"You should have woken me up. It's so late."

"You needed the rest."

She got out her boots from the closet. "Thank you," she whispered, her fingers tightening on the leather. "For finding my mother and bringing her back."

His gaze burned with a dark, intense emotion. "You should know by now, Shae, I'd do anything for you."

She swallowed hard and nodded. "She's so frail, Dagan, and her mind is so fragile. It terrifies me that she'll never recover."

"We'll be here for her," he said quietly. "We just have to be patient, it will take time."

Yes, she realized that. Her gaze lowered to her boots. And as she put them on, something about him, his manner troubled her. Normally, he would be holding her, comforting her—heck, Dagan always liked touching her. It seemed as if he wanted the distance.

She said, "You were up early."

"I had…things on my mind."

Frowning, she looked up. But when she met his brooding stare, uneasiness knotted her stomach. Something was definitely up—something dire. Her mind rushed through what happened the last time they were together…oh crap! Club Anarchy. Luka!

Deciding it was safer not to ask, maybe— hopefully—she was overreacting, she straightened from zipping her boots and ran her hands down her brown tartan skirt, smoothing the pleats.

Inhaling deeply, she made her way to him, and with him watching her, she felt like a convict on his last mile. His hand lowered to her waist as they walked out into the bedroom. "Nice outfit."

Huh? Cautiously, she eyed him. "Er, thanks."

The butterflies in her stomach fluttering wildly, she reached for the door, he stopped her. He pushed her damp hair away from her face and trailed open-mouthed kisses along her jaw and down her neck. *Ohhh.* Her breath hitched as if his mouth had a direct line to her core. He slipped his hand under her short skirt, and her eyes widened as he hooked his fingers into her underwear.

She grabbed his thick wrist. "We can't, I have to go see my mother."

"We aren't. In a moment, you will," he said, tone unemotional. Her panties still slid down her legs even though she still grasped his wrist. Oh, hell.

"Did you think I'd forgotten about what happened that night at Club Anarchy?" he asked pleasantly.

Shae bit back a curse. She had hoped he did. "Dagan, look, I didn't know Luka—"

"You blatantly disregarded my warnings," he cut her

off, "and put yourself in danger when I distinctly told you not to waste time and get that demon out of there. His two blood-demons followed closely. Had anything waylaid me, you could have been in grave peril."

Damn. "Nothing happened."

"The bastard had his hand under your dress, he put his fucking mouth on you. I wouldn't call that *nothing*."

Ugh, he'd seen everything. But being bait, those things were bound to happen. However, she refrained from saying so. Considering his pissy mood, it could just end up worse for her. "So I'm to go around without underwear?"

"It's so you'd think about how recklessly close you came to being harmed." He held out his other hand, expression implacable. "Give them to me."

Scowling, she stepped out of her fallen panties and thrust them at him. "I really hate that stupid ability of yours."

The black silk in his hand, he shrugged.

Thoroughly infuriated with him, Shae pivoted for the door, pulling her long tawny sweater down to her hips. He put his palm on the wood, stopping her. The warm length of his body settled against hers. Her breath caught in her throat as his semi-erect sex pressed through his sweats against her bottom.

Dammit! She bit her lip, struggling to shut off her traitorous body's reaction to him.

He lowered his head, his warm breath caressing her ear, a total contrast to his cool tone. "You need to understand that when it comes to you, I'll do whatever it takes to keep you safe. Break the rules, then there are reprisals, even if it means you aren't happy with my methods. And don't think of replacing your underwear with another pair, or I'll spank that lovely ass of yours, and it won't be fun."

She glared at him over her shoulder instead. "Are you done?"

He cut her a droll stare then straightened and waited for her to leave the room before he followed and said casually, "I'll return these later." He pocketed her underwear.

How could she want him so much and still want to strangle him.

Chapter 21

The late morning sun did little to warm the icy air in the kitchen—more precisely, the one emitting off his mate.

Dagan set his empty mug on the table. A smile tugged his mouth as he watched Shae. He found he enjoyed being with her when she had her meals. Just because he didn't eat, didn't mean his mate had to take her repasts alone.

But the ire coming from her held all the threat of several swords about to pierce him in the heart. Nope, she wasn't happy with him.

But she had to learn that she couldn't put her life at risk like she'd done two nights ago by not following his orders. Anger and fear resurged when he remembered the demon, Luka, trapping her in the alley with his blood-demons close behind.

And the damn kiss. He'd almost blown everything apart and killed the bastard right there.

Her chair scraped back on the marble tiles. Shae rose, carrying her cereal bowl and glass to the sink. She rinsed her dishes then packed them in the dishwasher.

Dagan strolled over and left his mug in the sink. Before she stalked off, he grasped her hand. "I'll be clearing my old workshop during the morning, then training with Blaéz later this afternoon if you need me."

She already knew his schedule for the day, but he wanted to get a reaction out of her.

Aaand, did he get one.

"I don't think I'll be looking for you much today, thanks."

With that caustic parting shot, she marched out, leaving behind a trail of frosty air.

Yeah, he'd asked for that, he thought wryly, rubbing his jaw…

A few minutes past two, Dagan headed for the massive training arena in the basement. As he jogged down, he grimaced, gingerly pressing his side. The wound still hurt like hell. With his healing abilities almost flatlining, he couldn't afford to sustain any more injures. Michael would surely bench his ass for as long as the damn wound took to heal. But he needed to train and keep physically fit since he was draining psychically, too.

In the empty arena, he selected a sword. At a shimmer in the air, he spun and barely missed decapitation at the deadly obsidian blade winging past his head. Considering whom he partnered this afternoon, not paying attention was asking for trouble.

The Celt had a masochistic streak a mile wide and appeared to be in a mood—summoning that damn Gaian weapon without cause was like reaching into your body and pulling out a rib.

Blaéz grinned, but it didn't reach his eyes. "Mating

has made you soft."

Dagan snorted and lunged at him. Blaéz countered with cold cunning deliberation, reminding Dagan of a time when the warrior hadn't been in possession of his soul. Dagan didn't let emotions crowd him either. Next on his to-do list: get rid of the Fallen after his mate, find the bastard who'd killed Shae's father and if he got ahold of Samael along the way, he'd take pleasure in annihilating the scourge.

Soon, the fierce clashing of steel reverberated off the walls. Time passed, and still, they fought. Long, hard, and brutally…

"Blaéz?"

At the soft, feminine voice, he spun toward the door instead of blocking the strike. Dagan's sword rammed him in the side. The Celt stumbled back, a curse flying free, but it didn't stop him from striding to his mate.

"Blaéz!" she gasped, darting across to him, fear darkening her eyes.

"Dammit, Darci—" he growled. "I told you, this place is off-limits."

Before she saw her mate's blood coating his sword, Dagan headed to the opposite side of the arena and got out a cleaning cloth from the shelf. Despite their low voices, he could clearly hear their conversation.

"You walked away before we finished talking. I gave you time to cool off. *You* didn't come back."

"What's there to talk about?" His tone terse, Blaéz pulled off his shirt, revealing the vicious scars crisscrossing his back, a horrific reminder of his brutal imprisonment in Tartarus. He wiped his face and chest. The place where Dagan had accidentally pierced him already healing. "You don't want to get married, fine."

Darci snorted. "The way you say *fine*, it sure is.

Look, all I said was two weeks is too little time to prepare for a wedding. Maybe early next year—April?"

"December...the first weekend."

"But that's just under four weeks," she protested. Then a sigh drifted out of her. "Okay."

His good mood apparently restored, his obsidian sword settled on his biceps. "Sumerian," he called as he ushered his mate out. "Rematch. Tomorrow."

Dagan nodded, putting his sword away.

***

Ten minutes later, showered and changed for patrol, Dagan left his room. He jogged down the gloomy, narrow side stairs, glancing out the darkened window. Dusk had settled in. With the onset of winter, daylight faded fast, and the job started too damn early.

As he hit ground floor, hunger cramped his belly. His teeth ground down. Later, he'd get that seen to. He had to go find Shae first. For now, he retrieved a cigar from his pocket and lit it, inhaling deeply to tamp down his thirst.

He cut through an empty kitchen. As he walked past the pantry for Hedori's quarters, his mate's scent drifted to him. He pivoted. And there, in the brightly lit pantry, he found her reaching for a canister on the top shelf. Her skirt lifted a little higher, exposing more of her thighs. Her long sweater, unfortunately, stayed in place.

He walked inside, and went motionless. The scene of her tears hit him like a dagger in the chest. "Shae?"

Hastily, her hand moved as if wiping her cheek. She didn't turn. "I can't reach the canister."

He got the tin and left it on the counter. "What's wrong?"

She lifted her damp eyes to his. "I'm trying to be

strong for Mom. It's so hard seeing her this way. She barely speaks and doesn't eat. Hedori made her favorite cake and…nothing. I don't know what to do. I-I thought making her favorite drink would help…" Her lips trembled. "What did that angel do to her, Dagan?"

His gut twisted to see her so distressed. He set his cigar on the shelf edge and drew her close. She buried her face against his chest.

How did he tell her about the horror he'd sensed in that damn place? It would devastate her. He said instead, "Samael took away her memories. It's why she's in this state. When she's physically stronger, we'll help her heal any way we can."

Silence lengthened. Just when Dagan thought she wouldn't speak, she said, "She held my hand for hours." A whisper of pain.

"Because you being there gives her strength."

Her arms tightened around his waist. "I'm glad."

He stroked her back, lending her *his* strength. After several minutes, a shuddering breath escaping her, she stirred and touched the damp patch on his black, crewneck shirt. "It's wet."

Hell, he didn't care about his shirt. He tucked a coppery-red strand behind her ear. "You okay?"

She nodded. Her gaze lifted to his. "You're going out on patrol?"

"In a few minutes, but I'll wait until I know for sure you're all right."

She sighed, her fingers smoothing his shirt. "No, don't do that. It's important that you go out there—"

"No, Shae, nothing is more important than you…" He kissed her tenderly, tasting her tears in the kiss. Then he pressed his lips to her right damp cheek. "Absolutely nothing…" Finally, he trailed his mouth over the bumpy lesion on her left cheek. "Not one damn thing."

A tremulous smile curved her mouth. It was like the sun peeking out after a bad storm. His heart settled. He caressed her back, her hips, still soothing her. Curious, he slid his palms under her skirt and encountered the smooth, bare curves of her bottom. "You didn't put on underwear?"

She glowered. "When you looked like a thundercloud"—he lifted a brow at that—"it seemed best to placate you."

Placate? He snorted, squeezing her bum cheeks. And bit off his own groan, his cock stirring in anticipation. But it felt damn good to see her back to her old self.

Shae grasped his shirt, tugged him down, and kissed him. "Thank you."

It was hard to ignore the hardening fucker with her mouth on his, and his hands cupping her sexy bottom. "For?"

"Bringing Mom back, for being my mate—for everything."

Ah fuck! His heart went gooey in his chest like a teen with his first crush. He kissed her deeper. She leaned against him. Her warmth and the musky perfume of her arousal tormented his senses, agitating his hunger for her. "You undo me, Shae. Every time."

"I need you," she whispered, meeting his gaze. Her eyes still held fragments of bleakness, something he never wanted to see again. "It's been a horrible, horrible day."

Much as he wished he could make everything better straight off with her mother, he wasn't a miracle worker. But this, he could give her.

With his mind, he shut the door.

He picked her up, set her on the counter. Her hands lowered to his leathers. And as she unbuttoned and undid his zipper, he slid his hand between her thighs, parted her folds, and stroked a finger down her tempting cleft. She shuddered.

His cock freed, she grasped him, flicking the head with her thumb. His balls jerked. Damn. He drew her to the edge of the counter and kissed her, his tongue sliding into her mouth. Her hand dropped away, and her legs wrapped around his hips, her seductively wet core sliding against his sex.

Aaand he lost whatever remained of his common sense. In one hard thrust, he sank into her.

"Ohhhh…" she breathed as her body stretched to accommodate him. A groan of pure need garroted him, her intimate muscles locking around him like a fist. And then he was thrusting inside her with hard strokes then slow drags.

"More," she whimpered. "Faster." The wet sounds of flesh hitting flesh filled the quiet pantry. Voices drifted from the kitchen. The warriors would be getting ready to leave on patrol now. And he could care less.

"Dagan—"

"Ignore them."

"The door—"

"Forget it."

He didn't bother to lock the door as he pulled out and thrust back into her. It could be done in an instant. And he wanted her on the edge to give her what she needed.

She braced her hands on the counter. Her gaze lowered to where they were joined. At the sight of his cock sliding into her tight body, arousal burned deeper.

He rolled her clit with his thumb, and she shuddered, her feminine muscles clamping around him. He gripped the tiny point of pleasure and tugged.

"God, Dagan!" She came fast, squeezing him like a vise as he pumped into her.

"Come here, baby." He pulled out, set her down, and spun her around. She grasped the counter. He slid his cock back into her, bent his knees, and drew her against him, his erection sliding deeper into her still spasming sheath. Wrapping her hair in his fist, he tilted her face to his and kissed her. His own orgasm barreling furiously down his spine, his balls tightened. His fangs lengthened.

Fuuuck! He pulled away and buried his face in her hair, his incisors piercing the flesh of his lip instead. He shuddered, releasing into her.

Several harsh breaths later, he eased away from her wet warmth and bit off a groan.

Shae staggered back against the shelves and then grabbed them, her skirt falling back into place and concealing her.

He hadn't meant to take her so hard. Obviously, his brain had hiked off into the land of the dead when it came to her. But hell, he didn't regret it for one damn second.

He reached for his cigar and inhaled the sedative smoke deeply…aware her eyes were fixed on him. But she didn't say anything. His throbbing incisors finally receding, he clenched the cigar between his teeth and glanced around. Grabbing a couple of paper napkins from another shelf, he cleaned her since she seemed to lack the strength to stand or do anything.

"Are you all right?" she asked as he took care of himself.

Always about him. Yet she'd been the one hurting so badly.

"I'm good." He zipped up and pushed the used tissues and dead stub into his pocket and felt her panties. "Here."

She pulled on her underwear, her wary gaze flickering past him to the shut door. "Are they still in the kitchen?"

Cutting her an amused smile, he shook his head. "They left." He picked up the hot chocolate from the counter, put his hand on her waist, and ushered her out.

In the kitchen, she got out the milk from the fridge and glanced at him where he leaned against the window counter. "Aren't you leaving now?"

"In a few minutes."

"I'm okay. Honest."

Yes, their passionate encounter had replaced desolation in her eyes. But he knew, too, the moment she went back to her mother, it would resurface.

Hedori entered through the open French doors. He'd seemed a little rattled after their rescue of Jenna in the Dark Realm. Dagan couldn't blame him, it had been centuries since the Empyrean took up arms as a warrior and killed.

Hedori cast a quick look at Shae then back to Dagan. "May I have a word?"

Dagan followed him out into the small terrace rich with the smell of herbs and stuff that grew in pots. Damn, he had to tell him the truth about Jenna.

Since Shae was still in the kitchen, Dagan lowered his voice, "Jenna is whom I've been searching for. She's the psychic killer."

"What?" Shock paled Hedori's tan features. "That means…"

"The seraphim will demand justice, and Michael will have to carry out the execution."

"No!" Hedori spat in vehemence. "She has been through hell—trapped in that godsforgotten place. The heavens only know what horrors occurred there. Besides, what reason would she have to kill those males?"

"To protect Shae. Samael probably blackmailed Jenna then blocked or wiped her memories of the kills—godsdamn these fucking angel wars!" Dagan cursed. "We'll need a miracle to stay that sentence."

Shae would be devastated.

Hedori's features morphed into hard, angry lines. "I won't let any harm come to her. Not again."

"Me either." Dagan exhaled a rough breath. "Shae doesn't know anything yet, and I'd like to keep it that way for now until I speak with Michael."

Hedori remained silent, his gaze on the trellised walkway, then those orange-green eyes came back to Dagan. "There's something I meant to tell you, but it slipped my mind with everything that occurred. The marking you asked about? The one that resembles a rope with one side unknotted? It's normally used as a brand of claiming by immortals. Once the deed's done, the knot closes off."

Fury like wildfire raged through Dagan. The bastard! He slammed his palms on the wrought-iron table there. That was why the fucking thing repulsed him.

"What is it?"

"Shae has a marking like that on her wrist." It was a miracle he could force the words out, considering how hard his teeth were clamped. "She has no idea what it is, thinks *she* got the damn tatt done. Aza must have wiped her mind of the incident."

"It's a tricky situation," Hedori said. "He will come for her."

Dagan's eyes narrowed dangerously as he straightened. "Shae's mine. We mated."

"True. The Fates chose her as yours. But he claimed her first. After Blaéz's dangerous encounter with the law-keepers a few months ago, I got the tome of the Absolute Laws to look for loopholes. It's all there. You didn't get rid of the mark when you mated her, so your soul-joining will not be at full strength. You'll probably experience everything a soul-joining bestows with her—telepathic communications, sense her emotions, etcetera—but all will be faint. If he mates her, it *will* override your bonding…"

Hedori brushed back a loose strand of hair that had escaped his metallic-gray braid, lines creasing his brow. "Though the Morrigan has ruled that the Absolute Laws do not affect the Guardians, you know the law-keepers will still keep watch. If Aza goes to them, you'll lose her."

Godsdammit! She was his mate. *His*!

Dagan paced the length of the terrace, his fury amping. Now Shae could be taken from him? *No!* Not fucking happening!

"You have two options. Find a way to get the mark off her before it's too late. Or kill him," Hedori said, like he didn't know that. "And tell her the truth, Dagan. She needs to know."

Dagan. Downtown. We have a situation near Club Nocte. At Blaéz's telepathic message, he bit back a curse. Hell, he should have left for patrol a half hour ago.

"I have to go, work emergency," he told Hedori. "I'll speak to Shae when I get back. Keep her—keep them both safe for me."

"With my life."

***

Dagan took form deep in the alley where he'd first met Shae and crossed to Blaéz, who waited near a boarded-up building with a *For Sale* sign.

Blaéz nodded to the door. "Inside."

Dagan followed him in then slowed to a halt, keeping his breathing shallow at the scent of fresh blood drenching the air. There, on the wall, the blond band member Shae had hugged was nailed to the surface, blood dripping down his body to pool on the grimy floor.

"Found this on him." Blaéz held out a smeared note, his expression grim.

The families of the Guardians' mates will soon join him, all nailed to this wall. You took what belongs to me. I want her back.

Jenna or Shae?

Dagan's jaw clamped down at the bastard's warning.

If Shae found out about this, she'd give herself up in a heartbeat. Not only was her friend's life on the line, but the families of the Guardians' mates, too.

He frowned at the note in his hand, and it finally registered. He couldn't pick up shit—his ability was dead like a damn doorknob.

A shimmer in the air, and Michael appeared. His eyes glowed silver as he looked at the crucified male. Dagan showed him the note while Blaéz eased the huge steel nails out of the unconscious man's limbs and laid him on the floor.

"Everything's blurry; can't pick up a reading," Dagan said.

His features cast in steel, Michael knelt beside the

human and swept his palm down his body. An eerie, silvery-white light, almost like a shroud, coalesced around the man as the Arc started the healing.

Dagan pulled his mind back to the job at hand. With little hope, he tracked for the psychic signature of the one responsible for this torture. A faint flicker of fury touched him. "I'm going to follow the trail, I can still feel the energy of whoever did this."

He headed for the door, his stomach constricting in hunger, reminding him that he had to go feed. As soon as he checked out the trail, he would.

As he traversed the alley, thousands of heartbeats crowded his head, the draw tugging him. His fangs throbbed at the temptation. Dammit. He fell against the wall, breathing hard, fighting for control. Before he went on a rampage, with shaky hands, he pulled out a cigar, lit the thing, and inhaled deeply.

A few minutes later, his hunger dulled, he cut through a thoroughfare into another grimy backstreet. The psychic vibration had gone cold.

About to head back to Blaéz and Michael, a piercing pain tore into his abs, and he stumbled backward. Cursing, Dagan yanked the sword free, but his palms stung as if acid were eating his flesh. *What the hell?* He flung the weapon away.

"Did you think I didn't know which of you assholes had my mate?" A tall, familiar blond emerged from the shadows. Aza.

"She's not yours. She will never be," Dagan snapped, his vision blurring a little. "How did you trick her into getting branded?"

Aza ignored that and circled Dagan. "The mighty Guardian, now at my mercy."

"You marked her against her will—" He wavered,

but steadied just as fast. "I'm going to kill you for that."

The Fallen slid his hands into his pockets and laughed. "Strange, I'm here, and you're fumbling around like a feeble human. Feeling a little frail there, Guardian? It hurts, doesn't it? You see, that's an angel's blade spelled with demon's blood. Can't heal that in a hurry, vampire."

Dagan leaped for the bastard, but he shimmered away. Something else about the Fallen nagged at Dagan, and it wasn't just him branding Shae.

A cacophony erupted deeper in the alley. Harsh grunts and snarls drifted to Dagan. A familiar flash of swords briefly brightened the alley. The other warriors appeared.

"Pity my fun's cut short," Aza drawled, reforming again. "Those blood-demons are hungry—you should be right at home with them. But know this, Guardian, Shae is mine. I will get her back." In a flash, Aza vanished.

Dagan snarled in frustration, wanting to go after the bastard. But with his Guardian oath too ingrained, he stumbled down the alley instead. He summoned his sword and dove into the horde, his weapon swinging— fuck! He faltered, pain gouging him as he stretched his injured muscles.

Shield, Aethan's voice drifted into his mind. At the familiar wave of white light flowing out from the middle of the chaos, demoniis scattered from Aethan like roaches. Dagan stood there. He couldn't move, couldn't dematerialize. His ability didn't worked. He shut his eyes.

"Dammit, Dag!" Tough arms snatched him away from certain death and dematerialized them to a rooftop. As they took corporeal form, Dagan slid to the cemented floor.

His chest heaving, Týr faced him, his obsidian sword still in his hand, the moon highlighting the concern on his face. His nostrils flared, and then he lowered to his heels and pulled up Dagan's t-shirt, exposing his abs and the wound Aza had inflicted. Before Dagan could stop him, Týr ripped off the dressing on his side. Horror darkened his face. "This demon-bolt wound is days old. You're not healing?"

Struggling to breathe through the excruciating pain, Dagan pulled his shirt down and closed his eyes. What could he say to the one person he didn't want seeing him this way? He wasn't healing because his abilities were now dead and he needed a *true* feed? Yeah, right.

"Dammit, Dag," Týr shook him. "Tell me what the hell to do."

He forced his eyelids open. "You can't do anything. The blade was…it's nothing. The Fallen bastard wants Shae back." Then he finally said the words, "If anything happens to me, ask Nik to keep her safe."

Týr's expression tightened at the shutdown of Dagan not asking him for help, but he'd trusted Týr once. The pain still lived in him.

"Well…" Týr retorted, "I would, but seeing as it's a soul-joining, maybe you'd want to give her a last message, too, before she joins you?"

Fuck, he'd forgotten about that. He bit back a pained groan and pressed a hand to the new wound.

"Here." Týr held out a thick wrist, stunning all hell out of him. "You need blood, take mine."

"I don't know what the hell you're talking about."

"I know." His mouth firming, Týr's obsidian dagger appeared in his palm. He sliced his wrist, blood gushed, thick and rich, snagging Dagan attention like a lure. "After we became Guardians, I followed you once, to talk to you…I saw you feed from a mountain lion."

"You're always where you shouldn't fucking be," Dagan muttered. "By the heavens, Týr, how could you let that happen? I thought you cared about her—"

A thick wrist was slapped against his mouth. Hunger gnawing his gut, Dagan clamped his lips around Týr's profusely bleeding wound and sucked. But at Týr's fast healing abilities, the lesion closed. Too ravenous to care, Dagan's fangs dropped. He licked the warrior's skin and sank his incisors deep again.

Týr inhaled sharply. A groan escaped him. "Fuck me! Is that what they all feel when you feed from them?"

Like a blast of icy water, Týr's words froze him. What the hell was he doing? He jerked away, shame rushing through him. Týr's blood would stop his thirst for a while, but it wouldn't give him what he truly needed.

Týr cut a quick look at the puncture marks in his wrist as they closed, then checked Dagan's wound again. His brow creased. Those pale brown eyes nailed him. "Why aren't you healing?"

He rubbed a weary hand over his face. "Because it's female blood I need."

"Shae—"

Dagan shook his head and lowered his hand. "I cannot. She's human. I'll kill her…that's my fucking curse."

"Tartarus sure screwed us over," Týr muttered. His eyes darkened, hollowed as if pulled back into the past. "What about the goddess I sensed you with over the centuries?"

Call Kaerys again? His entire being revolted. "No."

"Then find another female to feed from. You need to heal."

"No."

"What the hell do you mean, *no?*"

Dagan cast him a tired look. "Not at the price it comes with. My saliva being an aphrodisiac, they'll want more than I'm prepared to give. I can't—I *won't* betray Shae. I'll heal like humans do."

"Dag, we fight fucking evil and other shit every night. You cannot be at mortal strength."

"I've fought well enough in the past month."

"You haven't fed for that long?" Týr growled, reminding Dagan so much of how they'd once been. An ache formed in his sternum.

"I have, just not from a female of our genus. Animals sustain my hunger for a few hours." He shifted against the pillar and winced as pain speared him. "Why do you care anyway?"

"Because no matter what, you're still my friend. I know I fucked up damn bad. I wish to the heavens I knew what happened that day. I spent millennia going through the events…" His fingers tunneled through his shaggy hair. "I was patrolling the temple area when one of the handmaidens said that Inara wanted to see me. I recall waiting for her in her chamber. She arrived, seemed happy I was there, and she wanted to go to the river. I refused. She wasn't pleased but accepted it. After that, nothing…"

When Dagan remained silent, Týr's mouth pressed into a tight line. "I know no apology will ever be enough…" He rose to his feet. "Let me check what's going on down below, I'll be back to take you to the castle."

After Týr had left, with humiliation and guilt churning his gut, Dagan felt like shit. He wished he could let go of the past. But every time he thought about the brutal battle in the Sumerian temple, his mind turned hazy with agony and betrayal, and all he saw was Týr—the sole survivor in that blood-soaked room.

Pain strummed through his belly as he moved again. He bit back a curse and pushed against the cemented pillar. Using the thing as a crutch, he shoved to his feet, breathing hard through his nose, and braced a hand on the wall.

"Why do you do this to yourself?"

At the soft voice, his gaze snapped to his left. A shadowy, feminine figure appeared at his side, her scent achingly familiar. His heart pounded against his sternum. He dropped to his ass, shock nailing him in place. "No. *No*, it cannot be…

"Aye, it's me." A broken laugh echoed in the light breeze. Gentle hands touched his face. "I missed you, *ahu.*"

Brother? He blinked his blurry gaze, so sure he was hallucinating from blood loss. "Inara? How—why?"

The mirage merely shook her head. She appeared older. Thinner. No longer the teenage girl he'd once known. "You suffer greatly, when all you have to do is trust yourself."

"What are you talking about?" Her vision wavered. "No, don't leave—please don't—" He tried to grab her. Instead, his hand flayed through air. "Where are you?"

"I am…where I choose to be." Her ethereal image kneeled before him, and she stroked his hair. Then she fingered one of the ropey lengths and smiled. "Eons have passed, and you still wear your hair this way. She likes it, you know."

"What?" He shook his head again, trying to clear the dizziness. "Inara—"

"Shh, brother. Go back to your mate and do what you must."

He heaved a sigh at her words. Damn, he pressed a hand to his new injury. Even breathing fucking hurt. "I can't. She'll die, and that I cannot bear."

"How quickly you forget. *I* am the Goddess of Life. Aye, I've accepted what I am." A wry laugh. "Death is not in the cards today." She laid a hand on his arm. The intense pain eased as his body shimmered and the decrepit rooftop vanished.

Eyes clenched tight, Dagan staggered as he took form, not on the portico of the castle but on his own balcony.

"Be at peace, *ahu*," her fading apparition whispered. "You cannot blame yourself for something you had no control over."

"Inara, wait!"

"Alas, I cannot linger..."

At the sadness in her voice, Dagan's chest hurt. "Tell me where you are. I'll come get you—"

"No, brother mine, this time, it's my burden to endure. Penance for my mistake." Her misty form enfolded him in a sweet hug he couldn't feel. Her familiar scent of honey and some musky flower surrounded him, filling his mind with images of a time of innocence and laughter. Then, he was alone.

"Forgive your old friend." Her last words penetrated the fog in his mind. "Things are not what they seem...the dark angel, Lucifer, was my mistake."

Chapter 22

Dagan stood on the dimly lit balcony, the dissonance of night insects replacing the roar of traffic from the city. How many more hells would he have to endure before he found a modicum of peace?

With Inara's sudden appearance and her asking him to forgive Týr, but then refusing to say where she was and telling him that Lucifer was her mistake? What the hell did that even mean? And with the threats to his mate, who could be taken from him…his sanity hung by a thread.

He had to go find Shae. Needed her. Only her presence calmed the madness taking over his mind. But if she saw him like this, punctured with holes and bleeding again, it wouldn't go well. He pulled his blood-drenched shirt away from his wounds, teeth clenching at the spiking pain.

As he opened the French door into his room, a shift in the air had him glancing back. Kaerys took form. He bit back a curse. "What do you want?"

Her dark eyes glittered hungrily, sliding over him. "I,

er, saw you get hurt."

Anger buzzed through his veins and roared in his head, he barely heard her. "You're stalking me?"

"I missed you, so yes, I followed you, hoping you'd get over your snit..." She glided across to him, a sultry smile on her lips. Flicking back her brown hair, she swiped a fingernail over her neck. A thin, red line appeared. Blood seeped. Rich and decadent, the scent drew him. His incisors throbbed.

"Come, Dagan. Take. You need me, but you know what *I* want."

He was so sick of this shit. Her games. Keeping his breathing shallow, he pivoted for the door. "Leave."

"What?" Shock resonated in her voice. "It's been several weeks, Dagan. Just how long can animal blood sustain you? You should be grateful I'm looking past your callous disregard of me."

Callous disregard? The last time he saw her, he'd been hurt, exhausted, and only wanted to feed and rest. But she'd refused, miffed at whatever he'd supposedly done—wait! That's right, he didn't want to fuck her. Hell, he hadn't wanted her in that way for decades.

"I feel your hunger. Now take me," she ordered, impatience tainting her tone.

Best to get this over with. He leaned a hand on the doorjamb, his gaze hard. "We're done. Have been for decades. This arrangement between us is over."

"What? Why would you say that?" Her eyes narrowed. "Oh, I see, you're making me pay because I didn't come when you called recently. Very well, I'm chastised. Besides, animal blood isn't going to help you now. It's been too long, you're famished." Her gaze skimmed over his sweaty appearance and blood-drenched clothes in distaste.

He'd fed from Týr earlier, and it had tamped down the thirst. Except his starved psyche nailed him like a fist in the gut, demanding her energy-giving blood. His fangs ached. But Shae's smile when he'd finally claimed her filled his mind and was imprinted on his heart. She was all that mattered to him, the light to his darkness.

"Look, I'm grateful you came when I called you through the centuries. But I'm mated now."

"What?" Her jaw dropped. "Mated? Why would you do something that foolish when you have me?"

Yes, because she was so fucking good to him, taking away his dignity, making him crawl just to eat.

Shae made him feel many things—anger, frustration at her stubbornness that he wanted to shake her at times—and, hell, she could give as good as she got when angry, but not once did she belittle or demean him. More, it was the way she smiled, the way she looked at him, like he was her entire world... She made him whole again.

Kaerys' glared at him. He held her stare. Though she didn't deserve his honesty, he gave it anyway. "It's a soul-joining."

"What?" she blinked, fury brightening her eyes. Darts of power pierced him like needles before fading. Then she waved his comment aside and smiled like Bob finding a bowl of cream. "It doesn't matter. You didn't choose her like you did me. I mean, your sire didn't want your mother either."

She dared compare him to his old man? He ground his teeth, struggling not to let his temper erupt.

"Dagan, we were betrothed once. Even though you broke it, I waited for you for centuries. Then I found you again when Michael called me. *I* gave you a way out. She obviously cannot fulfill this—your most vital need."

"I don't care. Just go." He entered his room, relieved that she couldn't follow with the wards in place. Hedori was ever vigilant in changing them weekly.

"Aaargh!" She stomped her foot, finding her way obstructed. "This isn't over."

It was. Dagan didn't bother repeating himself. He headed for his closet to change his bloodied shirt before he went after Shae.

***

Panting like a landed fish, Shae drew to a halt just past the lake near a wooden bench, hands on her knees, gulping in copious amounts of air. The moon peering from behind thick rainclouds cast a silvery light over everything.

"Coming?" Elytani asked, swiping the sweat from her brow, reminding Shae that she hadn't been able to go for a run alone. Hell, she hadn't cared. She needed to work out her anger and helplessness at seeing her traumatized mother.

"In a moment." She inhaled another lungful of air. "Go on, I'll catch up in a minute."

Since they were close to the castle, Elytani nodded and jogged off. Gah, immortals and their insane stamina! She drank more water from her bottle, then reached down and rubbed her burning calf muscles. Her thoughts back on her mother, she hoped she'd get a few hours of sleep at least. With her memories of her time in captivity blocked, it terrified Shae what might occur when they returned.

"Excuse me."

At the strange voice, Shae straightened and frowned at the tall woman approaching her in a dark green, tunic-style dress that hugged her curvy figure. She could only be another immortal. Silky, cinnamon-brown hair framed her striking face and flowed down her back. There was something vaguely familiar about her.

Shae swiped away a strand of hair that stuck to her sweaty brow, suddenly feeling too grubby in her knee-length black tights and gray tank.

Dark brown eyes skimmed over her in disdain. "We must talk."

"About?"

"You are Dagan's mate, no?"

Her spine stiffened. She narrowed her eyes. "I am. Who are you?"

A knowing smile crossed the other woman's face. "I introduced myself to you in the mountains."

What the hell was she talking about? Then it clicked. "The dream—*you*!"

"Indeed. I'm Kaerys, goddess of chaos. His betrothed."

"Really?" Shae countered. "Yet, he mated me."

Kaerys flicked her comment off with a wave of her hand. "It means nothing. *He* knows that better than anyone." Her expression hardened. Power rolled off her and stung Shae like pinpricks. "Because of *you* and some noble self-oath he's taken, *he* now suffers, and will continue to hunger since he refuses to feed from me."

Her stomach twisted into an excruciating knot at the woman's words, but it didn't stop her. "So you're saying you're willing to be a donor for him without demanding more?"

"Why would I do that? He's mine. *My* betrothed. He stayed faithful to me through the ages." She stalked up to Shae, her dark eyes steaming with hostility. "But now, because of you, he'll soon be at mortal strength. With his honor so ingrained, he'll continue fighting never-ending evil until his last breath. Yes, human, he will die because you are selfish."

And *that* struck her in the chest like an arrow as her fears were given words. Because everything the witch said was true. *She* was nothing but a liability. And because of her, Dagan would lose so much. He could...die.

Oh, God! Her knees buckled. The bottle fell from her hand. Shae grabbed the backrest of the bench, terror stealing her breath.

"I'm glad you see sense, human—"

"What the hell are you doing here, Kaerys?"

At Dagan's roar, Shae turned. His chest heaved, like he'd run all the way to her. He probably had, but she could barely think straight at the pain seeping through her.

He could die, the words ricocheted inside her head.

The goddess cast him a sultry smile. "There you are, my love. After we parted, I thought it only fair to find her and explain the way things are."

What? He'd been with her? No-no, she rubbed her burning eyes.

"Shae—" He grasped her arms, making her look at him. "Whatever she's implied hasn't happened."

Shae struggled to get her thoughts away from the yawning chasm that would reel her into darkness. "Then why?"

Those yellow eyes flared with suppressed fury. "She's been keeping track—"

"Oh, for heaven's sake," Kaerys burst out, stomping closer to him as if to break their intimacy. "I came because you're hurt. Again."

"Shut the hell up, Kaerys!"

"What?" Shae hurriedly searched his black t-shirt but couldn't see anything. She grasped the hem of his tee. He caught her hands, his lips compressing. His usually sexy bronze skin appeared pallid and stretched taut over the bones of his face. And she knew. "You're hurt."

"I'm fine."

"Don't." She pulled away, feeling as if her heart would shatter. "Everything she said is true anyway. I-I can never give you what you need. Only she can. You even stayed with her through the millennia."

The hard set of his features realigned into one of frustration. "Because it was easier. For that reason alone and no other!"

"That's what you think," she whispered. "For her, it was a commitment."

As illogical and painful as it was, she would have far preferred if he'd gone to different women. Then this goddess wouldn't be gloating at how he'd stayed faithful to her through the centuries.

"The others wouldn't come when I requested. They...they were scared of me, of what I'd become and done."

At the deadness in his eyes, the self-loathing there, confusion overtook Shae's unhappiness. "How would they know any of this if they didn't..." She broke off, her gaze zipping to the smirking woman standing a few feet away. "You bitch! It was you! *You* turned them against him!"

Kaerys' smile vanished, replaced by an innocent look. "I didn't. The first time when I sought to help Dagan, he-he ravaged me..."

A dark red stained Dagan's face. His gaze flickered away. Anger swept through Shae like a gale force. He'd told her he had no control in those early days. She, more than anyone, knew just how tightly leashed his restraint was now, helped by those sedative cigars he smoked so he wouldn't hurt her—wouldn't hurt anyone.

"It took me days to heal. You know it's true, Dagan," Kaerys told him. "The others saw my ruined throat. It's why they wouldn't come."

Shae's power battered against her mental shields for release, to avenge him. She hung on by a breath. "You're a damn goddess, you couldn't self-heal?"

"Not from what he'd done. But it didn't matter to me, I loved him, I still do—"

"Love?" Dagan's cold gaze flashed to Kaerys, his handsome features like stone. "What you love is the excitement, the thrill of knowing you're fucking a dangerous creature born from the horrors of Tartarus, one who could tear you apart in a single heartbeat," he said, tone flat. Emotionless. And all the more lethal for it. "I let it slide because it suited my purpose. You were never faithful to me, not that I asked you to be."

"How dare you?" she cried. "I remained loyal through the ages!"

"Really? Then explain Nab, Astor, and Caelif to me? Those were the latest ones in a long list. And Michael? You told him I was too dangerous to be allowed among mortals? Did you think he'd boot me out of the job so you could have me at your mercy?"

Her mouth opened then shut. Color drained from her face. "How…what, I don't know what you mean. Yes, I spoke to Michael. I was concerned—"

"Cork it, Kaerys." A cynical smile rode his mouth. "I

have the gift of touch. I see things…incidents when I touch someone's possessions. You didn't know that, did you? And you left your trinkets from your lovers behind a few times. But I digress. Yes, my sire was a whoring bastard. He didn't care about the sanctity of his mate-bond. Unlike me. *She…*" He pulled Shae close again, pressing her against him, his mouth caressing her head. "I took one look at her, and I knew she was mine."

Shae froze, her heart pounding like a Ping-Pong ball against her ribs at his confession. Yes, Dagan cared about her, wanted her, but it was the first time he'd said something like this.

He glanced at her. Despite his coldness, his eyes blazed with a deep-seated emotion. "Hell, you drive me crazy at times, Shae-cat, but this heart of mine beats only for you."

A smile trembled on her lips, warmth replacing her pain. And she fell deeper into him.

"Aaargh, you males are so foolish!" Kaerys stamped her foot, her face flushed in rage. "When you find she cannot fulfill you and you come crawling back, I will make you beg before I accept you."

"Fuck off, Kae, before I really lose my temper—"

"You ungrateful wretch! After all I've done. You will pay for that!" Power crackled in her.

Dagan shoved Shae behind him just as Kaerys flung out her hands, a sizzling shard of light arrowing toward him instead.

"No!" Shae dashed in front of him, her own power unleashing, shattering through her mental shields like lightning. "Don't you freakin' dare! I'm so sick of your damn shit—for everything you've done to him!"

The winds started, picking up speed around her in a

tempest, a red haze stealing her mind. Then, everything slowed down. The goddess's bolt of power distorted into a shower of blue sparks. If she wanted, she could flick each firefly gleam away. Instead, the power slid straight into her and continued to flow…

From a distance, a disembodied shriek echoed. "She's gone crazy, she's draining me. Dagan, stop her!"

"Shae, lock down your mind shields," Dagan yelled, his voice rife with panic. "C'mon—c'mon, baby, shut down, now!"

Feeling as if her mind would explode at the energy roiling inside her, Shae grabbed her head, struggling to re-erect her fallen shields. Suddenly, the link between her and the goddess snapped.

Kaerys went flying to land hard on her back some distance away. She lurched to her feet. "You won't get away with this! The law-keepers will know about you and this mortal." In a furious shimmer, she vanished.

Threat's gone…gone… The words resonated inside her head. As her conscious mind flew back into her, her knees buckled. Powerful arms gathered her and lowered her to the grass.

She opened her eyes and stared into anxious sun-bright ones. Something warm and wet dripped down her mouth. Hastily, she sat up and her head swam. Clenching her teeth against the dizziness, she tugged free the hoodie she'd tied around her waist and wiped away the blood. Her gaze rushed to his. "I'm sorry."

His eyes glowed a yellowy red when his darker side came to the forefront. But he just shook his head and hugged her. His hoarse voice muffled in her hair. "Never do that again. I don't think my heart would survive it."

"I got mad. She would have hurt you." She pushed away from him and swiped her nose again.

"Lie back and keep your head up until it stops—"

"Allow me." Another voice surprised them both. Týr crouched beside them. She had no idea he'd been there. He held his hand above her nose, and a blue healing light coalesced into her, stopping the flow.

"Thank you," she whispered in gratitude.

"I'm glad I could help." Týr lowered his hand. "I came by to make sure things were okay when I didn't find you on the roof. Caught the tail-end of the drama—" He nodded to where Kaerys had been. "Good job, Shae. You terrified the hell out of that female."

She smiled, but her anxious gaze flicked back to Dagan. Before she could ask him about his new injury, he said, "This power of yours is different."

That derailed her thoughts. She frowned. "I felt the same as I did in the alley the first time…only stronger. This time, I could see everything in slow motion, see her power as it headed for us… Then I stopped it. Right?"

"No. You absorbed her ability."

"What?"

"It seems you have quite a unique capability."

What? Stealing another's—an *immortal's*—power? Christ! She could barely handle her teleporting. Worried, her gaze darted between Dagan and Týr. "Does this mean I'm psionic?"

Dagan rose and helped her to her feet. "It's the only thing that makes sense. Your powers appeared a few months after the first psi rose, as stated by the Watcher's prophecy—that once the Healer awakened, the rest would soon follow. And no ordinary mortal would have those kinds of abilities."

Týr nodded in agreement, pushing to his feet. "Echo can confirm that. She can see auras and knows a psi from a normal psychic—something about the color."

A shiver slid through her like some kind of precursor. She rubbed her arms, thrusting away the thought, recalling something else the goddess had said. "Dagan, what did Kaerys mean when she said she'd send the law-keepers after us?"

His expression hardened. "She thinks the law-keepers will execute us since immortals and mortals aren't allowed to mate and soul-join. She has no idea you're a psi and that she's wasting her time."

"It shouldn't be a problem anyway," Týr said, flanking her other side as they headed for the castle. "Blaéz got The Morrigan's promise. We should no longer be affected by the Absolute Laws."

"So we're safe then?" she asked, pressing her fingers to her churning stomach.

Dagan glanced down at her, his ashen features softening. He put his hand on her waist, his thumb stroking the inch of skin her tank top exposed. "Yes."

Shae inhaled deeply. God, she hoped he was right.

Chapter 23

Dagan opened the door to their quarters, but Shae stopped at the entrance to the bedroom, her gaze shifting to the enormous bed. He ushered her inside and said quietly, "My entire quarters were redone while we were in Romania. I asked Hedori. I wanted something better for you, and a fresh start for us."

She blinked, her throat tightening at his thoughtfulness, and she was damn glad he had. She pivoted and put her hand on his abdomen. Something warm and wet coated her fingers. She reared back, staring at her blood-smeared fingers. "You're bleeding."

He looked down at his shirt, now glossy with blood and sighed. "Give me a minute."

Shae inhaled a shaky breath as he disappeared into the bathroom. How many more of these injuries could he take? He looked far too pale. At human strength, he wouldn't last long, not with the kind of job he had.

Soft noise drifted to her, cupboards opening and closing, a dull thud…then silence. Her stomach pitching, she hurried inside.

Dagan had stripped off his shirt and was trying, rather awkwardly, to clean his wound. She washed her hands of the blood, wiped them dry, and turned to him. "Let me."

Pushing his fingers away and struggling to keep her emotions locked down at the steady flow of blood from the latest injury, she swabbed the lesion with disinfectant, then applied the green, mossy ointment and taped a dressing over it.

Lines of pain bracketed the corners of his mouth.

"Does it hurt?"

Those citrine eyes lifted to hers. He didn't answer, just hauled her into his arms and buried his head against her nape. "For a moment out there, I thought I'd lost you."

Shae put her arms around him, careful not to touch his injuries, and hugged him. "I couldn't let her hurt you—I just couldn't."

He trailed his lips along her jaw then nipped her chin, hard. "You put yourself in danger again. Kaerys could have killed you!"

Ugh, the man had an elephant's memory. "She didn't, okay?" she grumbled, stepping away and rubbing her sore chin.

"Just because you possess those abilities, doesn't mean you're infallible—"

"I'm aware of that. But you were hurt, and I'll do anything to make sure you're safe!"

With a growl of frustration, he hauled her back and kissed her. No matter how mad she got with him, just a touch, and her anger melted. Before she lost herself in him, she pulled away. "Dagan, wait."

A low, displeased growl rumbled from him. "What?"

"Look…" She petted his bare chest. "Kaerys is a manipulative bitch, there's no doubt about that. But she spoke the truth. I can never give you what you need—"

"Shae," he sighed heavily. "We've been through this."

"And concluded nothing."

He walked out of the dressing room.

Fighting not to snap, she followed and stepped in front of him near the huge fireplace. "The times we made love, I saw how hard it was for you, yet your control never broke. Not once. I'm not saying this will be easy. Just take a little at first..." Taking a deep breath, she held out her wrist, her heart thudding like a drumroll.

He stared at her for a long second as if considering her words—she hoped. He took her hand and pressed his lips to the blue veins clearly visible beneath her pale skin. "I'll be fine."

Her heart sank. No matter what she said, he refused to listen. Shae stiffened her spine. Hell, this was their life she was fighting for. "Is Nik here?"

Eyes narrowing, he shook his head.

He could wonder all he wanted, she wasn't telling him crap, didn't want him to arm-up. But there was someone else. "Týr!" she yelled.

"Dammit, Shae!"

She folded her arms and met his glare dead-on. Seconds later, the door flew open, and Týr thundered inside, a thick sandwich in his hand. "What? What's wrong?"

"Will you stand guard while Dagan feeds from me? He's scared he'll hurt me."

Týr halted a few feet from them and cut Dagan an unreadable look. "Yeah. Sure."

At Dagan's obdurate expression, she looked him dead in the eye. "You need female blood, it's vital for you. If you won't do this, then we can't be together. I won't stand by and watch you put your health—your *life*—on the line because of me."

"You aren't leaving," he said, his tone cold. Resolute.

Hers turned flat. Determined. "The castle, no. You, yes."

Her words were harsh, but it was a risk she had to take. More, she understood if this failed, Dagan would need a donor, but not Kaerys. Never that witch again. She'd find someone who wouldn't expect him to pay in carnal pleasures. Yet, the very thought made her stomach hurt.

She held out her wrist again.

"I can hold out for a while," he muttered wearily as if she were the difficult one.

"Yeah?" She lowered her hand, trailing her fingers down his ripped, lickable abs. His tummy muscles flexed, and his breathing deepened as she lightly traced the edges of the dressing she'd taped over his injury. Yes, she affected him the same way he did her. But her threats weren't working. This was probably the only way to *talk* sense into his stubborn head.

She whacked him on the wound. Hard.

"Fuck." Dagan staggered back, his eyes scalding her.

"Oh, did that hurt? I wonder why that is?" She arched a brow at his scowling features, daring him to comment. But bile rushed to her throat at hurting him.

He didn't say a word, his hand on his wound. Obviously, he knew what she was about.

Damn stubborn immortal.

She said airily, "Maybe I should join the Guardians,

hunt demoniis and other evil out there. Heck, I'm probably stronger anyway. Dagan can stay home and help Hedori—"

A terrifying snarl, like an animal finally snapping erupted. Shae had no idea what had hit her. One minute, she'd been taunting him; and the next, she was slammed into a wall, the air whooshing out of her flattened lungs. His hand wrapped around her hair, yanking her head back and baring her throat.

"Whoa, man!" Týr's alarmed voice cut between them. "Easy there with your girl!"

"Back the fuck off." His eyes a burning predator yellow edged with red focused solely on her. He dragged his warm tongue over her pulse, then his mouth fastened on her. Shae tensed. A sudden sharp pinch, and his fangs sank into her neck, then his tongue coaxed her blood to the surface as he sucked on her vein, each pull of her blood a delicious sensation.

Oh, dear God. Warmth filled her. Impossible desire took hold, spreading through her in a tremendous wave...

***

Dagan shifted his grip on her hair, tightening his hold on her body as he swallowed. His mind focused solely on the thick, warm nectar sliding down his throat... She was so damn delicious, he couldn't feed fast enough—more—he wanted more. He sucked harder on her vein, another deep pull, and his starving psyche shuddered.

A gasp cut through his feeding haze. Nails digging into his biceps—*no!* Dammit—no!

He leaped away, his heart hurtling in his chest as if it were attached to a **defibrillator**. His back hit the window, his terrified gaze pinned on Shae.

A hand on her throat, she watched him warily. "It's okay, I'm okay. You didn't hurt me."

He shook his head to clear the miasma. His body too tense, he prowled the length of the windowed wall and rolled his shoulders. No, he hadn't hurt her…didn't get caught up in bloodlust. But he felt odd…as if poised on the edge of a mountain, his skin all that held him together. His fangs throbbed in need, he wanted more so fucking bad. He scented blood.

"Dagan? What's wrong?"

At the fear in her husky voice, his head snapped to her. She was still bleeding. Týr hurried to her side and laid his hand on her throat.

"You okay, man?" Týr asked, watching him intently.

Frowning, Dagan scratched the gauze taped to his side. He tore off the dressings and stared. The hellfire lesion from few days ago had knitted together. All that remained was a pink scab, and even the new injury was just a fading mark.

"You're healing so fast?" Týr's eyes widened. "Injuries from hellfire bolts take at least a day or so to mend when aided with Lila's potions."

Dagan snagged a dagger from the wall and sliced his palm. Blood welled, and just as fast, the wound closed. More, the lethargy that had held him in its grip for days had dissipated. He felt…revived. Stronger. His sight sharper, his smell heightened once more. Shae's delicious fruity-spice fragrance crowded his senses, along with the tempting scent of her arousal. His own body tightened in response.

He lifted his gaze to where she stood, frozen. Tossing the dagger away, he crossed to her and pulled her into his arms, burying his face in the crook of her neck.

"You did this," he whispered, voice raw and thick with emotions. There were no words to describe this rush of gratitude, of sheer happiness sweeping through him. "You healed me—saved me."

Her arms tightened around him, and her shoulders shuddered. He stilled. But at the wetness on his bare chest, anxiety brutally hacked his joy. "Shae?" He cupped her face in his palms. "What's wrong?"

"Nothing," she whispered, her eyes wet. "I'm just so happy. I dreamed of this, wanted to be everything for you, and now...now, it's finally happened." More tears slipped free.

Gently, he wiped her wet cheeks with his thumbs. "I'm eternally grateful for whichever Fate decreed this. And that it's you. I love you, my beautiful wildcat."

He put his mouth on hers in a tender kiss, and she melted into him...

"Guess you don't need me around any longer," Týr's dry voice came from afar.

Shae pulled away from him, making Dagan growl. A deep red flooded her cheeks. "You make me forget myself," she muttered.

Hell, he'd forgotten about Týr, too, but he refrained from saying so.

The warrior grinned and picked up the scattered sandwich he'd dropped on the small table near the door. "Man, this is a mess. Later."

"Týr, wait."

He lifted a dark blond eyebrow and smirked. "What? You want a threesome?"

Even through the years, the bastard hadn't changed with that dry—at times annoying—wit. But, hell, Dagan had really missed his old friend. He snorted. "Yeah, right."

Laughing, Týr headed for the door.

"Thank you," Dagan said quietly.

The warrior glanced back. Nodded. One corner of his mouth quirked. "I'll be around for a while before I leave for patrol again. Need another sandwich."

Dagan understood exactly what he meant; he'd wait until he knew all was safe with him and Shae. "I know."

Týr froze. The shock and pain crossing his face at those two words—as if Dagan had yanked him out from an abyss—felt like a kick in his gut. So much hurt and enmity through the centuries.

"I need my sandwich," Týr muttered and walked out.

***

As the door shut behind Týr, Shae turned to Dagan. "I'm glad you found your friend again."

He nodded, his expression brooding. "All that agony, rage, and animosity for something I could have ended eons ago. But given the mess I was, I couldn't see clearly. I was too steeped in bloodlust and anger."

"You mended things now, and that's what matters."

He stroked her upper arms and lowered his brow to hers. "I think you had to come into my life and whack me upside the head first."

Shae smiled and lightly ran her fingers over his healed wound. Then said softly, "I was so scared when you started shaking. Are you sure you're okay?"

He brushed her hair away from her face. "Yeah."

"But you didn't feed long enough."

He pressed his lips to her pulse in a tender kiss. "Stop worrying, I'm good for now."

But she recalled the horrid demon-bolt wound on his side and knew it always carried an evil taint until completely healed.

"Dagan—" She pushed away from him. He was too distracting when she was trying to think. "You should feed a little more. It will give me peace of mind." She gestured at the scab on his torso. "That wound still carries a stain..."

He stared at her for a long moment before he nodded. Taking her hand, he led her to the chaise lounge set near the undraped, night-dark windows. He sat down and pulled her onto his lap, the soft lights reflecting their images on the windowpane.

He smoothed her hair away from her neck. When she realized this was it, her lungs nearly shut down.

"Ready?"

"Jeez, don't warn me, just do it."

"And you sliced your wrist?" he drawled, amusement brightening his eyes.

She grimaced. "Yes, well, escaping from evil demons and such, the adrenaline rush can make you do things..."

Smiling, he lowered his mouth to her throat. At the sensation of his warm tongue circling her pulse in a predatory way, her heart rate escalated. His fangs lightly grazed her skin, the erotic teasing making her shiver. His mouth fastened over it and he sucked as if drawing her vein closer to the surface.

His fangs sank into her neck, and a delicious warmth spread through her, she barely felt the sting. Shae wrapped her arms around his neck, her fingers tangled in his long hair, holding him close. He drank deeply. With every pull, it felt as if he were thrusting inside her. She rubbed herself against his rock-hard groin, a low moan escaping her.

Her fingers tugged on his hair, the edges of her consciousness clouding, and she sagged against him...

Shae's motionless body cut through Dagan's blood high. He tore his mouth away from her throat and licked the puncture wounds closed.

"Shae?" He grasped her face, her normally fair skin gone chalk-white.

Her eyelids fluttered open. "I'm okay… Just a little lightheaded."

"Fuck! I took too much."

"Yes, there was that risk, but you stopped, didn't you?" She patted his chest. "Now I know you'll be safe."

"At your expense?" he snapped, furious at himself then he narrowed his eyes. "Did you eat?"

Her eyelids drifted closed. "I will…in a moment."

"Godsdammit, Shae!" Choking back a violent volley of curses, he rose from the chaise lounge and carried her across to the massive bed. He set her on the cover and stacked the pillows behind her. "Don't move."

Pulling open the bedside drawer, he found her stash of candies, retrieved two, and gave them to her. "I'll be right back."

He flashed to the kitchen and grabbed a tray.

Hedori appeared from his quarters. "Sire, may I be of help?

"Yes. I need food for Shae. Her sugar level's low," he explained, his frustration at himself still riding high. Heavens, he was so damn grateful to be able to control his bloodlust and feed from his mate. But dammit, he had to be more careful with her and not aggravate her hypoglycemia.

Dagan stared through the window, rubbing the ache in his chest. She cared enough about him to put her life on the line—no one had ever done that for him.

The job didn't count, they were all brothers in their fight against evil, and their fealty belonged to Gaia. Hell, he'd survived Tartarus, and he'd thought he could survive this too, living an almost mortal life. Truth was, he would have died far sooner. And Shae knew it, too.

"Dagan?"

He turned. Hedori nodded to the tray. "Thanks. How's Jenna?" he asked.

"She sleeps…but in fitful snatches." An undercurrent of anger scored the male's stoic tone.

After being trapped in the Dark Realm, Dagan couldn't blame her. The emotional and mental trauma she'd gone through—would continue to go through—hell, it was going to be a long haul. But knowing Shae was with her, he hoped it gave her some peace, at least.

Dagan headed upstairs to his quarters and found the bed empty. Dammit! He dropped the tray on the coffee table in the turret living room and headed for the dressing room. There she was, looking into the closet.

When she saw him, her lips curved in a smile.

"For godsakes, Shae! What the hell are you doing? Didn't I tell you to stay put?" He swept her up into his arms and crossed to the living room.

"Dagan," she sighed, curling her arms around his neck. "I want to change and go see Mom."

"Later, when you've rested. You're not going to be any good to her if you're sick."

Her loud exhale sounded a lot like a grumble as he set her on the settee. "You know best, oh master."

He popped the soda and handed it to her. "It's good you know that."

She rolled her eyes. It didn't deter him. He waited. Once she'd drunk some, he took the can, set it aside, then put the tray on her lap. "Eat."

"You know I'm not an invalid, right?"

At her argumentative tone, he cut her a dark look. "If you won't take care of yourself, then I will."

Scrunching her nose at him, she uncovered the plate, picked up the spoon, and paused. "You know what's weird? I haven't eaten any Dextrose in the last two days, and I didn't feel dizzy at all. Actually, all I felt was this energy and heat spiking inside me until you took my blood."

He stared at her for a second. With her growing powers, it could be possible that parts of her were changing. "No matter, I'm not taking chances with your health. Eat."

As she made inroads in her meal, Dagan sat on the coffee table, his mind on something else. Hell, he still wasn't sure if he'd imagined it. "Shae, what did you eat earlier today?"

Lines puckered her brow. "Hmmm, I had a peanut butter sandwich and a banana. Why?"

His mouth kicked up in the corners. "Because I tasted it in your blood."

"What?" Her spoon clattered to her plate, her eyes darkening in worry. "Is that a bad thing?"

"No. Just strange after all these millennia. It has just a hint of flavor…" he paused, trying to think of how to explain it to her. And failed. Hell, the only other thing he'd ever consumed was weak black coffee, water, or red wine. He'd completely forgotten the taste of solid food.

"Like blood-flavored red wine?" she teased.

Smiling, he kissed her on the pulse point that had given him the blessed relief he'd sought for a hundred lifetimes.

"What about the goddess? Didn't you taste food with hers?" she asked.

"No." He sat back and studied her. Shae was beautiful with that coppery-red hair, porcelain skin, and her gold-gray eyes. More, she completed him on so many levels, and now this. "I don't know what it is about you. You're human, yet your blood fulfills me in more ways than I expected."

"Well, I'm your mate," she said, picking up her spoon again. "And I also have these abilities, maybe that's why."

Perhaps.

After she'd eaten, he scooped her into his arms and put her back on the bed, pulling the covers over her. "I'll be gone for the remainder of the night. And you rest."

"All right." She covered her mouth, smothering a yawn. "But I should check on Mom first."

"Your mother's asleep. Hedori told me. It's been one helluva night with your new power emerging, then me feeding from you. So try and sleep, Shae-cat, 'cause when I return, you'll wish you had." He kissed her brow. "I'll see you later."

She lifted her hand and stroked his whiskered jaw, her bracelets sliding back. "Okay."

He pressed his lips to her wrist and saw the—*fuck*! With everything that had happened, he hadn't had a chance to speak to her about the marking.

"Shae—" He drew her hand away from his face and sat on the bed. "When did you get this tattoo?"

She glanced at the thing, shrugged. "Probably after my dad died. I don't recall."

He had to unclench his jaw to explain what he'd learned. "This isn't a tattoo. It's a mating mark. Aza put it on you, and since you have no recollection, he probably blocked your memory of the incident."

"What?" Her eyes widened in horror, then she glanced at the brand and went motionless.

"What is it?"

She chewed her lip.

His eyes narrowed, and his gut twisted. She knew something. "Shae?"

Her gaze lowered. She tugged her bracelets, before lining the three in a row and blocking the mark. "When my mom disappeared, I was devastated," she said quietly. "Aza was at the penthouse the day after. He offered to help me find her, then asked me out on a date. I agreed, only because he was Other and I thought he could—"

Dagan jerked to his feet, unable to keep still, his fingers clenching so he wouldn't ram his fist through something.

Her gaze rushed to him, then she continued, "As the weeks passed, he had no news, but he often came to the penthouse. I started to avoid him. Then Harvey said he'd help me find Mom. He told me about the broker demon. It was a sure thing to getting a lead on Mom. I told Aza I couldn't date him anymore. He was a little upset when I broke it off, but he seemed to accept it. Dagan, I lost one parent, I couldn't lose her, too."

He didn't say anything because if he spoke now, he'd probably yell at her for being so damn impulsive, and now she'd tied herself to a fucking psychotic Fallen.

He headed for the door then stopped. *Shit*. He couldn't just leave her like this. It wasn't her fault but that damn fucker. He rubbed his jaw and turned back. She hadn't moved an inch, her expression pained.

"Dagan—"

"It's okay, baby. I'll deal with this. I just want you to be careful. Anything that requires you being out of the castle, you call me. If he gets ahold of you, he'll claim you, and that mark will nullify our bonding."

"No!"

"Yes," he said grimly. "I don't have the patience to look for a way to remove that damn brand. I'm going to have to kill him."

Chapter 24

Dagan stood to one side of the living room in Hedori's quarters while Michael spoke to Jenna. He'd discarded his shades, and she didn't react to his eerie irises. Her gaze clouded with pain and confusion, darting between him and the archangel.

Hell, Dagan wanted her to have a little more time, but Michael insisted it was imperative to speak to her, find out what he could about Samael's plans.

And why he was here instead of out on patrol.

"I don't know who took me...I don't know anything," she whispered again, curling into the corner of the couch, her knuckles white beneath her tan skin as she continued tugging at a lock of dull red hair. Ten minutes of questions, and still nothing.

Thank the stars Shae had been spared from seeing her mother this way.

Suddenly, Jenna jerked to her feet, her hands clenching together. "Please, I don't want to talk. I don't want to do this anymore."

A coppery whiff drifted to him. His gaze snapped to

her hands. Shit. *She's hurting herself,* he telepathed to Michael.

"Jenna," he said quietly. "Look at me." Hell, the power in the Arc's voice made Dagan want to crawl over and stare at him. "Calm down, we won't hurt you. We simply want to find out what happened."

Her agitated movements slowed.

"You're safe here," he reiterated, his tone softer now, which surprised Dagan, considering he was sure the Arc was created from solid rock.

"No one will harm you again. Will you come and sit down?"

As she lowered to the couch once more, Michael sat on the armchair across from her, keeping a distance. Hedori walked in and stood adjacent to her, near the windows overlooking the herb garden.

Her wary gaze shifted to Hedori, then to Dagan and stayed on him. "You rescued me from that dark place."

Dagan nodded. "Yes, we did. The Guardians and I—everyone here, will keep you safe." He cut a quick look to Hedori, who resembled a statue. His eyes, the only things showing emotion, blazed a deep, deadly orange.

"Jenna, can you recall what happened?" Michael asked. "How you ended up in this dark place?"

She remained silent for an endless moment, and just when Dagan thought she'd retreated into herself, tears rolled down her almost pallid face. "We had an argument, Shae and I, over that musician. Every time he called, she would go, and then she'd come home hurting because he would be with some other woman. Though she denied it, I knew—she's my child. How could I not?"

Jenna inhaled a shuddering breath. "Shae didn't go that evening. She worked instead and was on her laptop. Everything happened so fast—there was a crackling noise, then an explosion. The blast threw me across the room, and I hit my head on the wall…" Her fingers plucked at the ends of the sweater sleeves. "I don't remember what happened after that, all I recall is waking up in that dark place."

Dagan jammed his fist into his pants pocket. Shae hadn't told him the reason for the fight, and hearing Jenna reveal how much the human had hurt her pissed him off. His territorial nature demanded that he kill the bastard. His Guardian oath kept him glued to the floor.

He stilled, a thought that had been nagging him surfacing again. He summoned the pewter dagger. He hadn't had a chance to read it again. Maybe she'd know something.

The moment it took shape in his palm, he crossed to her and held out the weapon. "Jenna, do you recognize this blade?"

She stared blankly at the dagger, then her eyes widened. She snatched it from him. "Where did you get this?"

"So you've seen it before?"

A sob broke free. "This belonged to my h-husband. It disappeared when he was killed." Her gaze lifted to him. "We thought the murderer had taken it."

At her revelation, Dagan rose to his feet. This was a damn shitfest. The blade belonged to an angel, one who'd apparently still possessed his wings when he mated Jenna. It was why Shae had inherited those kinds of abilities—*no*! Terror crashed through him at the truth—at what it meant for Shae.

Born of an angel and a psi, it made her extremely powerful. A nephilim.

Michael and his band of warrior angels had

annihilated all the Watchers *and* their half-angel offspring. The Arc cut him an unreadable look, obviously picking up his violent emotions.

It's not my call to make a decision about Shae. But I'll do what I can, he telepathed him then returned to his questioning as if this were some godsdamn tea party. "What was your husband's name?"

Too edgy to remain still, Dagan paced back to the door, his rioting mind trying to recall any laws with loopholes to keep Shae safe.

Another long pause before Jenna answered. "Gus Ion."

That distracted Dagan. Not two names. *One*. Gusion. A throne. A powerful damn killer. And the other rogue Michael had been hunting.

Dagan frowned. Wait, just how had the throne escaped the law-keepers all those years ago? His mating to Jenna should have blinked on their radar.

"How did Gusion block your mating?" Michael leaned forward, his powerful forearms braced on his thighs. "I'm sure he would have explained the dangers about immortal-mortal mating to you? And about the law-keepers?"

A slow nod, she whispered, "He found an Oracle, she helped us with a concealment incantation."

She'd have had to be a very powerful one. Dagan knew only— "Lila," he said.

Her breathing quickened, terror whitening her face. "Please, I can't…"

It didn't matter. They had their answer.

Michael stared at her for a long second. Then, "Do you know who I am, Jenna?"

Her gaze lowered again to her fingers destroying the edges of her sleeves.

"I am Michael."

"No!" she shrieked, jumping to her feet, startling Dagan and Hedori to move closer. "You—*you're* responsible for my husband's death—"

Power sizzled. Her hands flashed out. Michael flew off the seat, hitting the bookshelf opposite him hard and breaking the wood. The silvery light in his shattered blue irises flared brightly.

Hedori grabbed her wrist. "My lady, stop."

Jenna elbowed him in the belly, stupefying him. Her eyes pinned on Michael became charcoal-gray holes.

Dagan leaped for her before she turned the Arc into a sack of skin. Except Michael straightened, the glow around him intensifying. She groaned, losing her concentration, and swayed, her eyes closing.

Hedori swept her up into his arms and headed for the guest bedroom.

"Someone's not only tampered with her mind but also set you up as a target," Dagan said.

"I figured that." Michael stalked out.

The Arc had many enemies, especially of the winged variety, so this didn't surprise him.

In the kitchen, Dagan crossed to the Sub-Zero fridge, got out a bottle of water and a Coke, and tossed the latter to Michael.

"There're a few rogue angels I've been hunting," he said, staring at the can in his hand. "They absconded from the Celestial Realm, thinking to avoid the final step."

Dagan unscrewed the bottle and sucked back half the liquid. Yes, the loss of their wings and powers as demanded by angelic law for *falling* would do that. He didn't envy the Arc his deadly job.

"You cannot let the seraphim pass judgment. They

will demand Jenna's death."

Michael cut him an irritated look. "You think I don't know that? Why the hell couldn't this job be straightforward?"

"*You* can stay their verdict," Dagan pointed out. No way would he allow his mate to be hurt again, just when she'd found her mother. "All she'll need is a protector until her mortal life ends."

"You can't be hers. Protecting one psi is a helluva undertaking, and being what Shae is, you'll have your work cut out. As for Jenna, it's unlikely the seraphim will be swayed."

"Not if *I* am her protector," Hedori said, walking into the kitchen. He put the kettle on. "Before you say I'm not a Guardian, I'll ask you to remember what I once was. And why the mage of Empyrea ordered me to keep an eye on its exiled prince. Aethan may no longer need me, but that doesn't mean I cannot do the job."

Hedori was a damn good fighter and a male still in his prime. Hell, training with this Empyrean kept the Guardians on their toes.

Michael nodded. "I will make your thoughts known when I meet with the seraphs."

"Make it known to them, too, that she is mine."

The Arc's eyes narrowed. He slowly set his Coke down. "I see."

His features inflexible, Hedori started preparing a tea tray. "The moment I sensed her in the room at the penthouse, I knew."

Well, damn! No wonder he'd been so determined to be a part of this.

"Explain something," Dagan said, screwing the cap back on the bottle. "How did Jenna survive Gusion's demise? A soul-joining always takes the remaining mate when death occurs."

Michael scratched his shadowy jaw. Yeah, he knew something, because he sure as hell hadn't seemed surprised by Jenna's revelation.

"Gusion didn't soul-join with Jenna," Michael finally said. "Celestial angels can't soul-join with anyone unless they fall. But spawn offspring? Yes, they can do that, just like the Watchers did."

Dagan remained silent for a moment then setting his water bottle on the table, he met the Arc's shattered blue stare. His expression implacable, he laid down his decree. "I won't let any harm come to Shae."

Michael exhaled a heavy breath. "I know."

Dagan headed outside to go back on patrol and stopped on the terrace. Despite the soothing sounds of the night insects, his mind churned. It was obvious Shae had no idea what her father was—what *she* was.

A nephilim, one marked for death if the seraphs had their way.

Not in his lifetime. And since his life was eternal, never.

***

Shae woke an hour before dawn in an empty bed. Dagan hadn't returned from patrol yet.

Rubbing her drowsy eyes, she looked out the darkened window. *Mom*!

Darn it. She was supposed to check on her mother, not sleep for so long.

A short while later, showered and changed, she ran downstairs.

Hedori glanced up as she entered the kitchen, in the middle of preparing the morning's meal—or more precisely, dinner for the returning warriors.

"Good morning." She gave him a quick smile. "I'm

going to see if Mom's up."

"Your mother had a restless night," Hedori told her gently. "Michael sent her to sleep. He thinks it better she rests." He hesitated, then said, "It will take her time to recover, she's been through…a lot."

"What did they do to her?" she whispered, dread squeezing her chest, her mind wavering between thoughts of emotional and psychical torture, and…rape? Oh, dear God! She pressed a hand to her cramping stomach. The warriors could have healed her bruises, but the trauma? The memories?

"I don't know," he said roughly as if he were in pain. "Your name was the only thing that stirred her back to life back when we found her in the Dark Realm."

Her eyes burned with tears. Dagan hadn't said much, just that her memories were blocked and she'd been locked in an empty house. And they'd killed the demons guarding her.

"Thank you for bringing her back."

He inclined his head.

Shae hurried into the dimly lit room and quietly approached the bedside to kneel on the floor. Her mother resembled a shell of the woman she'd once been. Her face gaunt, her tan skin appeared pasty and stretched tautly over her cheekbones, and her once beautiful auburn hair lay over the pillow like dull, lifeless weeds.

Gently, Shae grasped the cold hand lying on the cover. Tears started to flow.

More than anything, she wanted the bastard Samael to pay for hurting her mother. With an angry dash of her knuckles, she swiped her eyes, not wanting her mother to see her this way if she awakened.

Sensing a presence behind her, Shae glanced back.

Hedori approached, his features grave, but those striking orange-green eyes were soft with understanding.

He set a tray on the table with cocoa and her usual cereal. "Thought you might want to eat while you waited for her to awaken."

More tears lodged in her throat. She couldn't speak, but nodded.

His gaze rested briefly on the bed where her mother slept, a shadow passing over his stern features. Quietly, he walked out.

***

The night had been endlessly long and far too quiet. Daybreak was a mere hour away.

Normally, it would have made Dagan uneasy, because it just meant more shit would ensure when evil rose again.

Right then, he didn't care, restlessness taking hold as he traipsed the still dark alley downtown his mind on everything that had transpired from finding Jenna and the horrid outcome there, to Shae and the wonder of her.

Hell, he should have trusted himself. He'd never hurt her. She was his very life. It took her thumping him to show him the truth. A corner of his mouth kicked up. Only she would dare.

The smile faded, his mind looping back to Týr. A thought struck him like a punch to the gut, stealing his breath. He stumbled to a stop—*no*! No way!

Exhaling harshly, he whipped around in the gloomy alley. He had to speak to him. He sent his senses out, found Týr, and dematerialized to Dante's Bar. Several Harleys were lined up outside the all-night bikers' bar.

Týr's latest haunt. Which he didn't get since he'd

heard about the warrior's penchant for clubs and the females there. And this place? Mostly just bikers and their women hung out.

The moment he entered, the noise cut off. Heads turned. Ignoring them, he made his way to Týr, who was engaged in a tense game of pool with a heavyset, bearded biker, who sported more leather than the Guardians did. And was surrounded by more of his leather-clad pals.

You sure know how to make things come to a halt, Týr telepathed him, his tone bone-dry as he cued his shot.

Dagan snorted. *You done?*

In a moment, as soon as I get my hundred bucks from this human. Týr shot the last striped ball into the pocket and smirked. He didn't even notice the waitress nearby eyeing him hopefully as he collected his winnings. They headed outside.

"So. What's up?" he asked, pocketing the dollars. "Thought you'd be tracking back to the castle and your mate. Wait, did Michael reach a decision about Jenna?"

"No. Her mind's too fragile for a mental search, so that's on hold for now…" Briefly, Dagan filled him in at what had occurred earlier. About Jenna and Gusion.

"Man, that's the shits."

It sure was. "But there's something else I need to talk to you about. Let's head back to the castle first."

They took form on the kitchen terrace, heavy with the fragrant herbs growing there. The lights from the kitchen spilled out onto the paved patio and the wrought-iron table.

Týr removed his biker jacket and tossed it on the table, cocked a brow, and waited.

Despite the chilly fall breeze coasting over him,

Dagan barely felt the cold. But he had to start wearing a coat soon to blend in with mortals. "Something's been on my mind since we spoke on the rooftop. That last day in the pantheon, when you were with Inara, did you drink anything?"

He scowled. "I wasn't drunk——"

"No, I meant anything else. Do you recall?"

"Of course, I remember. I've replayed that scene a zillion times since then, searching every detail of that day, trying figure out where it went wrong..." Týr frowned. "Inara offered me a drink like she always did, only the cup was different...a gold goblet. Why? What do you——?" His eyes widened. *"Hell, no!"* He staggered back, hitting the table, a vein throbbing violently on his brow. "She fucking laced the drink because I wouldn't let her go to the damn river?" He slammed his palms on the wrought-iron table. "How could she?"

Dagan felt like pounding something, too. But the anguish in Týr's face, the pain there, garroted him. No words of apology could ever make things right——not with five hundred years of having lived the horrors of Tartarus between them.

"How could she?" a tortured whisper.

There was only one thing he could do. *"Hefnd* rite is yours. I will pay the debt for Inara, for what happened. And for what I did to you."

His words seemed to stir Týr from the dark desolation he appeared trapped inside. He straightened from the table, the furious color in his face ebbing to leave his usually tan skin pale. "You want me to take *revenge* on you?" he asked, tone flat. "Why? You weren't in charge that day."

"Don't give me that crap," Dagan snapped. "Because

of my sister's actions and my anger, I mortally wounded you. If the ruling council hadn't intervened, and we weren't hauled to the Gates of the Gods in that moment for judgment, you *would* have died."

Týr sat on the edge of the table, his gaze on his boots. Asked instead, "Did *you* ever regret what you did?"

"In that blood-drenched room, all I knew was that Inara was dead, and I was beside myself with grief. In Tartarus, I was still so angry...then my change occurred within weeks of being imprisoned, and all I could think of was my next feed. Sometimes, I think what happened to me there was just and fitting."

Týr's brow rose. "Becoming a vampire?"

He shrugged. "When we were sentenced, one of those persecuting gods telepathed my judgment into my mind. *For the lifeblood you shed, it will be your downfall*," he paraphrased. "At the time, I had no idea what it meant..."

"Which one?"

"The goddess Hel."

Týr surged to his feet and paced to the trellis, staring into the darkened archway.

"Týr—" Dagan touched his arm, and an image shot through his mind. *Endless gray skies, no sign of life, just ending heat and sands—* No! He yanked free, bile rushing to his throat. Týr couldn't have faced the same fate as he did. "You were trapped in Reapers Hell, too?" he rasped.

Týr cut him an unreadable look before glancing away. "No."

What the hell had he seen then? His abilities never lied.

The murmur of voices drew closer, breaking the

Georgia Lyn Hunter

thick tension. The other Guardians and their mates entered the kitchen. Shae would come looking for him soon.

"Had I a sister, I probably would have done the same," Týr murmured, sliding his hands into his pants pockets. "I already live with too many regrets. Furious as I am with her now, Inara was like a sister to me, too. But she was too young, probably didn't realize the consequence of her actions. I guess the only way to know why is to find her." His gaze shifted to the kitchen window and the other warriors there, the bright lights underscoring his taut features. "No one needs to know what occurred. Ever."

"You are much more forgiving than I. But you know what our laws demand. There's no way around it. Retribution is yours. It's been the ways of the pantheons for eons."

Týr shook his head tiredly. "Another bloody battle to the death? It's all our lives have ever been—even here. You have a mate now. Would you so readily take her into death with you?"

Dagan groaned, swallowing a curse. Grateful Shae wasn't here to hear this. With their weak mate-bond, he'd probably die alone, leaving her vulnerable for that fucker Aza to stroll in and take her.

"Thought not," Týr drawled. Then said, "We may no longer be a part of the pantheons, but the *hefnd* fee is mine. You aren't getting off scot-free."

Dagan narrowed his eyes.

"What? Unlike you, I'm not all that noble and self-sacrificing. Your cabin in the Adirondacks is mine..." he paused. "And a life-size carving of myself."

The tension eased from Dagan a little. "The cabin, yes, and a blood debt I hope I can one day repay. But the sculpture...not happening."

The French door opened, and Shae walked out, the chilly winds stirring her waist-length, coppery hair. Hastily, she buttoned her jacket. "What are you doing out here, it's so cold—oh, hi, Týr." She smiled at the warrior.

"Shae." He nodded, snagged his jacket, and headed for the door, then slowed and cut Dagan a droll stare. "Too bad, you just missed out on having my awesomeness set in stone."

"It would have been wood and used as kindling after," Dagan retorted.

Týr's chuckle drifted to them as he disappeared into the kitchen. Dagan's amused expression morphed into remorse. He leaned against the table and exhaled wearily.

Tender fingers stroked his jaw. "What is it?" Shae asked softly.

Dagan just reached out and pulled her between his thighs, needing to hold her. Feeling as if he were shattering inside.

After a long minute, when he could breathe again, he said, "My sister, Inara, spiked Týr's drink with a sleeping draft. That's why he was unconscious when she was abducted."

Her worried gaze searched his face. "You both okay?"

Dagan doubted it would ever be *okay*, but he nodded. "I don't deserve his decency. When I thought Inara was dead, I took my sword to his throat, Shae. And he forgave me."

"I know. But he's alive. The heavens must favor him," she said softly. "I like him." Dagan cut her a dark look, his territorial nature racing to the forefront.

She laughed. "He has a good heart."

A sigh. "I messed up badly and will always regret it." His expression turned grim again. "By the stars, I could wring Inara's neck! She had no idea what her folly would do. She wanted to go to the damn river on the day the attacks occurred. Týr refused, and she gave him the damn draft—hell!"

"She was still a child, Dagan. She didn't know any better."

"The warriors suffered, Shae. They all suffered." He scrubbed a hand over his face, his thoughts troubled, recalling his sister's pale, thin features. "But she didn't escape unscathed either. She'd paid a price, too, being trapped in Tartarus for five centuries. The heavens knew what kind of hell she'd endured with Lucifer."

Chapter 25

It was close to five when Shae left her mother and headed for her bedroom later that afternoon. The new living room door Dagan was behind remained closed the entire day, to keep the dust and paint fumes contained, he'd said.

She understood it would take time for him to assimilate after learning the truth of what had occurred on that fateful day eons ago.

Her cell rang on the nightstand rang. She snatched it. At the name on the display, she smiled. "Uncle Lem?"

"Yes, my dear. You didn't call, so I was wondering if you're still coming tonight? Don't tell me you've got other plans."

Aw crap. She bit off a groan, recalling the promise she'd made him a while ago about attending the election debate speech he was giving to kick off his mayoral campaign. "No, I don't."

"Good. Do you still want to look over my speech?" he teased.

She laughed. "I trust your judgment, you won't

embarrass us. I know you'll knock them right into voting for you."

His chuckle floated through the line. "You sound…happier."

She heard the question, and Dagan had already cautioned her against mentioning that they'd found her mother until they caught Samael. She didn't want Lem caught in the crossfire with this knowledge.

"Yes. *National Geographic* bought my Nightlife series." At least it wasn't a lie.

"Well done. All right, then, I'll see you tonight at Cooper's Union. At eight."

Rubbing her temple, she ended the call as Dagan walked out of the workroom. Perspiration beaded his brow, and his faded gray tee, darkened with sweat was stuck to his chest. Darn, the man simply smoldered sexiness, even in his clammy clothes.

"Shae?" He stopped in surprise. "I thought you'd be with your mother."

"I was. I came up to check on you."

A dark eyebrow arched. "Me?"

"Yes. That room got done faster than I blinked," she teased. "It says a lot."

A wry smile lifted the corners of his mouth. He stepped closer and pressed his lips on hers. "I'm okay, Shae-cat." Then he nodded to the cell in her hand. "Who was that?"

"Uncle Lem. It's his big speech today. Remember I told you about him running for mayor?"

"And he wants you there?"

"Yes." When he frowned, she added, "I'd like to go, Dagan, he's family. And this is really important to him."

He rubbed his jaw, his brow still furrowed then he

tipped his head. "Okay. Let me get ready for work and we can leave. But after the speech, I'm bringing you straight back."

"Okay." Not like she wanted to linger there when Aza would be about. Besides, she had her abilities if anything happened. She could teleport.

***

A short while later, dressed in boots, black jeans, and a cream sweater, Shae pulled on her leather jacket and ran downstairs to check on her mother.

In Hedori's quarters, she hurried through the living room and paused in the guestroom doorway. The TV was on but muted while her mother stared at her clasped hands. The pile of magazines Shae had set on the nightstand earlier remained untouched. Once, years ago, they'd used to love looking at the latest fashions. Then her father died, and everything changed.

"Shae?" Her mother's panicked voice pulled her back from her troubled thoughts.

"I'm here, Mom." She hurried across the room and grasped the hands tearing at the covers. Dull gray eyes blinked as if waking up from a nightmare. Shae's smile quivered, her chest hurting at the fear in them. "How do you feel?"

"Happier when I see you."

Her eyes burned as she stacked another pillow behind her mother. She forced a smile. "I missed you, too, Mom. Would you like me to get some tea? There's cake—chocolate cake. Hedori made it earlier—"

"I'm not hungry… He's the other man who rescued me," she said, her tone quiet. Eyes emotionless.

"Not exactly a man." Shae sat on the bed, watching her mother anxiously. "He's immortal, like all the men here. He takes care of everything at the castle. And he's an excellent trainer."

Her mom didn't say anything, her gaze drifting to the television.

Unable to stop herself, Shae blurted, "I'm so sorry."

Slowly, her mother glanced back at her. "Why?"

"For terrifying you when the laptop exploded. For hurting you."

"It's not your fault…" She frowned and rubbed her brow then shook her head.

Shae hated that lost look on her mother's face and tried to think of happier things she could talk about.

"Mom," she began quietly. "There's something I want to tell you. That tall Guardian with the warrior braids? We're uh…together."

Her mother stared at her steadily for several seconds then nodded. "I'm glad."

She couldn't help the smile curving her mouth thinking of her man. "Dagan makes me happy."

Her happiness faded a little. She hated having to leave her mom this evening, but Uncle Lem needed family with him.

Voices drifted from the kitchen, followed by the sound of clattering dishes. Shae cut a quick look at the doorway. The warriors would be leaving on patrol, and Dagan would be waiting for her.

"Shae—" Her mother grasped her wrist tightly, panic surging over her wan features. "Ash, he must leave this place."

Shae had no idea what to make of that. Her mother didn't have strong precognition, but she occasionally dreamed things. "Did you have a vision?"

She winced and rubbed her head, her eyes gone dull again. "I haven't had any of those for a long time. I just feel…uneasy about him."

Ash had always been "that musician" to her mother. The fact that she'd actually mentioned his name worried Shae. "Okay. I'm going out with Dagan to see Uncle Lem for a short while, I'll speak to Ash then."

The blank look back in her eyes, she nodded. "I'm tired… You'll come see me when you come back?"

"I'll be here." Her chest aching, Shae pulled the covers over her. The speech shouldn't take too long.

Leaving the bedroom door slightly ajar, she cut through the living room and made her way to the kitchen. As she entered, Dagan turned from the French doors, his black cigar case in his hand. Leathers covered his muscular thighs, and a black dress shirt fitted his wide chest, the sleeves rolled to his elbows. His brow furrowing in concern, he crossed to her. "What happened?"

"Mom feels Ash could be in trouble."

He stared at her for a second. Then, setting his case on the table, he grasped her hands. "Shae, there's something you should know."

His quiet tone sent alarm bells ringing. "What is it?"

"We found Ash a few days ago in a warehouse. He'd been hurt badly. Michael healed him, removed his memories, and sent him off. I didn't tell you because you'd already been through a lot."

"Who?" she asked, too worried to get upset that he'd kept it from her.

"We think Samael could have been behind it, for rescuing Jenna."

"Oh, God!"

His grip tightened on hers. "Your friend's okay. Go ahead and call him."

Dagan wouldn't lie to her. Her hands shaking like a leaf, she rang Ash.

He answered on the first ring. "Thank God, you live! You left the club so suddenly that night, then you just disappeared for work to the ends of the world without a word for weeks? Yeah-yeah, called your friend Harvey, he told me. When are you coming back, doll?"

Tears of relief stung her eyes at his lengthy speech. A shaky laugh left her. "When I'm done. Anchorage is hardly the end of the world. And there wasn't any Wi-Fi coverage where I was—" She grimaced at the lie. "Are you're still in New York?"

"Yeah, the gig will run for another week, then we're off to Miami."

Damn. There was no way Ash would pack up and leave now. "Just be careful, okay?"

"Careful's my middle name, doll. How's Alaska?"

"Cold."

"Shae?"

"Yes?"

A slight hesitation, then a sigh drifted through the line. "Come see me before I leave, okay?"

Something sounded off with him. She cut Dagan a quick look, knowing he could clearly hear their conversation. "I'll try. Bye, Ash."

She ended the call, and at his unreadable expression, she had a feeling Dagan somehow knew about her unrequited feelings for Ash. So she just said it, "Yes, I did like him, but I realize now it was a pale comparison to what I feel for you." Her eyes searched his. "Meeting you showed me that. I still care about him, but only as a friend. You know that, right?"

His gaze softened. "It's why he still breathes."

She huffed out a laugh, then immediately sobered. "Dagan, you have to get Ash to leave New York."

"I'll drop in on your friend later tonight and give him

a little nudge."

"Thank you."

He removed two cigars and pushed them into his pocket.

She frowned. "You still need them?"

"Not in *that* way anymore. But it has been centuries, and it is a narcotic smoke. I guess it will take time to ease off. These have a lower dose of the sedative leaf. Come on, let's go."

Out on the terrace, the moment his arms came around her, she inhaled deeply, his scent and his warmth calming her as he dematerialized them.

***

They took form in a small grove of trees not far from Cooper's Union. Clasping Shae's hand, Dagan headed for the brick building across the street. At the sight of the crowds rallying there, he slowed.

Shae tightened her grip on his hand as if he would leave—he *would*, but not without her. So he was stuck until the meet and greet was done. And the speech.

Inside the building, he ignored the stares coming his way and he and Shae headed down the busy corridor. The loud chatter in the place crowded his ears. Two hours—that wasn't long, he tried to convince himself. Yeah, that shit didn't work. His teeth clenched.

"Shae?"

They both turned. Her demon friend dodged the crowd and jogged to them. "Harvey." She grinned. "I hoped you'd come."

"Said I would." He cast Dagan a guarded look.

Shae introduced them. "This is Harvey, my best friend—Harv, my mate, Dagan."

The demon nodded. He didn't seem surprised at that bit of info.

Dagan stared, doing little to put him at ease. This male was there for her in all the times she needed someone, taught her to fight—yeah, he should be grateful—hell, he was, but bottom line? He was a territorial bastard, and there it was.

Shae elbowed him in the ribs. He merely folded his arms.

She rolled her eyes and turned away. "Come with us," she told the demon. "I'm just going to say hello to my uncle then we can find our seats."

Harvey groaned. "Fine, as long as I don't have to see that damn Fallen drooling over you."

Dagan couldn't fault the demon there; he was going to make that fucker wish for death for what he'd done.

"Your mother?" Harvey asked her then.

"The Guardians rescued her." She inhaled deeply, lowered her voice. "A rogue angel, Samael, held her prisoner in the Dark Realm."

"Shit. I'm sorry. But I'm glad you have her back."

"Me, too." Shae slowed after navigating the corridor to the back and stared at the few doors there, all shut. "Excuse me." She stopped a human male shuffling past, eyes glued to a file in his hand. "Leamas Hale? Do you know where I can find him?"

The guy looked up then frowned when his gaze settled on Shae's scar, lips curling in distaste. Her mouth tightened. A low growl rumbled out of Dagan. The human stepped back and hastily flicked his thumb over his shoulder. "Last office." And giving Dagan a wide berth, he scurried off.

"Asshole," Harvey muttered, climbing just a little higher in Dagan's estimation.

Shae didn't respond, heading for the last room instead. Dagan scanned and picked up four heartbeats.

Humans. She knocked and opened the door.

As they entered, the scent of coffee and liquor flooded his nose. A young, suited guy seated behind the desk was going through something on his laptop. Three more men sat at a round table, talking and looking over notes. Silence fell at their entrance. The man at the desk scratched his close-shaven hair, looked up, and a bright smile split his dusky face. "Shae."

"Hey, Rashaad. How are you?" Shae asked with a friendly smile Dagan didn't care for.

"I'm good, girl. We haven't seen you in a while."

"Been busy—work. I don't see my uncle around."

"He stepped out for a minute. I'll go alert him you're here." He jumped up and rushed off.

Harvey remained near the shut door. Dagan looked out the window into the darkened street choked with parked cars and scanned the area. Nothing. Even though there wasn't much supernatural activity here, he didn't trust the quiet.

People hustled toward the building, obviously not wanting to miss the speech. He slid his hands into his pockets, itching to get back on the street.

"You're like a caged tiger," Shae said, appearing at his side, a mug of coffee in her hand and a smile on her beautiful face. "He's stuck in the other office with last-minute things, he'll be here soon. I just messaged him that I wanted him to meet someone important to me."

Dagan cut off a snort and declined the coffee she held out. He was the last person to inspire confidence in anyone. With his height, long hair, and clad in leathers, he probably appeared more like the Grim Reaper. However, he wasn't concerned. If her uncle didn't like him, he'd simply change his mind.

We need you here, man, Aethan's clipped voice

sounded in his mind, sending him into tense alert. *Shit's flying everywhere.*

Dammit. The other warriors could help out for now.

The door opened, and an older man of average height with light brown hair wearing a black designer suit strode in, frowning at some papers in his hand. Two men, as well as Rashaad who seemed to hang onto his every word, followed him. The man sure had a presence about him…

The human looked up, a smile warming his austere features. "Shae."

"Uncle Lem." She set the mug on the windowsill and hurried over to hug him. "I'm so sorry, but the job took longer than expected. I want you to meet someone." She eased back and held out her hand. Dagan crossed to her, and she laced their fingers. "This is Dagan."

The man turned then, eyes narrowing. Before Dagan could take hold of his mind and soothe him, he smiled. "I'm Leamas Hale, her uncle. I guess you already knew that. Call me Lem."

Thankfully, her kin didn't offer a handshake. It suited Dagan since he didn't much like touching anyone.

Lem turned to the desk and put down his notes. "Let's have a drink." He nodded to someone. A server with a tray appeared. Dagan declined, watching as Lem offered Shae a glass and waved Harvey over then handed him one, as well.

D-man, where the hell are you? Nik telepathed him now. These damn mind-links were going to crash his brain. He shut them out, said to Lem, "I'm sorry about this, but something's come up—work. I have to go. Shae?"

The older man frowned.

"Dagan works security," Shae quickly covered.

"You can't leave," Lem told her, disappointment pulling his mouth down.

Dagan? she mind-linked him, her voice faint, but he heard the plea.

"Shae, see me off?" Since he didn't want to argue with her telepathically either, he ushered her out into the corridor and to the end of the passage slowly clearing of the crowd.

"Dagan, he needs me."

Dammit, he didn't want to leave her here alone. But her pleading tugged at him. He pulled out his cell and shot off a text. Put his phone away. "I'm not happy about this—hell, I just want to cart you back to the castle, but I know how important this is to you. Hedori will be here in a moment or so—go wait with your demon friend. I'll be back as soon as I can. If anything makes you uneasy, I don't care how insignificant, you teleport out of here back to the castle and telepath me."

"Okay, okay, be safe." Her eyes searched his. "Is everything all right?"

He didn't want her to worry about the shit happening out there. "The usual crap, but just a little more tonight." He cupped her face and kissed her, hard. "Be safe for me, Shae-cat."

"I will, and you be safe, too." She bunched the fabric of his dress shirt as if to keep him there. Her smile wavered. "I love you."

Dagan stood there like some damn stiff, unable to speak as a rush of emotions crowded his throat at those three simple words. "Now you tell me? When I'm about to leave."

A smile curved her mouth. A teasing light brightening her beautiful eyes, she whispered, "I'll tell you again later…in bed, when we're naked."

"Fuck, woman, don't put those thoughts into my head when I'm leaving. Cause right now, all I can think about is dragging you off to the nearest dark corner—" Growling, because talking about it sure wasn't helping his unruly body when he had to get back on the job, he gave her another hard kiss. "Go back to the office, I'll see you soon."

In the grove of trees, he scanned for trouble. Like pinpoints of icy prickles, it broke over him, abrading his mind. Shit, it wasn't just one spot but several places throughout the city.

Hedori materialized.

"Good, you're here. She's in the office at the back, last one."

***

Dagan rematerialized in the Bowery. The cacophony of guttural sounds rebounded off the grimy building walls deep in the alley downtown. Damn scourges would turn up now and distract him when he had things to do. Summoning his mystical sword, he dove into the horde.

With barely a ripple in the air, Týr appeared beside him, his sword blazing a deadly orange gleam, a smirk on his face.

"Damn fuckers!" Dagan growled, pain searing his right arm from a sword slash. With Shae's blood in him, he healed fast.

"Hey, fun times," Týr grinned, ducking a blow that would have severed his head. A flash of his hand, and the demon screamed as a blazing fire consumed him in seconds.

Dagan kicked a sneering demon in the chest, sending him flying. With his mind, he grabbed the lot in front of him and held them immobile. Using their own weapons, he compelled them to slice their own carotids. The bodies crumbled and disappeared. Hell, it felt damn good to have his abilities as backup.

Inhaling lungfuls of the decaying alley air, he scanned again. Sensing more of them deeper in the shadows, he flashed. In the dead-end, a shimmering portal hovered, and the scourges vanished through it. The gateway hissed shut. "Shit!"

Dagan searched the eerily quiet thoroughfare. Nothing. He dismissed his sword, but the itch bearing down his spine warned him that it wasn't over. Since he was close to Club Nocte, he'd go get that friend of Shae's to leave before he wound up dead.

"Where's Shae?" Týr asked, joining him.

"Waiting to hear her uncle's speech." It was strange that he hadn't laid eyes on Aza there. "I'm heading back as soon as this mess is dealt with. Got Hedori guarding her. And I have to get Shae's friend to leave the city tonight."

"Who?"

"A musician from RockinHell."

"Yeah, I heard them, they're good."

Dagan snorted, then explained about finding Ash tortured in the warehouse and Jenna's premonition. Týr nodded as he got out a pack of M&M's from his jacket pocket. He poured the candies onto his palm, and taking his time, he finally selected several reds.

"Really? Are you five?"

"Don't mock my method, you uninformed vampire."

"There's insanity to your method."

"Maybe…" Týr smirked, tossing the lot into his mouth.

Shaking his head, Dagan rubbed his jaw as they

headed up the alley, his mind back on Shae's uncle. "Leamas Hale… There's something about the human that bugs me."

"Could be that he's Shae's guardian, not blood, and maybe because he's young? You know, like that dumbass, Damon, who was Echo's?" Týr drawled.

"Not that young," Dagan grunted. "It's not just his excessive confidence…he's too smooth. Hell. It would hurt Shae if she found out I don't like the man."

"Leamas. That's a strange name. Leamaaas," Týr dragged out the name. "L. E. A. M. A. S.," he spelled slowly, eyes narrowing. "Motherfucker!" he snarled. "Leamas is Samael spelled backward. The bastard must have been laughing at us the whole time, being right under our noses. No wonder he was able to shield himself so well."

"Samael?" Dagan froze, feet nailed to the grimy asphalt. "Shae's *uncle*?" Just as fast, he yelled through their mind-link. *Shae!* Nothing, just unending silence.

"She's not answering my mind-link," he gasped. Then he couldn't breathe, feeling as if his strength had drained. Týr grabbed his biceps and shook him. "Dag—calm down, man. Gotta keep your shit together!"

He shrugged Týr off. "I left her with him. I didn't even know, and I met the fucker!" His fangs bared, his stomached roiled in dread.

"Go. I'll alert the others and see to the human." Týr flashed.

Dagan dematerialized, except he couldn't. An eerie sensation snaked around him, unlike anything he'd ever experienced before. Energy seeped into him. He stiffened. *What the—?*

His thoughts scattered as a riptide hauled him into a

vortex of impossible power.

Georgia Lyn Hunter

Chapter 26

Shae left Dagan and headed back to the office, empty champagne glass in her hand. She really wished he'd stayed. But innocent lives could be lost, and she didn't want that.

Ugh. She rubbed her temples, blinking at the sudden buzz in her head. She must have drunk the champagne too fast. Several people left the office, and Shae stepped aside to let them pass. It was probably time for the speech to start.

As she walked into the room, she found two strange men inside. They flanked her uncle, who sat behind the table, staring blankly at her. And Harvey stood stony-faced near the window.

"Uncle Lem?" she said, a slight sense of unease sweeping through her as she set the glass down, but he didn't respond.

Red tinged the eyes of the suited men beside him. Demons. What the hell was going on?

"Harvey?" she called out, fear rising, but her friend stood rigid near the window, looking like he'd been drained of every drop of blood as he glared at something behind her.

"Finally." The sleek voice caressed her nape, and the hairs on her arms rose.

Shae spun around and winced. Her head spun. She grabbed a chair for support, blinking at the stranger silhouetted in the entrance. Tall, blond, nothing was familiar about him. And she knew most of Lem's associates.

Sea-blue eyes met hers. Strangely, they were the only things about him that she felt a bizarre connection to. A hint of power radiated from him and slithered around her like a lasso, squeezing her chest. Another immortal.

Her own abilities swirled in response, but hands grabbed her by the upper arms and hauled her backward. Harvey stepped protectively in front of her, only then she understood the stranger was testing the strength of her capabilities, and she clamped her shields down. Dammit, what was it with her today? The dizziness creeping over her made her really slow.

"You think you can protect her, demon?" With a wave of his hand, the immortal shut the door. "The only one who can is her annoying watchdog." He laughed, the sound like crackling ice. "Now, isn't it nice that he got called away to an emergency? Something that's more important than you? By the way, your champagne? It was spelled. Just a precaution to keep out unwanted immortal interference, you understand."

Fear coasting through her like a gale-force, she mind-linked with Dagan, *Where are you? I need you!* Except she hit a dead zone. Silence echoed in her mind. Dear, God!

"If you touch her—"

"You try my patience, demon." The stranger's strident voice cut Harvey off, his eyes flaming in anger. "I'm so close to taking out your kind. Filth that doesn't belong here and mars my city."

"Why are you doing this?" Shae whispered, her gaze darting back to her still unmoving uncle. "What did you do to him?"

"That is the least of your concerns." Aza walked in like he owned the place and stood beside the stranger, a triumphant expression on his narrow features.

Shae stared, her lungs flattening in fear. "You're doing this because I didn't want to date you?"

Aza said nothing. The blond stepped forward, his hard stare pinning her. "You shouldn't have run or lied, Shae."

Lied? She'd never met the man before. "Who are you?"

"You wound me, my dear. For such a clever girl, you genuinely have no clue? And I had you and you mother under my care for so many years."

What the hell was he talking about? She'd never seen him before. But those eyes...

"You really don't know, do you?" He exhaled, his cool expression morphing to mock disappointment. Then his eyes began to glow with such lethal intent, Shae shuddered. Harvey held her arms as if lending her his courage.

"Come here, Lem," he commanded in a voice that didn't leave room for resistance. As her uncle rose and shuffled over like some wooden doll, the blond smiled. A dagger appeared in his hand, and without warning, he plunged it into Lem's chest.

"No!" she screamed. Breaking free of Harvey, she

sprinted forward and reached for her uncle, but he dissipated into the air. She stood there, staring at the spot where he'd been, pain searing through every facet of her being. *Dagan*, she cried through their telepathic link. But just unending silence answered her.

"Don't grieve him, he served his purpose. Let me introduce myself, my dear," the murdering bastard said, smiling. "I'm Samael."

"You godsdamn, asshole!" Harvey forged past Shae. Samael flung him back with a flick of his hand, and he hit the wall.

At the small, secret smirk on Samael's face, Shae snapped out of her shocked stupor, something cold materializing in her palm. With no idea how her obsidian dagger appeared in her hand, she flung it with every ounce of agony inside her. Samael shifted at the last minute, and the blade embedded in his sternum, missing his black heart.

The demons in the room rushed forward, but Samael stopped them with a wave of his hand as if he didn't need their help.

Harvey grabbed her by the shoulders and pulled her back.

Those familiar eyes narrowed on her. "Someone's been brushing up on her fighting skills." With a derisive laugh, he grabbed the obsidian dagger, yanking it out with a brief wince. "I knew I should have killed you ages ago, Harvey." Cold anger swirling in his eyes, he flung Shae's dagger at Aza, who grabbed it mid-air. "Finish him."

"I've been waiting for this." Aza leaped for Harvey, who jumped away.

Blood thundering in her head, Shae shoved Aza with all her strength. He lurched back a step. Snarling, he flashed, came up behind Harvey, and sliced her best friend's throat.

Harvey's eyes darkened in shock. He gurgled. Blood sprayed from the wound like a fountain as he fell.

"Nooo!" An agonizing sob tore free. She dropped to her knees on the hard, cold floor and held her friend, tears dripping down her face. Harvey's body shimmered from her blood-drenched arms, and he vanished, hauled back to the Dark Realm in death.

"Everything else is on track, too," Aza reported to Samael then strolled past Shae and returned her dagger to him with a satisfied smirk. "The asshole Guardians are back on the streets, the butler's busy outside. My demons play a good game of chaos. The ruckus should keep them busy for most of the night."

"Good." Samael stepped in front of Shae. "Get off the floor, my dear."

Two demons came forward and lifted her by her arms when she didn't move. "Why?" she cried. "Why are you killing my family—my friend? My uncle, what did he ever do to you?"

"You still haven't guessed? I'm disappointed, Shae. Very well…" He waved his hand over himself, and the next instant, he shrank to average height, his features morphing to the familiar ones of Uncle Lem. Two seconds later, he was the blond man again. "For years, I've stayed this way, using the alter ego. Revolting really, wearing a weak human skin, but necessary."

Oh, God. The pain of betrayal corroded her insides as it all began to make sense.

She loved a phantom, an uncle who didn't exist. She cut Samael a stare of utter loathing. "Mom didn't leave because of *me* six months ago, did she? *You* took her. Why?"

"Because you and your mother belong to me. Only she forced my hand, refused me. It's really bothersome having to recount everything." With a touch of his hand on her forehead, memories spilled free.

Shae staggered against the wall, grabbing her skull as images erupted. Her dreams. She pulled out the dagger from her father's chest, and in a flash, he too disappeared. "My father—" The truth cleaved her in half. "*You* killed him."

"Oh no, my dear," he said, his face void of emotions. "Not me, but he had to go."

"Why?" She gripped the edges of the desk so her knees wouldn't buckle, the sight of Harvey's blood spilled on the floor rendering her helpless.

"You don't know what he was?" Surprise colored his tone. "All these years, and they kept your heritage hidden from you?" He laughed. "Your father was a throne—a third-level angel created for war. But in this world, Gusion forgot our plans and vanished. When I found him again a decade later, he was preparing to go back to the Celestial Realm, to give up his wings and fall." Samael's highly polished shoes came into her line of view. "Imagine my surprise when I found out that he'd mated a mortal and spawned you. I wanted to kill you to teach him a lesson, but then I realized you were a nephilim. You had to have some of his powers. So I waited."

Her gaze snapped to him. "A nephi—what?"

"A half-angel, dear girl. However, except for sensing demons, your abilities never showed. You took after your human mother. And just when I thought I was wasting my time with the both of you, it happened. Who would have guessed that all it took was a fight between you two? Mother and daughter. Then your laptop short-circuited and exploded, sending her flying across the room."

He laughed. "That evening, one of my minions thought to have his way with Jenna, and a miracle occurred. Her powers awakened. She destroyed him within seconds, melting every muscle and bone. I realized then that she was the long-awaited psionic, a descendant of the powerful Watchers. Finally, I knew I could still have it all with her."

His chilling smile grew. "You see, that's why I had to separate you two, so she would do whatever I wanted. I laid out little traps, had her killing humans and Others alike, but Michael thought himself too lofty to investigate their deaths. He sent those pissy Guardians to snoop around instead." Samael ambled to the window, reached behind him, and scratched his back. "No matter, today I shall be free."

How could she not have known? Not guessed the truth? For so many years, she'd lived with this monster. And all the while, he'd been using her mother to kill. Her stomach churned, her hands shook, sweat beading on her brow. "And you think you can defeat *the* archangel?"

"I don't have to." He pivoted to her. "Jenna will kill him. And she can. Why do you think I let the demon, Luka, leak where she was? It was time to get this damn show on the road." Sinister laughter echoed in the room like splintered glass. "Because Michael is responsible for what's been done to me, and he will fix it, or he dies."

"Samael. We had a deal," Aza said from across the room. "I took care of Gusion. Gave you my demons when you required them. Now, give me the girl."

His words barely registered, her throat swollen with

tears as she grieved for her parents, for an uncle that didn't exist, and for her friend. And more, at how easily Samael had played everyone from her to the archangel.

Samael sauntered closer to Aza. "You've waited several months for her, you can tolerate a few more minutes."

"Your fight with the archangel isn't mine. Give her to me, or I will send all my demons back to the Dark Realm, even the ones on the street." Aza stalked over to Shae, then tripped, crashing into the desk. He grabbed his throat. His eyes bulged, choking sounds filling the air.

"Never threaten me, Azaul," Samael murmured, cool boredom on his flawless face—and all the more terrifying for it.

Aza rubbed his throat, his dark eyes becoming black holes as he straightened. In a blur, he moved toward her. Shae jumped back, evading him by a hair's breadth as he knocked into the desk, scattering papers everywhere. Someone grabbed her from behind.

Snarling, she elbowed the minion hard in the belly. A raucous growl blasted her ears. His huge fist came flying toward her face, landing with the impact of a boulder. Pain exploded from her jaw and into her head in a kaleidoscope of stars as she crashed to the ground.

"Very well, you want the girl? Go get me her mother," Samael's words echoed in her mind as it all went dark.

Chapter 27

Shae's head pounded like someone had slammed a jackhammer into her skull. A moan caught in her throat, she forced her eyelids open. Darkness surrounded her, along with a biting chill. Her damp sweater stuck to her back from lying on the dew-drenched ground. And it all rushed back as if an unending nightmare.

They were no longer at the office. Blurred, indistinct shapes swarmed her vision for several seconds. The moon underscored everything in an odd, silvery-blue light.

"Welcome back, dear girl. This place is so fitting, don't you think? Where it all started."

At the dreaded voice, she blinked to clear her fuzzy sight. The crisp scent of apples teased her nose. With some effort, she focused, and at the sight of the sloped red-roof house to her right, her breath hitched painfully.

He'd brought her to her old home near Stone Ridge, behind which lay the apple orchard she'd always loved so much.

Shae pushed herself off the ground and sat up, shivering in the frigid air. Her jacket had vanished. Did they think she had a stash of weapons hidden in it? Queasiness churned her stomach and tracked up her throat, the sounds of clinking crowding her ears. She rubbed her bleary eyes, except something heavy weighed her arms down. Metal manacles shackled her wrists, the chain fastened around a tree trunk.

At her helpless state, another bout of nausea bubbled up her throat.

Aza crouched near her, his eyes glittering in avarice as they swept up her body to linger on her breasts.

"You freakin' chained me?" She yanked at the restraints.

"So you can't teleport. The chains will keep you docile. It's why you'll remain shackled until we complete the mating," he murmured, his tone an icky caress. *Now you are mine, Shae,* his words trickled into her mind.

He was the one sending those insidious whispers to torment her. Shae heaved.

Aza smirked, rose to his feet, and faced Samael. "I brought you the other female, now I shall leave with Shae."

"You will wait until I decide you can go, Azaul."

"Never forget, I'm a Fallen, too," Aza retorted. "I could just take her from you."

Aza clearly had no idea about the truth of this rogue.

Samael laughed, the ominous sounds chafing her bruised psyche. He unbuttoned his jacket and flung it away. At the sudden rip in the night, Shae blinked. Samael groaned. Rustling filled the air, and in a flash of light, wings burst free from his back. Six feet of iridescent white wings gleamed in the moonlight—so beautiful, they put the stars to shame. And they belonged to this psychotic asshole.

"I am no *Fallen*." He cut Aza the smallest of smiles, all the more menacing for it. "Yes, I kept this truth from you. Losing my wings was not part of my plan. It's why I needed Jenna to corral Michael here. He'd come for her, thinking the *evil* Fallens had a powerful psionic in their grips. But then he would already be keeping tabs on *you*"—he glared at Aza—"after your idiotic stunt to restrain Shae by shooting her."

"She belongs to me. It was a mere retrieval and not intended to kill her, but who could have expected that asshole to protect her?"

"You're a fool." Samael's wings fluttered in annoyance. "They are Guardians. It's what they do. I didn't plan for eons to let *you* fuck up all my hard work. Do you honestly think I don't know why you put money into my mayoral campaign? You want a psychic, except Jenna is *mine*, as is Shae. She may be of no value to me, only a cog to be used to get her mother to play nice, but she's still mine. And you dared to put a mating mark on *my* property."

"I'm no one's damn property," Shae pushed through gritted her teeth, wrenching at her restraints.

Sea-blue eyes flickered to her briefly. "But you are, my dear, very much so."

Aza snarled, a sword appearing in his hand, braced for attack. Shit! Shae hastily scrambled backward on her ass to get out of the way. Power sizzled in Samael's hands. His wings flapped, casting a halo of light around him. "I could kill you before you blinked. Bear that in mind, Azaul. And don't even think of recalling these demons."

Scowling, Aza lowered his sword.

Swallowing hard, Shae leaned against the tree trunk. Hordes of demons, like jittering dark roaches, stood off to the side and polluted the overgrown lawn of her home.

"Now, where were we?" Samael strolled to her. "Ah, yes... It's time for a new regime of power in this world. Call Michael."

She glared at him. "No."

Samael shook his head. "You're a tough one. Why didn't I notice it before? Let's see how rebellious you are then, shall we?" His focus shifted to the house. "Jenna."

Mom? Her gaze snapped to the front door.

"Surprised, are you?" Amusement tinged his voice. "I simply got her here with a command in her mind. You see, I never took her cell. It wasn't like she could use it in the Dark Realm. When I called her, she answered. And made her way to the nearest watery spot."

The lake?

He gave the shortest of laughs. "It's so easy to conceal any mystical happenings, even at the Guardians' abode."

Her mother stepped out of their old home, the vacant look back in her eyes. Like a zombie, she shuffled toward Samael.

"Mom—no!" Shae pushed to her feet, desperately trying to mind-link with Dagan again. And still, nothing.

Samael drew her to him and fastened his mouth over hers in a lascivious kiss. Her mother stood there like a limp doll. And Shae knew. He'd used her sexually, too.

With a flick of his hand, her mother fell to the

ground. She grabbed her head and screamed, a thin, keening sound, the cry piercing Shae in the heart.

"Stop, stop it!" she yelled, straining against her shackles, the energy inside her whipping viciously, looking for an outlet, but she couldn't set it free with the cursed chains blocking her abilities. Blood seeped from her nose. She coughed out, "Don't hurt her—please don't, I'll call Michael."

"Just him. I see any of the other warriors here, Jenna dies."

He held her cell phone next to her ear. Dagan had given her all the warriors' numbers the night they'd gone to trap Luka. The call was answered on the first ring. "Shae?"

"M-Michael?" her voice cracked.

"Where are you?" His tone was quiet, reassuring. But she had so little hope left. Even her stupid abilities had deserted her.

"At my old home…you have to come alone, or he'll kill my mother."

"I will. Where is it?"

She gave him the address. Then Samael snatched the cell away. "Good girl. Now we wait."

Shae barely heard him, her burning gaze fixed on her mother shuddering on the damp ground. She didn't want to think of what she must have endured for six months at the hands of this coldhearted bastard—couldn't bear it—and she broke.

An agonized cry tore free. The heat inside her exploded. Her shields crashed. The cuffs snapped from her wrists and fell to the ground with a clinking of metal.

Caught in a cyclone of power, Shae leaped up. Her obsidian dagger taking form in her hand, she pivoted and slashed the demon closest to her across the throat. His head fell to the ground and rolled away to the jittery demon horde standing on the fringes of the yard.

Several of the scourges rushed her. A cacophony of sounds erupted as she dodged and ducked between them, evading attacks, leaping up and slicing. Blood gushed as heads rolled, bodies piling…

With a shudder, Shae came into herself, breathing hard. She stood alone in the violent, blood-drenched grounds. Red sprayed her clothes, her skin sticky with gore, her hair stuck to her face. The bodies had all disappeared, leaving only the grisly front yard behind.

Samael sighed, an expression of utter delight on his face. "Oh, my dear, you've been keeping secrets. You are a weapon of beauty."

She flung out her hands. Power sizzled out of her fingers like lightning, striking Samael in the chest. He lurched back a step. His face twisted into a terrifying, hollowed-out skeleton, then smoothed back again into the lean features of her uncle. "Utterly perfect. Now shield that power and come to me, dear girl…" he coaxed softly, holding out his hand.

Her heart shuddered in pain. *No, he's not real.*

"Come, Shae. You know me. We've spent so many years together. You know I won't hurt you." His mind stroked hers, calming, soothing.

Her powers eased, receding back into her body. Her thoughts a smoky haze, she stumbled closer. "Uncle Lem?"

"Yes, child." He grasped her wrist, his thumb stroking her skin.

She looked down at her hands. Lem would never use this compelling voice on her. Never do this. With a desperate tug, she tried to break free, her fingers squeezing her dagger. "No, you're not my uncle."

Laughing, he held her with terrifying ease. "You cannot kill me with any weapon, Shae, because we are one. Six months ago, I bound you to me when I realized you'd begun to drift away after the incident with your mama. I couldn't have that."

"What did you do to me, you rotten heap of angel shit?"

His features morphed back to the chillingly handsome visage of Samael. "Dextrose, dear Shae. It was so easy to get you to eat it for your little *health problem*."

"You poisoned it!"

"It's been spelled, I'm afraid. Just a little precaution I had to take with you always going off somewhere for that silly job of yours. It keeps our binding nice and strong. You were always such a good little girl," he crooned. "You took the candies every day."

He let her go. Shae stared blankly at him. Her body still immobilized and held prisoner by his power, but her mind was hers again. Hatred and rage tore through her.

Samael strolled across the blood-drenched grass and stared down at her unconscious mother. "Pity. I didn't like hurting her. She's a fighter, like you. Aza needed his little mating mark to keep track of you, but I always knew where you were." He frowned, looked around. "Where is he?" Then he shook his head. "No matter. He'll be back for you."

Samael glanced back. "Do you know why he wants you? It's because you were a little psychic. He likes the extreme in his sexual encounters—sex with near asphyxiation. Before his usual place, Club Illudo, burned down a year ago, he killed several human women in his quest for the perfect partner. Being who you are, you'd probably survive suffocation. So you see, my dear, why I'm better?"

Havta kill him—havta!

"Ah, finally. The esteemed archangel himself has arrived."

Michael appeared in a shower of silvery sparks. Those fractured blue eyes swept over Shae and her mother in a swift glide. "Let them go, Samael."

"Why?" Power hissed out of his palm, hitting Michael straight in the chest, sending him a step back. "You want to save them, then I want something from you. Since you did this to me when you first tried to remove my wings, you will mend me! I know you've been gifted with the power of healing by your ancient goddess, Gaia. Perform that task, and you can have them once I leave."

"You can't run from justice. Release them," Michael said, tone calm.

"Justice?" Samael rumbled. "Amazing, archangel, how you continue to serve Him, hunting runaway angels even though you can no longer call the Celestial Realm home."

Michael's mouth tightened. "Release them. *Now*."

"Your word, archangel?"

A long silence. "Very well."

Samael narrowed his eyes. "Try anything, and Jenna dies. Shae will remain permanently frozen, like a statue, for the long life she'll have as a nephilim."

Nooo. Shae pushed and clawed at the psychic hold Samael had over her.

Samael turned and waited. Shae gaped. Through his shredded white shirt hanging loosely on him where his wings had shot out, red streaks marred the pristine feathers near the base of his left shoulder. The wings were bloodied and slowly disintegrating—they were dying. The plumage close to his skin had almost blackened. Dark, vein-like threads spread over his skin.

A silvery-white healing light left Michael's hands, coalescing on the damaged extremities. The once deformed wings slowly mended, becoming strong and healthy again.

Samael inhaled a deep breath of relief. Then he stepped back and smiled. "You should never have come after me, knowing what I was created to do. Soon, with a psionic and a nephilim bound to me, I'll have everything."

"I'm well aware of what you are…Death." Michael retied his loosened hair. "Once you are no longer, a new angel will assume the position." His hand flashed out. A sudden explosion of power, and a blinding light streamed across the night. Shae couldn't see for several seconds. Samael's snarl ricocheted through the air, his hold on her loosening. In the distance, swords clanged.

Shae lurched toward her mother. Out of nowhere, Aza appeared, clutching her upper arm. Before he could flash them away, Samael blasted him clear across the yard with a wave of his hand and grabbed Shae around her waist. *No!*

She tried to latch onto his abilities, drain him, but she hit a wall. His mind guards were too strong, like reinforced armor. A strange heat seeped into her, spiraling through her body…not hers. Frantically, she tried to teleport, but his power was too intense, overwhelming hers. At Samael's feral expression of delight, understanding pounded through her. *He* kept her here…he wanted her to kill again.

She coughed, pain ripping through her insides,

struggling to hold onto her own splintering shields.

"Go on, Shae, let that beautiful power out. End him. He doesn't deserve to live," Samael murmured. "Michael was the one who killed those *unfallen* angels who mated humans, as well as their offspring…"

Shae shook her head as Michael fought an invisible barrier to get to them.

"He killed your father, too," a whisper in her ear.

"Nooo!"

"Yesssss."

The storm inside her gathered force, spiking higher and higher. She would kill him. *Kill them all—*

With a blast of her mind, Michael flew through the air, a fiery power haze surrounding him.

"Good girl. Now the others, starting with him."

Her gaze followed to where Samael pointed. Amidst the rioting demons, under the silvery moon, she saw *him*.

She angled her head. Her powers churning like a geyser inside her and sparking in her palms, she stared silently as a demon charged him. The tall warrior whipped around, his long hair flying about him then he stumbled. More surrounded him, swords raised.

A blood-curdling scream left her. She threw out her hands, a bolt of power escaped, torpedoing straight to him. He flew back, crashing through the demons, toppling them like dominoes.

"Good girl," Samael crooned.

Chapter 28

What the hell? The power ensnaring Dagan in the alley finally released him, dumping him in a…warzone?

Grunts and screeches filled the night air. He spun around in the chaos. The looming mountains were a short distance off, so somewhere in the Catskills—there was a farmhouse on the other side of the riot.

His mystical tattoo shifted on his bicep, demanding release at the absolute evil surrounding him, but a hilt already rested in his fingers.

His obsidian? *What the fuck?* He could no longer summon the weapon, which meant…

His heart careened to his throat. Only when she was in absolute danger would the dagger summon him. She was here!

Frantically, he searched the crowd, feeling as if a huge hand were crushing his chest. *Shae,* he telepathed in a yell, *answer me, dammit!*

A demon charged him, and he stumbled. Several more circled him, closing in. They lunged, swords arching down as if he were that easy to defeat. Damn fuckers!

A scream tore through the chaos, wrenching his heart. Power slammed him in the sternum, sending him flying back, crashing into several demons. His breath rattled in his chest. And he knew.

Samael. The bastard was somehow controlling Shae.

Mindless with terror, he leaped to his feet. Inhaling harshly, his bruised lungs protesting violently at the action, he flung the demons out of his way with his mind. A path cleared, and he sprinted to the echo of Shae's scream. There, in the center of the lawn, a fiery glow surrounded her and Samael, who had her in a deadlock. The rogue flung a bolt, and a sizzle of energy thrust Dagan back several steps.

Resist him—lock your mind, Shae, he telepathed to her, praying she could hear him now that he was here. *Shut yourself off from him!*

A moment passed, then her thin, agonized voice seeped into him. *I'm so sorry...* She shut her eyes.

"Let her go, Samael!" Michael wrestled through the power storm, trying to get to them.

Dagan cleaved his way to her, feeling as if he were wading through molasses, desperation eating at him. *Hold on, baby, I'm going to get you out of this.*

Her eyelids snapped open, an eerie, swirling gold eclipsing her gray irises. *No, stay back, I don't want to hurt you again.* Her words echoed faintly inside his head.

You think I'm just gonna let you fucking die?

I-I can't break free of him. Somehow, he bound us together... I'm sorry...

Fear corroding his gut, his heart in his mouth, he pushed through the storm. A strange surge of power shot out of him, startling Dagan, and like lightning, it rammed through the barrier surrounding Shae and the rogue, splintering it apart.

Dagan lunged forward into the thickened haze. Blistering heat scorched his clothes and his skin as he fought to free her from Samael, who smiled like a maniac. A white eddy of light swirled, coalescing into him—as if the bastard was depleting Shae of her very essence.

Did he think he could reap her powers? *She* would to drain him dry!

Suddenly, Samael's eyes widened in confusion.

Yeah, the fucker got the message. Only his girl could steal another's abilities.

Samael started grappling with Shae, trying frantically to free himself. His wings fluttered furiously, his entire being pitching like a flaming wave. The force of energy flung Dagan several meters away.

Pain didn't deter him, he dashed forward, but Michael grabbed his arm. "Wait—"

"Fucking let go, Arc!" Dagan bared his fangs, close to ripping his leader's throat out. But the bloody angel didn't budge. Arms like bulldozers kept him nailed in place. His gaze shot back to Shae and the rogue, then all he could do was watch.

Samael's feathers caught on fire, flames soaring in a hiss. His roar of pain reverberated like fragmenting glass. Shae held onto him as if in an embrace as his essence flowed into her in a stream of firefly sparks, encompassing them both in a bright light.

Michael let Dagan go, a small ebony disc appearing in his hand. He threw the ring up, and the thing broke apart over Shae and Samael. A net flew out, and as it fell over Samael, a golden light glimmered through the links as if securing him.

"What the hell is that?"

"An angel snare."

As the flames died out, black bits of charred feathers floated about. The acrid smell of scorched hair hung heavy in the still night. At Samael's back, only ghostly, skeletal spines remained, like macabre antlers, before they crumbled into ashes. Trapped in the net, Samael's emaciated form collapsed to the ground in a tangled heap. Next to him, Shae swayed.

Dagan leaped and grabbed her around the waist. He lowered her to the blackened grass, holding her in his arms. The scorching heat emitting from her singed him. He barely noticed.

Her entire body glowed like the sun. Blood seeped from her nose.

Shae, go to the place inside you and lock your power down, bring your shields up, baby. C'mon—c'mon, do it!"

I...can't. So...tired.

Yes, you can, he ground out in desperation.

"Let me." Nik crouched. Dagan stared blankly at him. Only then did he become aware that the other warriors were there, too. The demons had been destroyed. Nik grabbed hold of both of Shae's hands and let his power loose. Ice crystalized the very air around them as he infused his own freezing abilities into her, trying to cool her down. But the heat radiating off her just sizzled through, melting the ice, steam hissing into the night.

"Dammit!" Nik sat back on the grass, breathing hard. "I'm sorry, D-man. Whatever this is, my abilities can't stop it."

Dagan, help me—her cry a faint, anguished plea

seeped through his mind. Her body shuddered as if convulsing. *It hurts so much...I'm burning inside.* Her obsidian dagger appeared, hovering between them. The yellow halo surrounding her body glowed even brighter. *End it, please, I beg you...*

Her words convulsed his heart like a power blast. *I cannot, don't ask me!*

Michael grabbed the airborne obsidian blade and plunged the deadly dagger into Shae's chest.

Her body jolted. Her mouth opened in a soundless cry.

"No!" Dagan slammed Michael aside with his mind and yanked the blade out, flinging it away. And watched in horror as her eyelids closed, her heaving chest slowed.

"Shae, no! Please!" he cried, willing his own life force into her.

Her body wavered, slipped his grasp, becoming luminous as she rose higher and higher...she was dying the way angels did.

Grief slid like a sword between his ribs, gouging out his shattering heart. His tortured cry rang out through the trees. And like a wounded animal, he dove for Michael, taking him down, a red haze saturating his thoughts. They both rolled on the ground. Curses erupted, hands tried to pull him off. With his mind, he flung them aside.

"Dammit, Dagan," Michael grunted, trying to hold him off. "It had to be done—"

"It wasn't your fucking choice to make!" His fist smashed into Michael abs. Bones cracked. He didn't care the archangel wasn't fighting back.

Michael growled. "Listen to me, you insane son of a bitch—" Dagan plowed his fist into the Arc's face, cutting off his words. Blood flowed from his split lip.

"You took her away—took her away from me." He punched Michael again, anguish tearing at his gut. "Didn't…give…her…a…chance."

Each word accompanied another blow. "Only she made sense in this fucking messed up life of mine. Now she's gone—"

Michael shoved him off with a bolt of power, sending him crashing into a tree. "It was so she can live again!"

"Bullshit!" Dagan snarled, leaping to his feet.

"She's nephilim. It was the only way," Michael rasped, pressing a hand to his ribs. "Think, man, think about it. You're still standing here, aren't you? Damn, your fucking fists should come with a warning sign!"

No, he was still standing because their fucking soul-joining was too weak.

"Shae!" Jenna's voice broke through the deadness inside him. Dagan's head snapped up. Shae's body hovered several feet above them in the air. His heart lurched. She hadn't gone up to the heavens yet?

Jenna broke free of Hedori's grip. She darted past Dagan, her terrified gaze pinned on her daughter. He barely registered that the female was different, more responsive.

"I'm going to anchor her—bring her down." Michael shot up into the air, reaching for Shae. A wave of power like an inferno exploded out of her, flinging him some distance away—the sheer heat burning the tops of the fir and oak trees nearby.

Her body encased in a white light, swallowed her whole, giving her a ghostly form. Shae's eyes remained closed. Her head slumped to her chest, her hair floated about her in the swirling power as if she were

Georgia Lyn Hunter

underwater. Dagan leaped up, fighting through the heat wave singeing his skin and his hair and grabbed her. Another explosion of energy. He flew back, skidded across the ground, scoring the earth like a boulder crashing, jarring every bone in his body.

Dagan lay there, staring helplessly at the pulsing white sphere engulfing her, tears blurring his sight. *Don't leave me, Shae-cat. I cannot survive in a world without you.*

The tall spiral of light shuddered. Then it began to reform into a shimmering female shape…solidifying.

His heart racing to his throat, he leaped to his feet. Prisms of light shot out of Shae's eyes, her mouth, and her fingertips. Whatever force held her suspended in the air, the sight was beyond breathtaking. Her hair floated out around her in waves of white. Her arms hung loosely at her sides as she became corporeal once more. Color seeped into her—and she was naked. Dammit!

Then Dagan forgot her nakedness, his eyes widening as branch-like appendages spread out from her back several feet wide. Feathers burst free…and two enormous coppery-red wings spread out.

"Oh, dear God," Jenna whispered, her hand on her mouth. "She has wings."

"She would," Michael said from beside her. "Her father was still an angel when Shae was conceived—"

"No!" Jenna rounded on him, her expression fierce in a way only a mother's could be. "You will not touch her. I know about the killings of half-angel children by you lot."

Hedori reached for her, but she shrugged him off. "She's suffered enough…" Her voice cracked.

Hearing Jenna's words, Dagan's jaw clenched. Yet

his gaze remained fixed on his mate still hovering several feet in the air.

Finally, the furious, spinning energy slowed, and Shae floated down.

Dagan dove forward, swept her into his arms, and lowered to his knees, her enormous wings fanning out on the ground. Gently, he laid her down and hauled off his button-down. The shirt was scorched in the front, the sleeves burned to his biceps, but it didn't matter. With her appendages in the way, he put the shirt on her backwards.

Then he simply held her, staring at her beautiful, serene face. His heart still hammering like crazy, his fear not leaving him, he stroked her smooth cheek, the Y-shaped scar there now a faint, white line and barely noticeable.

"No one will ever touch my mate. I don't care if she's psionic or a damn nephilim, she's mine!" Dagan lifted his gaze to Michael, his tone a stone cold promise. "They come near her, and I swear on every fucking star in the universe, I will kill them."

The other Guardians moved to stand beside him, their support evident in their granite expressions. "So will we."

"We're fed up with the Absolute Laws having dominion over us, always on our asses the moment one of us finds our mate," Aethan said coldly. "We are immortals who live under the radar, but this world is ours, too. We deserve a damn chance at happiness."

Michael remained silent for a long second then snorted. "You're one damn pack of boneheads." He glanced at Jenna. "Rest easy. The laws of the Watchers do not apply here. Shae's immortal now, she's safe. But her human self had to die for her immortal self to be born."

Jenna's shoulders sagged in relief, tears sliding down her cheeks. She dashed at them. "After living in fear for so long, it's so good to hear this."

Dagan held Shae close. There were no words to express his relief that he held her living body in his arms again. He rose to his feet, carrying her, her wings dragging down.

Too overwhelmed to speak to the warriors who'd rallied with him, Dagan nodded to them, then dematerialized with his mate back to the castle.

Chapter 29

Sweat running down his face and back, Dagan swiped it away with a towel and grabbed a bottle of water and an energy drink from the small fridge in the training arena where he'd spent three intense hours training with swords with Nik.

"How's Shae?" Nik asked, snatching the can Dagan tossed at him in midair.

Jaw tight, Dagan unscrewed the bottle and gulped half the contents. "She still sleeps."

"Guess with all the changes she's been through, it makes sense." Nik guzzled some of his drink. "I'm off. See you at the briefing."

Dagan nodded. Since their return from Stone Ridge three days ago, he'd left Shae under her mother's watchful eye when he went on patrol, hunting for that bastard Aza. In the furor of the fight, he'd obviously snuck away. None of the warriors had seen him either. So he probably had no idea Samael had been captured.

Wiping his face again, Dagan headed for his quarters. As he entered the bedroom, Jenna rose from the bedside. With a small nod, and as silent as usual, she walked out, the door closing softly behind her.

Dagan rubbed his palm over his whiskered jaw, exhaustion riding him hard. He should shower and get—

A soft sigh distracted him. He pivoted toward the bed and felt as if his knees would cave.

Shae's gaze flickered around then settled on him, and the smile he adored took life. It had been hell waiting for her to awaken. Three days seemed like years.

The sconces' lights above the bed cast a soft golden glow over her, bathing her in warmth and reflecting off her enormous wings fanned out on the massive bed like burnished copper. More, he worried at the heightened power he sensed churning inside her. "How do you feel?"

"Tired. Like I've been through a long sprint and still have too much energy inside me." Her smile died. "Dagan," her voice broke, tears flooding her eyes. "Samael killed Harvey. He killed him because he was trying to protect me."

"Harvey cared about you. He was a true friend. I'd do the same." Dagan sat on the mattress and wiped away her tears. "Samael had traps set for us all over the city. Demons attacked Hedori in a damn long fight when he arrived at the hall."

"It was so he could get me alone," she whispered.

"I realized that too late." Dagan wished he could get his hands on the bastard just so he could kill him this time. He lifted her fingers and brushed his mouth across her knuckles. "At least Týr got your friend Ash to leave."

"Thank you." She shifted on the mattress, distress

tightening her face. "All these years we were staying with a monster, pretending to be my father's friend. Oh, God, Mom?" She gripped his shirt.

"Your mother's fine. She's spent a lot of time here with you while you slept."

That seemed to break her out of her terror. "She did? She's okay?"

He recalled her silence. No, she wasn't. He merely said, "Samael's hold on her is broken. And since she's a powerful psi, Hedori took on the role of her protector. So she'll be safe now."

"Thank you." A shaky smile touched her lips. She shifted again and frowned. "The bed's lumpy. Did you change it?"

His mouth quirked. She still had no idea. "Not exactly."

She pushed up and groaned. "My back feels so heavy..." She reached behind her. Her eyes widened. "Dagan, what is this? What's wrong with me? There are tufts of—"

She stared at him as if she didn't believe what she felt. She glanced over her shoulder. "No-no way!" She scrambled off the mattress and nearly fell on her back again at the weight.

"Easy." He grasped her upper arms and helped her up. Before she unbalanced again with the added mass of wings, he guided her into the dressing room and over to the huge paneled mirror on the wooden wall.

Her mouth dropped open. "Oh, Jesus! I have wings. How?" She spun around to him and nearly tripped, her enormous extremities hitting the closet with a thud. "Ouch!"

"Slowly, baby." Dagan cupped her elbows. "It happened after you incinerated Samael."

"Tell me he's dead?"

"No, but he'll wish he was. He's been condemned to Purgatory for the deaths of so many. However, you did destroy his wings."

"Good." At her bloodthirsty satisfaction, he shook his head and continued, "You were encompassed in a white glow, it swallowed you whole..." His gut twisted, still haunted at how helpless he'd felt having to watch her fight a powerful angel then be consumed by her own power...and, finally, die. He rubbed his burning eyes.

"Dagan? What is it?"

He lifted his agonized gaze to hers. "I thought I'd lost you."

"I heard you," she whispered. "After the immense agony, I was finally in this place of calm and peace with radiant white lights. And a melodious whisper in my mind saying I would always be at peace there... I never wanted to leave. But, then I heard your voice and it tugged at my soul, I knew I couldn't stay..."

She stroked his left pecs as if to ease his grief. "I tried to reach for you, but you were so far away. The voice continued to tempt me to stay, but my heart wanted you. I fought to break free, but it was like trying to fight through quicksand... I don't recall anything after that. Just immense white light surrounding me."

She'd heard him, and she came back.

He grasped her hands from his chest and pressed them to his lips. Emotions choked him. It took a moment, maybe several before he could speak again. "You became an orb of light and rose into the air. It swirled and started to reform. When you took shape again, those wings grew out of you..." Dagan shook his head, still awed at her rebirth. Then he grasped her wrist and turned it over while Shae warily eyed her wings in the mirror again.

The fucking mating mark was still there.

"They feel odd...heavy," she said, tentatively reaching behind her to touch the downy feathers. "How on earth am I to walk without falling?"

"Practice."

"Dagan—" Wild-eyed, she stared at him in the mirror. "How can I leave the castle with these things in view?"

"You'll have to learn to conceal them. Angels who come to Earth do it all the time. Draw them close to your body," he encouraged.

After several grunts, she managed to fold them against her back.

"That's good." He stroked the arches of her wings, and she stiffened, a low moan escaping her. Her pale cheeks took on a deep flush, and her pupils dilated. He went motionless. "It turns you on when I stroke you here?"

She bit her lip and nodded. "Like you have your fingers..."

"Where?" he teased. "Here?" He stroked the arches again.

"Between my thighs," she growled, her voice huskier than normal.

And just as fast, he lost his smile, a thought kicking him in the gut. He cursed under his breath. "No one must touch your wings there. It's essential you learn to conceal them."

Her shoulders heaving in a huge sigh, she nodded. "I know. Or you'll probably kill them all."

He frowned. Even though she'd been in a healing

sleep, she looked paler than normal. "I'm an idiot, dumping this on you when you've just awakened. We can wait a day or so."

"No. I don't want anyone making me feel this way— ugh." She grimaced. "What must I do?"

He stroked her upper arms and considered his options. "Remember how you shielded your powers? Let's try the same way here. It should work. If not, Michael will have to teach you."

Shae shut her eyes, a shimmer, and her wings vanished. Her eyelids snapped open, shining with wonder. "They're gone, I don't feel them anymore. I'm normal again."

"Normal?" A smile tugged his lips in wry amusement. "Hardly." He grasped her hand, drew her back into the bedroom and stopped in front of the fireplace. "I don't want you to hurt yourself. The dressing room wouldn't take your open wings easily. Go ahead."

Dagan stepped to her front. She inhaled deeply, and in a swoosh of feathers, her wings emerged. She stumbled back at the added weight, her hands grabbing his shirt for purchase, and she grinned up at him. "I did it!"

At her happiness, he pulled her close and kissed her, dying to touch her, to make love to her after all that had occurred over the past few days, but he still had a damn Fallen to annihilate.

He didn't want to worry her about that just yet. He would find the bastard soon enough.

"Can I fly now?"

He struggled to contain his smile as she stood there, hands on her hips, her wings held close to her body before they vanished. It must be an inherent angel thing at how easily she learned to hide them.

"Well?"

"So impatient." He laughed. "Probably. However, *that* I can't teach you. Michael will have to get one of the angels to show you."

Suddenly, her gaze widened, her wish to fly seemingly wiped from her mind. "Dagan!" She rushed behind him. "Your beautiful hair!"

"What?" He turned with her as she pulled some of the remaining long braids to the front.

"So much burned off," she whispered, gently touching the singed ends. He stared at it for a second. Right. He'd forgotten about getting them cut off. "How?" she asked.

"When I tried to save you. The white glow emitting from you as the changes took place, exploded, and I got caught in the crossfire. My hair paid the price."

Her face fell. "I'm so sorry."

At her distress, he drew her into his arms. "I don't care about my hair. You are all that matters. I love you, Shae. I'd give my life for you, don't you realize that?"

"I know." A smile hovered on her lips. "Let me even them for you."

He headed back into the dressing room, got a pair of scissors from a drawer, and handed them to her. With his mind, he undid his ropey hair then sat on a wooden chest. She gathered his uneven mane to the back, and the sounds of snipping echoed. Burnt ends and longer tails fell to the floor like black ribbons, but his chest constricted. She was so close, and he couldn't sense her—couldn't feel her spirit anymore, faint as their mate-bond had been.

She set the scissors on the trunk and dusted his back. "There. All done."

Before she stepped back, Dagan grasped her arm and rose to his feet. He drew her close and wrapped in his arms, wanting to keep her right there forever. When she died, their faint bonding had severed, probably aided by the damn mate brand on her wrist. But the loss clawed at his soul.

As if sensing his despair, her worried gaze searched his face. "What is it?"

He shook his head. She pushed away and wrinkled her nose. "Ugh—I smell terrible, like charred dead things, and you didn't tell me. I'm going to shower."

"No." He swept her off her feet, startling a squeal out of her as he headed for the bathroom. "We both are. You were in a healing sleep, how you smelled was of little importance, but to make up, I'll pay careful attention to every part of you and make sure it's all washed."

"Oh…" Then she smiled. "I like your idea far better, and I get to do the same." She kissed him.

A half hour later, they stepped out of the shower. Shae made her way into the dressing room, her face flushed from the intimacy they'd just shared.

Dagan inhaled deeply, rubbing a hand over his chest where her light resided inside him once more. Shae hadn't even realized that their mating bond was back, probably because of so much energy churning inside her. Except Dagan felt the difference. It was still faint because of the damn mating mark obstructing the completion of their soul-joining.

It was almost midnight when they headed downstairs. Aware of the furtive glances she kept throwing him, he arched a brow. "What?"

"Nothin'…" A smile ghosted her mouth as she raked back her damp hair.

Yeah, she was up to no good. He pressed her up against the balustrade with his hips, his hands on the railing, caging her. He lowered his head and ran his tongue over her pulse point. "Tell me. Or... I'll bite you."

"Really?" She leaned back, casting him a sultry look. "Go ahead, I love your mouth on me."

Amusement tugged his lips. Her smile turned into a sigh. She patted his chest and relented. "It's just that you look so different. Before, with your long hair, you sported that dangerous, get-the-hell-away vibe. Now, you look really, really hot and sorta have this badass, please-do-me look."

"Is that so?" He trailed his mouth over the faint lines where the bumpy scar had once been in a slow kiss. "Oh, I plan to *do* you, Shae-cat. In every way possible, as soon as I can..."

***

"Samael tried to kill me when I was a child?" Shae shouldn't be shocked, considering all she'd learned about her *uncle*.

"Yes," Jenna said quietly, her eyes dark with pain and anger. "I recall it all now. Samael was unaware that your father had cast a protection spell on you when he first attempted to end your life and failed. You were three. That incantation was to keep you from being detected by the archangel and thrones. But something must have released you from its protection..." She cast a glance at Michael before continuing, "He believes it could have happened when you met your mate."

They'd gathered in the kitchen. Dagan stood near the open French doors, his arms folded across his chest. The other warriors were still out on patrol, leaving only Michael and Hedori. Echo sat opposite them.

As her mother revealed the horror of Samael's reach—of him killing her father and wiping out Shae's memories of the incident—Dagan's expression turned darker.

"Samael lied to me about Gus being killed in a mugging." Her mother stared at the teacup she wrapped her fingers around. "He had Aza do it. An angel killing another would instantly draw Michael to him, and that he couldn't have. He used to tell me all these things every time he came to the Dark Realm where he'd imprisoned me. I hated him. I wanted to hurt him so badly, but I couldn't do anything, I-I was helpless—" She broke off, wiping her wet cheeks.

"He paid, Jenna, and he'll be paying for eternity where he's now trapped," Michael said from the opposite end of the long dining table. "There is no escape from Purgatory."

After a long moment, she nodded. "He deserves no less." Her gray eyes lifted to Shae's. "You were fifteen when your father decided to fall. He didn't want us to be hunted for the rest of our lives, and you had to be protected at all costs. It was a dangerous time for us. He trusted no one and wanted us shielded while he was gone to the Celestial Realm. We were going to tell you the truth after he came back, Shae."

She pushed her cocoa mug aside and rubbed her brow wearily. After everything they'd been through, anger was so pointless when her parents were only trying to protect her. She lowered her hand. "I'm so glad you're safe, but I wish I'd known about Dad." Just thinking about her father, and her chest compressed. She'd known all about her parents' first meeting, bumping into each other on the street, and it was love at first sight. "Dad was wonderful."

"He was." A trembling smile touched her mother's lips. She tucked an auburn strand of hair behind her ear. "He simply wanted a quiet life with us. He was tired of the heavenly wars, the bloodshed, and Samael's plans to take over this city. He was furious at Gus' decision. I guess that's when he decided to kill him." She picked up her tea. She didn't drink and set it down again.

No one spoke.

Hedori stood near the island counter, adjacent to Michael. He appeared pale, his features drawn. Eyes unreadable.

"When I saw your powers consume you three days ago, I thought I'd lost you, too."

At the immense pain in her mother's eyes, and knowing she was still grieving for her father, Shae leaped off her seat, lowered to her knees, and hugged her. "I'm here, Mom."

"Now. But you died, Shae."

She frowned, letting her mother go as memories of the violent night at her old home resurfaced. "If I'm a nephilim…then the seraphs would want me dead." Her gaze rushed to Dagan. "You told me that in Romania."

"I know." He straightened from the doorjamb, the night silhouetting him like some deadly being ready to destroy "Now it no longer applies."

"I don't understand."

"You were already incinerating from the immense power," Michael explained. "Your human body couldn't handle it. I stabbed you in the heart to end it faster, and to give you a chance at rebirth. Given who your sire was and your inherited abilities, you absorbed Samael's powers and angelhood.

"He was the Angel of Death, but he also possessed a

singular ability, too—one he never used—to *restart* life because then it would mean giving up his status as Death. It's what happened to you. You sensed it and rebirthed yourself. You are an exception. Not a divine angel, but still immortal. You made it through the change, which can be…excruciating."

Excruciating? Shae sagged on her heels, her mind reeling. She'd been in hell, burning alive.

Remembering the impossible agony coursing through her and begging Dagan to end her life, she shuddered. But the unadulterated torment in his eyes that she'd asked him to do such a thing would always remain with her. She jumped up and hurried to him, sliding her arms around his waist.

"I couldn't," he whispered. "I just couldn't…"

"It's okay. But it's not something I ever want to experience again." Her fingers bunched his shirt. "I know what Michael said, that he gave me a chance at rebirth, but it was *you* who pulled me back—*you*."

He stroked her healed cheek, his eyes damp with tenderness. Before he could speak, a shift in the air signaled Aethan's and Týr's appearance on the terrace. They entered the kitchen, bringing in the chilly night air with them. Aethan instantly headed for Echo and drew her up into his arms, kissing her on her nape. Týr dropped onto a chair and tilted it back on two back legs.

"It makes sense now," Echo said, leaning against her mate and brushing away her overlong bangs from her eyes. "Why I couldn't get a proper reading of your aura. It's a lot like Michael's—a silvery white. Before, it was almost translucent. Hidden. I guess it was the protection spell keeping it at bay." She smiled, her bi-colored eyes gleaming in mischief. "If I'm the Healer, what will you do as an immortal who—ugh, it's simpler to say—who's an angel?"

"I don't know..." Shae blinked. She hadn't thought that far ahead, except for cataloguing Dagan's work for sale. But what she'd taunted him with, about being a Guardian... That idea perked her up. Not just yet, though. Heck, she had to get used to being who she was now first before she gave Dagan a coronary. Besides, her mother was going to need help to get well again.

"I'll find something, I'm sure," she said instead.

Michael picked up his Coke, took a swallow, and glanced at the warriors. "Seems like this is something we need to pay attention to if there is another."

"Man," Týr groaned and rose, his tilted chair hitting the floor with a thud. "Hope the next one is way in the future." He headed for the fridge.

Michael set down his drink, lines creasing his brow. "Jenna? About those killings from months ago..."

Her lips pressed tightly for a second. "I'm really sorry about their deaths. But I had to. Samael threatened to hurt Shae and mate her to that horrible Aza. I lived in constant terror. There was no escape from that place. Then he started to take away my memories when I became h-hysterical, or he'd put me under in a deep sleep. As time passed, I didn't know what was real or not anymore. I thought the killings were a nightmare..." She swiped her damp cheeks with the long sleeves of her green sweater. "Now that I know Shae's safe, I'll accept whatever the punishment is for taking the lives of those innocent men."

"Mom, no!"

The sudden fierceness of the emotions in the room was so thick, light a match, and it would explode like an H-bomb. "No one will touch her," Hedori said, his voice harsh with resolve.

Jenna frowned at him then looked away.

Michael shook his head. "Since Samael was behind the killings, I'll speak to the seraphs and request a pardon. But, those abilities will be bound," he warned Jenna.

She shut her eyes and nodded. "Thank you. I don't want them anyway. I don't want to ever become a liability again."

"Okay. I'll go get this settled." Michael vanished in a swirl of silvery sparks.

Shae had to take several deep breaths to calm down. Unable to stay still, the power she'd consumed from Samael still riding high in her, she stepped away from Dagan and rubbed her arms. It was a struggle to keep her abilities leashed as anger pounded through her at what her family had endured at Samael's hands.

Dagan drew her to him, asked quietly, "You okay?"

She didn't want to worry him, so she just nodded.

"Good thing the bastard's been captured," Týr muttered, a half-empty bottle of water in his hand. "You have some great abilities there, Shae—" He broke off at the sudden draft of air blowing into the kitchen.

Shae frowned at the tall, snow-haired man on the terrace. Another immortal.

He didn't come inside. Dagan pushed her behind him. Aethan and Týr immediately flanked him, swords drawn, and moved Shae farther away from the door. They knew him, and he wasn't a friend. A shiver of unease slid down her spine.

"It's why we came back early," Aethan muttered. "Echo told me Shae had awoken, knew this asshole law-keeper would be by."

Týr grunted in agreement. "I'm quite happy to take his head."

"What do you want?" Dagan snapped.

The stranger held up a hand in the universal peace sign. "Before you all get your blades in a knot, the Fallen has demanded the female he marked as mate be handed over. I have come for her."

Oh, Lord. She'd barely had time to recover from what had happened, and now this? Her stomach churned.

"Not fucking happening."

At Dagan's snarl, Shae rubbed the brand on her wrist, wishing she could scour it off.

Without a doubt, Dagan would find Aza and kill him, but retribution burned deep inside her. He'd hurt the people she loved. *And* he'd killed her father and Harvey.

The Guardians and Dagan looked ready to hack the stranger into firewood, while he appeared determined not to leave without her.

At their standoff, Shae worried her lip between her teeth, and realized there was only one way to end this. "Dagan?"

"Yeah?"

"He wants me, let me go. I can handle myself."

His head snapped to her. Fury cracked through the ice in his gaze. "Not fucking happening!"

She wasn't surprised at his furious response. Then she remembered something pivotal from the commotion when Samael had her trapped in the power storm at Stone Ridge, and Dagan had fought his way to her. Not even Michael had broken through, yet Dagan had.

Without a word, she grasped her man's hand and tugged him from the kitchen. *Honey, you know I can do this, that I can kill him, right?* she mind-linked with Dagan, not wanting the law-keeper to hear her. *You can follow in your invisible state after I leave.*

No way. His snarl, though tinny and faint, reverberated through her head like nails as she hauled him down the hallway. *You're still struggling with all those new powers flowing through you, and you've barely gotten used to your wings. They are more a liability right now. They will appear in a fight and weaken you with their weight. Besides, the fucker will have backup.*

Shae bore his anger. It was no easy feat dragging an inflexible obelisk with her. *You know the law-keeper's not going to leave without me, and you guys can't kill him, not if you want to avoid another bloody battle on our doorstep with the gods. Besides, Aza can't be as scary as Samael was.* She slowed when she came to a door just past the rec room and opened it. It was a small closet with circuit boards and stuff. She shut them inside.

Dagan switched on the light, his jaw melded in that intractable jut. *No, it's too dangerous. Your powers still roil inside you, I can feel them, and I'm sure everyone here can, too. You'll draw every fucking evil out there to you.*

"We can speak aloud now," she teased.

His yellow eyes burned with deep-seated emotions. "I'm not handing you over."

God, she loved him so much. "Kiss me."

He scowled. "You brought me here for—dammit, Shae!"

"You don't want to?" She put on a hurt expression

and let her mouth tremble.

Growling, he pressed his lips to hers, and before he pulled back, she wrapped his shorter hair in her fists, keeping him there. "Bite me, take my blood."

"I'm not hungry."

"No, but you can reap my powers."

He reared back, tearing free of her grip. "What?"

She rolled her eyes. "I'll excuse you for not being aware of *that* because of everything that occurred. Dagan, I saw—I *know*. You not only taste food through my blood, you also harvest my powers when you take my blood. It's how you broke through the force field surrounding Samael and me. Furthermore, it's one surefire way to get this churning power inside me down a level, too, I think."

He stared at her, shock brightening his beautiful eyes. "I did, didn't I?"

"Yes. At least, this way, you'll always be gifted with the powers I drain. Though how long it lasts, I guess we'll have to see."

Without a word, he lowered his head and licked her on her pulse point once, twice.

Her breath caught, the feeling so sensual, her heart thudded in anticipation. His mouth pressed against her skin, and his fangs sank deep into her. He sucked hard, a pull she felt all the way to the spot between her thighs. A soft moan escaped her. She rubbed her aching core against his hardening cock. A growl rumbled low in his throat as he fed. All too soon, he licked her skin and pulled back.

"I love you, you crazy, impetuous woman, more than I ever believed possible." He caressed her face, his eyes filled with tenderness. "You are my smile—my heartbeat—my entire existence. So you damn well better survive this shit. Or I swear on every godsforsaken star that I will find you, and you will be sorry."

She laughed and hugged him with an airtight squeeze. "I love you, too, my dearest barbarian. Now let's go get Aza."

His gaze skimmed over her, and she knew he was scanning for the churning power inside her, but it had quieted. A sigh escaped him. He nodded and picked up her wrist. "This knot remains open because he hasn't completed the physical bonding. Don't engage him, Shae. He gets anywhere near you, he could flash you—"

"And I'll flash right back."

"Great." He pinched the bridge of his nose. "Just be safe, okay?"

Her heart melting with love, she stepped out of the closet. Good thing she hadn't told him what Samael had revealed about Aza and his twisted sexual needs or Club Illudo. Later, she'd tell him. Maybe.

Chapter 30

Dagan followed Shae into the silent kitchen, hating the thought of her meeting Aza on her own. And helpless to do anything about it. Her power rolled inside him now, but at least she wasn't sending out those deadly vibrations that would alert every evil bastard out there as to her whereabouts.

Jenna and Echo were no longer in the kitchen. The law-keeper—the same one Blaéz had nailed to the castle wall several months ago—waited out on the porch, having a stare-down with the Guardians. The lethal, black-tipped silver sword used to kill those who broke the Absolute Laws remained sheathed in a scabbard on his back. Like that would stop them from killing him. Nothing showed on the law-keeper's face as Shae crossed to him.

"You're just letting her go?" Týr barked, his expression incredulous.

Dagan didn't respond, mostly because his jaw was clenched so tight. The bastard touched her hand. She sent Dagan a little smile as if to say, "I'll be okay".

Not until he had her back with him and Aza was roasting in Hell, would it be *okay*. The moment Shae and the law-keeper vanished, he dematerialized.

So, what's the plan? Týr mind-linked with him.

You can't be with me.

We aren't, Nik shot back, joining them. Then Dagan sensed the others close.

Yeah, Aethan added. *We're going back on patrol.*

C'mon, let's go get the dumbass. Blaéz.

Damn stubborn bastards. One of the others must have told them what was happening.

Aza was a damn fool to think he would so easily let Shae go. Yeah, the fucker had put the mark on her, staking his claim, but that was just semantic bullshit, one Dagan planned to rectify in the next few minutes. Bastard probably had no idea he was no longer weakened from not feeding—and just how in the hell did Aza find out about *that*?

In his molecular state, Dagan coasted across the city. Connected through his blood-link with Shae, he tracked her to some small town in New Jersey, and a run-down, boarded-up factory slated for demolition near the bay.

I'll call if I need help, he telepathed the rest of the Guardians.

Hope she ices the dickhead, Týr retorted.

The warriors dispersed. Dagan couldn't feel their presences but knew they'd be close.

Still in his invisible state, he glided in through the broken window and into a silent, empty place. What the fuck?

Where the hell were they?

***

The law-keeper took form with her in some rundown

warehouse with a vaulted roof overlooking the bay. Shae didn't think they were in New York any longer. She shrugged off his hold but didn't move away from him. Bits of broken furniture and a few steel pipes scattered the ground.

On the other side of the old furniture factory, Aza stood with a demon minion whom he waved off. Wearing a dark suit, his dark blond hair in its typical neat, short style, he appeared more like a banker than an insane parasite. His dark gaze slid over her in a manner that made her want to take several baths.

She gritted her teeth, didn't say a word. No way would she add to his excitement by letting him see her smidgen of fear. But at the thought of what he'd done to her family and her friend, vengeance blazed deeper, burning away the last remnants of unease. With all the mind manipulation this monster and Samael had used on them, it was a miracle her brain and her mother's had remained intact.

The snow-haired law-keeper looming at her side said, "She's been delivered. One question, did she agree of her own free will to this mating?"

Aza ambled toward them and nodded, his unwavering gaze pinned on her. "Yes."

"Did you?" the law-keeper asked her.

Shae narrowed her eyes. "It's strange. I don't recall it at all."

The law-keeper didn't ask questions. He grasped Shae's wrist and Aza's, closed his eyes, and a faint glow appeared over the mating mark, then he nodded. "It is as he claims."

Of course, it would be. Her jaw clenched.

The law-keeper vanished.

"Finally." Aza strolled closer. "We're gonna have so

much fun."

She countered his moves, keeping her distance. She summoned her abilities, but only a faint heat remained. Had Dagan taken all of them? Shit, she was so screwed. She needed time. "What? You think I'm just going to lie back and let you fuck me while choking me?"

"You'll do anything I want. You see, I'm protected from your abilities, and I know Ash still lives. This time, I'll make sure he stays dead if you don't behave."

He'd hurt Ash? Fury tore through her. "You bastard!"

He shrugged. "At least I had the forethought to prevent you from mating anyone else with my mating mark. I wouldn't have been in this position, but the asshole Guardian just had to destroy Club Illudo, the one place I could have my needs fulfilled. Now, he thinks he can have *you* as his mate?" Aza glared at her like it was all her fault. Then he sighed. "Yes, providence is a wonderful thing. I will have it all now." He broke off, eyed her coldly. "You stink of him. You'll regret letting him touch what belongs to me!"

"Go to hell," Shae spat, sidestepping a broken table. "The only thing I regret is ever agreeing to go out with you."

"We'll both be going to Hell once the mating's completed," he murmured, trailing her. "You won't be residing in this world much longer."

"Dagan is my *mate*, the one thing you'll never be. I'm going to kill you."

He smiled, kicking a piece of wood out of his way. "You can try."

"And fail," a new voice added.

Kaerys appeared beside Aza in silvery-blue sparks.

Shit!

The viper wore a pretty navy sheath, but her eyes were hard, her smile vindictive.

"You couldn't face me, a mere mortal, on your own? You had to get this Fallen's help?" Shae taunted, wanting to tear the goddess from limb to limb. "And *you* told him about Dagan?"

"He deserved it." Kaerys' mouth twisted in anger. "Your bravado won't save you now. Dagan will not find you in this place. I cast a shielding spell, keeping us hidden from mortal and immortal alike in this dull little town."

"I'm going to kick your sorry ass, Kaerys!"

"Do not address me so informally, mortal," she snapped, circling Shae like a damn flea she desperately wanted to stomp out. "You should be begging for your worthless life. Did you really think I'd let you humiliate me and get away with it? After Aza mates you, Dagan will have no say in anything regarding you. My vengeance will be complete. He'll regret walking away from me."

"The only thing you regret is not being aligned with his family, the affluence of being joined to a powerful lineage," she shot back. "Except he didn't care for all that. He chose to be a *protector* to his sister."

"Do it, Aza," Kaerys snarled. "And don't be gentle when you mate her. I want to hear her screams. Then I'll let Dagan hear them, too."

Shae fisted her fingers.

"No, you don't." Aza flashed and grabbed her by her arms. He kept her hands pinned to her sides and lowered his head, dragging his mouth down her cheek, which no longer bore the bumpy scar. "We know what these can do. We don't want them to get in the way, do we, little psychic?"

Bile shot to her throat at his touch. "I'm sure you don't. Pity you didn't remain to see what else I could do before you slithered away from the fight like the snake you are."

He smirked. "All that matters is when you're struggling beneath me as I ram into you—"

Shae kneed him hard in the nuts. A keening howl broke loose. He doubled over, clutching his groin. She hoped she'd flattened his damn balls into pancakes. "Since you like pain, I hope you enjoyed that!"

A blast of power hit her right in the chest. Shae crumpled to the grimy floor, unable to breathe, so sure her lungs would never work again. Kaerys stood over her, beaming. "I really enjoyed that."

Wait, dammit! She was immortal now, and reborn, stronger than before, right? Going on instinct, she blocked out the pain. Instantly, her limbs functioned again, and her breathing didn't hurt like her lungs wanted to escape. Beautiful, familiar heat whirled through her once more.

Ugh, she had to get hurt to regenerate. Typical.

"You'll have to mate her here, Aza. Now. If you leave, Dagan will sense her," Kaerys warned.

"I hadn't planned to do it here." Aza grimaced. He dragged Shae up, grabbed her wrists and twisted them to her back, staying behind her this time. She flinched, pain wrenching her shoulders. "But I'm certainly going to enjoy this." He hauled her toward the open door of another room. A bed appeared with ropes tied to the four posts.

"A gift." Kaerys gave her a chilling smile. "So you don't teleport away." With a slash of her hand, she ripped Shae's top down the front.

Damn bitch. Teeth gritted, Shae's energy spun as if it would pull her into a vortex.

Wood exploded, shrapnel flying all over. Kaerys vanished. A deadly storm flew inside. Dagan. His eyes flaming like the sun latched on to them and burned with fury as they lowered to her torn clothes. "You will beg for mercy for this."

***

"Still, you threaten me?" The Fallen yanked Shae to his front, using her as a personal shield. He bellowed in a strange language. Several demons and demoniis rushed inside like a plague of rats, scuttling over the floor.

Stupid bastards. In one fell swoop, Dagan held them all immobile with his mind. He cut a quick look at Shae. Just her smile, and he breathed again.

A shift in the air and Kaerys appeared. She glared at him. "Did you really think, I'd ever forgive you for humiliating me by mating with this lowly mortal? I won't be laughed at in the pantheon."

No, he wasn't really surprised to see her here, used to her vindictive ways. He flung her aside with his mind, but she stayed put. Damn female must have used a shielding spell, not only on this place but on herself and Aza, as well. Except, he had help. Shae was right. With Samael's power still roiling in him, and since none could evade Death, he'd finally managed to crack the outside protection.

Kaerys probably had no idea he'd powered up on his mate's blood. He ignored her.

Aza sneered. "I've waited a long time for this."

Dagan lifted a brow. "To die? Then it's your lucky day."

"You still have no idea who I am, do you? And you can't kill me." Aza twisted Shae's hands harder, and she winced.

He was so going to rip the bastard's nuts off and shove them down his throat.

Through the open door, in the gloomy room beyond, Dagan spied the bed with the ropes tied to the posts. Another image from a year ago flickered through his mind. *A female tied to a bed, a dark-haired Fallen pumping into her...as she died.* Club Illudo! No wonder the fucker felt so familiar. Only his hair was blond now.

Dagan eyed the sadistic bastard. Didn't bother with a threat when death was his end.

Aza snorted and shook his head. "Here I have you at my mercy where not even your feeble group of Guardians can penetrate the spell the goddess has cast, and you think you're more powerful? I will have my revenge on you." A sword appeared in his hand. "Then I'll have her. Oh, the things I'm going to do to her before I fuck her—"

Aza shoved Shae aside and lunged, his sword arching toward Dagan. "Shae, leave!" he yelled.

"Can't, the shielding spell!"

Shit! He ducked the blow and stumbled over a steel pipe. That was far too close to his face for comfort. Evading another swing of the blade, Dagan smashed his fist into Aza's face, sending him flying back. Shae cried out. Dagan spun around as her wings unfurled in a furious flutter of burnished red, and she stumbled. Dammit, she wasn't used to her wings.

Fear riding him hard, Dagan grabbed a broken steel pipe from the ground and plunged it straight through Aza's belly, embedding it into the wall behind him. "You should have taken my offer of Purgatory at Club Illudo. Now, you'll wish for death."

The Fallen gurgled, his jaw dropping open in surprise.

Dagan pivoted sharply. Kaerys had snatched one of Shae's wings and was yanking on it. Feathers tore free and floated to the ground.

"No, you fucking don't!" Snatching Aza's dropped sword, Dagan went after the wretched female. He'd stake her right next to her accomplice before killing her.

"No!" Shae flashed out her hand, stopping him, her eyes stormy and wet with tears of pain. "She's mine."

With a cry of rage, she twisted free and dove for Kaerys. The weight of her appendages giving her the momentum she needed, Shae slammed the goddess into the wall, grabbed her upper arms, and then they both rose several feet into the air. Kaerys' eyes suddenly widened in terror. "Let go—let go!"

"You want mercy? Did you show my mate any?" Shae spat, her body glowing, a glimmering halo surrounding her. "This is for what you did to him, for the millennia of humiliation!"

"Noooo!"

A bright light enclosed them, and Dagan knew what would happen next as he'd discovered on the blood-drenched grounds of her home near Stone Ridge. He'd seen it with Samael.

"An angel," Aza moaned. "She's mine—*mine*!" He tugged at the pipe.

Dagan ignored the crazy fuck. Kaerys' body trembled, the white glow seeping into her, revealing a skeletal form. Then, her emaciated body vanished in a smoky haze. It would probably take her weeks, months to regenerate from this brutal encounter, if she were that lucky. But he doubted she'd ever be at full strength again.

Shae wavered, her wings fluttering in agitation as if forgetting their momentum. Dagan grabbed her before she fell and hurt herself. "I have you, baby."

Carefully, he brought her down and lowered her to the floor, easing her onto his lap.

"Everything okay?" Týr burst inside. "The place was locked as tight as a bloody fortress!"

Aethan, Blaéz, and Nik followed him inside seconds later.

"Kaerys aligned with Aza. She had a concealment spell over them and the warehouse," he said absently, his focus on Shae's still and utterly pale face. But the new power rolling inside her lashed at his psyche, her skin the only thing probably keeping it contained.

"And those frozen assholes?" Nik grunted.

"What?" Dagan dragged his gaze off Shae, only then remembering the dozen or so demons he'd immobilized with his mind. "They're all yours." He released them. Grunts and snarls erupted.

Týr and Nik flashed, their obsidian swords taking form in their hands as the demons rushed them. Blaéz and Aethan spread out, waiting. Watching.

"Is she okay?" Aethan asked over his shoulder.

Dagan nodded. These warriors truly were his brothers. "Thanks for having my back."

"Hell, we couldn't do much here, you both seemed to have it all in hand. Besides, your surly ass is always there for us." Aethan smirked. The cacophony of noise soon quieted down as the last guttural growl died away.

"What about this one?" Blaéz drawled, walking around an impaled Aza, studying the embedded pole.

"Mine-mine," Aza whimpered, his blood-drenched hands sliding over the post, eyes glued to Shae. "She's mine."

Dagan barely glanced at him. With his mind, he picked up the fallen sword and let it fly. The weapon winged in a deadly arc, millimeters from Blaéz's head. As he leaped back, the blade decapitated Aza. The Fallen's head rolled across the debris-covered floor.

"Damn! Your shit's fucking scary," Blaéz muttered. "Quite forgotten that—"

The concrete floor split open, stopping him short. An obscure dark mist flowed out. Greedy fingers took form, slithering out of the orifice. And in smoky agitation, they grabbed Aza's body and head, pulling him into the dark hole. Seconds later, it hissed shut.

A year late, but Purgatory was a fitting end for him. Dagan stroked Shae's bright hair.

"Okay, then." Nik strode over. "I'm gonna do a quick recon of the area, a few of them lit outta here like their asses were on fire."

"Indeed. Let's go kick some demon backside," Blaéz said, then glanced at Týr. "It's time you got your hard arse on track and claimed your rainbow."

"Celt, you're a damn pain in my ass. And keep your precog crap away from me." Týr glared at him. "The only reason you're still in one piece is because I like Darci. It baffles the hell outta me how she remains so good while sharing your black soul."

Laughing, Blaéz followed him out. "She adores me."

"Yeah, about that? I worry about her state of mind being mated to you."

"What rainbow?" Nik asked them.

"Nothing," Týr muttered. "The Celt's a demented fucker, that's all…"

As their voices faded, Shae stirred. Her eyes snapped open, and she pushed up, her gaze darting around the empty warehouse. "What happened? Aza? Kaerys?"

"He's dead. She's gone. You did a helluva job on Kaerys. Never seen anything like it." He shifted so she could lie more comfortably against him. But the new influx of powers roiling within her abraded his psyche like sharp pinpricks. "You okay?" he asked quietly.

She nodded, then whispered, "They're all finally gone—thank God. Mom's safe now."

"As are you, my wildcat, but you're not okay, Shae. I feel it." He tenderly stroked the arch of her spread wing, so grateful to have her in his arms again. She may be strong and possess incredible powers, but she was his entire life. "Those pilfered abilities consume you once more."

She inhaled sharply as he caressed the appendage's curve. He could hear her heart drum faster, and it had nothing to do with the battle she'd fought minutes ago.

"I didn't want to worry you."

"When it comes to you," he murmured, deliberately running his finger down her wing's arch again. "I'll always worry." A husky purr of need rolled out of her, and he couldn't wait to be the one to satisfy it. He slid his mouth along her jaw.

"Dagan—wait, Ash! Aza threatened to kill him."

"Done. Shot Týr a message to check on him. Home," he growled.

***

As they took form back in their room at the castle, Shae leapt for him, barely able to contain the tumultuous desire sweeping through her. Her momentum—and her heavy wings—thrust Dagan back, and he tripped, landing on the carpet near the fireplace, she on top of him.

Shae yanked at his shirt. He tore hers off. His mouth,

his hands sliding over every curve and dip on her body. "Conceal your wings, baby. Don't want you to injure them."

Drowning in sensations, Shae wanted him inside her but managed to pull in her wings and conceal them much easier this time.

Dagan flipped her, and she was on her back. Pushing to his knees, he tugged off her boots and jeans, slid down her body, and buried his face between her thighs. He licked and swirled around her clit. His arms under her hips, he tilted her up, his fangs lightly scraping her flesh.

She shuddered, her body throbbing with a burning ache. Her head fell back, her moans growing. "Dagan, please…"

With another decadent drag of his tongue over her throbbing flesh, he then sealed his mouth around her clit. Whatever he did with his tongue, liquid heat pulsed through her body. He sucked on her flesh with hard pulls. Caught in a haze of sensual pleasure, a sharp, hot fire exploded through her as his fangs sank into her. *Oh, God!* She nearly came off the floor. He held her down, a hand on her stomach as he pulled on her blood, his tongue on her clit. Shae grabbed his hair, pressing her core into his mouth, wanting more. Everything in her focused on the immensely delicious suction—the impossible pleasure building between her legs.

His pulls grew sharper, more intense. A heartbeat later, with a hoarse cry, she grabbed his hair, her orgasm erupting through her like a landslide as she fell…

When she finally got her breath back, and the roiling power inside her eased, and her heart no longer in danger of collapsing, it stunned her speechless that he would actually drink from her *there*—and that she'd actually liked it.

He licked her once more, then he crawled up her body, his expression tender, red streaking his yellow irises. "Feel better?" he asked, amusement brightening his eyes.

He seemed to enjoy her discomfort when he did something sexually unexpected and really wicked to her, but she didn't care. "Can you actually drink that way?"

"For a feeding, I usually prefer a vein. This was more for your pleasure and to ease the power inside you. There're so many other delicious places, Shae-cat." He rolled her nipple.

"Oh." Heat flooded her face, and he smirked, his fangs peeking out. It was the sexiest thing ever, his smile. She put her mouth on his and kissed him.

Dagan rose to his feet, and she wrapped her legs around his hips as he flashed them. Warm water splattered onto her face. "What the—" she spluttered, breaking their kiss.

They were in the shower, the faucet open full, water pouring down on them. Shae blinked away the droplets. "Really?"

He shrugged. "We need a bath after rolling on the grimy floors in that dilapidated building." He got rid of his boots, both landing with a wet thud on the tiles. He straightened, the water cascading in a rustle over him. Shae lowered to her knees and tried to undo the metal snaps of his jeans. But his rock-hard erection straining the wet denim seriously hampered her efforts. With a tiny growl, she fought the snaps, the water making it even more difficult to unfasten. "A little help would be good, you know."

"Why? When I enjoy your growly efforts so much more."

"Sadist."

He laughed, the sound warming her heart. She looked up, water running down her face, and at the absolute love in his eyes, her heart nearly faltered. The next minute, his pants disappeared.

"I love you undressing me but I can't wait any longer." He picked her up and pressed her back against the wall. Her legs came around him again. Pinning her to the shower stall with his body, he grasped his cock in one hand and, in one thrust, sank into her. And he groaned.

Shae gasped. His erection filling her, stretching her, and stealing her breath.

Those inhuman yellow eyes seared hers as he pulled out and slammed right back into her. Her gasp turned to a whimper, and he ground his hips into her, rubbing against her sensitive clit, his expression wild. Eyes intense. Exactly how she always wanted him.

Her orgasm close, she stiffened just as a bright, white light flowed through her, sweeping away her thoughts. It coalesced and merged inside her as unimaginable pleasure swept through her, hauling her up and over.

Warmth, tenderness, and so much love flooded her. "Dagan," she panted. "What is that?"

"It's our souls joining—how it should have been." *Now, you are all mine.* His words were clear in her head, not faint and tinny like before. He thrust back into her. Harder. Faster. Then his entire body went rigid. A low, aching groan escaped him.

It was the sexiest sound she'd ever heard. He

shuddered as he found his own release and spilled himself into her. *I love you, Shae-cat. Deeply…madly…desperately.* His avowal crowded her thoughts. *And when the sands of time fall no more for us, I'll love you beyond and forever.*

Finally, she had the man who made her whole. Completed her, melded with her in ways she couldn't begin to fathom. She loved him. Madly. Deeply. Desperately. And, yes, forever.

THE END…

ACKOWLEDGEMENTS

I can't end this book without an enormous Thank You to a special group of people.

My CPs: **Anna, Nancy, Celia,** and **Coleen,** for wading through all that is first draft and bringing out the best from me. This book is the better for it.

My editor: **Chelle**, for what you do to make this shine, and for enjoying my stories.

Annette, for reading the first draft, rereading chapter s, and then final beta/proof-reading. And for just being there. Your unfailing support means the world to me. A huge squishy hug!

Carolyn, for catching those misses, for your constant encouragement, and snarky messages—love them.

Sara, for relishing all those *juicy* parts and making me smile. You guys are truly amazing!

To my wonderful family, my other **Half**, I treasure your patience and understanding.

Ty: my Jiminy cricket, you are a-maze-balls with your keen mind and sharp eyes. I'm never gonna forget the Fibonacci lecture. Ever.

Finally, **Montana Jade**. Darling girl, without you this book—heck, the **Fallen Guardians** series—would not exist. Most of all, thank you for creating all my fabulously sexy covers, and for still adoring me despite the pester sessions. Hugs and sloppy kisses!

And to my readers: You guys have really been patient and incredibly supportive after the grueling and tragic past year as things slowed down a lot in my writing world. I do hope Dagan's story has made up for the wait. Love Georgia ♥

Also by Georgia Lyn Hunter

FALLEN GUARDIANS
Absolute Surrender 1
Echo, Mine: (Novella 1.5)
Breaking Fate 2
Tangled Sin (Standalone)
Guardian Unraveled 3

WARLORDS OF EMPYREA
Darkness Undone 1

CONTEMPORARY: PLAYERS TO MEN
Breathless

About the Author

Georgia Lyn Hunter loves to create characters who'll take you to the far and beyond to unforgettable adventures, steamy encounters and heart-stopping love stories...

She grew up in the sultry climate of South Africa and currently lives in the Middle East with her family. An avid reader from a young age, she devoured every book she got her hands on. When she's not writing or plotting her next novel, she loves trolling flea markets and buying things she'd never use (because they're so pretty,) traveling, painting, and being with her wonderfully supportive family.

And there you have it, all the boring stuff.

Want more? Then subscribe to her new release:

Newsletter: http://eepurl.com/bpHvET

Website: www.georgialynhunter.com

FB: https://www.facebook.com/GeorgiaLynHunter

Twitter: https://twitter.com/GeorgialynH

81230304R00259

Made in the USA
Columbia, SC
17 November 2017